M000221230

Victoria J. Price lives on England's breathtaking south coast. She loves fairy tales, myths and legends, and grew up creating stories both in words and pictures. When she's not writing you'll find her exploring with her husband and their two dogs, searching for beautiful hidden places and secret picnic spots.

Sign up to Victoria's mailing list:

www.victoriajprice.com

Follow on social media:

Instagram @victoriajprice

Twitter @victoria_jprice

Facebook @authorvictoriajprice

WITHDRAW
from records of
Mid-Continent Public Library

Books by Victoria J. Price

Daughter of the Phoenix Series

The Third Sun

The Eternal Dusk

The First Dawn

VICTORIA J. PRICE

A LEGACY OF STORMS AND STARLIGHT

Copyright ©2022 by Victoria J. Price

All rights reserved. No part of this publication may be reproduced, stored in a retrieval system, or transmitted in any form or by any means, electronic, mechanical, recording or otherwise, without the prior written permission of the copyright holder.

This is a work of fiction. Names, characters, businesses, places, events and incidents are either the products of the author's imagination or used in a fictitious manner. Any resemblance to actual persons, living or dead, or actual events is purely coincidental.

Editing services provided by Melanie Underwood

Cover and title design by Franziska Stern

Map by Andrés Aguirre Jurado

ISBN: 978-1-9163540-3-6

www.victoriajprice.com

For Amy Eversley—

for your unwavering support and friendship

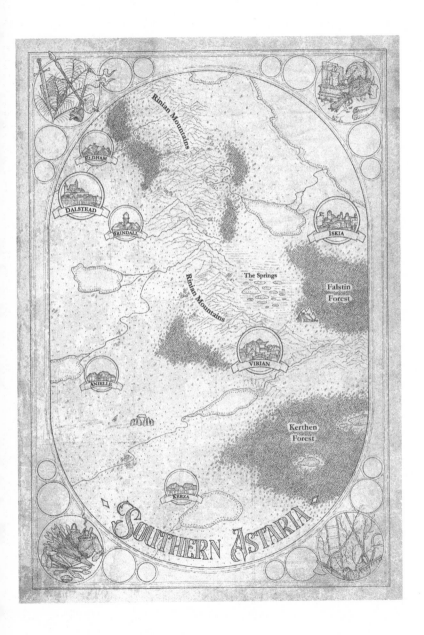

1

I didn't mean for him to die.

The scent of freshly baked bread drifted through the grate at the top of Zylah's cell, and her stomach growled in response. It was from the Andells' family bakery; she'd know it anywhere. There was no use climbing up to the grate—she'd almost broken her wrist trying to do it the day before. Instead, she folded her arms tightly around herself and pictured the bakery: the way the warmth hit you the moment you opened the door, the soft glow of the orblights, the mouth-watering smell of the canna cakes, and Mrs Andell behind the counter, flour brushed over her cheeks and green apron.

And the painting that hung on the wall behind her. She'd said it had been gifted to them by a traveller one day who couldn't pay for bread; it depicted a snowy mountain and verdant trees dusted in white snow, a blazing beacon in the background the only speck of colour. Somewhere in the Rinian mountain range, the traveller had told them. Zylah had never seen anything like it—no one she'd ever met had seen mountains. She knew the range began—or ended—somewhere upriver, but few people seemed to travel from that direction these days.

Someone in a nearby part of the prison threw up, and Zylah was brought right back to her cold cell, to her throat that was hoarse from screaming, her filthy uniform and the fetid stench of death. The last of her tears had dried up days ago.

I didn't mean for him to die. It was the only thought that stopped her hands from trembling. It was an accident. Surely they'd realise that soon enough?

A mouse shot out of the grimy hay beside her feet, scurrying away into the shadows to hide. Not that it was difficult, the grate only let in a thin shaft of light, and it was all she had to illuminate her cell, which she'd rather not have seen, anyway.

She shouldn't have even been in the prince's quarters, but when Kara had asked her to cover the evening shift, Zylah couldn't refuse. She already owed the girl for covering her back on more than one occasion, and besides, she'd do anything for her friend.

Zylah wrapped her hands around the iron bars of her cell, the cold biting into her fingers. The reek of the prison was worse here—on her first day it was so bad it had made her eyes water. But she needed to listen, and she pressed the side of her head against the bars, straining to hear the whisper of the guards in the darkness. Nothing.

I didn't mean for him to die. But he was hurting her. The moment Prince Jesper had caught her eye as she swept ash from the fireplace, Zylah had recognised the look that darkened his face. She'd seen it enough times on Theo's face to know precisely what the prince had intended, and the feeling had most certainly not been mutual.

"Please, please let us out," a woman from another cell called out. "We'll leave the city, we'll pack up and go, just please let us out."

But that was not the way things worked in the king's prison. Zylah ran her thumbnail over a flaking piece of rust, listening to the woman's quiet weeping, fighting with her own rising panic. If she hadn't already heaved her guts out in various parts of the rotting hay, she'd be sick again.

"Be quiet, Maren, or they'll kill us before our trial," a man hissed.

Footsteps sounded, and Zylah pressed the side of her head against the bars again. Two sets, at the top of the staircase that led down into the prison: one heavy and one light. No other prisoners would have heard them yet, they were too far away still. But Zylah had always been a little... *different,* not that she'd welcomed it—she'd always had keener hearing and sharper vision than the other children when she was a child. Had always been the fastest in races. And she'd been bullied for it, no matter how much she'd yelled at them that she wasn't different, not truly.

Unusual was not something you wanted to be in Dalstead or the villages, like hers, that surrounded it.

3

It hadn't always been a curse. Her father had taken her on as his apprentice because of her keen sense of smell. One afternoon in his apothecary, she'd caught a trader trying to sell perfumed tea leaves instead of crushed erti root. Zylah frowned at the memory. She would never see the apothecary again.

If only she'd had some erti root in her apron, or better yet, some besa leaves, anything to cover the stench of the prison, but she was fairly certain her clothes had soaked up the stink now, too. The footsteps were getting closer, almost to the door at the bottom of the spiral staircase, and Zylah heard the dainty sniffing of a woman. A maid, maybe? No, they wouldn't be sending a maid down for a prisoner the day before her execution.

A key turned in the lock, and the door swung open on creaking hinges. Zylah couldn't see along the corridor, could barely see to the next cell, but she heard the intake of breath, the stifled sob and the mumbled words from whoever accompanied the guard. It was Kara.

Zylah smoothed down her filthy tunic, huffing a quiet laugh at herself as her hands reached her sides. What good would it do? She most likely looked a complete mess, but it helped her hold onto her last shreds of sanity. Tomorrow, she'd never see anyone again. She took in a few deep breaths, practised her smile, and waited for Kara to reach her cell, for the soft glow of the orblight the guard carried to grow brighter.

"Oh, Zy," Kara said, the moment their eyes met. Kara's

tiny face was puffy from crying, her tight brown curls escaping haphazardly from the wrap she wore to keep her hair in check whilst she worked. She reached her hands out for Zylah's through the bars.

"How did you convince them to let you down here?" Zylah asked, placing her hands over Kara's tiny fingers. Everything about the girl was dainty. Her nut-brown eyes, her soft nose, the way her little curls brushed against her deep brown skin. Zylah tried to hide her shaky breathing, tried to keep her smile bright for her friend.

Kara wiped at a tear with the back of her sleeve. "Mama's friends with—" She looked up at the guard beside her, who had turned his back to the cell, but kept watch diligently, the orblight hovering above him. "Mama helped me," she said softly. "I'm so sorry, Zy. This is all my fault."

Kara's face blurred and Zylah saw the prince approaching again, saw the way he'd caught her off guard and taken the fire iron from her hand. She'd been stoking the fire as a pretence, just so she had a weapon to defend herself with. But when he'd stepped before her, she'd frozen. She didn't know why, but she was furious with herself for it. All her training with her brother had been for nothing when she needed it most. Well, almost.

"None of this is your fault, Kar, okay?" Zylah squeezed Kara's fingers gently. "You've covered my shifts a hundred times. I'd cover for you again in a heartbeat."

"But it was your last week," Kara said, her voice breaking on the last few words.

Zylah schooled her expression as best she could. It was true, she was only meant to be working for the royal family for another week before she went full time with her father. Business had been better than ever, and they could finally afford to go without her meagre salary from the palace—she could, at last, spend her days doing something she loved. But she wouldn't burden her friend with any of that.

"You did tell me my hips would get me in trouble one day," she said, with the closest thing to a smirk she could muster. There must have been a reason he'd attacked, some glance she'd given him, but no matter how many times she replayed it, she couldn't remember what had happened in the moments right before he'd confronted her; it was as if there was just a gap that she'd blocked out.

The prince had split her lip, and it still hadn't healed. It had broken open every time she'd spoken, every time she'd screamed in the darkness. Every time she'd thrown up.

Kara didn't return the smile. "Your face," she said quietly. "He did this to you?"

Zylah wondered how bad her eye must have looked if the bruising was still as bad as it felt. She swallowed, not wanting to think of the way Jesper had put his hands on her, the way his breath had reeked of avenberry liquor. "He did. I was defending myself; I didn't mean for—"

The guard shifted his weight beside Kara but didn't turn to look at Zylah. None of them had. They all knew the truth. It was impossible to take one look at her and not know. They were cowards, all of them.

"Have you heard from my father? I haven't seen him since they put me here. I'd hoped he'd come to see me before the execution," Zylah said. Her voice was quiet, but she tried her best to keep it hopeful, for Kara's sake. She was afraid to die, but dying was the easy part, wasn't it? After, it wouldn't matter for Zylah. But it would for her father. For her brother. For Kara.

Kara flexed her fingers in Zylah's hands. "They didn't tell you?" She shook her head. "Of course they wouldn't. He went to find Zack, to beg your pardon before the execution."

Zylah's chest tightened at Kara's words. She knew it would never work. The prince was dead, and the king would never pardon her, no matter how highly he thought of her brother. Zack was the King's Blade, but that wouldn't make any difference now. Still, she wouldn't let Kara know that. They'd been friends for as long as Zylah could remember—Kara was the only one who had never shied away from her strangeness, well, other than her brother.

She and Kara had grown up together, worked together, shared stories of first kisses together. Some things Zylah had kept to herself, even when she knew Kara wondered what a man's touch felt like. Her friend always seemed too pure for any of that. But one day soon she'd be married off, whether her mother wanted it or not. Women had little say in the city of Dalstead.

"Thank you," Zylah finally said. "You've given me hope. Something I thought I'd lost entirely." The truth was, she'd lost hope days ago.

"Did he—the prince?" Kara's eyes filled with tears again, and Zylah could only feel relief that it hadn't been her friend with Jesper that night.

"No. He tried." Zylah reached for her face in a poor attempt at disguising her wince. "It all happened so quickly. I was stirring the fire, and he crept up on me. I just knew his intentions were not—" She glanced up at the guard as he coughed uncomfortably. "*Honourable.* I asked to be excused. He told me to stay. When I made for the door, he threw me against the wall, and—" Zylah's heartbeat was like a raging drum in her chest, the sound filling her ears. But she knew Kara wouldn't have been able to hear it, or the guard. She willed herself not to be sick again, shoved aside the thoughts of the prince's hands tugging at her tunic.

"I was defending myself," she whispered. "I didn't mean for him to die."

"He deserved it, for what he tried to do to you." Kara pressed her face against the bars, her eyes wide and filled with tears.

"Kara, you'll get yourself thrown in here with me," Zylah said, shuffling closer to her friend.

The girl closed her eyes for a moment. "Do you mean it, Zy, nothing else happened?"

He'd tried. Gods, had he tried. That's how she'd got the split lip and the black eye—because she wouldn't go down without a fight. The minute he'd thrown her against the wall and broken eye contact, it was like she'd stepped out of quicksand and woken up all at once.

"Only this," Zylah said, waving at her face.

She'd replayed it all, over and over again. Enough times that every moment felt as if it were burned into her eyelids. She'd hesitated, and if she hadn't, she could have darted out of the room, and none of this would have happened. But she'd hesitated, and he'd seen it, waited for it—like she was nothing but his prey. The moment she'd snapped out of her stupor and realised he wasn't going to stop, she'd grabbed the fire iron out of instinct.

"This was enough," she said after a moment, her voice raspy.

Kara nodded in understanding. She looked up at the guard beside her, his gaze still fixed ahead of him, and reached into her apron. Zylah kept her eyes on the guard as Kara's delicate fingers slid something into hers against the bars. Something very small. Zylah flicked her attention back to her friend, and Kara tightened her grip.

At the end of the corridor, the rusty hinges squeaked as the door to the prison slammed open, the guard beside them reaching for Kara's arm.

"I'll wait up for your father," Kara said. "I'll tell him I've seen you. We'll get you out of here, Zy. I promise." The guard was already pulling her away, fresh tears glistening in the orblight.

Zylah didn't protest, didn't do anything that might put Kara in more danger than she already was, just kept quiet as whoever had entered the prison approached, praying they wouldn't throw her friend in the adjacent cell.

She slipped whatever Kara had given to her into the pocket of her apron, smoothing it down and steeling herself as the footsteps came closer. Kara and the guard left quietly, the door falling shut with a thud behind them.

Zylah counted three, maybe four sets of footsteps, and they seemed to be taking their time, delaying the inevitable. No one in the prison made a sound, even the quiet whimpers had stopped, as if the air had been sucked out of each cell.

Zylah didn't need to see to know who it was. King Arnir. He stank of the same avenberry liquor as his son had. Not that she could blame him, his only son was dead, the piece of shit. The orblights cast a soft glow across the corridor, but Zylah didn't let herself look into the surrounding cells. There was nothing within them that she'd want to see in her final hours. She took a step back from the bars and braced herself for the king's abuse, knowing all too well it could be more than just words.

"Any other bitch would have been grateful for his seed inside them," the king spat as he stepped up to her cell, wrinkling his nose in disgust. "Brought down by a maid," he seethed, banging his sceptre against the iron bars, his fat jowls vibrating as he spoke.

Zylah didn't flinch. She wouldn't let her fear show, not to him. She took steadying breaths in through her nose, ignoring the burn of the prison's putrid stench at the back of her throat. She said nothing—there was no use—not to the likes of him. He'd only silence her anyway, and that was precisely what he was trying to do, to rile her so he could cut her down in front

10

of his guards. She wouldn't give him the satisfaction.

"Fine. Have it your way," King Arnir hissed. "Guards. Take her to the gallows."

2

"Wait!" Zylah pleaded, taking a step back from the iron bars. She pressed her hands to her sides to hide her trembling. They couldn't take her, not now, not like this. "My father is coming. My brother. Please, Your Majesty, I know you value Zack's word." She hated that she had to beg, but she would do anything to see her family.

King Arnir's face was purple in the orblights as he slammed his sceptre against the cell bars again. This time, Zylah couldn't help but flinch.

"How dare you speak of what *I* value," Arnir spat. "My son is dead because of you. My only son!" He clasped a hand around the bars, narrowing his eyes at Zylah as the guard's key rattled in the lock.

She took another step back, sending more mice scurrying from the hay. This wasn't right. She was meant to have until tomorrow. Was meant to see her father. Her brother. A pathetic whimper escaped her as panic coiled in her chest. Not

12

at the approaching guards, but at the thought of never seeing her family again. It had never mattered that they weren't her *real* family—they were all she had. And she couldn't die without saying goodbye. Without thanking them for the life they'd given her.

Her back pressed against the cold stone, grazing against the knot on her spine she'd had for as long as she could remember. She reached a hand out to steady herself, her fingers brushing against something slick and slimy, and she fought to steady her breathing.

Two guards stepped into the cell, a third remaining beside the king. *They truly think I'm going to harm him.* She could try to snatch his sceptre… but she'd never be able to fight off the three guards *and* the king, heaving oaf that he was. And if Kara's guard had wanted to keep his job, he'd have locked the door to the prison behind him.

But she wouldn't beg again. Not to him. None of the citizens held much regard for Arnir, but Zylah had seen what a true tyrant he was during her time working in the palace. The brin fruit hadn't fallen far from the tree with Prince Jesper.

She wiped her hand against the back of her tunic and twined her fingers together to hide her shaking, fighting with the instinct to run. There was nowhere to go. One guard hooked his hand around her arm and tugged her forwards. His warm touch through her tunic brought her right back to Jesper's quarters, but she shook the thought away.

"Move!" The guard's voice reverberated in the small cell. The second stood at her other side as she stepped forwards.

They tugged her arms out from behind her, and the first guard locked heavy iron cuffs around her wrists, the chain dragging her hands against her body. No chance of snatching the sceptre now.

King Arnir mumbled something incoherent and stormed off, his personal guard close behind him, his sceptre scraping against every iron bar of every single cell as he left.

"Any sudden movements and we've orders to strike you down here and now. Understood?" the guard to Zylah's left said.

She looked up at his pockmarked face, his broken nose and the large scab on his cheek. He was just like the rest of them, blindly taking orders from their fool of a king.

That was why Zack had joined the guard—he'd wanted to make a difference. She'd trained with her brother every day before he'd joined, could match him blow for blow with a sword—well, a training sword, at least.

Everything he'd learnt, he'd taught her. Sword fighting, archery, how to disarm a man, how to strike him down without a weapon. Zylah ran through everything he'd taught her—any shred of information that might help her get out of this. They'd never covered *handcuffed and escorted by guards*.

If only she had a hairpin, or a needle, anything to work on the cuffs.

She bit back a hysterical laugh. Not that she'd ever be able to pick them anyway.

"Disgusting Fae," a woman spat as the guards dragged Zylah down the corridor. It was Maren, the woman from

14

earlier who had been begging to leave. Zylah recognised her voice.

"I'm human," she muttered to no one in particular. It didn't matter now, no one would believe her—but for killing the prince, they'd branded her as Fae regardless. To make an example, she suspected.

The last of the Fae had been wiped out a little over two decades before when she was a baby. Humans had had enough of their kind—of the power they flaunted, and an uprising had nearly destroyed everything. Everyone fled, for a time, human and faeries alike. It was most likely the reason she'd been dumped in the bushes for her brother to find.

He'd brought her back to their father, days after Zack's mother had been killed. Their father had taken one look at her and brought her up as his own—maybe it was the grief, maybe it was just because he was a good person, Zylah would never know. But she was just as human as the rest of them. There was no hint of Fae about her—no pointed ears, no powers, no ethereal beauty. Nothing.

And for the first time in her life, she wished she truly was different. Something more.

Something else.

The man beside Maren spat, and the glob of phlegm narrowly missed Zylah's feet.

"Oi, that's enough of that," the guard to her right snapped. She didn't bother to look at him. He'd only said it because the snot had only just missed *him*. It wasn't for her benefit.

The king and his guard had already disappeared up the

stairs, their orblights leaving a ghostly luminescence in their wake.

Pockmark made his way through the door first, and the second guard shoved her towards him, taking up his position at the back of their miserable procession.

Zylah's breaths felt shorter with each intake of fetid air. Before, she'd somehow found a sense of calm about having one more day, some sense of order to it all. But this was random, the king's command had come out of nowhere, and it had shattered her self-control. She wasn't ready to die. She had too much living still to do. She had to see the world beyond Dalstead and her little village, had to discover for herself all the things she'd only ever read about in books.

Tears pressed at the corners of her eyes, but she blinked them back as she shuffled up the stone staircase. The orblights hovered above them as if they had a mind of their own, but Zylah knew there had to be a science behind them, somehow. Some small parts inside them that allowed them to move, an insect, perhaps? She'd never figured it out, never been allowed close enough to one to inspect them. Only the palace had them, the rest of the city used lamps and candles.

The staircase seemed to narrow as they ascended, each turn of the spiral pressing in on Zylah, swallowing all the air that was left in the tiny space. Soon they'd reach the top, reach the corridor at the back of the palace.

She wished she had some besa leaves to dull her panic, dull everything. She could picture them in a jar beside the counter in her father's apothecary, grey and crumbling in the yellow tinted glass. He'd taught her all he knew about plants—which she could eat raw, which she could cook, which had uses for medicine, for poison. She'd spent every spare moment poring over his textbooks, forgetting her other chores and responsibilities.

Zylah Alyssa Renfall, she could hear her father say. *The broth is boiling over again!*

He'd named her Zylah after his mother. Alyssa after the alyssina flowers that matched the dark violet of her eyes—eyes she'd learnt to hide from inquisitive people who entered their apothecary.

Since the other children had branded her as different, she had quickly learnt how to make herself invisible. They all knew her brother and father weren't her true family, and she didn't want to draw further attention to herself. So she'd taught herself to be small, to shrink in a crowd or to be silent at a gathering, to go unheard and unseen in plain sight.

She could outrun anyone; it had always been her and Zack's secret weapon as children stealing brin fruit from carts. He'd distract the stall owners and she'd swipe the goods and run. No one could ever catch her. But she'd soon learnt not to outrun the other children. She taught herself to stumble, to huff and puff the way they did. To pretend she'd twisted an ankle or simply couldn't keep up with the rest.

But her stumble on the last step up into the palace was no charade, and the guard behind her yanked at her tunic to right her, shoving her the rest of the way. She would never see Zack and her father again. Never hear her father call her name. An

17

acid taste coated her tongue, and if she'd had anything left to bring up, she'd have heaved all over the guard in front of her. She choked back a gagging cough instead.

"Don't you hurl your bloody guts up on me," Pockmark barked. "I only got this uniform last week."

The guard behind her laughed. "Just like a piece of shit Fae to ruin a good uniform."

If she'd thought she could open her mouth without being sick, Zylah would have snapped back with an objection. But she didn't have it in her. They were marching her straight to the gallows. No one would listen to her cries for help.

A noise echoed off the walls, one she wondered if only she could hear, a thumping, rhythmic sound that matched her quickening heartbeat. The chains rattled with the shake of her hands. The sweat at the back of her neck sent a chill down her spine. There was so much she had wanted to do still. So much to see. So many new plants and remedies to discover. The last shreds of composure she'd found over the past few days seemed to fall away from her with each shuffle forwards.

The palace was a blur in the glow of the orblights, her feet pressing into the plush golden carpet. She'd expected the guards to lead her through the back corridors and down to the river where the gallows were, but instead, they were heading for the front of the palace. Zylah imagined maids running in the moment they left, burning the carpet she'd walked on and replacing it with something new and equally garish. Gods, she truly did stink. The thumping grew louder, so loud Zylah couldn't feel her heartbeat anymore.

Pockmark pushed open the doors to the great hall, and Zylah turned away from the assault of light. Her cuffed hands were too heavy to raise to her face; all she could do was let her eyes slowly adjust. The hall was lined with great windows, a winding staircase rose on either side, lavish purple drapes and pictures three times as tall as her lining the walls—though most things were taller than her, she'd found.

It was a spectacular entrance, precisely the kind of grandiose display she'd expected the first time she'd set foot in the palace, dripping with privilege and echoing with the sound of cheers and clapping from outside. That explained the thumping.

It was just like Arnir to turn the event into a spectacle.

A spicy aroma filled the room, saffa spice mixed with besa leaves, Zylah guessed, presumably to hide the stench of prison she carried with her. Up ahead, King Arnir watched her approach, as if he were waiting just for her.

"Now," he commanded, and more guards threw open the doors, the sound of the city erupting into the palace.

Half the city had come out to watch. The roar of the crowd seemed to shake even the ground beneath Zylah's feet. They'd come to witness her death, to watch the one who had killed their prince hang on the gallows like the murderer they all thought she was. She stopped, but the second guard shoved her forwards into Pockmark, and he spun around and sneered.

She felt as if the world was tilting, as if the air was being sucked from everything and already she couldn't breathe. Already she was gone.

Her father had told her once that the dead look over us, that our purpose was to give them something to watch. That we are their legacy. Zylah had never agreed. She'd always thought her purpose was to live. To exist. To experience everything she could, for no one but herself. She came into the world alone, and now she would leave it that way, with no legacy and nothing to leave behind but her name.

Pockmark shoved her through the palace doors, the crowd erupting into cheers. Gallows had been built halfway down the steps, and Zylah knew precisely why. So the king could tower over them all as she hanged before his citizens.

She was dragged down a dozen stone steps, her feet refusing to obey her, and shoved straight onto the wooden planks of the gallows. Pockmark positioned her over the trapdoor, and a rough rope was thrown over her head and angled behind her. Zylah barely registered it. She was searching the crowd for her father and brother, even though she knew there was little chance of finding them.

Instead, she caught sight of brown curls and a delicate face, eyes bright with tears. *Kara.* Kara met her gaze, her hands clasped over her mouth, shoulders shaking. Zylah bit her lip, tried to keep her resolve, but the sight of her friend was almost too much to bear.

Look away, Zylah mouthed. But Kara wouldn't, her shoulders still shaking as she sobbed.

"Look away," Zylah called out, her throat hoarse, her own tears streaming freely down her cheeks.

"Zylah!" A voice cried out from the crowd. Her father.

20

She searched for him among the faces staring back at her, and his eyes found hers.

"My girl! Zylah!" His eyes were glassy with tears as he fought his way through the throng towards her.

Arnir was saying something, but Zylah focused on her father's face as he called her name. He'd come for her, and the thought knocked the last of the breath from her in a pained gasp.

She heard the crank of the lever, the hinges of the trap doors opening beneath her, and then she was falling, the rope burning against her skin, the crowd cheering, her throat tightening, death approaching.

And then it all spiralled away from her, like water down a drain.

3

Zylah had expected death would be cold, but she hadn't expected it to be so windy. Her throat ached from the burn of the rope, and she dragged a hand through something cold and wet as she reached out to grasp it.

Only she couldn't because they were handcuffed.

This isn't right.

She opened her eyes to a blizzard raging around her, felt the chill of snow rush through her clothes.

What happened?

She forced herself to her feet, trying to shield her face from the snow, but the cuffs weighed her arms down. Her heartbeat still thundered in her chest. She tasted blood. Her neck wasn't broken, so at least there was that. But that didn't answer her question, didn't explain how she was standing in the middle of—

She spun around to get her bearings. White, as far as she could see in the dim grey. She could just about make out the snow-capped mountains beyond and… her breath snagged in her throat. It was a beacon. Not just any beacon, it was the exact scene from the picture in the Andells' bakery, the flame bright orange against the stark white snow. *Gods above.*

She wiped an arm at the tears that had frozen to her face, trying to clear the snowflakes from her eyelashes to get a better look. It had to be the Rinian mountains, but how?

Snow soaked through her thin shoes and every part of her shook from the cold, her teeth chattering. She'd narrowly escaped death once; she wasn't about to let herself die from frostbite.

Zylah urged herself up the snowy slope to the only landmark she could see—the beacon—as a fresh wave of panic hit her. She wouldn't last long like this. She paused, frantically trying to squeeze her hands out of the cuffs, but it was no use, and she needed to keep moving.

Each step sank her into the powdery snow, piling in around her, the cold seeping into her bones. She stumbled, but forced herself back to her feet, narrowing her gaze on the beacon until it spiralled away from her, a rushing sensation tugging at her insides before she fell face first into the snow. Her apron and trousers were already soaked, right the way through to her tunic.

When she looked up again, she was only a short distance from the balefire, the pyre almost as tall as the king's palace.

What is happening to me?

It wasn't just the cold that had her trembling, the cuff chains rattling against each other. Her panic was all consuming, and she closed her eyes to try and steady herself. That strange sensation washed over her again, and when she opened her eyes, she was right next to the beacon, could feel the heat against her skin, the solid rock beneath her wet shoes where the flames had melted away the snow.

Okay. Okay. I can figure this out.

But she was too cold to think straight. She soaked up the heat from the fire, wishing she could bottle it somehow. Snow melted from her tunic and trousers; her cheeks began to flush from the warmth. Her teeth stopped chattering. But the blizzard still raged on around her. She couldn't stay; it was unlikely the beacon was left unguarded. But she didn't know where she could go, either. Or how long she'd last out in the snow.

As the chill began to ease from her bones, she forced herself to walk around the pyre, squinting out into the grey for any other landmarks. Her neck and throat burned from the noose Pockmark had slung around it. She tried to piece together the moments before she'd arrived out in the snow, but nothing made sense. A blast of heat gusted around her shoulders and Zylah shuddered. She'd survived.

Her braid had come loose, but there was nothing she could do about it now. Wisps of blonde hair brushed her cheeks as she surveyed the mountain range beyond. How big could a mountain range be? There was nothing but snow and rock as far as she could see, that, and the next beacon along the mountain range, a tiny fleck of orange against the white.

She thought of the way the trapdoor had opened beneath

her feet. The way the rope had tightened around her neck. The way she had *fallen*. A second longer and she'd have died. She pictured Kara's face, tears streaming down her friend's cheeks. She'd told her to look away, but she hadn't. What did Kara think of her now? Or her father?

Zylah walked further around the beacon, sucking in deep breaths of icy air to calm herself. The blizzard was only getting worse, but there, in the distance, the expanse of snow gave way to trees. She tried to order her thoughts. She'd been the one to… *travel* though she didn't know how she'd done it. But it had been her, no one else. She could do it again. Get away from the mountains.

Zylah closed her eyes. Willed the world to fall away from her.

Nothing happened.

Shit. It would be dark soon. She couldn't linger.

"Oi!" a voice called out from somewhere nearby.

Oh, gods.

She spun around in the direction of the voice. A young man, dressed in the uniform of the King's Guard, and he was running right for her.

Zylah looked at the trees in the distance again and scrunched her eyes shut, focusing on the sound of her heartbeat drumming in her ears. "Come *on*," she whispered, her voice raspy. The feeling of the world spiralling had her coughing back bile until she stumbled, her feet landing in snow again.

She flicked her eyes open. Trees. Godsdamned trees. She'd

done it. Zylah choked back a sob as she ran into the forest, tripping and stumbling in deep pockets of snow, the iron cuffs cutting deep into her wrists. She didn't care. She was alive, and she wouldn't stop running until she was dead.

She darted through the trees, jumping over branches and *travelling* ahead in spurts to whichever trees she could see in the near distance. Each time it was easier, the world didn't spin; she didn't stumble as much when she reappeared, but she didn't know what happened in the space between two locations. One moment she was in one spot, the next she was in another. She didn't allow herself to think about it either, because the light was fading, and soon she wouldn't be able to see anything to *travel* to.

The scent of the fir trees and snow flooded her senses, along with the disturbed earth beneath her feet. The world was eerily still amongst the trees; every time she *travelled* and paused, it was as if the world was holding its breath.

Zylah's own breathing was ragged and broken, and she leaned forward to rest, drops of blood falling into the snow where the cuffs had sliced into her wrists. *Find shelter. Warmth. Somewhere to rest.* Her brother's voice echoed in her head. It was one of the first things he'd taught her when he was training to be a guard.

A piercing howl cut through the still of the forest, and every hair on Zylah's arms stood on end. Wolves. She was fast, but not so fast that she could outrun an entire pack. One lone wolf, maybe. But she doubted very much that the wolf was alone.

She looked ahead to a cluster of trees in the distance, willing herself to *travel* to them. When she landed, more howls sounded in the half-light. She had to keep going, no matter how much her wrists hurt, how much her chest ached, how much the snow had soaked through her clothes.

Zylah urged herself to keep travelling, again and again, in short bursts to the next cluster of trees ahead of her. After the fifth burst, her knees buckled beneath her, her hands trembling. Adrenaline was the only thing keeping her going; if she stopped, let it fade, she didn't think she'd get back up again.

The wolves howled again. Further away this time. But she couldn't stop. For the first time in her life, the knot on her spine ached; up until now, it had only ever been a small lump she chose to ignore. Why give attention to something she couldn't change?

Zylah didn't want to think about her list of ever-growing ailments; whether she'd still have all her toes when she finally took off her shoes. If her heart was still beating, then she'd endure it. She travelled again and again until her head pounded so loud she couldn't think straight. The trees had begun to thin, and for a moment she wasn't sure if it would be safer to risk the night in the forest than to chance being seen by the king's guards with chains around her wrists and rope marks at her neck.

Don't be ridiculous, Zy, her brother would say. She half ran, half stumbled ahead to where the trees thinned out further, the forest falling away and a strong gust of wind hitting her. Zylah staggered to a stop as a steep drop cut away from the rock just ahead, and below, patches of jewel-bright water beneath a layer of fog spread as far as she could see, until the fog was too thick and the light too poor to make out anything further.

It was a long way down. But she closed her eyes, took a steadying breath, and thought of standing on the stone beside the water.

Her feet touched down on something warm, and she opened one eye. Relief washed over her, and if the cuffs hadn't weighed so much, she'd have thrown her arms up in the air. She knelt down and held her hands above water as bright as the sky on a clear day. *It's warm.* A single tear of relief rolled down her cheek. It wasn't fog she'd seen. It was steam.

Zylah tentatively dipped a finger into the liquid to test it. It felt like bathwater, but she didn't succumb to the thoughts that screamed for her to submerge herself, not yet. Instead, she sniffed at the water to try and detect anything that might be contaminating it.

Besides, she could bathe for a while, but then what? Every muscle ached. She plunged her hands into the blue and watched it turn rusty as some of the blood washed away from her wrists. The pain in her back was worse. The lump was small, no bigger than a pebble, but since she'd learnt others were afraid of anything strange or different in Dalstead, Zylah had always covered it up as best she could.

She cast her gaze from the edge of the water, back to the base of the rock face she'd travelled from. Dark shadows dotted the rock. *Caves.* Small islands of moss-covered rock peppered the space between her and the shore, the water bright and peculiar beside it. Some of the distances between islands were too far for her to jump, and she thought of the stories from her childhood and imagined water sprites and spirits snatching her from the air and into the water. She hadn't come all this way just to be taken by a sprite. Zylah pushed herself to her feet, her body trembling with the effort as she willed herself to travel one last time.

Her feet slipped on wet moss as she landed at the shore, the steam easing her aching muscles. Other animals could be using the caves, and she stilled, tilting her head to listen in the twilight. She heard nothing but her own thumping heart.

With quiet steps, she made her way towards a cave with a sputter of steam in the entrance, where the warm vapour billowed from a hole in the ground. The rock beneath her feet warmed her toes, and as she stepped around the geyser the heat of the cave cocooned her.

Zylah fell to her knees, her hands pressing against the warm rock, and let her sobs shake through her. She stayed like that for a moment, letting the tears fall and her cries echo in the darkness.

Then she took a deep breath and sat tall, smoothed the front of her clothes as best she could with her cuffed hands and then—her fingers brushed against something in her apron. It was whatever Kara had slipped her, back in the cell.

Zylah shoved her hands into the pocket, her fingers closing around the tiny piece of paper and she unravelled it as carefully as she could, the warmth slowly returning to her fingertips.

Her breath snagged. It was a hairpin. "Kara, you sly little thing," Zylah whispered, a smile breaking across her face and quickly turning into a cough as she choked on the pain in her throat and her lip split open again.

She angled the pin in her fingers, bringing the cuffs together so that she could work at the first lock. She'd never picked a lock before, only read about it in the storybooks Kara was always letting her borrow. Zylah turned the pin slowly, afraid it might snap, listening carefully for any sounds inside the lock that might tell her it had caught in the right place. She wouldn't survive long with her hands cuffed together. And anyone she saw would know her at once for what she was: a prisoner on the run.

Her fingers began to shake, and she drew in a deep breath. *Concentrate.* She listened to the sound of the pin scraping inside the barrel of the lock, to the way it dragged against the tumblers inside it.

Carefully, slowly, she angled her makeshift lockpick, running it along each of those pins one by one until—the cuff clicked open. She fought down the whimper threatening to escape, rubbing at her freed wrist where the bruises had turned it purple. *One down, one to go.*

Zylah slid the hairpin into the second cuff, listening carefully for the drag of the cylinders. She twisted it slowly; it just needed a little more and then—the pin snapped inside the lock.

"No!" she groaned, clawing at the broken metal. But it was no use. She angled her wrist, banging the cuff against the ground to try and shake the pin loose, but nothing worked.

So close. She'd been so close. Every part of her ached. Her head, her back, her legs. She knew the moment she stopped she wouldn't be able to get back up, but she hadn't expected the exhaustion to be so all consuming. The warmth from the cave was making her drowsy, too.

Her lip trembled, but she was too exhausted to cry. Zylah lay down in the dirt, her head resting on her uncuffed arm, and closed her eyes.

In the morning she would come up with a plan. In the morning she would figure out how to get her life back. But for now, all Zylah wanted was to sleep.

4

A piercing howl had Zylah bolting upright from her resting place in the dirt. It could have come from anywhere, but she uncoiled to her feet regardless. Something seemed to whisper, carried into the cave on the wind. Or maybe it was the wind itself.

Everything still ached. The lump in her back. Her head, her wrists, her throat. Her legs. Her chest. Worse than the time she had fallen through every single branch of the weeping eye tree in Kara's parents' garden.

An odd odour lingered in the warm air of her little cave, something she suspected might be an animal's dwelling if she were to explore further into the darkness. But Zylah's thoughts were occupied with survival. She'd need food and water if she was going to keep running. To where, she hadn't figured out yet, but all she knew was that she couldn't risk staying in one place for too long.

She couldn't *travel* again just yet though. She felt it in the searing pain in her head, and the way her chest burned, no matter how or why the travelling had happened the way it had. She stepped tentatively out of the cave, holding the loose cuff in her still-cuffed hand, her eyes adjusting to the brightness of the water.

Pampa reeds jutted out of the rock here and there, bent over double from the weight of their seed pods. They were completely inedible, a fact she'd discovered as a child when she'd hurled up half her guts after tasting one, but that wasn't what Zylah was considering.

She knelt beside the reed closest to her, her hands pressing into the moss at her feet, the loose cuff dragging beside her. The morning dew had collected along the curve of the reed in perfect droplets and would be a far safer option for her to drink than risking the jewel-blue water.

The droplets trickled down her lips, cool against the burn in her throat. It was the cleanest water she'd drunk since this whole mess began, and she almost shed a tear at the freshness of it. Water might be hard to come by in the days ahead, and already her mind was playing over ways she might be able to contain it without a vessel.

Her stomach grumbled, moving her thoughts onto other pressing matters. She'd never eaten moss before, but it was harmless and better than nothing. She tugged at a handful, shoving it in her mouth without hesitation before she had time to consider the taste. It wasn't too bad, but it scraped against her fragile throat. A little bit like seaweed, but chewier.

She shoved another handful into her apron out of habit

from working in her father's apothecary before pushing herself to her feet.

Stories of water sprites tugged at her memories again as she looked out at the expanse of blue. None of it made sense. The travelling. She'd never heard of anyone with such an ability. They were probably calling her all kinds of names back in Dalstead. Fae. Witch. Sprite. If the guard hadn't seen her at the beacon, she might have been safe for a while, but she knew it would be foolish to risk more than another day here.

If Kara were smart, she'd have left the moment Zylah disappeared from the gallows. Zylah hoped that's what had happened, for her friend's sake. And her father... Zack's position would protect him, wouldn't it? She took in a deep breath of the steamy air, testing the feel of it against her throat. If only she had some honey and alea blossom to soothe the pain.

She should keep moving, shouldn't stop to indulge herself in a bath, but the warm water would help ease her aches, could help her keep mobile for a little while longer. The azure water seemed to beckon to Zylah, whispering to her to cocoon herself in its warmth. She wrapped the loose cuff and chain around her wrist, removing her apron and the rest of her clothes as best she could with her free hand. The movement opened up some of the cuts on her cuffed wrist, and she winced in pain, eager to dip into the water. If anything or anyone came near, she'd hear them first. At least, she hoped she would.

The cliff face reached up behind her, the water stretched out ahead of her. To her left, the rock shielded her from the open, jutting right out into the water. But to the right, the rock could be traversed by anyone light-footed and steady enough. Anyone with the will to reach her part of the shore.

Zylah paused, ears pricked for any sounds out of the ordinary. Water lapped against the rocks. A bird called out from somewhere above. But everything else was as eerily quiet as it had been the night before. A shiver traced its way down her spine, and she carefully stepped down to the water's edge.

She stared back at her reflection, at her tired violet eyes and her wild hair. The undeniable line of the rope mark at her throat, her black eye and her split lip. It was enough to shake off her hesitation. She stepped into the water, sighing with satisfaction as the warmth swirled around her.

Zylah closed her eyes, let herself be held by the soothing water, and bit back the tears that burned her eyes. *You survived. Don't give up now.* A single sob shook her shoulders, but she held her hand to her mouth to keep herself in check. *You can do this.*

She rubbed at the dried blood on her wrists, the water muddying a little as she worked gently at her pale skin. Once she was dry, she would pack moss between her wrist and the remaining cuff to protect herself from more damage. Simple, logical thoughts about each step she had to take kept her tears at bay, stopping the fear that had firmly taken root in her heart from spreading.

Her aches began to ease, and she let herself think further ahead than the moment. Where did escaped convicts go? She could cover the rope wounds easily enough, but the remaining cuff was going to be a problem if she couldn't remove it.

She sank her shoulders beneath the warm water; the air still had a bite to it, and she was eager to soak up the warmth. Steam swirled above the surface, and with the grey sky, she couldn't see far. Only blue water and a few small rocks ahead, the odd pampa reed poking out here and there.

Every time she thought she had a grasp on her panic, that sense of dread seemed to work its way under her skin again. *An escaped convict on the run.* She wouldn't get far before someone turned her in for a handsome finder's fee. She'd seen enough bounty hunters pass in and out of the palace to know they'd be after her soon enough.

Zylah held her breath and submerged herself. She kept her eyes open, wary that any animal returning to the cave might sneak up on her, but of course, there was nothing in the clear water. Nothing but the sound of her heartbeat, and the feel of the warm liquid between her fingertips as her hair swirled around her.

And a shape, forming in the blue. Zylah blinked once, twice. A translucent figure began to appear.

She shot up out of the water, wiping her hands across her eyes to clear her vision. Nothing. Of course there was nothing. But she didn't need a second warning. She climbed out of the water, grabbed her clothes and another handful of moss, and padded back to her cave, the root of fear spreading deeper. *It was nothing.* And yet, she couldn't help the shiver that danced down her spine.

The stories of sprites played on repeat as she dressed and

chewed at her moss. She pulled on her apron as best she could and slipped her feet into her shoes one by one, her thoughts darting between the water sprites and what she was going to do next. The lump in her back had become an acute pain, and something seemed to pull at her insides. *Hold it together, Zy.*

When she looked up, a young man stood before her, and she fought back an alarmed squeak. Only he couldn't have been a man, because he had the beauty of a god and the pre-ternatural silence of one. Raw, ancient power seemed to roll off of him, and yet she hadn't heard him approach, which was, well, impossible. She'd have heard anyone come anywhere near her cave. Zylah held her breath as the man bit into a brin fruit, his brow furrowed as if he were thinking her situation over.

Shit. She was blocked in. Even if she could slip past him and outrun him, which, with someone else, might have been possible, she already knew that with him there would be no chance. She exhaled through her nostrils, willing her heartbeat to steady, determined that her fear wouldn't show to the god before her, assuming he couldn't somehow sense it already.

He wiped a sleeve at the brin juice that rolled down his chin and folded his arms across his chest. Gods, the brin fruit looked good. And it would feel so much better than the scrape of the moss on her throat. The god caught her eyeing his snack and gently tossed it towards her.

She caught it instinctively, silently chastising herself for letting her guard slip, but the man didn't make a run for her. Just folded his arms across his chest again and watched her.

Zylah took a bite of the brin fruit and tried not to moan. She pictured the way the outside of the cave looked while she chewed, the cut of the cliff, the space at the end of the rocks that she could travel to, looking within herself for enough energy to do it. What she was looking for, she didn't know. But she wasn't about to take her chances with the silent god.

His dark hair was dripping wet, and he ran a bronzed hand through it as he watched her, his forest-green eyes bright and inquisitive. Was this his attempt to unnerve her? To be silent until she spoke and confessed her situation? She wouldn't break. She'd played this game with her brother many times as a child. She'd always won.

It wasn't the only game she'd played with her brother, and Zylah had learnt the hard way that often the only way to win was to switch up the rules. She took the last bite of the brin fruit, turned to throw it into the darkness of the cave behind her, and pulled on whatever force it was that allowed her to travel. It was energy, neither hot nor cold, but she felt it flow beneath her skin as she called on it.

When the world came back into focus, she was out of the cave and away from the god, the brin fruit and moss in her stomach turning over themselves. She looked ahead and could just make out a line of trees before the fog thickened, and willed herself to travel to them.

The world went dark for a second before she reappeared beside the trees, and a warm hand clamped down on her shoulder. Every muscle in her body tightened. She'd been a fool to think she could outrun a god, but still, she ducked

38

down from his grasp and swung the loose cuff behind his knees as hard as she could.

With an inhuman speed she'd never hope to match, he grabbed the cuff, wrapped the chain around his wrist and pulled her towards him, the air escaping from her throat in a *whoosh*.

Zylah pressed a hand to his hard chest to put distance between them, his shirt wet against his skin, the faint scent of earthy acani berries drifting from him.

"I'll kill you," she breathed, pushing a stick against his ribs. It was all she'd been able to reach when she'd ducked.

"With a pointy stick?" He arched a brow and a smirk tugged at his lips. "What is a young woman doing out here alone, with no weapon, rope marks around her neck, injuries that by all accounts tell me you should be dead, and one broken handcuff?" the god asked, his voice deep and husky.

His breath was sweet with brin fruit, and this close, Zylah could make out the honey-coloured flecks in his eyes. *So this is how it ends. Sucked in by a god's eyes and handsome face. Think, Zy.*

Before she could reply, he placed a hand around her cuffed wrist, and it clicked open beneath his touch. He cast the cuff aside and took a step back. Zylah felt the cold rush back in, ignored the treacherous thoughts that she wanted to feel his body heat again just so she wouldn't freeze to death, and rubbed at her wrist.

She held his gaze, summoning a shred of the confidence that she knew was quickly disappearing. "What is a god doing out here, talking to a young woman, who by all rights most definitely *should* be dead, and is very much hoping to live?" There was no point in trying to deny anything. He'd have taken one look at her and known she was on the run. Did gods punish mortals for escaping death?

He didn't answer, just laughed and folded his arms across his chest again. It was a gesture that had already started to grate on her.

"A god?" he asked, huffing out a breath. "I've never been called that before."

Zylah's cheeks flushed. *If not a god, then what?* She took a step back, trying to make it look as she had when she was a child, as if she were adjusting her balance, just awkward on her feet. Her wet hair dripped down her back and she was certain, if she could see it, the ends would already have turned to icicles. She didn't let go of her stick though.

"I'm no god," he said softly. "But I'm someone you can't outrun. And someone who's had a lot more practice at evanescing than you."

"Evanesce? You mean the travelling?" She looked up at him, hating that she had to tilt her head up so much to meet his gaze, hating that he already knew more about her than she did. "I only discovered I could do it yesterday."

"This also happened yesterday, I take it?" He waved a hand at her neck and face, and his expression seemed to darken.

Zylah reached up instinctively, rubbing at the tender skin around her throat and thought of the moment the trapdoors had opened. She nodded. If she hadn't been with him, whoever he was, she'd have taken a moment to close her eyes, to steady herself. She pulled her hand away and smoothed down the front of her apron to hide her trembling.

Think, think, think.

"Did anyone see you on your way here?" he asked, tilting his head towards the cliff that stretched up to one side of them.

"One guard. By the beacon," Zylah said. She could have lied, but what was the point? It wasn't going to get her out of this.

His eyes narrowed, his head tilting back to look up the cliff face as if he could hear something. "They're coming for you," he breathed, snatching her wrist in his hand.

Zylah didn't have a chance to object, didn't have time to shake him off. The world spun, and she knew at once that he had evanesced them both.

5

Zylah's feet landed in snow and she swore under her breath as it soaked through her shoes. They were part of her palace uniform and absolutely useless for anything outside of the lavishness of Arnir's palace. Her wet hair was far worse though, and she wrapped her arms around herself as she bit back nausea from the evanescing. He'd evanesced them *both*. How?

"Why are you helping me?" she asked as her teeth chattered together.

A few snowflakes had landed on the god-not-a-god's eyelashes and Zylah found herself thinking about how ridiculously long and thick they were. Gods above, the cold had really got to her.

He held her gaze for a moment until his eyes dropped to her arms wrapped around herself. "We need to keep moving," he said and grabbed her wrist again.

Shit. He was so fast, she didn't have a chance to duck out of the way. If not a god, then what? He looked like a human.

A witch, maybe?

The world spiralled around them before it stopped, and Zylah stumbled into snow again, the man's hand tighter around her wrist.

This time, she didn't hesitate, she spun around, swinging her elbow up to meet with his jaw. It wasn't as hard as she'd have liked, thanks to his outrageous height, but it was enough to take him by surprise and for him to release her wrist.

"What was that for?" he asked, running a hand over his jaw, his eyes narrowing.

Zylah rubbed at her wrist, still bruised from the iron cuffs. "You were hurting me."

His eyes flared for a moment, and realisation seemed to sink in. "I… I'm sorry. We can't stay here. The King's Guard patrols the forest." He reached out a hand for her, waiting.

Zylah tilted her head to one side, listening. The forest was quiet, melting snow dripped off branches, ferns rustled nearby and—*there*. The thunder of hooves in the distance. She looked to the man's outstretched hand, to the honey flecks sparkling in his eyes.

"Are you going to tell me your name?" She reached for his hand, irritated by how small hers was in his.

His fingers wrapped around hers. "Holt."

He'd barely finished the word before he evanesced them again, the warmth of his calloused hand spreading through hers, the only part of her body that didn't feel frozen.

When they stopped, Holt released her. "Put these on," he said.

Zylah spun to face him, just as a pair of boots *appeared* in his hand.

"How did you...?" She reached for the boots, kicking off her wet shoes without further argument. "These seem a little small to be yours," she muttered as she laced them up.

"They're not mine," Holt said, his back to her as he turned slowly to the forest. His shirt was still wet in patches, his trousers tight against the muscles of his legs and—

Pervert, she heard Kara's voice whisper in her head. Zylah felt her cheeks warm and turned her attention back to her laces. Theo had been a welcome distraction from the bleakness of Dalstead, cold nights and warm bodies had staved off the reality that she would never leave, never know anything else. But where Theo was lanky, Holt was twice his size, thick with muscle. What in Pallia's name was he?

When she stood, he was waiting, arms folded across his chest. She wanted to give him a second elbow to the face for how much the gesture irritated her but resisted.

He reached his hand out again, and she took it, the forest falling away from them.

They evanesced time and time again until Zylah thought she might hurl up whatever was left of the brin fruit. She was sick of the sight of the forest, of the trees that pressed in around them. And she was so godsdamned thirsty.

She fell to her knees in the snow, cupping some into her hands to get whatever liquid she could from it.

"What are you doing?" Holt asked. He sounded out of breath. *Not a god, after all.* Hours had passed and Zylah had lost all track of time, of how far they'd travelled. The forest seemed to stretch on for an eternity.

"What does it look like I'm doing? I'm thirsty." She didn't bother to look up at him as she pressed the ice-cold snow to her lips.

"Here," he said, handing her a water canister.

Zylah had no idea where it had come from. Probably the same place as the boots, which she was most definitely going to ask him about if they ever stopped running. But now was not a time for questions. She threw her head back as she gulped down the water, forcing herself to stop when she was about halfway.

"Thank you," she said, handing it back to him.

Holt held her gaze for a moment, and finally said, "Have I earned your trust enough for you to tell me *your* name now?" He took a swig and waited for her response.

Zylah studied the forest as she considered her options. *One: lie.* She watched the way the snow was beginning to melt from the trees, how more vegetation coloured the forest floor in a velvety green. Lying could backfire. He wasn't a god, but he was something. He seemed like the type to see a lie from a long way away. The trees had thinned out, but very little light broke through the canopy. An eerie silence still hung over everything. *Two: tell the truth.* And then what? What could he do with just her name? She didn't have to tell him the rest of it. *Gods.* There was no option three, she realised, as at last, she came full circle to face him.

"Zylah," she finally said.

Holt pressed his lips together. Was he hiding a smirk? Zylah didn't know, but she wondered if she'd be quick enough to elbow him again. Best not to test her luck, she decided.

He held out his hand. "Nice to meet you, *Zylah*."

He said it as if it wasn't her name, as if she'd just made up a word and given him that. But she didn't have the chance to argue, because he was already evanescing them to the next location.

When they stopped, Holt dropped her hand and staggered forwards a step. His shirt was damp with sweat, his shoulders heaving with laboured breaths.

"It's okay, we can stop for a bit," Zylah said, unsure how to comfort a stranger she didn't even know if she could trust yet.

Holt's breath clouded in front of him and he swallowed. "It's fine. We're here," he huffed, pointing to something behind her.

Zylah spun around to face a small cabin with a rickety old door and windows that looked as if a light breeze might blow the glass out.

"Go inside and get warm. I'll check the perimeter." Holt didn't wait for a response, just jogged away from her into the forest.

She stared after him for a moment, and then back at the cabin. For a second, the thought of the prince throwing her against the wall in his chambers flashed before her eyes, his hand making contact with her face. If that was Holt's intention, he'd have tried that already, wouldn't he? She pushed out a breath and made her way to the porch.

The door creaked on old hinges as she opened it, her eyes adjusting to the dim space. It was sparsely furnished: a small wooden table with benches, an old, beige, upholstered lounger like the ones she'd seen in the palace, only this one had seen far better days, a bookcase with a handful of tattered books, a fireplace.

She knelt before the hearth, searching for a tinderbox. Fresh logs were already stacked and waiting in the fire. Zylah found the box tucked behind the fire tools, pieces of tinder folded neatly beside the flint. She shoved some into the grate and struck the flint against the side of the box, watching as the sparks caught alight.

Her hand closed around the fire iron, and in the flames, she saw the prince, surrounded by his own blood.

The door creaked open, and she swung around, her weapon raised and ready.

Holt turned his back to her as he closed the door, bolting each of the three locks shut. Zylah tightened her grip.

"You're fast," he said, turning to face her. "But we both know I'm faster. And I have no intention of harming you. Or touching you in any way."

His eyes fell to the marks at her neck, and Zylah wondered if he could hear her heart as loudly as she could. If he somehow knew what had happened to her.

"There's a bath through there." Holt pointed to a door. "It will be warm."

Zylah rested the fire iron back beside the fire. "I've already bathed today."

Holt raised an eyebrow. "You have, but you didn't wash your clothes."

Heat rushed to Zylah's cheeks. The prison stench was rather offensive, but she'd gotten so used to it now. And gods, did she ache still. She shot him a death stare and walked through the door without saying another word, letting it swing shut behind her.

It was a small bathroom, barely any bigger than the bath, full of steaming water, the vapour clouding the air. *How?* Zylah paused to listen for whatever Holt might be doing in the cabin, questioning whether it was wise to jump into a bath with him in the next room. She bit down on her lip and instantly regretted it. *There is still kindness left in this world, Zylah*, her father would say to her, when he'd give free poultices to those who couldn't afford to pay. *We just have to be willing to offer it.* Maybe Holt felt the same way. But it had never sat well with her to accept help, no matter what her father had taught her.

She rubbed at her wrists. There were a hundred different alternative situations Zylah knew she could have been in at that moment, but instead, Holt had spent all day bringing her here. She glanced at the wooden panels of the bathroom. Somewhere safe. She kicked off her boots, untied her apron, pulled off the rest of her clothes and let them all fall to the floor. She didn't need to sniff them to know how fetid the stench was, it was ingrained into her nose.

She stepped into the bath, facing the door so she could keep an eye on it, the water so warm she stifled a moan. A bar

48

of soap sat on the metal rim, and she sniffed at it. Acani berries. She listened for any sound of footsteps outside the door, but Holt was on the other side of the cabin, busying himself with something.

She closed her eyes, wrapping her arms around her knees. She'd survived another day. Zylah breathed in the soothing steam as the adrenaline started to leave her body and saw her father calling out to her from the crowd again, his eyes wet with tears. Her brother's position would protect them both from Arnir, wouldn't it? The door clicked shut, and Zylah's eyes shot open, but the bathroom was empty, the disturbed steam the only sign of any movement.

"I just took your clothes to burn them. There's some clean clothes in the drawer beside the bath," Holt called out from the next room.

Zylah almost leapt out of the bath, water sloshing around her.

"Relax. I'm not really burning your clothes," he said from beyond the door, laughter lining his voice.

Asshole. Zylah sank back down, scrubbing herself with the earthy soap, careful not to disturb the scabs at her wrists before moving onto her hair as she worked her way through all the questions she had for him. Now she was free of the cuffs, she had a lot more options, but she had no idea how widespread Arnir's men would be stationed, how far the king's control reached.

Her aches had eased, the pain in her back almost gone entirely. Even her throat felt a little better. She submerged her head and shoulders beneath the water, holding her breath for a moment in the stillness.

I didn't mean for him to die.

Zylah thought of the way Jesper's blood had pooled on the golden rug, the way his body had stilled. She thought of the blows he'd landed to her face: a backhand to her mouth, a fist to her eye. The way his smooth hands had fumbled to slide up her tunic, his breath hot against her skin. She pushed herself out of the water, gasping for air.

He deserved it, for what he tried to do to you, Kara had told her. And Zylah would do it again if she had to. She ran a shaky hand through her hair to check the soap had rinsed away and stepped out of the bath. Kara was right, but that didn't change anything.

Zylah wrapped herself in the only towel and wiped a hand across the steamed-over mirror. She took in her black eye, her busted lip and the marks at her throat and shook her head. *He deserved it.*

She dried herself quickly and pulled open the drawer to search for clothes. Folded shirts and trousers—all for men. All with a musky smell, and a hint of the acani berries. She opted for a white shirt and a pair of grey trousers with cuffs at the hem, a pair she was certain would be cropped on Holt but came down to her ankles when she slipped them on. The shirt swamped her, but she tucked it in and rolled up the sleeves before towel drying her hair. There was no hope of re-braiding it without a brush. Instead, she combed her fingers through it as best she could before opening the door to the rest of the cabin, steam and the scent of acani berries billowing out around her.

Holt sat cross-legged on the lounger, eating something that looked a lot like a canna cake. Zylah sniffed at the air. It *was* a canna cake.

"There's one for you on the side. Be careful, it's hot," Holt said, waving his cake towards the small area that passed for the kitchen.

"Did you make this appear out of thin air, too?" Zylah asked, testing the heat of the cake before picking it up and blowing on it. She leaned back against the counter, casting her gaze around the cabin as she took a bite. Gods above, it was just as good as Mrs Andell's.

Holt laughed softly. "No," he said, brushing crumbs off his shirt. "I baked it."

Zylah arched a brow. "He looks and moves like a god. He trav... evanesces. Makes things appear from thin air, including, of all things, hot water. He bakes." She listed each item off with a finger as she spoke. "What are you?"

"The same as you, it would seem."

Zylah said nothing as she let his words sink in. There was no way they were alike, and besides, the cake was too good to keep talking through, so she waited for an answer.

"Fae." Holt swung his feet onto the floor, waving a hand at the space on the lounger. Zylah didn't move. "Well, you're half Fae by the looks of things."

She almost choked on the canna cake. "You're not a Fae. Where are your pointy ears?"

His expression darkened for a moment. "I hide them. Best to in my profession."

"And what is that, exactly?" She looked anywhere but at him, scanning every inch of the cabin for—

"What are you looking for?" he asked.

"A weapon."

Holt laughed again, the sound so at odds with the deep tone of his voice. "Here."

He was on his feet so fast and so quietly, she wondered if before he'd been making noise just to reassure her whilst she took a bath. With a few steps he was in front of her, and she had to tilt her head up again to look at him. He reached over her; the musky smell mixed with acani berries drifting from him as he handed her a small dagger.

He must have noticed the way she'd stilled, and his mouth pressed into a firm line. "I won't touch you," he said softly. "You don't have to be afraid of me."

"Who said anything about being afraid?" Zylah asked, snatching the dagger from his hand and side-stepping out from under him, throwing herself on the lounger with as much confidence as she could muster. "The Fae are long dead. What are you *really*?"

He folded his muscled arms across his chest again, and Zylah considered throwing the dagger at him.

"Many died. Many fled. But some stayed," he said, holding her gaze.

Zylah had always thought it odd that not a single Fae had remained after the war but then, she'd never left Dalstead and the small villages that surrounded it; had only lived under Arnir's rule. And speaking of the Fae was forbidden, punishable by death—any record of them destroyed. "And what makes you think I'm half Fae?"

"Besides the evanescing, your speed, your heightened senses?"

She tested the weight of the dagger, her grip firm as she raised an eyebrow to him. "Fine. But those could be a coincidence. Apart from maybe the evanescing. Can all Fae do that?"

"What happened to you?" Holt asked, leaning back against the counter as she had been moments before.

Zylah was quiet, her gaze settling on the flames in the hearth. It would be different telling him than Kara. Kara understood. Kara knew her.

"We can talk more in the morning. Get some rest," Holt said, as if he'd sensed her discomfort. He made his way over to the bookcase, grabbed a book and took a seat at the table.

The motion pulled Zylah from her thoughts. "Alright, *old man*." But she *was* exhausted, physically and emotionally, and she was still ten kinds of uncomfortable that she couldn't figure Holt out. She'd been doing just fine before he showed up. She could have evanesced away from the king's men. *But for how long?* Zylah wasn't used to relying on others, least of all strangers, and yet there was no denying she'd be spending the night in another cave, or worse if it weren't for Holt.

He rubbed at his neck, and for the first time, she saw a nasty scar poking out of the top of his shirt. "There's water on the table," he said, not even looking up, shifting his bench to turn away from her, as if he wanted to give her some privacy whilst she slept.

Zylah chewed at her lip, wincing when a tooth caught the place the split was healing. He looked exhausted from a day of evanescing, and her own exhaustion told her to leave her questions until the morning. He *had* helped her, there was no denying it. She just had to know why. No one did that in Dalstead.

There was little privacy to be had in the cabin. In two strides she could be in the *kitchen*, two strides in the other direction and she could open the door to the bathroom. But it was better than out there, in the snow.

Zylah took a swig of water and settled into the lounger, watching the flames as Holt's words sank in. *You're half Fae.* And if King Arnir thought as much, he wouldn't stop searching for her until she was dead.

6

Kara's favourite book was set in the forest. Faeries, of all things. Ethereal beauty, kind hearts, courage. Those were the qualities Kara had listed as her favourites. Zylah awoke from a strange dream, her fingers brushing against something soft and the images fading as soon as the fabric registered around her fingers. It was a blanket. Her eyes shot open, and she took in the sight of the cabin in the daylight, of the man asleep on the floor beside the lounger. The *Fae*.

Holt must have put the blanket over her when she'd fallen asleep. She sat up, a hand instinctively reaching to the rope burns at her neck. The skin felt normal; there was no ache. She caught sight of her wrist. The scabs were gone, and from her other wrist too. She reached a hand to her lip, her fingers tracing against smooth skin. Had he healed her, whilst she slept?

The dull ache around the knot in her spine remained, but that didn't surprise her, she was getting used to it already. She looked at the way Holt rested his head on his arm, his shoulders heaving with each breath. More of his scar escaped the collar of his shirt, up the back of his neck almost to his hairline. He'd helped her. But that didn't mean she owed him anything, did it?

She studied his face, the angle of his jaw, the way his mouth pressed into a firm line and his brows furrowed slightly. He seemed a little older than she was, mid-twenties perhaps, stubble peppered across his jaw. There was something familiar about him, but Zylah couldn't place what.

Morning light filtered in through the dirty glass of the cabin, dust motes dancing in the air. And clothes, hanging to dry. *Her* clothes. Gods. *All* of her clothes. Zylah leapt over Holt's sleeping body and grabbed her things from the line around the fireplace.

She spun around to find Holt awake, hands resting on his knees.

"You washed my undergarments?" she seethed, trying not to wave them at him. Her hair fell around her shoulders, and she was certain its messiness undermined her demeanour.

Holt ran a hand through his own tousled hair, but it did little to tame his bedhead. "They were dirty," he said with a shrug, and with one graceful movement, he was on his feet and in the kitchen, unwrapping another canna cake.

Where in the seven gods did these things keep coming from? How many godsdamned cakes had he baked whilst she was in the bath?

"I think we need to establish some ground rules," Zylah

said, eyeing the canna cake as her stomach unceremoniously broke the silence and hoping her face wasn't as red as it felt.

Holt threw her a cake, and Zylah shoved her clothes under her arm just in time to catch it. "Fine. Rule number one, no more touching Zylah's undergarments," Holt said, biting into a cake to hide his smirk.

Zylah remembered her dagger, but she'd foolishly left it on the lounger. She sat back down as casually as she could, casting her clothes to one side and biting into the cake. Gods, this Fae could bake.

"Rule number two," Holt continued, wiping his hands together. "No elbowing each other in the face." His eyes moved to her hand, already tight around the hilt. "No hurting each other at all." His mouth twitched, and she wondered if he ever actually truly smiled.

Zylah swallowed down the last of the cake and held her hand out to silence him. "Rule number three," she said, holding up three fingers for emphasis. "I'm not going anywhere else with you until you tell me what you want from me."

Holt had already turned his back to her, clattering around with something on the kitchen counter. He made his way over to the hearth, waving a hand across it and hanging a kettle with the other. The fire roared to life. "Tea?" he asked, not even turning to look at her.

"No, I don't want any tea. What I want is—"

"Are you sure? I use honey and alea blossom; it might help with that," he said, flicking his chin towards her throat again. Except it didn't hurt anymore, because it had somehow miraculously healed in the night, and she was sure *he* knew that, could see that. He got a point for the alea blossom, though.

Zylah crossed her legs on the sofa and busied herself with looking at her dagger. "Who are you, what are you, and why are you helping me?"

Holt pulled two cups down to the hearth, dropping in dried alea blossoms and spooning some honey into each. "I'm Holt. I'm Fae. And I'm not in the habit of just leaving people to die out in the wilderness."

Zylah ground her teeth. "There are others like you? More Fae?"

"You're here, aren't you?"

"But I'm not… I'm just ordinary." He had it wrong, surely. There were no Fae in Dalstead, Zylah had always been taught there were none left in Astaria at all.

The kettle whistled, and Holt poured steaming water into both cups. "I think we both know you're far from ordinary." A heartbeat of silence stretched out between them. "Do you know your real parents?"

"No."

He handed her a cup. "And you're what, let me guess, early twenties?"

Zylah nodded. "Twenty-three."

"Precisely the number of years ago that the Fae were driven out of Astaria."

Zylah blew against the hot tea, the aroma of the alea blossom pulling her back to her father's apothecary.

58

What if something had happened to him, just for knowing her? She cast the thought aside. "Discussing the Fae in Dalstead is punishable by death. All I know is that there were Fae, once, and now there are none."

Holt rolled his eyes. "Arnir and his rules. Is that what you did, to end up on the gallows, discuss the Fae?" He sat cross-legged before her, his back to the fire, his frame illuminated by the flames as he sipped at his tea, and for the second time, she noticed how absurdly big his hands were.

Zylah studied his hands as she fought back the memories of being in the prince's quarters, focusing on the way Holt's fingers rested around the cup. She swallowed as she recalled the prince's avenberry breath against her skin, the rage in his eyes as he struck her across the face. "I did not."

"And you won't tell me what you did?" Holt asked, meeting her eyes.

"I stabbed someone for asking too many questions," Zylah said, holding his gaze over the edge of her cup as she took a sip of her tea.

That elicited a smile, a real one. Ethereal beauty, Kara's books had said. They were right.

"Few Fae remain outside of Dalstead, but they still exist, scattered here and there. All keep a low profile, keep out of the way of Arnir's men," Holt said.

Gods, Kara would never believe it. So many times they had talked of meeting Fae as they sat in the tall grass in her father's garden. Her home. "You mentioned you hide your ears because of your profession. What is it, exactly?"

59

"One that I'll have to be getting back to. I'm on my way to Virian. I've connections there I can introduce you to. They'll help you get set up, get on your way."

Zylah felt a flicker of something at his words. Disappointment? *You barely know him.* No, not disappointment; it just felt as if she were trouble and he was trying to get rid of her. *It's the truth.* But she could look after herself. Could find work with the local apothecary, perhaps, just enough to save for onward travel. "Connections. Are they Fae?"

Holt was quiet as he drained his cup.

"Can they teach me about the evanescing?" Zylah asked, handing him the empty cup and scooping up her clothes.

"I'm starting to understand why you stabbed someone for asking too many questions." Holt was on his feet, tidying away their cups. He was far too big for the tiny cabin, but he moved with the grace of a wildcat and the silent footsteps to match.

He turned his back to her and Zylah considered throwing the dagger at the spot on the wall just in front of his head. Maybe later. She took her clothes to the bathroom instead, changing out of his and into the ones he'd washed for her. *Gods above.* But it felt good to have something familiar, something of home. Even if it was just the clothes on her back. *Half Fae.* And what did being Fae mean so far? They didn't seem to stick together, that much she could tell.

She studied her face in the mirror. Her wounds were entirely healed: no black eye, no split lip. No rope marks at her neck. She still looked half-starved, though. *A week in a rotting prison cell will do that for you.*

She'd need to change her appearance, she thought, working strands of her blonde hair into a braid. Perhaps some erti root to dye it brown; she could change the style too. Her eyes would be harder to disguise, but she'd once seen a traveller in the Andells' bakery with a pair of eyeglasses; she could look for a pair of those wherever Holt was taking her.

A new life. It was what she'd always wanted, wasn't it? But it felt meaningless without being able to see her father and brother, or Kara. Like this, there was no one to share it with. She trampled the seed of doubt before it could whisper at her further and pushed the door open to the rest of the cabin. Her freedom was all that mattered.

Holt was waiting for her, arms folded across his chest—*surprise, surprise*—and waved a hand at her boots. "It's another day's journey to Virian. We should be there by nightfall." He wore a dark leather coat that reached to his knees, a sword strapped across his back, the same shirt and trousers from the day before.

"Tell me," Zylah said as she knelt to slip on her boots. "Why don't you evanesce us all the way there? Is it too far for you?" Her fingers brushed against a sheath down the inside of one boot she'd noticed the day before, and she tucked her dagger securely inside it.

Holt straightened one of the benches beside the table with one hand. "No, it isn't too far. Different types of magic leave a different type of trace. We're trying to lose anyone who might be tracking us. Unless of course, you'd like me to lead the king's guards right to you?"

It was a question that needed no response. But she tucked the snippet about the magic away for another time. "What's the furthest you've ever evanesced?" Zylah asked, pushing herself to her feet, tilting her head back to meet his gaze.

An expression she couldn't name danced across his face for a moment, and he tugged gently at her braid. "You'll be too cold like this, and we need to cover your hair." He waved a hand and a cloak wrapped around her shoulders.

"How do you do that?" she asked, examining the fine black fabric between her fingers. "Are you just pulling this stuff from nowhere?"

He laughed, and gently hooked a fastening at her throat, those green eyes of his fixed on hers as his fingers adeptly took to their task. "Of course not. A thing has to exist for me to summon it. It helps if I know where it is too."

Zylah pictured her favourite dagger tucked under her bed back in her father's house and clicked her fingers. Nothing happened. She rolled her eyes. *Typical.*

Holt huffed another laugh again as he fastened something else on the cloak. How many godsdamned fastenings did this thing have?

"So this is yours?" she asked, sniffing at the fabric and trying to focus on anything but the warmth that radiated from him and the way the muscles in his arms flexed as he did whatever the seven gods he was doing with her new cloak.

He pulled up the hood and held a hand across his heart. "You wound me. I do bathe, you know."

"Do you?"

"Of course. What do you think I was doing at the springs when I found you?" That smirk was back, and a dangerous glint sparkled in Holt's eyes.

Zylah felt heat rise in her chest as she realised he *was* wet when he'd found her, as if he'd just got out of the water, and that he might have seen her bathing. "So this is yours?" she repeated, the only thing she could think of to change the subject.

"It's my sister's."

He stepped back, and Zylah knew at once that she'd asked the wrong thing. Holt waved a hand at the fire and it snuffed out immediately.

She made a mental note not to mention his family again, running her fingers along the hem of the cloak. "You healed me, didn't you?"

"I did."

And she'd hit him in the face. *Gods.* He'd deserved it though. *Who just runs off with someone like that, without a word? The nerve.* "Sorry for elbowing you in the face," she offered.

"No, you're not."

"No, I'm not." She wished he'd look at her, but he was busying himself with straightening the cabin, and she was just watching the way he moved through the world, the speed and precision in each movement. "But thank you for healing me, you didn't have to do that. Although I really would love it if you'd explain some of this Fae stuff to me. Starting with the evanescing."

"Look at you, accepting your heritage," he said, finally

turning to face her. He'd attempted to tame his unruly hair and she wondered if he'd cut it short around his ears on purpose. So that people saw their roundness, their humanness.

She wanted to see what he really looked like. What else had he changed about his appearance? "I'm not... I just, need to understand it," she said instead. It was the truth. She was used to being able to find things out for herself, to read, to learn, to practice, even if her knowledge was limited. Relying on information from someone else made her uneasy, but Arnir had made sure all knowledge of the Fae had been destroyed. Holding any possessions related to the Fae, books or any other objects would see you in his prison, too. All were forbidden to speak of them. She didn't mention that Kara had smuggled Fae novels and leant them to Zylah whenever she could.

"We need to get going. If you were meant for the gallows, Arnir's men won't stop until you're dead."

And there it was, the thought that Zylah had somehow managed to cast aside since the night before. She was an escaped convict who'd killed the prince, and no amount of learning anything would ever change that.

7

They evanesced for hours. When Zylah offered to give Holt a rest, he quizzed her on her knowledge of the Falstin forest that bordered Virian. She had no knowledge of either, and gods did it irritate her.

It was another item she tucked away for later, for when they made it to Virian and she could find a library to learn as much as possible of the geography of the world. Already she was beginning to realise how little she knew of it, and if she was to spend her life running, she had a great deal of learning to do. She was in no hurry to come back to the Falstin forest any time soon, of that she was certain.

"So you need to know what a place looks like to evanesce to it?" she asked as they stopped for Holt to catch his breath. It was another observation she held onto—that he had a limit to his power, and it explained the way she'd felt when she'd evanesced so many times consecutively after leaving the gallows. The ache in her back hadn't quite gone away, and she wondered now if it ever would.

Holt surveyed the forest, looking and listening, and Zylah did the same, taking in the way the sunlight filtered through the trees, how the snow thinned in patches, the scent of disturbed earth and fir needles. There were plants everywhere, and she wished she had her notebook with her, but her memory would have to do. Gods, it was cold.

He finally turned to face her. "You need to know what a place looks like, yes. For shorter distances, just having a visual is enough."

"And where do we go, when we're evanescing?" *Tree fern, fresh shoots, fascinating.* Zylah investigated every new plant she came across.

Holt had paused to look at her. "The space between worlds."

Zylah felt another pair of eyes on her, but when she looked through the trees, she saw nothing but shadows. Every forest had sprites of its own, her father had always taught her. Every patch of water, every stretch of marsh. All things in nature had a spirit, and they were to be treated with respect. "Between... worlds?" she asked, turning her attention back to Holt. He was about a second away from folding his arms across his chest, she thought, one eyebrow raised as he watched her.

"The aether," Holt replied, folding his arms across his chest, the muscles in his arms pushing against his coat sleeves. *Called it.*

Zylah ran her fingers through the tree ferns, shaking off the last of the snow that still dusted them. "I understand the

66

concept of aether. But are there truly other worlds out there?"

"There are many." His breath clouded in front of him as he spoke, and again she thought of how wild he seemed, as if he were half animal. It wasn't just the way he moved, but how he held himself when he was still. As if that power she'd sensed the day before seemed to simmer beneath his skin.

"So it works exactly the same in reverse, with the items," Zylah mused. "You said you need to know where a thing is to summon it."

"I said *it helps* if I know where it is." He'd turned away from her, looking out into the forest again, listening.

That explained the boots, and the water canister, and the cloak, but… "How did you get the hot water in the bath then?"

Holt still didn't face her, just observed the forest quietly. He had to be some kind of hunter. Maybe a mercenary. He had enough muscle for someone to hire it anyway.

"From the springs," he said, in answer to her question.

That was… *impressive*, but Zylah wasn't about to confess as much. "Can all Fae do this?"

"No." His voice had become even deeper during their conversation, and she stifled a laugh as she realised it was with irritation.

An owl hooted somewhere nearby. *Isn't it too early for owls?* Zylah had no idea. She'd lost all track of time. The Goddess Pallia was always depicted with an owl, and although Zylah never truly believed in the deities she'd been taught at school, it was Pallia she whispered to when she was alone. She was the Goddess of Wisdom and Knowledge, and that always appealed to Zylah. Never mind that she was also the Goddess of War and Heroism. And of Sacrifice, although Zylah supposed she already knew a little of that.

"Ah, jupinus amataxus," Zylah mused, reaching for a flower. Her fingers were freezing, but this find was worth the cold. "Fascinating. I've never seen it in the wild."

"You are strange. You know that, don't you?"

"Jupe for short. The flower can be used for sniffles and coughs. The leaves are highly poisonous. No odour, either. Here." She waved the flower at him, and he took a step back. Zylah shrugged and shoved a handful into her apron out of habit.

"That explains the moss," Holt said. "In your apron."

Zylah rolled her eyes and held up four fingers. "Rule number four... no going through my things."

"I'd hardly call moss *a belonging*, Zylah."

It was the second time he'd said her name, and it sent a shiver down her spine. "Moss has many uses. If you must know, I was keeping it for a snack, and to pack inside my cuff so it wouldn't rub." She turned away from him, busying herself with looking at the ferns again to hide the flush in her cheeks.

"How did you get the first one open?" He'd taken a step closer as Zylah crouched down to inspect a fern frond, her left hand hovering near her boot and the hilt of her knife. Just in case.

She examined the fern, but she was listening to the sound of his breathing, to how even each breath was. They'd be on the move again soon. "My friend gave me a hairpin."

"You picked a lock with a hairpin?" he asked. He crouched down beside her, but his gaze was somewhere else, off into the shadows of the forest. Heat radiated from him, and she resisted the urge to shuffle closer, just for the warmth.

Zylah couldn't see whatever he'd seen—only more trees and shadows, broken up by the odd beam of light here and there. *And a few pairs of eyes*, her mind whispered. But when she blinked, they were gone. "That's what I just said, yes."

"How?" Even crouching, it was ridiculous how much he towered over her.

A twig snapped in the bushes, and her hand instinctively closed on the hilt of her dagger, but Holt seemed unfazed. "By feel and sound. I could hear the pin catching inside the lock. But it broke inside the second one."

A rabbit hopped out of the bushes, and Holt arched a brow. "You're tenacious, I'll give you that."

She'd been called far worse, she supposed. The owl cried out again, and Holt was on his feet, sword drawn in one graceful, practised movement. Zylah pulled her knife free, and as she stood with her back to him, it wasn't lost on her just how much she looked like a child beside him, her tiny frame and her small dagger next to him and his enormous sword. Not that it mattered, she knew how to do plenty of damage with what she had.

"Stay together," Holt said almost inaudibly.

"Where in Pallia's name do you think I would go?" she muttered.

An arrow whistled through the air, a sound Zylah had

heard many times practising with her brother, but before she could step out of the way, Holt had spun out in front of her with preternatural speed, swiping the arrow away with a sword.

A flash of metal caught Zylah's eye, and she pivoted away just as someone charged at her with a blade. Holt was already occupied with another of their attackers. Zylah held her dagger steady, easily ducking and twisting out of the reach of the sword. Its owner was a beast of a man; where Holt was toned and muscular, this man was brutish, a nasty scar running from his eyebrow across the corner of his right eye and down to his cheek.

Zylah spotted an opening in the brute's stance, swung around and shoved her dagger into the flesh beneath his ribs. It wasn't a fatal wound, but it was the only opening she had. With a grunt, she yanked the dagger back out and almost lost her footing backing away from him.

"A tiny knife for a tiny girl. I've had whores cut me deeper than that," he spat, pressing a hand to his wound.

Tiny girl? Zylah clicked her tongue. She wasn't *that* short, well, maybe. And she'd had the body of a woman since she was thirteen, another reason she'd learnt to hide herself in a crowd. For a time, she'd even considered binding her chest to better disguise her shape.

She weighed up her options. He was striking to kill, not merely to injure her or knock her off her feet. He pressed a hand to his wound and pulled it away to examine the blood, and when his gaze met hers, Zylah knew whoever landed the next blow would be the one to walk away from this. She swallowed back her fear at the thought.

A sword clashed against another behind her, but Zylah didn't dare turn her back from the brute as she circled him, studying his hideous face for any signs of a tell; the moment before he might swipe at her next.

He lunged forwards with his sword and Zylah spun around him, leaping onto his back and dragging her dagger across his throat. She tried not to think about how easily the blade cut through flesh. Instead, she pushed herself off as he fell to his knees and landed face first amongst the jupe flowers. *What a waste.* She whispered a quiet prayer to Pallia, her breaths uneven and shaky.

It took her only a moment to spot the third attacker firing arrows from amongst the trees, and she was loath to part with her dagger from this distance. With a glance at Holt, she counted three arrows protruding from his frame. *Not a god, he says.*

The archer's attention was on Holt, and Zylah took the opportunity to crouch out of sight, low amongst the ferns as she caught her breath. If she was quick enough... She didn't think it through, just evanesced herself to the space behind the archer, throwing herself onto his back as she had with the brute. But the archer was swifter, and in one fluid motion, he threw her over his shoulder.

All her breath was knocked out of her as she hit the cold, hard ground, opening her eyes to the archer's bow slamming down towards her. *Shit.* There was no time to roll out of the way. She brought her hands up over her eyes, but no impact came. The archer made a choking sound, and when she looked up, vines wrapped tightly around his bow, trapping it between his arms and his body. His mouth hung open as he choked, and hundreds of grub beetles erupted from it.

What in the—?

Zylah didn't stay to watch. She rolled away and shoved herself to her feet, still trying to catch her breath.

More insects came from the forest and Zylah backed away as they covered the archer entirely, turning his body into a swarming mass of black and brown. *By the gods.* She stepped back again, slamming into something hard. And warm. A person. She spun around, swiping her dagger, but Holt caught her wrist.

He released her the moment their eyes met. "I'm sorry," he said, flicking his chin at her wrist where he'd touched her. "I thought you were going to stab me."

"I was." Zylah lowered her weapon, wiping it in the snow to hide her trembling as the fight caught up with her. *Steady breaths, Zy.* Two lives she'd taken now, and a third, sort of. "Why did you wait so long to do that?" she asked, assuming it could only have been magic that had the archer crawling with half the forest over his body. Zylah could barely make out the outline of his frame under the mound of vines and insects that covered it.

"The last part wasn't me," Holt said, watching her as she cleaned her blade, his gaze moving from her to the brute, face first amongst the ferns beyond them.

Zylah pushed herself to her feet, tilting her head back to look at him. "But the vines were?"

"Yes. Like I told you. Magic can be traced. I keep mine muted. For good reason." He sheathed his sword. Zylah didn't need to ask if the third attacker was dead.

"Are you going to do anything about those?" she asked, pointing at the arrows protruding from his arm and back.

Holt waved a hand and the arrows fell away. "You're bleeding," he said, his brow scrunching in concern. "May I?" He stepped closer, his hand hovering over her cheek. It must have been the archer when he'd thrown her over his shoulder.

It was her own fault for not thinking it through. Zack would have chastised her for her foolishness. Zylah blinked as she registered how close Holt was, the warmth from his hand as it rested an inch away from her cheek. He held her gaze, waiting, and she nodded.

She felt the warmth flow from his hand into her, the sting of the wound as he healed it. She cleared her throat as he stepped away. "Thank you." He was already observing the forest, his gaze anywhere but her.

"If only the first part was you, who was the second part?" Zylah asked. She took in the forest as he did, listening for any sounds that might indicate more bounty hunters were on their way. Something cried nearby, a bird, maybe.

Holt looked in the same direction as the pained sound, his mouth a firm line. If the arrows had bothered him, he showed no sign of pain, but then he'd healed her, so she assumed he'd healed himself.

73

"The sprites. They're drawn to my powers," Holt said as the creature cried out again. "We need to leave." He reached out his hand for hers but didn't take it.

"Wait," Zylah said, stepping towards the creature's cries. "Look, an elf owl." *Just like Pallia's.* Zylah knelt next to the frail thing, one wing lying awkwardly to the side. "It warned us," she breathed. "He's the one that warned us right before the attack." She scooped the owl into her palms, stroking the peppered feathers with a thumb. He was so small she could almost cup her hands around him entirely.

"I understand why you want to save it," Holt said with an edge to his voice that hadn't been there before. "You just killed a man. But—"

"He wasn't the first man I've killed." Zylah swallowed the ache in her throat. "Please." She hated the way her voice wavered. Hated that he wouldn't help. But she couldn't leave the owl to die. Its eyes fluttered as she stroked its head.

Holt sighed. A heartbeat later he held a hand over the owl, its wing healing right before Zylah's eyes.

"We need to go, now," Holt said, his head jerking at a sound in the forest. "They were Arnir's men. More will be following."

The little owl didn't leave Zylah's palms as Holt's hand closed around her wrist, the forest spinning away from them.

8

They reappeared outside the walls of a great city, amongst a cluster of trees set back from the road. Zylah tried to hide her wonder at just how high the walls stretched from the outside. Dalstead was big, but this was something else, and she found herself wondering why Arnir hadn't chosen this one for his capital.

There were no traces of snow here, and as soon as Zylah could get her hands on a map she intended to study it, if only to learn how far they'd travelled. Holt was alert, as she'd become accustomed to, his eyes taking in everything from the caravan shuffling by on the dirt road to the guards pacing back and forth.

"The quicker we get inside, the better. It's too busy to evanesce unseen into the city. Leave the owl here, he'll be fine." He waved a hand but then held it out for her to wait.

"Absolutely not. Kopi's coming with us," Zylah hissed as a guard passed them. She knew this game well: wait for the right moment to blend in with the crowd, to become one of them. For the moment, they were just any old pair having an argument in the shade.

Holt's eyebrow raised. "You named the owl?"

If he folded his arms across his chest now, Zylah decided she was going to stab him for it. "He saved us. We owe him." Kopi stirred in her palms as she ran a thumb across his soft feathers. Two children ran by, chasing a lizard through the dirt.

Holt folded his arms across his chest, those ridiculous muscles of his pushing against his coat and puffed out a quiet breath. "I don't think owls believe in life debts. Besides, I healed him, we're even."

"Fine, the two of you are even, but I still owe him a debt. I can't just leave him here." Stabbing Holt was off the cards with her hands full. He'd be onto her the moment she set Kopi down, and that wasn't about to happen any time soon. Holt might have healed the little owl, but Kopi still seemed too drowsy to be left alone.

A muscle in Holt's jaw flickered. "I can't believe we're discussing whether or not you can bring an owl into Virian."

Gods it was irritating how much she had to tilt her head back to look up at him.

She gently tucked Kopi into the pocket of her apron, readjusting her cloak over the front of it. "What do you do? For your job. You handled the sword rather efficiently for a baker."

Sunlight cut through the trees and cast a soft glow onto his bronze skin. His eyes were bright as he tilted his head to one side, as if he were covering a smile. "A baker?"

Zylah shrugged as she watched a man pass, leading a horse carrying his heavily pregnant partner towards the city gates. "The canna cakes. It's all I had to go on."

"I'm not a baker," Holt said. She could hear the amusement in his voice, but she wouldn't look up at him. She wouldn't give him the satisfaction.

She pushed up the hood of her cloak instead, making sure her hair was tucked away. "Then what?" The guards had long gone and now was as good a moment as any to step out of the cover of the trees, to join the bustle of traffic to and from the city.

Holt moved out of the shadows first, ushering her to follow him. "Why is it so important that you know?" he asked, the moment she was beside him again.

"Because I like to figure things out for myself," Zylah mused, her gaze fixed ahead on another caravan, an old man sitting at the back of the last wagon staring back at her.

"Asking me doesn't really count then, does it?" Holt had moved his sword to a sheath at his waist, his fingertips dancing over the hilt as they walked, eyes darting about the crowd.

One of the carts must have been carrying livestock, and as the breeze picked up, it carried the stench of confined animals and dung towards them in a warm gust.

Zylah waved a hand across her face. "Fine, I'll keep guessing." She would figure him out, she was determined to.

"You only get three guesses. And you've used up one with baker. Two left," Holt said with a smirk, watching her waft the stench away.

There was something so familiar about walking beside him. As if they'd done it before. *Good gods, Zy, listen to yourself.* Kara's books had finally started to affect her. They fell into an easy silence as they joined the queue shuffling into the city across a great cobblestone bridge so wide Zylah couldn't see off either side. All she could see was the perfect blue sky, not a cloud in sight.

Holt tensed beside her. "Keep your hood up and loop your arm through mine."

There was still a bite in the air here, enough to warrant her keeping her hood up, anyway, not that she'd confess to him that she'd had any intention of taking it down. "Oh, good sir, you flatter me."

"Just do it," Holt muttered, but not unkindly, holding his arm out for her to take.

Zylah hummed in agreement as she looped her arm through his. It was difficult not to press against him with the height difference, but she managed to keep an inch of space between them. "I must look like your child beside you."

"Papers, get your papers ready!" a guard called out at the gates.

Holt swallowed. Was he worried about getting her inside the city? "You... most certainly do not."

"Most certainly? What's that supposed to mean?" She chanced a look up at him, but if he felt her gaze, he didn't glance down, just frowned and looked ahead to the gates.

Other people seemed to be paying for entrance to the city,

but Holt merely nodded at the guards as they passed, dropping Zylah's arm for a moment and pressing lightly at her back as they stepped through the gates. His warmth flowed through her clothes, but as soon as it was there, it was gone, and she felt the cold draw in immediately. When she didn't move to reach for him, he looped her arm through his again to keep them moving. The guards hadn't asked him for papers... which meant he could have been someone important, or perhaps he'd just bribed them... Zylah ran through options, but she wasn't ready to waste another guess just yet.

Kopi stirred in her apron as if the sounds of the city had woken him, but he made no move to scramble for freedom. The main street from the gates was a wide expanse of cobblestones, paler than those on the bridge, some with dark patterns Zylah had never seen before. There were too many people to get a good look at them; there were people everywhere. The two caravans had come to a stop, and an argument had broken out up ahead.

Holt tugged her down a side street, too narrow for wagons but just as bustling. She wanted to look up, to take everything in, but didn't dare. She kept her gaze to the cobblestones, to the feet of the people walking by, listening to the sounds of chattering and laughter, to pedlars pushing wares as they pressed on. Different aromas drifted to them as they walked, and Zylah struggled to keep up with Holt's irritatingly long strides as she slowed to take in each new scent; this one, a florist, she smelt the venti lilies before she saw them, purple and in full bloom in wooden buckets along the pavement. She didn't dare look any higher. "This is so different to Dalstead."

"You walk like someone who's had a lot of practice being invisible," Holt said quietly at her side.

She glared up at him. If she stabbed him here in the street, no one would notice, would they? "You're just full of compliments today, aren't you?"

"Why?" Holt asked.

"Why what?"

"Why are you so good at hiding yourself?" He glanced down at her for a moment, before his attention went back to, well, everything else.

"I learnt not to draw attention to myself from a young age," she admitted as the scent of freshly baked bread carried to her. The noise and the aromas were overwhelming, but she wasn't about to admit that to Holt.

"And yet you only just discovered you're half Fae?"

"So you tell me, oh wise one. Hunter?" It was a long shot, but he observed the world like a hunter might watch its prey.

"One guess remaining," he mumbled. Was that a smile tugging at the corner of his mouth?

Zylah could play this game. "I'll figure you out, Holt, you'll see."

Holt didn't answer; he had stopped beside her and gone utterly still.

"What is it?" she asked, chancing another look up at him.

Even Kopi was stirring as if he wanted to peek out of her clothes. Holt was staring ahead, jaw clenched, and she followed his gaze to a patch of posters plastered against a wall.

There were posters for shows, musical productions, even a botanical garden—that alone under any other circumstances would have had her jumping for joy—but right beside them, dotted in every space, were wanted posters, with a rather too close for comfort rendering of her face.

Fear clutched at Zylah's chest. *Dye your hair. Find some eyeglasses.* She repeated the instructions over and over to herself to remain calm.

She released Holt's arm and walked right up to the posters, tugging at the one closest to her. *Calling all Bounty Hunters. Fugitive Fae wanted for the murder of Prince Jesper. Highly dangerous. Use caution. Bonus rewarded if the subject is brought to the king alive.* She didn't dare look up. What if someone recognised her? She felt for any stray hairs poking out of her hood, readjusting them as subtly as she could.

"How... it's only been a few days, how are these already here?" Zylah swallowed. She wanted to tear off her cloak, needed to feel the fresh air on her face, but she didn't dare.

Holt took the poster from her hand and slapped it back on the wall. "Arnir has trained eagles. They'd have been here before nightfall the same day you escaped. Let's go," he said, with a gentle hand to her back again.

They were silent as they walked the next few streets. Zylah didn't hold onto his arm as he'd asked, and he didn't reach for her either. Just as well, because she didn't feel like hanging onto him like some desperate lover. She repeated her plan over and over, her thoughts drifting to the botanical gardens—she could try for a job there, or at the apothecary—a city of this size might even have two. But the botanical gardens interested her most. That was an opportunity to learn something new.

Holt said nothing of the poster. She supposed he probably believed it after she'd killed the bounty hunter back in the forest, and neither of the two facts seemed to bother him. He stopped at a wooden door and pushed it aside. Laughter and the tang of ale hit Zylah, along with the same smell that seemed to cling to all taverns and drinking houses: spilt drinks and sweat.

Holt's hand rested lightly against her back as he guided them to the bar, where an old man cleaning a tankard with a filthy rag beamed at them as they approached.

"Holter, my boy!" The old man slammed the tankard down and wiped his hands on his apron.

"Holter?" Zylah murmured.

"Just play along," he mumbled back. "I'll be needing my room for a few nights, possibly longer," he said brightly to the barman, tilting his head in Zylah's direction.

The barman gave her a wide smile. "Of course, dear boy. It's ready and waiting for you."

"Do you bring a lot of women here?" Zylah muttered, heat rising to her cheeks as the barman winked at her. She was barely tall enough to rest her arms on the bar, not that she'd have wanted to, it was filthy, and whilst she didn't mind getting her hands dirty, she saw no use in ruining Holt's sister's fine cloak.

"Can I borrow your map, Arran? I've got some deliveries to plan."

"Anything for you, dear boy." Arran hobbled to the end of the bar and returned with a scroll of parchment and a rusty key. "Keep the map, I have another. Breakfast at the usual time?"

Holt nodded and gave his thanks, steering Zylah away from the bar.

"Deliveries? Hmm, nice try, but I'm not going to waste a guess for that," Zylah teased, but Holt didn't reply.

They zigzagged between the busy tables, up a narrow wooden staircase and to the end of a dark corridor, until they reached a door that had once been green but had now faded almost entirely. Holt turned the key in the lock, and Kopi stirred again in Zylah's apron.

She cast aside thoughts of being alone in the prince's chambers. *I won't touch you... you don't have to be afraid of me.* Holt's words played on repeat. He'd had plenty of opportunities before now if that was his intention.

He ushered her into the room, closing the door behind them, and for the first time since entering the city, Zylah removed her hood and looked around.

A large, neatly made bed covered in a green blanket took up most of the room. A threadbare grey rug covered the floor, wooden side tables, a lounger like the one back at Holt's cabin, a few pieces of furniture in the same style as the side tables, and in the corner by the window, a small table and chairs just big enough to seat two completed the interior. About as fine as Zylah would expect for a tavern... but he'd referred to it as his.

The light was fading fast, and outside, lamps had started to flicker on. Zylah resisted the urge to look out of the window just yet, in case someone recognised her still.

Holt had sat on the end of the bed, spreading out the map and Zylah's hands shot to her mouth when she took in the distance they'd travelled.

"Oh, gods. How did we get so far from home? My family, I didn't expect to be so far away from them." Kopi stirred in Zylah's apron at her outburst, and she gently reached for the owl to check on him.

Holt sighed. "Better for them that you are. They'll be safer this way."

She saw the prince's blood pooling on the floor of his bed chamber and scrunched her eyes shut for a moment. When she opened them, Kopi blinked up at her from her palm and made a quiet *hoo* that sounded more like a purr.

"You seem better," she said softly and set him down on the chest of drawers before pulling her hood back up. "Thank you for helping us. You saved us." She stroked his head, and the little owl made another quiet *hoo*. "Are you well? Can you fly now?"

Holt cleared his throat behind her. "He can't understand you; he's an owl."

Zylah waved a hand at him dismissively. "Can you fly, little one?" she asked, turning back to Kopi.

Kopi stretched his wings out, flapping them once, twice, three times.

"See," Zylah said pointedly, glaring at Holt. "He gets it."

Holt merely shook his head.

Of course he *doesn't get it. Oaf.* "Thank you for what you did for us," Zylah said, making her way to the window. She tucked in a few loose strands of hair before pushing the window wide open. "I won't forget it."

Kopi made one final small hoot and shot out the window into the dusk.

"Well," Holt said from his seat on the bed. "Clearly all the evanescing has started to take its toll on you." He pushed himself to his feet. "There's a bathroom through there, a tray of food will be here in a moment."

A knock sounded at the door and Zylah instinctively reached for her dagger.

"Relax. It's just our food."

But Zylah was thinking about the wanted poster. *Dye your hair. Find some eyeglasses.* She repeated the instructions to herself as Holt brought the tray to the small table and gestured for her to join him. She didn't feel like eating. She grabbed a bread roll and stepped into the bathroom, letting the door shut behind her.

She couldn't sit and eat with him like nothing had happened. Like it wasn't all just some strange game they'd been playing. Zylah let out a breath and left the bread roll on a set of wooden drawers beside the door.

Two full kettles hung over the fireplace beside the bath and she tipped them into the tub, steam rising from the water. Had he done that? She didn't call out to ask. He'd done so much already. First thing in the morning, she was going to figure out a way to get hold of some erti root and some eye-glasses, and then she was going to find a job. The quicker she could repay Holt, the better. He had work to get back to, anyway, he'd made that clear, and she wouldn't be a burden any longer.

She undressed and grabbed her roll to nibble at in the bath. She wasn't hungry, but she could never pass up bread, and she didn't know when the next meal would be and if he would provide breakfast, or if Arran would, that is.

Calling all Bounty Hunters. Fugitive Fae wanted for the murder of Prince Jesper. Highly dangerous. Use caution. Bonus rewarded if the subject is brought to the king alive. Zylah didn't know how far Arnir's men would be searching for her, but she had to stop somewhere, couldn't run forever with nothing.

The days had passed by in a blur. It had only been a few nights since she'd escaped the gallows, and yet they'd travelled so far already. How was she to repay Holt for that? Would money be enough? She'd always hated accepting help, had always done whatever she could by herself, even to her own detriment.

She forced herself to finish the bread, unbraided her hair and scrubbed at her skin with the questionable-looking soap that sat beside the bath. Venti lilies, she thought, with a sniff. There were worse things to smell of.

Leaving was an option. But where would she run to without any money, without any supplies? Better to save up and equip herself for the life of a fugitive. Because that was what lay ahead of her now, whether she had fully admitted it to herself or not. She'd always be looking over her shoulder, wherever she went.

She stayed in the bath until her skin wrinkled and the bathwater was cold, hugging at her knees as her thoughts went round in circles. With any luck, Holt would be asleep by the time she left the bathroom.

She dried quickly and dressed, pausing to listen for any sound from the room. It was quiet. She reached for her dagger and carefully pushed open the door. The sound of Holt's steady breathing was all she could hear. The tavern below had fallen quiet some time ago.

He was fast asleep on the lounger, his hulking frame far too big for it, one arm under his head and the other brushing the floor. *Holter, my boy.* Arran seemed to think a lot of him. *I'll figure you out.* Zylah tucked the dagger under a pillow and climbed into bed, shoving aside the thoughts of the wanted poster that seemed imprinted into her eyelids.

Jesper was laughing, blood dripping from his head, his eyes, his mouth. His hands were covered in it as he stepped closer, reaching out to her as he called her name, "*Zylah...*"

"Zylah, Zylah wake up."

Zylah's hand closed around her dagger, and she instinctively brought it to the neck of the man leaning over her as awareness crept in, the scent of acani berries and musk filling her senses as the nightmare slipped away from her.

Holt didn't flinch at the dagger or make any move to stop her. His hands were warm on her shoulders, his gaze fixed on hers. His green eyes were wide as he murmured, "It's okay, Zylah, I'm not going to hurt you."

Her heart was racing so loud she was certain he could hear it. But what was there to say? She'd had a nightmare about a dead man? She focused on steadying her breaths but didn't lower her weapon.

Holt made no effort to move. His eyes flicked lower for a moment, and then back to hers. "I'm going to step away now, okay?"

Zylah nodded once, and Holt released her shoulders and sat beside her, running a hand through his sleep-tousled hair as he released a quiet breath.

"That's it, no questions?" Zylah asked, clutching the dagger to her chest to try and hide her unsteady breathing.

"No questions. But you realise you almost broke rule number two," he said with a tight smile, flicking his chin at her dagger.

She knew he was trying to make her feel better, but the shadow of Jesper, dripping in blood, still danced before her eyes. "Why are you helping me, Holt?"

"Because it could have been my sister."

Seven gods. I remind him of his sister.

"I know what they do to women in prison. I saw your black eye and split lip." He looked away, and she knew there was more to it, more about his sister he wasn't letting on, but just like before, something told her not to press him on the matter.

88

She said nothing as she watched him, the moonlight casting a pale glow across his face, and she wondered what he truly looked like. He'd said he hid his ears. What else, then?

"If I'm not here when you wake up and the door is locked, the spare key is in the top of the dresser. I shouldn't be gone for long. Someone will knock with breakfast."

"Your deliveries?" Zylah asked, raising an eyebrow.

Holt nodded. "Do you want me to wait here until you fall asleep?"

Gods above. He really did think her a child. "I'll be fine. Thank you."

In one graceful movement, he pushed off from the bed and returned to the lounger, lying down with his back to her, and again she thought of how the way he moved seemed so at odds with his size. That power she'd felt on the first day they'd met... the rawness of it. Yet he'd woken her so gently, his eyes soft and full of concern.

"Goodnight, Zylah," Holt murmured.

Zylah still clutched the dagger to her chest. "Goodnight, Holt," she said, as flatly as she could manage.

She silently went through her plan for the morning. *Dye your hair. Find some eyeglasses.* Only a few days of running and she was exhausted. Could she be a fugitive forever? She wasn't sure. But she would not live in fear.

She listened in the dark as Holt's breathing grew steady, going over and over her plan until exhaustion pulled her back to sleep.

9

A tapping sound woke Zylah. She shot up, dagger in hand as she blinked at the daylight. The room was empty. The tapping started again. She looked to the window, and there, face buried against the glass was Kopi.

She ran over to let him in, keeping out of sight as best she could. The little owl swooped in and settled on the dresser, a quiet *hoo* escaping him as he flew.

"Didn't like the city much, huh?" Zylah asked as she closed the window behind him.

He *hooed* again.

Zylah sighed. "I get it. It's much busier than I'm used to. You can stay here for as long as you need," she said, stroking his head lightly as he nestled into his wings.

Beside him on the dresser was a bottle of erti root and a pair of eyeglasses, and a note scribbled onto a piece of parchment in beautiful, slanted writing.

You talk in your sleep, was all the note said.

Heat rushed to Zylah's cheeks. What else had she said? Had she mentioned Jesper's name?

She took the erti root to the bathroom and gathered towels for her hair. The list of things she owed Holt for was adding up, and she didn't like it one bit. She'd never even asked her father for help, or her brother. Had always made her own way and had contributed to the household bills as soon as she'd been old enough to work.

Owing someone so much didn't sit well with Zylah. And she owed Holt her life.

She hoped the erti root wouldn't take much scrubbing to remove from her hands; it wasn't the kind of impression she wanted to make looking for jobs. Not that she was really dressed for it, but at least her apron would make her look more work ready. The fine cloak would be a little at odds with the rest of her attire; her apron and tunic had certainly seen better days. She rinsed out the dye and towel-dried her hair, examining her work. It was a dull shade of brown, the kind no one would stop to look at twice. With the glasses, it would be enough for now. It would have to be.

Voices chattered down the hallway, growing closer as she tidied the bathroom.

"I'm sorry it's late, I knocked earlier, but there was no answer," an old woman said.

"My wife is a deep sleeper," she heard Holt say.

Wife! In Pallia's name...

The door to their room clicked shut, followed by the sound of a tray being placed on the little table. Zylah pushed open the bathroom door, her hair dampening her shirt.

"Wife?" she asked, a hand on her hip, the other gesturing to the door and the woman beyond it.

Holt smirked as he bit into a piece of toast. "Better to look like husband and wife. The duller the story, the less likely people are to talk. And what could be more tedious to the city gossips than a married couple?" He reached into the pocket of his coat and pulled out a small paper bag, placing it on the table.

Zylah sniffed at the air. It was a canna cake, but she made no move to sit down, despite the hunger that gnawed at her stomach.

Kopi *hooed* beside her.

"I see your friend returned." Holt sipped at a steaming mug of tea, the slightest hint of amusement lining his voice.

Zylah turned away from him, stroking Kopi on the head and noticing Holt's note and the eyeglasses again. *You talk in your sleep.* She put the glasses on and inspected herself in the mirror, angling herself out of Holt's line of sight. If she thought the hair colour was dull, the eyeglasses were even duller. They were perfectly round and a little too large for her face, and she hated the way they blocked out half the world around her, how the tint took the edge off the colour of things. But they would have to do.

No one would recognise her from the poster now. Not unless they held it right up to her face. And she was too quick to let that happen any time soon.

She loosed a breath in relief and took the seat opposite

him, unwrapping the canna cake and picking at a small piece. "Tell me more about my Fae abilities. Train me. I'll pay you."

"With what money? I've seen your undergarments."

Zylah snorted. "I fail to see how that is relevant."

"There are no secret pockets stashed with notes." His face gave nothing away as he sipped at his tea, not a hint of amusement flickering in his eyes. Oh, he was good.

"Rule number five: no mention of my undergarments, whatsoever. I'll earn money when I get a job. And I'll pay you to train me. I'll pay you back for everything."

He'd gone quiet, and she wondered if he was waiting to crack another joke. But she wanted him to know she meant it.

"Thank you," she said, looking up at him. "For all of this." She waved the cake at the room, at her hair and glasses. "I'm going to look for work today, and I'll repay you for all of it."

"You were serious? About looking for work?"

"Why wouldn't I be? Just existing is not enough, Holt. I want to live. I've seen what a half-life does to people. It's torture. I do not accept that fate. Even if I have to run from Arnir for the rest of my life, I will do it, and see the godsdamned world while I'm at it. But I need money first." She didn't ask him about the connections he'd mentioned, the ones that could help her get set up. She could do this by herself: find work, repay him.

Holt rested an arm over the back of his chair as he watched her eat her canna cake, but he didn't say anything. She suddenly found herself fascinated with her breakfast, unwilling to meet the intensity of his gaze. If he was going to ask what happened to get her into all this, she still wasn't ready to tell him.

He reached into his pocket and placed a small vial on the table. "Naptha oil. To remove the dye from your hands." He leant across the table and brushed a feather-light thumb across her temple. "And from here," he said, with a smirk.

Zylah stopped mid-chew, trying to come up with a response and failing. Holt had already pulled away and pushed himself up from the table.

"I'm going to take a bath, then I've got some deliveries to make across the city. I can point out a few places on the way and meet you back here this evening." He didn't wait for an answer, had already made his way to the bathroom in half a stride and closed the door behind him.

Well then. That went well. Zylah twirled the bottle of naptha oil in her fingers as she finished her canna cake and her toast, resisting the urge to touch her face where Holt's thumb had brushed it. She shoved aside her wandering thoughts about how her situation had progressed—sharing a room with a hulking Fae who'd referred to her as his wife. It was like the plot of one of Kara's Fae novels, and if Zylah ever saw her friend again, she was going to make her promise to stop reading those ridiculous romance books to her.

Zylah sighed. It was most likely she'd never see Kara again, or her father, or her brother… She walked over to the window. Water sloshed in the tub next door, and Zylah focused on every detail of the city she could see; anything not to think about the fact that Holt was sitting in the tub on the other side of a very thin wall. A tub that was entirely too small for him, and how much of him would even be covered in water anyway, and what did—*Gods above, Zylah.* She opened the window a crack, suddenly too hot in her clothes, the fabric scratching against her skin.

Fresh morning air cooled her face. The city was densely packed with familiar grey stone buildings, and from here she had a view across rooftops and towards a few grander structures with pillars and carved fascias, the details of which were too far away to see. She meant what she'd said to Holt. She would not live a half-life. It was the way all the women of Eldham, her father's village, lived. And it had always frightened her. She had always longed to see the world, and now she had a reason to put as much distance between her and Arnir as possible, even if it meant looking over her shoulder for the rest of her life.

In the street below, a pedlar pushed just about every variety of household item Zylah could imagine, from buckets to taps, stools and brooms, he seemed to have it all in the little cart he dragged along behind him. But he soon quietened down when a group of soldiers entered the street, and at their lead, a golden-haired young man who looked... *No.*

Zylah took a step back and knocked over a chair. *Jesper is dead.* Her heart beat wildly in her chest, her breaths came too fast and her palms turned clammy. *He's dead.*

"Zylah?" Holt asked from beside her. He'd moved so fast, and she hadn't heard a thing.

Zylah peered out of the window again, taking a closer look

at the man leading the soldiers. She let out a broken breath in relief, resting a hand over her heart. *Not Jesper. Just your imagination.* "I thought I... saw someone I recognised."

Holt peered out beside her, following her gaze down the street and frowning. He was shirtless, his hair and skin dripping and only a towel clinging to his waist.

Zylah cleared her throat, trying not to look at the thick muscles of his arms and chest. Her eyes fell to the vicious scars along his right arm that reached to his neck and her breath snagged in her throat. "How did that happen?" she asked, unable to look away.

Holt was still looking out of the window, down into the street below. "I got in a fight I couldn't win," he murmured, not even bothering to ask what she was looking at. "I'll be ready in five minutes," he said, pulling some fresh clothes from the drawers Kopi sat atop.

She chanced a look at him in the mirror, at the way his muscles were sculpted across his stomach and suddenly remembered the naptha oil in her hands. "I'll need a moment just to clean up the erti root," she said quietly, averting her gaze.

But the bathroom door had already clicked shut behind Holt again.

Zylah sighed, stroking Kopi on the top of his head as she waited for the bathroom to be free. "You'll be alright napping here for the day, won't you?" she asked quietly.

Kopi made his quiet *hoo* sound, nudging his head up to her fingers.

"I thought so," Zylah murmured. "What do you think of the new look?" she waved a hand at her damp hair and her glasses. The eyeglasses were ever so slightly tinted, just enough to make her eyes look dark blue or grey, but the glass didn't change her vision at all, just did a good job of hiding her features.

She noticed the smudge of erti root Holt had pointed out over breakfast just as he stepped back into the room.

If he saw her inspecting her new look in the mirror, he didn't say anything, and she ducked under his arm to towel dry her hair some more and clean the erti root off her skin. Her heartbeat still hadn't quite returned to normal, and she drew in a few deep breaths to try and calm her nerves.

"What's Kopi got planned for the day?" Holt called out from the next room.

Zylah smiled as she dabbed oil at the dark stain on her face. "Napping."

"Tsk. *Lazy.* Some of us have to work, you know, Kopi," Holt said quietly.

She could hear the laughter in his voice as she dried her hair and Kopi's quiet *hoo* in response. She smiled again. It hadn't taken Holt long to warm to the little owl, and the thought of the two of them side by side had her biting back a laugh.

She scrubbed at her hands with the naptha oil, rinsing off the stain in the sink.

"What's so funny?" Holt asked from behind her in the doorway.

She threw her towel at him. "I'm going to get you a bell if you don't stop creeping up on me like that."

Holt peeled the wet towel from his face and dropped it on the floor with a *thwack*, one eyebrow raised at her. "Rule number six: no bells. Ready?"

"I just need my—"

He held out his hand and her cloak, his sister's cloak, appeared in it.

"You really don't want to miss these *deliveries*, do you?" Zylah asked as she shrugged into the garment.

Amusement danced across Holt's face. If she knew him better, she might think he was enjoying himself. "Don't forget your key." He patted Kopi's chest of drawers as they passed.

She whispered a goodbye to Kopi as she pocketed her key, following Holt out of the room. Their room. *Gods*. He locked the door behind them, and Zylah sucked in a deep breath as she braced herself for the city.

The start of a new life. A fresh chance. Or... the prelude to her new life. The part where she gathered up her supplies to make a clean break and explore the world, laughing at the king who'd never be able to find her. Gods above. No more books. But it was an easier thought than the reality of her situation. The posters didn't bode well for life in Virian, and she'd been lucky this far, but how long would her luck last?

"You'll need to use a fake name. *Another* fake name," Holt said quietly behind her as if he'd known where her thoughts had taken her.

Zylah clicked her tongue. "And what makes you think

Zylah's not my real name?"

"Better to keep switching it up." He shrugged as he glanced down at her, and she turned her attention back to the corridor.

"Liss."

"You came up with that rather quickly." He tugged her hood up, squeezing past her as he did so, close enough that she could feel the warmth radiate from him.

"It's short for Alyssa. My middle name." She swatted him away and adjusted the hood herself.

"Do I get to know your full name?" he asked over his shoulder.

"Do I get to know yours, husband?" she muttered.

"Point taken." Holt waved a hand at Arran as they passed and held the door open for Zylah as she stepped out onto the street.

"You certainly behave like a husband." Zylah looked up at him and smiled sweetly, her head angled just so Arran would see.

Holt narrowed his eyes and his jaw seemed to tighten. "Now, now, *Liss*, let's not argue right before work."

But Zylah wasn't listening. She was too busy taking everything in. Now that she didn't have to hide her face, she looked up and spun around to take in the front of the tavern and the sign that swung above the door. The Pedlar's Charm. Fitting.

She marked the details of the street; the tailors opposite, the streets that ran off of this one.

"If you get lost, just look for the old bell tower." Zylah looked up at the tavern as Holt pointed. "It's lit up blue at night, you can't miss it." He held nothing to deliver, but she knew it was just as likely to be words or information as it was to be wares.

Not that it mattered. Holt had explained himself to her, and despite her reservations, she trusted him. Better that he looked at her like a little sister than the way Jesper had.

"Perfect." She looped her arm through his. "Now to find myself a job because my husband doesn't get paid well enough to afford my fine tastes." She brushed a hand against an invisible crumb on her cloak as she looked ahead.

The banter came easy. It smoothed over the cracks, helped her shove down her feelings. Her fear. Everything with Holt had an ease to it she'd rarely experienced. And for a moment, she could almost pretend she hadn't just left her life behind. For a moment, she could pretend she wasn't wanted for the murder of the prince.

And for just one moment, she could pretend she'd made the right choice.

10

After Holt pointed out the direction of the two apothecaries in the city, Zylah wasted no time heading straight for the botanical gardens. The domes were impossible to miss.

Once she'd made it off the side streets, Virian's main streets were wide and lined with leafy poplar trees. Regal buildings of grey stone housed shops and restaurants and theatres. Zylah took her time studying each one and committing landmarks and street names to memory, all the while trying to look as if she'd always belonged there. Nothing drew the attention of unwanted eyes faster than someone who looked lost. She'd learnt that the hard way on more than one occasion back in Dalstead.

She had her dagger tucked in her boot, but as soon as she could save up enough money, she intended to find some bracers. She'd customise her own if she had to, but she'd feel better when she could have a knife on each forearm. Zack had been promising to bring her some from Arnir's armoury for months, but she'd always turned him down because she wanted to pay for her own.

Her dagger under her pillow back home was the only thing she'd managed to save up for herself, and she pushed aside thoughts of the home she'd never see again. She'd have to ask Holt where she could get some weapons.

Zylah puffed out a breath as she ducked past a woman carrying a bucket on her shoulder. She flexed her fingers in an attempt to shake off the unease that had settled in her, worrying her lip as she realised finding a job in a new city might not be as easy as she'd hoped. What if it put her more at risk of being discovered? What if her new boss gave her away? She swallowed back the lump in her throat, dismissing the thought.

"Papers! Get ya papers!" a pedlar cried out on the opposite pavement, individuals ignoring him as they stormed by on their way to work.

The first dome of the botanical gardens seemed to grow larger as she approached, and she realised just how much she'd misjudged the size of the gardens. The sound of marching feet cut through the familiar racket of the city, and Zylah willed herself not to look up, to keep her pace steady and not to change direction.

It's just a patrol. Just a regular morning patrol. She'd seen them do it enough times in Dalstead to know it was commonplace. Still, it took a few moments for her heartbeat to return to normal.

Light bounced off the glass dome as she made her way to

the entrance, not letting herself be put off by the fact that the ticket booth was closed and didn't open for another hour. That wasn't the way she'd intended on going in anyway. On this side the glass was tinted a dark blue, and although Zylah had never seen anything like it, she suspected that this close to the entrance it was just for the spectacle of it. As far as she knew, only clear glass would be beneficial for the plants, but she made a note to ask someone about it later if the opportunity arose.

She followed the glass wall around a curve until she found what she was looking for: a delivery entrance. A scruffy child carried a pile of boxes twice his height, and Zylah padded silently behind him.

"Can I help you with those?" she asked, stepping into place beside him as he made his way inside the dome.

Zylah didn't wait for an answer, just took the top three boxes off the child's pile, revealing a small face swamped almost entirely in a mop of dark hair.

"Um, thanks." The boy blew a piece of hair out of his face as he looked up at her.

"Oh! Maranta cuttings!" Zylah examined the contents of the top box she held. "How wonderful, they'll love the conditions here." The heat was already sweltering under her cloak, but she'd expected as much from a glasshouse. She breathed in the familiar fragrance of the maranta cuttings, staring openmouthed at the plants before her.

This might have been the delivery entrance, but it did not disappoint. Weeping eye trees lined the pathway, their broad, waxy leaves holding dew droplets and shading tillaries beneath them, the distinctive bell-shaped flowers easy to spot anywhere.

"Beautiful tillaries, they're wonderful specimens." Moss not unlike the variety she'd snacked on at the springs lined the beds beneath it all, the earthy scent filling her nostrils.

"So um, who are you?" the boy asked as he shuffled alongside her.

Zylah had almost forgotten he was there.

"Kihlan, who are you talking to over there?" an old man's voice called out. A hand pushed aside some hanging bead vines and a wrinkled old face followed.

Zylah cleared her throat. "Good morning, sir. My name's... Liss. Beautiful tillaries. And these marantas are truly wonderful." She placed her boxes down beside Kihlan's and brushed her hand against her cloak before offering it to the old man. "Pleased to meet you."

"Jilah," the old man said by way of introduction. "You've met my son. My daughter's around here somewhere." He shook her hand lightly, his skin rough, likely from years of tending to the garden. He wore a dirty black apron over a dark green tunic, sleeves rolled up to the elbows, and beige trousers with dirty patches on each knee.

"Is this... are you the owner of the gardens, sir?" Zylah asked, noticing new plants every time she looked.

"I am."

She could feel Jilah's eyes on her as she spun around to take it all in and didn't make any effort to hide her sense of wonder as she pushed back her hood. She pressed her eyeglasses up her nose to resist tearing them off, hoping the movement seemed natural.

"Care for a tour?" Jilah asked, holding out his arm for her to take. "It's not every day someone comes in here and lists off any of my plants by name."

Zylah smiled and looped her arm through the old man's, fighting the urge to tell him how much a job at the gardens would be a dream come true for her. More than that, it felt like her new life depended on it. She couldn't keep relying on Holt.

Jilah led her through an archway of yellow crawlers, their tendrils brushing Zylah's shoulders as they walked. The sound of trickling water and chirping birds filled the space, along with the occasional flap of wings.

"My owl would love it here. Well, he's not really mine. He's just my friend," Zylah said, reaching out to inspect a dewglove petal.

Jilah picked at a lily stem and handed it to her. "Friends with an owl, aye? Are you Pallia in disguise, come to test me?"

Zylah inhaled the lily, wondering what to say to that. There were many tales of the gods coming to test the mortals, but then, she was only half mortal now, wasn't she? Zylah hadn't stopped to think about what that meant for her lifespan and made a mental note to ask Holt about it later.

Jilah pointed out some plants she didn't recognise, as if he could sense her discomfort. Blooms of red and orange dusted a bed of blue cloud violas, but Zylah's favourites were the wood strings hanging down from the winnow trees. *When I die, I want to end up in a botanical garden just like this.*

They left the first dome, the fresh air welcome on Zylah's face, but she still pulled up her hood, just in case. Jilah didn't mention it, just carried on pointing out his plants to her. They were between the two domes, in an open expanse of garden dotted with trees and shrubs. Zylah couldn't help but study the trees for any signs of life, but it was just the two of them as far as she could see.

"Worry not, this is secure from the rest of the city," Jilah said, ushering her down a narrow path between some trees until they reached a rocky opening. "This is my favourite spot in the gardens."

The sound of laughter echoed from the rock within, and Zylah followed Jilah into the entrance. It was a grotto. A small cut-out in the rock revealed a small expanse of water, nothing but the occasional drip breaking the silence. And then more laughter. The lump in Zylah's back ached, but she shoved the feeling aside as she stared in silent awe.

Kihlan darted by, followed by a smaller girl with the same dark hair, but even longer and more unruly. The girl tucked her hair behind an ear, an elegant, pointed ear, and Zylah realised Kihlan's were the same.

"By the gods, they're Fae," she said with an intake of breath.

Jilah rested against the rough rock of the grotto. "I won't have them hide themselves as I have, at least, not here. Here they can be themselves."

That explained why Kihlan hadn't looked that way outside; his ears had been normal. Zylah studied Jilah's face. Inside the grotto, his ears were pointed, his features slightly sharper, grey eyes brighter, even his beard and hair seemed silver rather than the dull grey it had been moments before. "You're Fae," she murmured.

The old man nodded. "There are many of us still in the city. Many who would not give up their home."

"Niara, come back! You can't keep it hidden from me forever!" Kihlan yelled as the two children shot past.

Zylah watched the siblings playing as if they didn't have a care for the outside world that hated all things Fae. "You hide in plain sight."

"Yes. Just as you do. Do not think you can trick me, young lady." He smiled reassuringly at her as he spoke.

Zylah tucked a piece of hair in her hood, but Jilah's expression was still warm. How had he known? If Jilah could take one look at her and know she was half Fae, that meant others could, too. Or maybe Holt had sent him a message… but Holt couldn't possibly have known she would find her way to the gardens.

The old man waved a hand. "Come, you'll love the flowers in the second dome."

They left the grotto—Zylah hoped she'd get to explore more of its dark corridors another time, if she returned. Her thoughts were filled with questions about the Fae and herself, but she refrained from blurting everything out to Jilah. She could tell he was kind, but he was still a stranger. She followed him into the second dome, Niara and Kihlan rushing by, their ears now soft and round, like a human's.

"I've brought you on the shortest route, I'm afraid." Jilah pressed a hand to his lower back. "The waterfall back in the first dome is my favourite, but it takes a while to reach it. This dome is for the plants that prefer the drier climate." He waved a hand, and Zylah followed his gaze to the edge of the platform they were standing on.

Tiers of beds stretched out below them, and a winding staircase rose out of the middle. So many plants Zylah had never seen before covered every tier as far as she could see.

The children came rushing back in from outside, eyes wide, and Zylah knew at once that something was wrong.

"Guards," Kihlan called out, dragging Niara back up the steps.

Zylah reached for her dagger, but Jilah caught her wrist. "There'll be too many of them. Take the children to the grotto and stay out of sight."

"But I can—"

"Go!"

She nodded once at Jilah, and ushered the children back out of the dome to the grotto, her heart thundering in her chest. *You led the guards here. You put them all at risk.* They ran into the grotto, and she followed Kihlan and Niara through the winding corridors she'd been wishing to search moments before. Kihlan ducked under a low rock that opened out into a larger cave, and Zylah followed the children under it. She tried not to grit her teeth at the ache in her back.

"It's alright, they won't find us here," Niara whispered, squeezing Zylah's hand, mistaking her grimace for fear.

The girl's pointed ears had reappeared, and Zylah wondered what it was about the grotto that revealed the children's true identity.

"Father will be back soon," Niara said when Zylah didn't reply.

What was there to say? These children had spent their whole lives doing what she was trying to do. Only they were innocent.

They sat in silence, Zylah straining to hear any sounds of a struggle back in the dome. After what felt like an eternity, the soft thump of Jilah's steady footsteps made their way into the grotto.

"It's alright, they're gone," he called out.

The children shot out first, and Zylah followed. "I attracted the guards. I'm so sorry."

"You? Don't be ridiculous, child. Guards come this way at least once a month. It's a way of life here in Virian."

"Seven gods." Zylah smoothed down the front of her cloak to steady her hands.

"You and your gods. I would love to bear witness the day Arnir learns his beloved gods are Fae," Jilah mumbled as he led her back out in the gardens.

Zylah's hands stilled on her cloak. "What?"

"The guards are always searching for Fae," Jilah said, leading the way into the second dome as if he hadn't just dropped such a wild nugget of information about the gods. "They know we didn't all leave. But we do love to give them the runaround, don't we, children?"

"Yeah!" Niara and Kihlan called out in unison from the level below.

Zylah followed the old man into a small gift shop at the far end of the dome. He seemed too old to be their father, but Zylah kept her thoughts on the matter to herself as she looked around the shop. "Have you ever considered selling a few remedies, just a few basic ones so as not to offend the apothecaries, the whimsical type perhaps? You've got all the ingredients here."

"Whimsical?

"For broken hearts, rainy days, for the brin fruit of one's eye, that kind of thing."

Jilah smiled. "You're smart, Liss. I'll give you that. You've come here for a job, I take it, or are you into the habit of letting old men talk your ear off every morning?"

This guy doesn't miss a trick.

"Well, I—"

"It's alright. I've been looking for a way to give the children more time for their studies for a while, but trustworthy people are so difficult to come by," Jilah said.

Trustworthy. She was far from trustworthy. *You're getting them tangled up in your mess.* But she needed this job. Needed to stand on her own two feet, and she looked nothing like the wanted poster now. No one would recognise her, would they?

"And even more difficult to meet someone with knowledge of the plants, and some love for them too. You had the job the

110

moment you complimented my tillaries." Jilah's smile was bright as he looked at her. "But I'm afraid this morning I'll need you to start with the more tedious job of manning the ticket booth. We're quieter at lunch. We'll be able to talk more then."

>>>>> <<<<<

It was already dark by the time Zylah made her way back to the tavern. Jilah had given her a vegetable muffin, and she nibbled at it as she navigated her way through the streets, a cool breeze kissing her face.

Two men turned a corner ahead of her, walking in the same direction she was headed.

"Arnir's men are being slaughtered. Every single one he sends out for the girl, they all end up dead," one said quietly to the other.

Zylah instinctively tucked her hair inside her hood, focused on keeping her steps as even as they'd been before.

"I've told you before, Sarson, it's that damned Fae uprising."

Zylah almost choked on her muffin, and she kept her head down as one of the men looked over a shoulder.

An uprising. And they were helping her?

"Tch, uprising my arse. The Fae are long gone. It's the Black Veil, I'm telling you."

The men turned a corner, and Zylah kept on walking. The tavern was only one more street away. The city orblights were dull, but she'd always had keen eyesight. What more was there to learn about her Fae heritage?

She pushed open the door to the tavern, hood up and head down so no one would bother looking her way. *A Fae uprising.* It was all she could think of. The tavern was packed, the smell of *fyrsha*, a homegrown liquor made from potatoes, thick in the air. Zylah had tasted it once with Kara, hiding in her father's garden, and they'd both nearly choked up their insides after one mouthful.

She made her way up the narrow staircase with nothing more than a wayward elbow from one of the patrons, her fingers dragging along the coarse wood that lined the corridor. Holt wasn't back when she let herself into the room, but Kopi made a quiet *hoo* in greeting.

"Oh hey, buddy, I'm so sorry it's late. We'll need to get some ribbon attached to this window for you." She shoved open the window for the little owl, but he made no move to shoot out. Zylah reached into her apron for the grub beetles she'd collected from the arid dome earlier on. "Here, I brought you some snacks."

She left Kopi to munch on the beetles as she rummaged through the drawers for something to sleep in. Holt's scent was everywhere. She found an old shirt at the bottom of the last drawer and shrugged it on after discarding her clothes on the dresser.

Acani berries and Holt's musky scent invaded her senses. *Damn Fae.* She climbed into bed, thinking about Jilah and his children. *You hide in plain sight.* How many more of them were there in the city? And the guards barging in. It was no surprise that there was a Fae uprising, but were they truly helping her? The Black Veil seemed a little more unsettling.

Her head spun and her back ached from hauling boxes of bulbs from one dome to the other all afternoon. But it had been a good day. She'd made progress with her new life. Her new beginning.

A key turned in the door, and Zylah reached for her dagger.

It was only Holt. But something was a little off about him. She scrunched her nose at a metallic tang in the air. It was blood, but whether it was his or not, she couldn't be certain.

"I'm sorry, I didn't mean to startle you," he said as he locked the door behind him. He looked tired, and for the second time that day, she found herself wondering what he truly looked like, whether his ears were pointed like Kihlan and Niara's.

"I got the job!" she said, shoving the dagger back beneath her pillow.

"I didn't doubt you for a moment. Where?" He edged his way closer to the bathroom, and Zylah didn't miss the way he didn't turn his back to her.

"Botanical gardens." She straightened the blanket across her lap, suddenly aware of the fact that she was wearing his shirt without asking.

"Impressive. Jilah's a hard nut to crack."

"You know him?" Perhaps she had been right to suspect Holt's intervention, after all.

113

"In passing." Holt stood in the bathroom doorway, one arm awkwardly held behind his back. If he was hiding something, he was doing a terrible job of it.

"Do you need your *wife* to look at that?" she asked, flicking her chin at him.

He pressed his lips together as if he were about to say something, but just huffed a quiet laugh instead. What had happened?

"I meant what I said before, about training. I want to learn more about what I can do, and I want to learn to use a sword like you can. I've only ever practised with, well sticks, essentially," Zylah said, thinking about the training swords she'd used with her brother and all she'd learnt in the last few hours.

"And I'm sure you're lethal with one." Holt ran a hand through his messy hair as he looked at her, every inch of him seeming tightly wound.

"A pointy stick doesn't really do much damage." She was referring to the one she'd threatened to kill him with the day they'd met, hoping to elicit a laugh from him.

His eyes seemed to brighten for a moment. "Goodnight, Zylah. And congratulations." The bathroom door clicked shut behind him, and Zylah was left blinking at the peeling wood.

She'd let it go, for now, because he looked like he'd had a bad night and she felt just as exhausted as he looked. But she wouldn't be brushed off so easily. If there was a Fae uprising, she could help, couldn't she? She could fight, make poultices. She could meet more of her kind.

Zylah lay down to sleep, clutching her dagger as Holt

splashed around in the bathroom. Something was definitely off about him. But she didn't want to press him again when he'd seemed so unwilling to talk about it.

She thought of the conversation she'd overheard on her way home from work as sleep tugged at her. *Work.* She couldn't believe Jilah had given her the job so quickly, and she felt safe at the botanical gardens.

She felt safe with Holt, too.

11

A week rolled by, and then another. It felt as if Zylah had always worked at the botanical gardens, as if she'd always come home exhausted and satisfied every night from a day working with plants.

And there were moments, every now and then, that she could forget she wasn't wanted for murdering the prince. Could forget what he'd tried to do to her.

The guards had returned twice more, but Zylah had stopped hiding. She'd decided on their second visit that she wouldn't spend the rest of her life cowering in fear.

If Jilah could hide in plain sight, so would she.

She was thinking of Jilah and the children as she tucked into a canna cake that Holt had just handed her. He'd brought her one every day, without fail, regardless of what the tavern staff brought them for breakfast.

"Train me," she said through a mouthful of warm canna cake. It wasn't as good as Mrs Andell's. It wasn't as good as

116

his, either, but she'd never admit that.

"Train me so I can join the Fae uprising." Perhaps she wouldn't have to run. Perhaps she could join a cause worthy of risking her life for.

"I don't make promises I can't keep."

"Then don't promise. Just do it."

Holt gazed out of the window, eyes darting across the rooftops. "I thought you wanted to live."

"I do. But I also want to make a difference."

"It's dangerous," he said, turning his attention to her.

Zylah pushed away from the table. "Well, it's a good thing you're not really my husband, because it isn't your decision to make."

He blinked, but she couldn't read his expression. A few weeks with him and she still couldn't read him at all.

"You're right. It isn't," he said softly.

But she wouldn't let his tone soften her anger. She stormed into the bathroom to get herself ready for the day. *It's dangerous.* She was well acquainted with danger.

"What is this?" Holt asked from the bedroom, irritation lining his voice.

So he'd found the money, then.

"I told you, I wanted to start repaying you as soon as I could. Jilah just gave me my first pay yesterday." She needed to spend it on supplies. Needed to save if she was going to keep moving, but she owed him. She fixed her hair, checking the roots. The erti root would need to be topped up soon.

Holt rested against the door frame, watching her in the

mirror, hands sliding into his pockets. "Do you repay all your friends in coin?"

"I… I only had one friend." The fire fell away from her words when she thought of Kara's dainty face.

"Well now you have two," Holt said, holding out the money for her.

She squeezed past him without taking the money from his hand. She had no intention of taking it back. Even if she had to wash the same clothes in the bath for a month. "Please, Holt. I need to do this. I—"

"I've no need for your money, Zylah. Just live your life, that's repayment enough." He was still in the bathroom doorway, this time facing out into the room, eyes following her as she gathered her things.

She hated that she relied on him for so much. That she couldn't provide for herself. "What about *your* life? Surely you don't intend to keep this up forever. Soon enough Arran will realise we're not married." She straightened her bedsheets, trying to hide her frustration.

"Has it ever occurred to you that I like the company? That I like seeing that little pile of feathers on the dresser when I come back at the end of the day, or hearing you clatter around in the bathroom, or knowing someone else is here when I wake in the middle of the night, is—" he took a step closer.

"I do not clatter," she said, heat flushing her cheeks.

He put the money back on the dresser, slid his hands back in his pockets again. "You do clatter. And you get water everywhere."

Zylah rolled her eyes, scooped up the coins and tugged at one of the hands he'd shoved into his pockets. "I can't rely on you; I have to do this."

Holt didn't budge. "Oh, you can't?"

Gods. Now you've offended him. "Just take it, Holt."

Kopi hooed from his spot on the dresser.

"Will you also insist on giving Kopi coin?" Holt asked.

Zylah chewed her lip. At least one of them was helping to turn the conversation around. "Are you hearing this, Kopi? You've melted Holt's cold, dark heart."

But any trace of humour left Holt's face at that. "There's nothing left of my heart to melt, Zylah. I have a delivery to make; I'll be back later. Lock the door—"

"Behind me, yes I know. I'm sorry—" *Shit.*

But he'd already left.

There's nothing left of my heart to melt.

She opened the window for Kopi to fly on ahead to the gardens. He often joined her, snoozing throughout the day. Sometimes he even slept on her shoulder. In the evenings he flew on ahead of her, but she always knew he was nearby, keeping an eye out.

She closed the window as she watched him fly away, trying to work out how the last five minutes had gone so badly. She had to be independent, surely Holt could understand that?

Shit. She ran a hand over her hair. *Well now you have two,* he'd said when she told him she only had one friend. Somehow she'd managed to offend him multiple times in the space of a few minutes. *Excellent work, Zy.*

119

She locked the door behind her and made her way out into the streets, listing off all the ways she'd insulted him. *One: asking for training.* Although she still maintained he didn't get to decide what was dangerous for her and what wasn't. *Two: she'd tried to repay him.* Why couldn't he just take the money like any normal person would? *Three: she'd said he had a cold, dark heart.* Which he clearly didn't; he was just so godsdamned difficult to read.

A heavy feeling settled in her stomach. The truth was, she liked his company, too. She liked seeing his things in their room. The canna cakes he brought her for breakfast. And knowing he was there in the night when she woke. For how difficult he was to read, he'd revealed quite a big piece of himself: he didn't like to be alone. *Maybe he misses his sister.* She kicked at a stone. She'd try to smooth things over later and suggest he go visit her. Maybe being with family would be good for him.

Kopi hooed from somewhere above, and Zylah realised she'd taken a wrong turn. She smiled at the sky as she turned back in the right direction, but the owl was already out of sight. A priestess and her acolytes paraded by, but Zylah wasn't afraid. They were a common sight in Dalstead, and Virian's governor answered to King Arnir, who was well known for his reverence of the gods. As far as Zylah knew, all of Astaria was under Arnir's control, and by default, the priestesses that paraded around in his name.

Kihlan was outside the first dome when she arrived, unloading deliveries with a young man. His shirt sleeves were rolled up to reveal toned arms, his long, messy hair hanging over his shoulders in waves. He looked up and caught her gaze, offering her a polished smile, but Kopi flew down and landed on her shoulder before she had a chance to say anything.

"You were right, Kihlan, like a true goddess," the young man said, oozing with practised charm. His face was striking, his blue eyes a bright contrast to his jet-black hair. While he was taller than her, which wasn't difficult, he didn't quite match up to Holt's enormous frame.

Gods above, Zy. Are you really comparing them? Clearly, she'd missed her nights with Theo more than she'd cared to admit to herself.

Kopi flew on ahead into the dome, and the young man watched the owl go with a raised eyebrow.

"Does it come when you whistle for it?" he asked, rubbing a hand against his shirt. "I'm Raif." Corded muscle flexed in his arm as he extended a hand in greeting.

"Liss. And no, Kopi does whatever he wants. He isn't mine." She shook his hand with as much vigour as she could, and though his calloused hand enveloped hers, he was gentle. She pulled away as the corner of his mouth tugged into the beginning of a smile and scooped up several boxes full of bulbs.

"Spoken like a goddess," Raif said with a wink at Kihlan.

Zylah shook her head. She'd met his type before. Too aware of his looks for his own good. Always trouble.

Jilah greeted them as they carried their boxes in, his apron already covered in fresh dirt. He wiped his hands on a clean patch. "Raif, I wasn't expecting you today. Is everything well?" A look of concern flickered across his face as he looked to his son and back to Raif again, waiting for an answer.

"Everything's fine, my friend." Raif set down his boxes and steered Jilah towards the waterfall, no doubt so they could speak away from prying ears.

Zylah observed the leather bracers at Raif's wrists as he walked away, and the shadow of a dagger hilt pressing against his trousers just above one of his boots. He moved like Holt did, like he was wild and lethal.

"Raif's a warrior. He's teaching us how to fight." Niara bit into a brin fruit as she watched Raif and her father walk away. Where in Pallia's name had the girl appeared from?

Kihlan snatched the brin fruit from her fingers and took a bite. "We're not supposed to tell anyone, remember?"

"Hey! Give it back!" Niara yelled, and with that, they were chasing each other through the dome, boxes forgotten.

Zylah frowned at the discarded boxes. Maybe Raif was part of the uprising. He certainly moved like someone who could fight. *Or he's part of the Black Veil.* But she knew Jilah would only align himself with someone good, someone fighting for the right cause. If he was teaching the children how to fight, then why not her?

It would help smooth things over with Holt, to not have to keep asking him for help. She finished bringing in the last of the deliveries and began unpacking them, planning what she was going to say when Raif returned. Kopi hooed somewhere nearby. He preferred this dome to the second, hotter one, but

122

he was usually outside in the gardens. He mostly slept, but now and then he'd join her.

Zylah looked up just as Raif stepped out from behind the wood strings, swiping at the loose strands of hair that had fallen into his eyes. "So you're new here?"

Her planned speech turned to ash on her tongue. "Train me," she blurted out. Her father had always chided her for making brash decisions. "I know you're training the children. I can fight... a little. I just need to be better. I can help in other ways, like making healing poultices and I can—"

"Whoa. Slow down there. Help with what?" Raif folded his arms across his chest as he waited for an answer. He stood with a stillness that reminded her of Holt. *He has to be Fae.*

Zylah cleared her throat. "You're part of the Fae uprising, aren't you? I want to help."

Raif took a step towards her; somehow he'd moved so fast he'd closed the distance between them entirely. "Are you out of your fucking mind? That kind of question can get you killed here. So much for being subtle," he said quietly, those blue eyes bright as he stared down at her, a mint and lemongrass scent drifting from him.

"I don't have time for subtle. I want to help." If he was trying to intimidate her, to get a rise out of her, it wasn't going to work. She'd faced Jesper. Raif was nothing in comparison to that monster, even with his matching height and his muscles.

Raif arched a brow. "To help? What can a little thing like you do to help?"

"Thing?" It was Zylah's turn to fold her arms across her chest.

"You know what I meant."

"I can fight. I'm fast. And I can help with ailments. I worked in an apothecary before I came to Virian." She held her ground as Raif began to circle her, his expression gloriously bored. More intimidation. She wouldn't baulk.

"And what brought you to Virian exactly?" Another lock of hair fell into his eyes and he swiped it away. Zylah resisted the urge to offer him a hair tie.

"I wanted to start over," she said, averting her gaze from his, thankful for the eyeglasses that hid most of her face.

"And you think joining an uprising is the best way to do that?"

"I've nothing to lose," Zylah said, holding her head high as she met his gaze again.

"Only your life."

What was it with Fae males thinking they had a say in her life? "I could be useful to you."

"I don't doubt that." Raif dragged his gaze up her body, a dimple appearing on one side of his mouth as if he were fighting back a smile. "Same time tomorrow, *Liss*?"

He didn't wait for an answer. And she didn't give him the satisfaction of watching him go—she wouldn't be caught out gawking after him if he turned back to look at her. He hadn't exactly agreed to training her either. Or answered her question about the Fae uprising. He hadn't given anything away at all.

But Jilah trusted him, and that was enough, for now.

12

Plants had always fascinated Zylah. Even before she'd learnt to speak, her father told her, she would help with the plants he'd hang drying in his apothecary, holding them carefully and passing them to him one by one. He said they seemed to calm her. She'd tried to cling to that calm the moment she arrived at work.

She occupied herself with the insect ferns throughout the day; they'd settled in the pond at the bottom of the waterfall in the first dome and had taken over in the last few weeks. It was good work to keep her hands busy and her thoughts at bay, but she kept playing over her argument with Holt whenever she stopped for a moment. First, she was going to apologise for her comment about his heart, she'd decided.

By the time she made it back to the tavern in the evening, she was exhausted, but she preferred it that way. The less time she had to think about Arnir and Jesper, the better.

She'd gotten used to ignoring the patrons and the tang of

ale as she let her feet carry her up the narrow staircase, unlocking the door to the room and pushing open the window for Kopi to fly back through when he was ready.

The Black Veil. Something had been nagging her about it since she'd overheard those two men in the street. A Fae uprising *and* the Black Veil. What was the Black Veil's purpose?

She made her way into the bathroom and started preparing for a bath. She was too tired for the old kettles to boil, but she carried on, nonetheless. *Gods.* Zylah caught sight of herself in the mirror. She'd forgotten the erti root. Her blonde roots were going to be obvious soon.

A key turned in the lock to the bedroom door, and she took a deep breath. She was too tired for this conversation, too, but they needed to clear things up.

"Look, Holt, I just wanted to say—" Zylah began, but the moment she turned to face the bathroom doorway she knew something wasn't right. The way a floorboard creaked ever so slightly, the spicy fragrance that hit her faintly.

She reached down for her dagger, and in the split second it took for her to get back to her feet, a cloaked figure stood in the doorway, looking over her. Zylah didn't give them the upper hand—she slashed out, but the intruder leapt back and shook their head.

Zylah slashed again, but the hooded figure was too fast, disarming her and spinning her around, her back to their chest and a hand clamped around her mouth. Their breath was hot in her hair, and she froze, her mind taken back to that night in Jesper's room.

126

Then she heard Kopi's cry.

Her assailant shoved her away, and she fell, head smacking against the corner of the table and her vision spotting. Kopi's cries mingled with the man's as Zylah realised the little owl was attacking. Blood sprayed across the room when Kopi's claws found flesh, the intruder swatting at Kopi and shoving him back against the wall, feathers fluttering down around him.

No! Zylah's senses returned to her, and she grabbed for her dagger and launched herself at the hooded figure. He threw her over the top of his shoulder—an evasive move, part of her mind registered—and she rolled out of the way just as the hilt of a weapon came towards her.

She was on her feet faster than him, and she used the moment that he was off balance to shove him out the door, slamming it shut behind him and fumbling with her key in the lock. She pushed Kopi's dresser in front of the door for good measure, straining to listen for the assailant, but all she heard was the sound of footsteps getting further away.

Zylah released a shaky breath. With trembling hands, she grabbed her dagger again and checked on Kopi. "Hey, buddy," she whispered. "That's two I owe you now."

Kopi *hooed* in response, head buried in his wings.

"Did he hurt you?" Zylah asked quietly.

The little owl flexed his wings; there was no damage, just a few out of place feathers.

"You did good. Thank you."

Zylah leaned against the wall beside the door, listening for any signs of the intruder returning. The corridor beyond was quiet, the only sound her heartbeat, heavy in her ears. If he was one of Arnir's men... but how could it be? Maybe they'd just seen her walk up the stairs from the tavern alone and thought her an easy target.

She'd almost let it happen again. Had frozen, again. Her head was pounding, and she inhaled slowly through pursed lips to steady her breathing. The room felt as if it were sliding away from her, and she pressed a hand to her stomach. Her thoughts jumped from one thing to the next. Had she done something that could have invited attention? What had she been doing just a few moments before? Zylah couldn't think straight.

Her bath, she'd been preparing a bath. She listened again: laughter from the tavern, the slam of tankards on tables, nothing out of the ordinary. Whoever it was, they were long gone. She stroked Kopi's soft head and his eyes closed at her touch. "Keep watch for me?"

Zylah shut the bathroom door behind her. It had no lock, but it was another wall between her and the outside world. The kettles had long since boiled, and she tried to still her shaking hands as she filled the bath with steaming water. She caught sight of her face in the mirror, the gash above her eye where she'd hit the table. If Kopi hadn't been there... She'd have evanesced away, wouldn't she? Then why hadn't she? Why had she frozen, again?

Nausea roiled threateningly in her stomach, and she gripped the edge of the bath for support, sucking in a breath.

Her bones felt weak. Like her body was still being slammed to the floor by her assailant, over and over.

Zylah blinked, stripped out of her clothes and sank into the bath. She pulled her knees to her chest, one hand still clasped tightly around the hilt of her dagger, and closed her eyes, replaying everything over and over until her heartbeat returned to normal and the water became tepid.

Kopi's soft *hoo* and the sound of a key in the lock tore her from her thoughts. Holt. Her grip still tightened around her dagger.

The door hit the dresser. "Zylah?" Holt called out.

She didn't answer. Didn't think she could find her voice.

"Zylah!" His voice was more frantic this time as she heard the scrape of the dresser being shoved out of the way.

He'd have taken one look at the blood and the feathers and known enough of what had happened.

Zylah took a deep breath. "I'm fi—"

The bathroom door flew open with such force, she couldn't help but flinch when it hit the wall and pulled her knees tighter to herself. "Fine," she said in a whisper.

Holt was beside her at once, an expression she'd never seen painted across his face. He was on his knees beside the tub, knuckles white as his hands gripped the edge, the metal groaning beneath his touch. His eyes searched her face as her fingers tightened around her dagger.

"They didn't hurt me," she said quietly.

"This tells me otherwise," he said, his eyes darkening as he raised a hand to the gash above her eye.

Zylah flinched away from his touch and he pulled back his hand.

"You look cold. And your wound is still bleeding. May I?" He gestured towards her cut but didn't reach out for her again.

She nodded, watching him as he brought his hand close to her face, the warmth of the power pouring from him mixed with his familiar scent. She felt the trickle of blood clotting, the sting of the skin knitting back together.

"No other wounds?" Holt asked softly.

Zylah shook her head.

He held a towel out for her. "Come on, you're cold."

She stood facing away from him, not caring what he saw, clutching her dagger as he placed a towel around her shoulders.

His breath caught almost inaudibly at the last moment. He'd seen the knot in her spine, Zylah assumed. That was most people's reaction, anyway.

"I've had it since I was a child," she murmured as she stepped out of the bath, pulling the towel tighter around herself.

"Is it painful?" He didn't reach out to help her, just watched her intently as if she might explode in front of him.

Zylah shivered. "Only when I was evanescing away from Arnir. And a little since." A half-truth, because she was too tired for the whole of it. She sat on the edge of the bed, vaguely registering the dip of the mattress as Holt sat down beside her.

"What happened tonight?"

She'd been a fool to think she could outrun this. She'd

killed a man. Two. She was a criminal.

"Zylah?" Holt's fingers carefully prised her own from the dagger. His skin was warm and rough with callouses, and she looked up at his face as he placed the dagger on the bedside table. His throat bobbed as he stared back at her, his brow etched with concern.

Zylah cleared her throat. "I thought it was you. I—" She pulled the towel tighter around herself, watching the drips of water that landed on the rug. "By the time I realised it wasn't, they were already in here. A guy with a hood—I didn't see his face. It all happened so fast. He grabbed me and I…" She looked at Kopi, fast asleep in the corner. "He saved me."

"I doubt Kopi locked the door and pushed the dresser in front of it," Holt said with the hint of a smile.

"That part was me."

Holt rummaged through the dresser for some clothes. "And you thought getting in the bath was a good idea?"

"I just… I wasn't thinking." He was right, though. It was a stupid thing to do. Her assailant could have returned and then what?

Her heartbeat quickened again, her breaths coming faster.

"Hey, it's alright. It doesn't matter now." Holt handed her the bundle of clothes. His clothes. "I'm sorry about this morning." He drew in a deep breath. "I've lost a lot of friends over the years. I'm not ready to lose another."

He turned away as she shuffled into the clothes, not bothering to roll up the ridiculous sleeves or do anything with the shirt hem.

She sat back down on the edge of the bed in a daze. "I killed Prince Jesper." It was more for herself than for Holt; he'd already seen the posters.

He sat beside her again, and she could feel the warmth that radiated from him.

"I was working a shift for my friend at the palace. I'm never normally in his room. But I knew the look on his face the moment he saw me. And when—I just *froze*." She swallowed, remembering Jesper's hands tugging against her tunic and the avenberry liquor on his breath.

"Did he—?"

"He got me in the face. Well, you saw my lip and my eye. And then I got him with the fire poker after that." She looked up at Holt, who had gone utterly still, his face darkened again with another expression she couldn't read.

"Tenacious," Holt murmured, but Zylah wasn't really listening.

"I'm sorry, too," she said quietly. "For the things I said this morning."

"No, you were right. I didn't mean to make a decision for you." He glanced around the room, signs of a struggle everywhere. "I should have started training you the first time you asked."

"This wasn't your fault, Holt."

He lifted the table with one hand and righted it, placing the chairs back neatly beside it.

"Do you need anything?" he asked softly.

Zylah let out another shaky breath. "Can you sit here for a

while, until I go to sleep?"

The bed was big enough for two, even though Holt had slept on the lounger every night. She missed hugs from her father and Kara. Missed Kara grabbing her hand to show her another book or squeezing up against her to whisper one of their stupid shared jokes. Zylah even missed messing around with Theo—just to feel someone's touch, she realised, not because she missed *him*.

She climbed into bed and shifted herself to one side, twisting her fingers together without her dagger to keep them still.

"Here," Holt said as he sat beside her, handing over her dagger, now cleaned of blood. "You sleep better when you hold onto it."

Zylah huffed a quiet laugh. "I do not." She held it tightly all the same.

"Training starts at dawn, unless you're taking the day off, that is." He leaned back, resting a hand behind his head for a pillow and closed his eyes.

"Why would I? No, dawn is perfect." She took one last look at him, at the way his muscles were emphasised in this position, at the square of his jaw. *Who sleeps with an arm up like that, anyway?*

Zylah rolled onto her side away from Holt, focusing on the sound of his steady breaths until she fell asleep.

She woke once in the night. A dream, or a memory, startled her awake. She was warm. One leg wrapped over one of Holt's, her head on his chest. His arm wrapped tight around her. *Gods above.* She'd missed touch a whole lot more than she'd realised. She breathed in his scent and listened to his heartbeat until the memory of the assailant faded.

She played over his words from a few hours before. *I've lost a lot of friends over the years. I'm not ready to lose another.*

Neither was she.

13

The sound of the window clicking shut woke Zylah.

Holt had let Kopi in and was leaning against the wall, arms folded across his chest. "Good morning." He looked as if he'd slept well, and he seemed to be in good spirits.

"Good morning," Zylah said, with a stretch, wincing when she felt a bruise from the night before.

Holt's expression darkened. "We don't have to do this today if you don't want to."

There was no way Zylah was going to miss this opportunity. She threw the bedcovers aside. "I absolutely do. Just give me a minute," she said, padding into the bathroom to look for her clothes, which were nowhere to be found. "Did you break rule number one?"

"Arran's wife does my laundry. I thought you might prefer to go to work with clean clothes."

She was about to argue, but then she saw the dents in the side of the bath where he'd gripped it, and all her snappy retorts about him touching her undergarments fell away from her. She frowned at the marks in the metal as she combed her fingers through her hair, replaying the events of the night before.

"Your clothes will be ready by the time we're back from training," Holt called out from the bedroom when she didn't reply.

What would stop the hooded figure from trying to return? Was it one of Arnir's men? "That's all well and good," Zylah mused, "but I'm going to need something a bit more suitable for training in." She stormed back out into the bedroom and to the chest of drawers, rummaging through to find the shabbiest shirt she could lay eyes on. "Are you particularly fond of this one?" she asked, waving it in front of him.

He shook his head. He'd cleaned up the room. When did he find the time to do all of these things? Perhaps he barely slept at all, but then she remembered waking up wrapped around him in the night, his arm holding her tightly, and willed her cheeks not to flush.

She stomped back into the bathroom, ripping Holt's shirt into strips to fasten around her chest. Rags were all she'd had as a girl until she'd saved up enough for her bralette—even that she still preferred to wrap tighter when necessity called for it.

What if the intruder had sent a message to Arnir?

She pulled the shirt she'd slept in back over her head, rolling up the sleeves and tucking it in at the waist. She rolled that over a few times too, and the hems of the trousers. There was no escaping the fact she was wearing his clothes, but at least they might stay on her now. Finally, she scooped up her hair into a messy bun; there was no time to braid it, she'd wasted enough time already wrapping her chest.

"I'd have woken you up an hour earlier if I'd known you were going to take this long."

Zylah felt Holt's gaze as she stepped back out into the bedroom, wondering if he'd woken up with her wrapped around him. Gods above. "I'm ready," she said, pulling on her boots and tucking her dagger into one of them.

"After you." Holt held the door open, and Zylah glanced between him and Kopi. The owl was fast asleep. At least one of them was.

Holt locked the door behind them, pocketing the key.

"I forgot my cloak," Zylah whispered, in case any other patrons were sleeping in the adjacent rooms. Come to think of it, she'd never seen any of the rooms at this end of the corridor occupied.

"You won't need it," Holt said quietly. She followed him soundlessly down the corridor and the narrow staircase, into the tavern, where instead of the door, he turned to the bar.

She didn't argue as she followed him behind it, just watched as he rolled up a rug, lifted a trapdoor, and waved a hand at a set of steps leading down in the darkness. Anticipation danced along her spine. A smile tugged at Holt's lips as an orblight flickered on below them, bathing the staircase in a soft light.

Zylah made her way down the steps until she reached a

door—locked. Holt pulled the hatch shut above them and followed her, squeezing his way past. He glanced down at her for a moment, his body close to hers, and Zylah wondered if she should apologise for how she'd slept. But what was there to say? *Sorry I slept on you?* In Pallia's name. He didn't look at her that way, he'd made it clear. Holt waved a hand over the locked door and it clicked open.

"You can use magic inside the city without it being traced?" she asked, tilting her head back to look up at him.

He pushed open the door and stepped inside. "The tavern and this area are warded heavily. It's where I come to train."

Alone. The implication was there. Maybe he wasn't part of the uprising, after all. She'd decided against telling him about Raif, for now. There was nothing to explain, yet. Raif hadn't agreed to or acknowledged anything—for all she knew, he was just dragging her along to occupy more of her time.

Zylah's thoughts were interrupted by the wall of weapons before her. It truly was a training room. Practice swords, swords of different lengths, knives, staffs, and weapons she didn't even have words for each had their own section along the brick wall, a wooden rack holding each.

Orblights cast their soft glow across the bloodied mat that covered most of the floor. In the far corner, a wooden door led elsewhere.

"What if he comes back, Holt? What if he was one of Arnir's men?" Zylah asked, resting her eyeglasses on a lip of brick and looking up at him once more. She could find somewhere else to stay, now that she had a job. But she didn't want to.

"He won't. He was dealt with. No one will disturb you here again." He watched her the way he always did, as though a caged animal sat just beneath his skin.

Dealt with. He could have caught her assailant leaving the tavern. Zylah had seen Holt with a sword, the way he moved; it was enough to know precisely what *dealt with* meant. She couldn't say she was sorry for the intruder. And she believed Holt when he said there would be no one else.

"We'll start with training swords," he said, throwing her a wooden sword. "Just to warm up."

Zylah had only ever used a training sword, and she wondered if he'd remembered that she'd told him that. She felt the weight of the weapon in her arms, took a split second to work out if it was suitable to use one-handed, and spun around Holt to try and land the first blow.

He pivoted out of the way, bringing his sword down to meet hers with a *thwack*. "Good, use your size," he said, taking a step back, completely unfazed. "Again."

She lunged again and again, and each time Holt commented on a way to improve her stance, to hold her sword, to observe his movements.

"Try not to give so much away," he said after a while when she was already huffing and puffing.

Zylah wiped sweat from her brow. "So much of what?"

"Everything. Your face, your body. You give everything away when you attack. I know precisely where you're going to lunge for me each time because you look right at the exact spot. Imagine yourself walking through the city unnoticed,

139

like the day we arrived in Virian."

Over and over he had her try to strike him until she was exhausted and bent over her knees to catch her breath. She hadn't landed a single blow.

"We'll stop there for today," he said, tugging the practice sword away from her. He'd barely even broken a sweat.

Zylah watched him place their weapons back on the wall as she snatched up her glasses, twirling them with her fingers. She followed him back out to the tavern as her breathing steadied. "It wasn't just fighting, if you recall. I want to know more about my Fae heritage. About what I can do."

Holt unrolled the carpet over the trapdoor in silence. He led the way back up to their room, handing Zylah the bag of laundry that was waiting for them beside the door with one hand and picking up their tray of food with the other.

Coming back to the room, knowing she didn't have to move out, was a bigger relief than she'd ever admit to Holt, and yet still, it irritated her that she couldn't depend entirely on herself.

Kopi was still fast asleep as Holt set the tray down on their little table.

"What's wrong?" he asked as Zylah pulled a face.

"There's no canna—"

A brown paper bag appeared in Holt's hand. Zylah sniffed at the air. "Did you just steal that?"

"Zylah, how little you think of me still. I *always* pay. The baker will find the correct amount in his till." He held a hand over his heart in mock offence and winked.

Ass.

Zylah bit into the warm cake, her eyes closing at how good it tasted. "I'm still waiting," she said, through a mouthful of cake.

Holt looked at her over his cup of tea, and she wished she had the eyeglasses on to give herself an extra layer of protection from the intensity of his stare. "What do you want to know?"

Zylah wiped the crumbs away from her face, resting her cake on the table. "Are the gods truly Fae?"

"So they say, if you believe them."

"Don't you?" She watched the way he drained his cup, the way he piled his eggs on top of his toast.

"The gods never came to *my* aid or to any who needed them. So no, I don't believe they are Fae. I refuse to believe they watched their own people suffer."

"But the Fae weren't truly wiped out. You're here, Holt, and so are Jilah and his children."

"We aren't the same Fae we once were, Zylah. We were given labels long ago. High Fae and Lesser Fae. After the first uprising, those titles were abolished, and the High Fae became the ones to be treated as nothing. Most concealed their powers. Some used them to make a living. Others were murdered in their sleep. The courts were ripped apart, their rulers murdered. We even had a few kings and queens, once."

"You talk about it like you remember it," Zylah said as he ate his toast in two mouthfuls.

Holt looked out of the window and loosed a breath. "I do."

He barely looked a day over twenty-five. She wanted to know... not just his age. She wanted to know more about him. "How old are you?"

"Three hundred and thirty-two. Fae age differently."

Zylah almost choked on her tea. *By the gods.* "Does that mean... Will I age differently?"

"Yes, most likely. You've already reached maturity by Fae standards, so you'll age at a much slower rate than humans."

"I'd always imagined Fae to be immortal," Zylah murmured. She didn't know why. It was the complete opposite of what she'd been told in Dalstead.

Holt looked away and rubbed at his chin. "Immortal, but not unbreakable. Some live a very long life. Others are not so fortunate."

She'd struck a nerve again, and quickly fought for words to change the subject. "I wondered if you could tell me where you got the erti root." She pointed to her hair, to where the blonde was beginning to peek through.

Holt looked back at her, a bottle of erti root appearing in his palm. "Also paid for," he said with the ghost of a smile as if he'd read her thoughts.

Zylah took the bottle from him, careful not to let her fingers brush against his. "Thank you." She cleared her throat, suddenly aware of the intensity of his stare and wishing she could read him better. "I've never fought with a real sword, you know."

"Really?" Holt arched a brow as he leaned back in his chair, fingertips resting against the table. The corner of his mouth twitched for a moment, but then it was gone.

"You knew all along, didn't you?" She picked up the remains of her cake, breaking off a piece and sticking it in her mouth. His hair was still messy from training, a shadow of stubble across his chin. Her thoughts drifted to how it had felt to wake beside him, his arm wrapped tightly around her and she looked out of the window, worried that he might somehow know what she was thinking just by looking at her.

Holt pushed off from the table, grabbing his coat. "I did, but I wanted to build your confidence. You need to know you can do it. Adjusting to a real sword is only about the weight difference; practice swords are heavier and build muscle. And you're strong, we'll find a sword that's a good fit for you." He gave Kopi a light stroke on his head and shot her a tight smile before he turned to the door. "I have to go, I'll be late."

"Yes, yes, for your deliveries. Go." She stood by the door, ready to lock it, waving a hand at him. He snatched the last piece of her canna cake and shoved it in his mouth just as he slipped through the door.

She turned her key in the lock, biting back a smile. He was right about building her confidence; it had worked. She grabbed the erti root from the dresser and dashed into the bathroom to touch up her hair before work, her head buzzing and her muscles aching with the morning's activities.

Whether he was part of the Fae uprising or not, Zylah had made up her mind; she was going to join them as soon as she figured out how. One thing she knew for certain: she would never be a victim again.

14

Kopi met her at the entrance to the first dome, where Zylah found Raif helping Kihlan unloading boxes again from a cart. His long hair was still loose and messy, and she caught his mint and lemongrass scent as she approached.

"Our goddess has arrived, Kihlan," Raif said by way of greeting, a bright smile breaking across his face. "Been busy this morning, have we?"

Zylah frowned at the sarcasm lining his voice. She was only a few minutes late. Not enough for Jilah to comment anyway.

"I've been exercising."

"Warming up for our session?" Raif asked with a wicked smile.

Gods. Zylah resisted the urge to sniff herself. She'd only had time to change her clothes after training. She supposed he was just being dramatic; he seemed like the type. "So you *will* train me then?"

"Raif is the best," Kihlan added. The boy puffed hair from

his eyes and Zylah took the pile of boxes from his arms.

"Correction. I learnt from the best." Raif nudged her lightly with his elbow. "But yes, I will."

Zylah shook her head, ignoring the way her muscles ached as she carried the boxes past the weeping eye trees and towards Jilah, kneeling beside more marantas he was already halfway through planting. His hands were covered in dirt, clothes crumpled, but the old man never rested.

"Ah, Jilah, you don't mind if I borrow Liss this morning, do you?" Raif asked as he placed his boxes down. His sleeves were rolled up, showing off the thick muscles of his arms and a banded tattoo around one bicep. He caught Zylah looking and winked.

She rolled her eyes as she put her boxes beside his and straightened her apron, biting back a retort in front of Jilah, the smell of turned soil hanging in the air where he'd disturbed it.

"If Liss would like to accompany you, I see no reason why not," Jilah said, raising an eyebrow to her as if waiting for her agreement.

At least one male she knew had the sense to let her make her own decisions.

Although, Holt had, too.

She kept demanding more of him when he'd already done so much.

Raif held out an arm for her to take, but Kopi flew down and landed on her shoulder.

"Ah, so he isn't yours, but you are his to watch over," he

mused, shrugging off his offer and leading the way back out of the dome.

He ducked under the wood strings that brushed his shoulders, their spiralling tendrils cascading from the trees above.

Kopi hooed in agreement, and Zylah laughed quietly at the owl's response. "Something like that." She noted the cloud violas looked a little lacklustre and might need their soil turning, making a mental note to address them when she returned. Anything to distract her from what might come next.

She absentmindedly brushed her hands against the rough hem of her apron to keep herself from fidgeting, hoping to appear as if she was used to joining uprisings every day of her life and that this was no exception.

Raif looked back and winked at her again. "Pallia's owl watched over her too, you know."

"I am well aware."

His eyes flickered to her hair for a moment, but he said nothing, leading the way out into the cobblestone streets and past the pedlars that always set up outside the dome, some of whom Zylah had come to know on a first-name basis.

Raif watched her silently as she greeted them. *Hiding in plain sight.*

"Care to share the joke?" he asked as she smiled to herself.

"Care to tell me where you're taking me?" Zylah ignored the way he dragged a hand through his godsdamned hair, cut short the thoughts that were leading her somewhere other than the streets of Virian, her aching muscles rooting her firmly in the moment.

A mischievous grin broke across his face, and for a moment, she wondered if some Fae had the ability to read thoughts. "You'll see."

She considered confessing that she'd already had one training session that morning but didn't want to risk losing this opportunity, no matter how much her muscles protested. Raif led the way down Virian's main street, past the pillars and arches of buildings Zylah recognised, taking different turns until they reached the river. The trees that lined the pavements stopped abruptly at the bridge. This was the furthest Zylah had been in the city so far.

Something about the river always sent Kopi into a fluster, and he started to flap his little wings in irritation as they approached.

"Your owl is wise to mistrust the river," Raif said as Kopi flew ahead to the first tree on the far side of the bridge, waiting.

Only a few people crossed the bridge, and all looked a little rougher than those walking the main streets, none of them meeting Zylah's eye. She could just about make out Kopi's little silhouette in the tree across the river, waiting, watching.

"Why is that?" she finally asked.

Raif rested a hand on the stone wall, looking into the murky water below. "Our dead were thrown into the river during the last uprising by Arnir's men. Many say they leave the water at night."

Zylah followed his gaze. Surely the dead were free to do whatever they wanted? "What is so wrong about that?"

Raif let out a quiet laugh, but Zylah doubted there was anything positive in it. "Because the dead should stay dead. Come on, we shouldn't linger here."

Zylah ignored the chill that raked its way down her spine as they crossed the bridge, Kopi landing on her shoulder the moment they reached the other side.

The buildings soon turned to boarded-up, rundown shells of brick and timber, wooden terraces half broken and fixed in multiple places. The sun disappeared behind the clouds and a dark shadow fell across everything.

Raif glanced up and down the street and pulled Zylah into a side alley, his hand around her wrist. He brought a finger to his lips, and Zylah's heart was like a drum inside her chest.

The alley was narrow, barely wide enough for the two of them and Zylah's back grazed across cold brick as she looked up at Raif in question.

"Just being cautious," he said with a smirk and tapped three times on a door behind him that Zylah hadn't even had the chance to notice.

Her stomach flipped as she wondered if this was a bad decision, but Kopi was quiet on her shoulder.

A shutter opened and closed, and the door swung wide, a young woman with black hair holding it open for them. "Another one?" she asked with a raised eyebrow.

Zylah glanced between the two of them; the similarity was undeniable. Raif and the young woman were related.

"Liss, meet my sister, Rosanna. Rosanna, meet Liss."

Rosanna took a step back to let them in, and Zylah tried

not to gawk at the space.

Brightly coloured fabric lined the walls, sections of it draped across the ceiling to a centrepiece made of coloured glass, no doubt lit with an orblight. Lanterns of green and blue glass dangled on chains, some shaped like stars and moons with lights inside. A wooden counter sat in one corner, a low lounger and a round wooden table beside it. Doors opened up at either end of the room, and Zylah guessed it was a reception area.

"Nice to meet you, Rosanna," Zylah said, at last, bringing her attention back to the Fae and doing her best to hide her intake of breath at Rosanna's delicately pointed ears, pierced from lobe to tip with silver rings and interconnecting chains, some with little moons and stars that dangled down.

Rosanna had the same striking blue eyes as Raif, and her mouth quirked into the same smile as she said, "Just call me Rose. My brother likes formalities—"

"But we're far too common for that, aren't we?" Another Fae stepped out from a beaded curtain behind the counter, running a hand lightly over the tight curls of her jet-black hair that was cut far shorter than Holt's, and wearing a matching set of earrings to Rose's. The Fae's amber eyes roved over Rose in a way that made Zylah want to step outside for some air.

"This is Saphielle," Rose said, leaning back into the Fae's embrace. "Saphi," she added quickly, after Saphi playfully touched a hand against Rose's ribs, her face pressed close to Rose's.

"Cute friend." Saphi held out her palm near Kopi, and a

worm appeared. The owl snapped it up and swallowed it whole. "Just like Pallia's owl," the Fae added, adjusting the bangles against her russet skin as a frown creased her brow. "You smell like—"

Raif laughed and shook a finger at the pair. "She was exercising this morning, be nice, girls."

Zylah feigned looking around the room again to sniff at her tunic. Gods above, did she need a bath that badly?

"Exercising?" Wide grins broke out across both the Faes' faces, but it was Saphi who spoke. They shared a look, but Zylah thought better than to snap back at them. It wouldn't be the best way to make a first impression.

"Liss and I are going to have a little one-to-one time, and then I'll send her your way for some kit, if that's alright?" Raif added, steering Zylah away from the two Fae.

Zylah raised an eyebrow at him, but he just winked and led her through a doorway at the far end of the room.

"Jilah tells me you only recently found out about your Fae heritage. Half Fae? Extraordinary," he said as they walked through a narrow corridor lined with wooden panels leading to another door.

"What is this place?" Zylah asked, tilting her head up to look at him as he paused by the door, covered in strange markings carved into the wood in a language she'd never seen before.

His gaze lingered on her for a heartbeat longer than it should have, until Kopi ruffled his feathers and broke the stillness. Raif pushed open the door, holding it open for Zylah.

"One of many. A place to train. A safe space, for you. For others."

It was a plain room. Orblights dotted here and there, a training mat in the centre, weapons on one wall, not unlike the room she'd trained in with Holt that morning. Her muscles still ached, but she wasn't about to admit that to Raif. This was what she wanted. To learn to fight. To stand up for who she was, even if she didn't fully understand herself yet. Kopi flew off her shoulder and perched on a wooden shelf above the racks of weapons, cosying down for a nap.

Zylah's head was full of questions. "What's the difference between the Fae uprising and the Black Veil?"

"One is the hand that feeds the other," Raif said, watching her as she walked along the wall of weapons. Here a sword, there an axe, beside it something with two balls attached to a wooden handle by a chain, a weapon that Zylah had never seen before.

"But which is which?" She hadn't considered before that he could be part of the Black Veil. Jilah didn't seem the type to involve himself with anything... *bad*, did he? But Raif certainly had a *quality* about him... She stopped in front of the training swords and reached out for one.

Raif held a hand out to stop her. "I'll withhold that information for a future lesson, I think." His fingers brushed against her wrist for a moment, and then he straightened the sword in its stand.

"Why?" Zylah asked, taking a step back to put space between them. He clearly had no sense of boundaries.

"Because I like the way your eyes light up when you think you've finally figured everything out," he said with polished charm, tugging at the end of her braid. He'd closed the distance between them again, his gaze playful as he looked down at her.

She gave a firm shove against his chest, and he didn't budge an inch. "You're kind of insufferable, you know that?"

"Most women find it charming." A corner of his mouth twitched as he said it, his blue eyes bright and playful.

Gods above, he was in love with himself. "I'm not most women, Raif." She wouldn't call it charm, but he certainly had a way of making her feel at ease. Maybe being around Holt so much had helped more than she realised, and yet for some reason, the thought sent a twinge of guilt through her.

Raif only smiled at her, a playful glint in his eyes. "You're right about that. You said you can fight. What can you do? Show me."

Zylah pulled off her cloak and apron and dropped them below Kopi's perch, saying a silent prayer to Pallia not to let her aching body fail her. "With no weapons?" Everything her brother had taught her blurred into one before her eyes. It wasn't much. But it was enough. It had to be.

"We'll work our way up to weapons," Raif said with a smirk.

At least Holt had the decency to trust her with a sword. "Worried I'll hurt you?"

"A tiny little thing like you? Never."

"Don't call me that again," Zylah muttered, spinning

152

around and kicking Raif behind a knee.

He barely staggered forward a step, but it had been enough to take him off guard. She used everything Holt had taught her that morning about not giving away her moves and trying to read Raif's, but she barely landed a punch.

Still, she didn't give up. If the man last night had been one of Arnir's, more could come. She had to be ready. She had to be prepared to move on, and this time she wouldn't have Holt to help her. She spun around again, using her size to her advantage as much as she could, but Raif dodged her at the last moment.

"I'm impressed," Raif said after a short while, blocking another strike. He moved as fast as Holt. Well, almost.

Zylah didn't believe for one second that he was impressed. Surprised, maybe. But not impressed. "I had a few pointers from a friend," she said, not ready to give up. Every muscle in her body was burning, and an idea occurred to her—he'd said no weapons, but if this was her only chance to show what she could do…

"Am I not a friend?" Raif tried to grab her wrist, but Zylah saw his intent and spun out of his grasp.

She took a step back to catch her breath. "We've only just met."

"I think we'll make good friends though, don't you?"

His expression told her exactly the kind of friend he wanted to be. And he could be fun, couldn't he? She needed something to take the edge off her nerves. *Gods above, Zy, why are you even considering it?*

His smirk turned to a grin, those godsdamned dimples of his making their appearance. "Am I distracting you with my charm?"

"I take it back, you're truly insufferable." She feigned dodging one of his blows to discreetly reach for the dagger in her boot, but the moment she was back on her feet, he was right in front of her, those ridiculous blue eyes burning as they looked down at her.

He held her chin lightly, but she already had her dagger pressed against his ribs.

"Don't," she rasped, hoping he couldn't hear her heartbeat as loudly as she could and willing herself not to lean into his touch. Raif was trouble. The kind of trouble she could get far too carried away with.

And now she had her whole extended half Fae life ahead of her to get carried away in as many ways as she wanted. He *could* be a good distraction, but what if he knew the truth? If he knew she'd killed Jesper, that the wanted posters all over the city were for her—then what? He'd most likely cut her loose. She'd be too much of a risk to the uprising, or the Black Veil, whichever godsdamned organisation he was part of.

Raif leaned closer, and her gaze lowered to his mouth for one traitorous second. She spun away, her dagger slicing through flesh, shock written all over Raif's face.

So much for not being a risk to the organisation.

15

"Oh shit, I'm so sorry." Zylah hadn't expected to land a blow, and it was a deep cut, crimson staining Raif's shirt, the copper tang already flooding her nostrils. "It looks like it's going to leave a scar." From the edge of her vision, Kopi ruffled his feathers.

Raif watched her intensely, one hand pressed to the wound on his arm, blood leaking through his fingers. "You did good. Don't worry, Fae don't scar. Not like humans, anyway," he said with a smirk. "Not unless someone's done some real nasty shit to keep the wound open."

"But I... my friend has a scar," she admitted, wiping her blade on a rag she kept in her apron and thinking of the vicious scars down Holt's neck and arm.

Raif clicked his tongue at that. "Only one Fae I know with a scar worth commenting on, and he's a mean bastard."

"You know Holt?" Zylah asked, shrugging her apron over her head.

"Everyone knows Holt."

Zylah stilled.

"Shit, don't tell me he's the friend you've been training with. Are you trying to get me killed, Liss?" Raif reached for Zylah's arm, but she shook him off. He'd taken enough liberties already today with his inability to respect her boundaries.

She grabbed her cloak and threw it over her shoulders, Kopi resuming his position and adjusting his wings as he settled. So Holt was part of the uprising? Why hadn't he told her that? *Everyone knows Holt.* He didn't owe her any explanations. He didn't owe her anything at all. *She* owed him. But he was so guarded with what he told her, as if... as if he still didn't trust her. And why would he? She was an escaped convict; that fact remained unchanged. Just because he'd helped her didn't mean he had to open up to her, did it? She could feel Raif's gaze on her but ignored it as she fastened her cloak. "Holt doesn't speak for me, Raif."

He laughed under his breath. "That doesn't surprise me." Raif led the way back to the reception area, his sister and Saphi appearing from behind the beaded curtain as they approached the counter. Zylah braced herself for their reaction to Raif's wound. She didn't know what she expected, but she was certain they'd have something to say about it.

Rose pressed a hand to her mouth to hide her laughter. "You did this?" she asked the moment her gaze landed on Raif's wound. Her sapphire eyes sparkled with delight, and it was those eyes that truly gave her away as Raif's sister. Zylah bit back her smile as she nodded once.

"Did I mention Liss only recently discovered she's half Fae?" Raif said with another of his infuriating, dimple-ridden grins. Blood had begun to clot and crust around his fingers, but he still hadn't released his pressure on the wound. Zylah pressed her lips together, fighting with the instinct to apologise again.

The girls shared a knowing look, smiles brightening both their faces.

"Very impressive, Liss. You'll fit right in here. We deal in armour and weapons, and pride ourselves on finding items that match their wearer's unique skill set," Saphi added, as Rose led Raif into another room.

Zylah watched them go for a moment, before turning her attention back to Saphi. "Skill set?"

A vanilla perfume drifted from the Fae as she rested her delicate chin on her hands above the counter. "Your Fae abilities," she said, arching a brow.

"Well, I... that's partly what the training is for. I only know about the evanescing," Zylah admitted. She looked away, focusing on the strings of glass beads that hung from the curtain Saphi and Rose had appeared through. There was no use in lying about what she knew, but there was still every chance it could weaken her position amongst them.

Saphi touched a hand lightly to Zylah's arm, her amber eyes widening. "Quietly. That's not something you want to throw around, even in here, warded though it is."

"Why?"

Wards. That was a question for another time, but one she'd been thinking of since Holt had mentioned them that morning.

"Because only a handful of High Fae can do that," Saphi whispered.

A shiver danced across Zylah's skin at the admission. "And are High Fae not well liked?"

"It's complicated." The bangles on her arms jingled as she straightened, but her expression was still warm. She had an easiness about her, a warmth that reminded Zylah of Kara.

"So I'm learning," Zylah said quietly, giving Kopi a little stroke.

Saphi produced a new worm for him, and he snatched it up from her palm. "You really are new to this, aren't you?"

"I found out by accident, really. And I'm here to start fresh, to make friends."

"Oh, I've no doubt you'll do that quickly enough," Saphi said with a smile as the sound of Raif's laughter drifted from another room.

Zylah rolled her eyes, thinking about how he'd tried to kiss her and how she'd almost let him. How she'd wanted to. "He seems like trouble."

"He just likes women to think that. He's got a good heart though."

That was something, at least. But Zylah wasn't looking for commitment. She couldn't even consider it, burdening someone else with her fate.

Though Raif didn't exactly strike her as the type looking for commitment either. What *she* was looking for, after what happened with Jesper, was control. Life on her own terms, and no one else's. "What can you tell me about the uprising?"

"Where did you say you came from?" Saphi asked, lifting a jug from beneath the counter and pouring a drink for them both. Her thin sweater dipped with her movement, and Zylah caught a glimpse of a scar at the centre of the Fae's chest, disappearing into the cobalt folds of fabric. Raif had said Fae only scarred badly if the wound was kept open, and Zylah's eyes narrowed at the sight of it.

She tucked her observation away for another time and sniffed at the air. Only water. She swallowed it down gratefully. "Brindall, just outside of Dalstead. Any discussion of Fae is punishable by death. Arnir's orders." Brindall wasn't her village, it was the next one along. Even though she wanted to trust them, it didn't seem sensible to tell them the whole truth. Not yet.

Saphi glanced down, toying with her cup. "Arnir's orders are supposed to extend to Virian. But it's a little difficult for him to follow through on that in the old capital."

Zylah tried not to choke on her water. "Virian was the capital?"

"At one time, yes." Thick lashes framed Saphi's eyes, and Zylah could have sworn some flicker of sadness settled for a moment, and then it was gone.

So Virian was the old capital. That explained a lot. But it still left Zylah with so many questions. Too many.

She knew she'd have to be careful. "What I don't understand is, you all seem so powerful. How could the Fae have

159

been taken down by humans?"

Kopi hopped down onto the counter between them, and Saphi gently stroked his head. "It didn't happen all at once. What happened just over two decades ago was the tipping of the cup. For generations of human kings and queens, the Fae and our ways were... eroded. They sought to chip away at us, little by little."

Zylah pieced the information together with what Holt had told her. "Do you intend to take back what's yours with the uprising?"

"*Ours*," Saphi said with a smile. "And no. The Fae abused their power for years. We just want the balance to be restored. To walk the streets freely without fear of guards striking us down for who we are."

Zylah knew the feeling all too well. But she *had* committed a crime. Whereas the Fae, as far as she knew, had not. They were being attacked simply for who they were. "How do you hope to achieve that?"

Raif strolled into the room before Saphi could answer. "All in good time, Liss. Jilah will be wondering where you are. Shall I walk you back to the gardens?"

Rose returned a heartbeat after her brother, and for the first time, Zylah noticed the glimmer of something where one of her feet should have been.

"Beautiful, isn't it?" Rose asked, tugging on her trouser leg to reveal an obsidian blade in place of a limb, delicately curved at the tip like a pointed foot.

Zylah had never seen anything like it, but it truly was

beautiful. "Incredible," she replied, resisting the urge to ask if she could look at it more closely. Rose dropped her trouser leg back down, already sliding into place at Saphi's side.

A question. Raif had asked her a question, and she'd been busy gawking at Rose and Saphi's otherworldliness, a world she was now very much a part of. "It was nice to meet you both," she said with a smile, Kopi flapping his wings once to resume his position on her shoulder.

Raif waved a hand in goodbye as he ushered Zylah out of the door, letting it fall shut behind them with a soft click. A heartbeat later, Zylah heard locks sliding into position. Five of them.

"I don't see how Arnir fits into all of this," she said as Raif stalked out into the street. Kopi flew on ahead as always; she knew he wouldn't go far, even if she couldn't see him.

A guttural sound rumbled from Raif. "He doesn't. The king is a fool and the sooner he's disposed of, the better all of our lives will be."

A new king wouldn't care about retribution. On wasting men to hunt her down. She'd truly be free if Arnir was gone, and a chill ran down her spine at the thought. "I want to learn more about my abilities. Is that something you can help with?"

Raif raised an eyebrow as he glanced down at her. "Just say the word, love, and I'll show you anything you like."

In Pallia's name. "Do you really think those lines work?"

Raif shrugged. "They make you laugh. That's enough for me."

Kopi swooped down to land on her shoulder as the sound

of many footsteps reached them. Guards. Without even thinking, she tugged up her hood, a quiet sense of foreboding washing over her.

"Ah, so he is a guard dog," Raif murmured at her side as the guards passed.

Zylah's thoughts drifted to the night before, when Kopi had clawed her attacker's face and sent blood spraying across the room. She swallowed. "Something like that."

Raif nudged her with an elbow. "Did I say something wrong?"

"No. But I do owe Kopi a life debt. Two, in fact."

He huffed a quiet laugh. "A life debt. Ah, so you do know a little of Fae culture."

"Life debts extend into our… into human culture, you know."

"Oh yes, I'm well aware of the watered-down promises humans call life debts. A life debt for a Fae is binding: a life for a life. Nothing less will repay the debt." His brow scrunched a little as he said it, but as if he caught her gaze, his expression quickly returned to cool neutrality.

"Well, Kopi's saved my life twice now so, I guess I'll have to figure out some way to repay him. Same time tomorrow?" she asked, as they strode for the goods' entrance of the botanical gardens.

Raif's smile was feral. "For a chance to see you in action again? You bet." He didn't follow her in. Just shoved his hands in his pockets and walked away, as if they were total strangers. Which they were, she supposed. She still barely knew him.

With muscles protesting her every movement, she willed herself to finish off her work for the day, almost yelping with relief when it was time to go home for the evening. When she returned to the tavern, Holt was already back in *their* room, hair wet, a clean shirt revealing a glimpse of the scar along the muscles of his neck. She swallowed as she thought of Raif's words about how difficult Fae were to scar.

Holt frowned. "You smell different," was all he said as they stared at each other.

Zylah willed her blood not to rush to her cheeks. "What is it with everyone commenting on how I smell today?" She ducked past him, pushing the bathroom door shut behind her and sniffing at her clothes. Sweaty, but not terrible. She'd have to wash them in the bath after she was done.

She set about filling the kettles, her hands working automatically without any thought now that she was used to the routine, finally allowing herself a moment to work through the events of the day. Her muscles screamed as she peeled off her clothes. She couldn't train twice every day. She'd have to think of something. Perhaps one of them could focus on magic and the other on combat. She wasn't sure yet, but she'd figure it out.

All that mattered was that she was learning—it didn't matter who taught her. The faster she could learn, the better chance she stood of making it out of Virian and moving on with her life. She'd been studying Holt's map in the evenings: the world was vast. And she intended to see as much of it as she could. But she knew it would be a mistake if she tried to keep running now. She'd only end up captured or killed by Arnir's men. She had to be patient.

But the sense of foreboding she'd felt earlier still lingered. How long could she go on hiding in Virian, how long could she push her luck? It felt unwise to dance with fate, to toy with the time she'd been given, time that stretched out before her in a way she still hadn't truly grasped.

Raif's words played on repeat as she fastened her hair in a messy bun above her head. *The king is a fool and the sooner he's disposed of, the better all of our lives will be.*

Zylah couldn't agree more.

16

After a second training session with Holt, every step on the way to work had sent searing pain through Zylah's body. By the late afternoon, she hid by the waterfall in the first dome to stretch her aching muscles, working through what he'd taught her. It hadn't even been a full one-hour session, but after the previous day, it was enough. The roar of the water drowned out everything else, the smell of wet rock and moss flooding her senses. Holt had been quieter than usual, but so had she, focused on absorbing as much of his teaching as she could. On improving.

The humidity of the dome helped her a little with the aches, but she still rested a hand on the wooden rail beneath the waterfall, her arm thrown over her head to stretch as gently as she could. Her pruning shears banged against her knees through her apron pocket, but she was busy sifting through all the information she'd learnt in the last few days.

"I know an excellent technique to ease muscle tightness," a

voice said from behind her.

Zylah spun around, the pruning shears already in her raised hand, ready to strike. Raif leant against a tree trunk—part of the support structure for the waterfall—his blue eyes lit up with amusement, one of those irritating dimples already visible as he bit back at a smile.

Even if it was all a front, as Saphi had suggested, Raif seemed to be enjoying himself. Techniques, indeed.

"I'll bet you do." Zylah didn't put away the shears though, not yet. She'd wounded him once; she'd do it again if he overstepped.

Raif raised a brow at the shears. "Hoping to wound me two days in a row?" He pushed off the tree, closing the distance between them. Zylah had barely even blinked and he was in front of her, far too close for someone she'd only just met. She tilted her chin back to look up at him, at the amused expression that still danced across his face. His mint and lemongrass scent drifted from him, mingling with the wet rock and moss.

"No," she murmured, following his gaze to her raised hand. She took a step back, returning the shears to her apron. She needed to phrase her request carefully about alternating her training. If she showed too little interest in combat training, he might deem her a waste of time for the uprising, too unreliable.

"Pity," he said softly, his eyes flicking down for a moment before settling back on hers. "You said you wanted to learn more about your Fae heritage. I hear the grotto has perfect acoustics at this time of day."

Gods above. He was relentless. But if he knew how ridiculous his lines were, he didn't let it show. Zylah wondered if he even cared. *They make you laugh, that's enough for me.* Maybe he did have a good heart.

The humid air suddenly became stifling, and she resisted the urge to tug off her apron. "You love to hear yourself talk, don't you?" Zylah finally asked, pushing past him to walk down the ramp that led out of the dome. Kopi's quiet hoot told her he was watching close by, but she still scanned the gardens for any signs of... well, anyone else.

She caught Raif watching her but refused to catch his gaze. She'd never stop looking over her shoulder, checking the shadows for any signs of Arnir's men. She knew the moment she did would be the moment they'd take her. A quick glance at Kopi told her nothing was amiss. She could barely distinguish his head from his body; if he was perfectly at ease, she should be, too.

Raif fell into step with her as she made her way down the narrow path to the grotto. "How about an information exchange. You already know a little bit about me. If you want me to trust you, tell me about yourself."

She paused to look up at him, one hand on her hip. "I know nothing about you, other than that you're an arrogant bastard."

That godsdamned dimple made an appearance as his gaze drifted from Zylah's hand to her face and back up again, slowly. "You know I have a sister. Do you have any siblings?"

Did they count if she could never see her family again? "A

brother." Zylah pressed on to the entrance of the grotto, hidden amongst the bushes. "Well, he's not my real brother. I was adopted."

The cool air of the grotto enveloped Zylah as she made her way to the rocky window that overlooked the pond. Jilah called it a lake, but it was far too small for that.

"Interesting." Raif rested against the opposite side of the window, nothing more than a cut-out in the rock, and Zylah tried to hide her surprise as she saw the tips of his pointed ears for the first time. Like Jilah and the children, the grotto revealed his true appearance. His eyes were brighter, his movements even more fluid, as if he kept the way he moved through the world a secret.

Zylah realised she'd been staring, grasping for the first thing that came to mind. "Rose and Saphi, they seem…"

Raif chuckled. "They are very into each other, yes. But it's a good thing. Rose and I don't always see eye to eye, and Saphi acts as a… buffer."

"Why?"

Raif looked out to the water. "I was good friends with Rose's mate. Before she rejected the bond. It drove him mad. Saphi found her after the first uprising, lying in the mud with one leg missing, and saved her life. The rest, as they say, is history."

There was so much information packed into those few sentences. Kara had often spoken of Fae having mates, had made Zylah read enough of her books about them. Zylah had always laughed it off. Kara was the romantic one out of the two of them, that was certain. And as for the rest, about Rose and Saphi… it didn't seem right to ask Raif about their story. "Do you have any other family?"

"Our mother is dead." He turned his attention back to her, those cobalt eyes dimming a little.

"And your father?" She was pushing her luck. But she wanted to know more about him—she wanted to trust him.

Raif folded his arms across his chest, and the movement reminded her of Holt. "We try not to speak about our father. For fear that it summons him." He laughed quietly. "And you? What of your adoptive parents?"

Zylah looked out at the water again, at the dragonflies skimming above the surface. "My father. I won't be seeing him for some time." And there it was. The reminder that this, whatever *this* was, was temporary. That as soon as she had the means, she'd be leaving Virian for good and getting as far away from those wanted posters as possible, further away from her family, too.

"Ah, the starting over. So why the uprising? Why our cause, why not another?"

"Because no one should have to live in fear just because of who they are."

Raif's hand lightly touched her elbow, his calloused fingers brushing against the sleeve of her tunic. "And you know a little of that, do you?"

Zylah hadn't noticed he'd pushed off the wall. She looked up at him, at the way his eyes darkened with that all too familiar glaze. He leaned into her, his hand trailing up her arm, and she fought against her warring emotions. Jesper had taken something from her, something she knew she could take back when she was ready, but Zylah hadn't made her decision about Raif, not yet. She evanesced out of his touch, back towards the entrance of the grotto.

His eyes widened as he spun around to face her. "How—"

Jilah called out from somewhere in the second dome, and a muscle flickered in Raif's jaw. "Don't let anyone in the city see you do that. Ever."

Zylah ignored his outburst, straining to listen. "Guard search, I'll go back to work, they're used to seeing me here now."

Raif grabbed her elbow, pulling her away from the entrance, and Zylah shrugged out of his grasp.

"Wait here," he said and stalked out of the grotto.

Zylah listened to his footsteps as he stormed away, debating whether to march out there after him. That would draw the guards' attention, though. She paced, pausing every few steps to listen for any exchange between the guards. She'd evanesced in front of him. Saphi had warned her, and that look on his face, as if he was appalled by it, by *her*. Maybe she'd read the situation wrong. Maybe he wasn't interested, and he was just overly flirtatious with everyone. And what would he do with that information, now that he knew she could evanesce? She still had no idea if she could trust him.

Kopi's quiet hoot told Zylah Raif was returning, but she already recognised the sound of his gait upon the path.

"We should continue your training at the safe house. The

wards are stronger." He seemed completely at ease, as if the guards hadn't just marched in for a check, but then Zylah supposed Raif wasn't the type to baulk at anything.

She followed him out of the grotto, glancing up to Kopi's favourite tree. He was still there. "I thought you hadn't decided whether you trust me enough to train me."

"I decided the moment you told me you wanted to help. Plus we could use someone with your knowledge of plants."

"Ah, I see, so I'm a means to an end." She tried to hide the elation from her voice, to keep her tone casual.

A smile tugged at his mouth. "Were you expecting a grand initiation ceremony?"

"I…" Zylah shook her head. She didn't know what she'd expected. "What do you need to know?" They returned to the first dome. She wouldn't be seen on the streets without her cloak, no matter who walked beside her.

"Healing poultices are difficult to come by in large quantities—the apothecaries' inventories are monitored by Arnir's men. Do you think you could make some for us, provide instructions for how to make more?" He watched her as she carefully shrugged into her cloak, the hint of a dimple appearing as his mouth twitched.

Gods, her body ached. "I find it difficult to believe you can't all heal yourselves."

"Not all Fae have powers like yours, Liss."

She tugged up her hood as they reached the goods' entrance. "I can't heal," she said, tilting her chin to look up at him.

171

He was already surveying the streets, but there was no sign of any guards. "Have you ever tried?"

The usual pedlars were working their regular spots outside the gardens, and Zylah gave them each a polite wave as she and Raif strode past. She caught Kopi's silhouette darting off to the rooftops. "No. That's where you come in, remember?" The aroma of frying meat hung in the crisp air from a relatively new addition to the street vendors. Zylah had taken one look at how much oil he used to cook the meat and decided it wasn't for her.

"Fine. Seeing as your other training seems to be taking its toll, we can focus on your Fae abilities for now."

Zylah paused to look up at him again. "You noticed." Of course he had. These Fae didn't miss a thing.

He took a step closer, the glazed look returning to his eyes, the one she'd seen enough times on Theo to know precisely where his thoughts had taken him. "Every wince and sigh. Oh, I noticed," he said under his breath.

Her traitorous heart skipped a beat, and her thoughts were almost as bad. Zylah shook her head and took a step back from him, her gaze landing on a couple feverishly kissing outside a restaurant. Oh, there was no doubting Raif's intentions, and she was grateful for the hood covering her face, certain she was unable to hide the inevitable flush creeping up her neck.

Up ahead, she could already make out the silhouette of the trees lining the bridge, Kopi's tiny body swooping down amongst the branches. Zylah quietly drew in a breath. Something told her that how she chose to reply would set the tone for their training session. She waited until they reached the wall overlooking the river before she allowed herself a look up at him.

Raif's hands were shoved deep in his pockets as he leaned back against the wall, his sleeves rolled up past his elbows, high enough that she could just glimpse a peek of the band tattooed around one of his biceps. A breeze blew a few wisps of midnight hair across his face, but he didn't swipe it away, just held her gaze, waiting.

"I—" Zylah began, but Kopi's warning cry cut her off.

Raif pulled her behind him, and she ducked to grab her dagger from her boot as a knife clinked off the stone wall beside her. She snatched it up as she pushed herself to her feet. Two hooded figures attacked Raif, a third ran for her. They weren't guards, but that didn't mean they weren't Arnir's men. They could be mercenaries, willing to split whatever coin the king had offered them for her capture.

Zylah threw the knife and it sank to the hilt into her assailant's shoulder but didn't stop them. They lunged for her and she pivoted out of the way, catching sight of Raif fighting with nothing but his hands against the two who faced him. He'd learnt from the best, he'd said.

Kopi called out again, and Zylah spun back around just as her attacker held out the knife, dripping with blood and ready to strike. She took less than a heartbeat to decide, launching towards them, shoulder barrelling into their waist and shoving them back against the wall. They stumbled back and Zylah ducked down at the last moment, just as her assailant went tumbling over the wall, rolling down the slope to the river. She didn't wait to see what had become of them, she turned back to Raif, just as one of his attackers turned to ash at his touch, and the second turned on his heels and ran.

The breeze picked up and the ash scattered, just as Zylah reached him. "What did you do?" she whispered.

"We need to get back to the safe house. Now." He turned to look at her, and Zylah could have sworn his eyes were different, but he blinked and they returned to normal. "You're alright?"

"Thanks to Kopi." She flicked her chin in the owl's direction, her heartbeat still far too loud in her chest.

"Nice job, with the river," Raif said, his wicked grin returning, all hint of whatever it was that had cast over him gone. "I think we can count that as your initiation."

Zylah laughed. He didn't have a single mark on him. And he hadn't used a weapon. Perhaps she should have picked him for combat training instead. She needed to get those bracers as quickly as possible, she couldn't rely on walking around the city with just her dagger any longer. That would be her first request to Saphi and Rose.

She rested a hand on her shoulder and rolled it gently. She'd need a long, hot bath the moment she got back. She looked up to find Raif looking at her but cut him off. "Let me guess, you know more than one excellent technique to ease muscle tightness." She couldn't help the smile that tugged at her mouth as she said it.

Raif offered a knowing smile in return as he turned down

an alley she recognised, the narrow space between buildings and the door to the safe house nestled out of sight of the street. He reached to knock on the door but turned back to face her instead, his dimple dangerously close to being fully on display.

"That's three times you've stared at my mouth today," he said with a smirk.

"Asshole." Zylah reached up on her toes, hands curling into his hair and pressed her mouth to his. She'd made her decision. And it was her choice, this kiss. Not his. But Raif didn't hesitate; he pulled her to him, the hard muscle of his body pressed against hers as he kissed her back. His hand wrapped around the back of her neck, eliciting a gasp from Zylah as his tongue swept in and their kiss quickened. Somehow, she'd backed up against the wall, not an inch of space between her body and Raif's. *Gods above.*

Zylah pulled back to catch a breath, pushed at his chest. His eyes sparkled, no doubt with all the *techniques* he intended to demonstrate to her. She pushed again when he didn't move, her hand remaining until he took a step back, his hands unwinding from her hair. She could go through that door with him, and this would continue. Gods, did she want it to continue.

Kopi flew down from the rooftops and landed on Zylah's shoulder as she fought to control her ragged breathing. "Same time tomorrow?" she said with a smile. Zylah didn't wait for a response; she evanesced back to the tavern before she could follow Raif inside the safe house.

"Zylah?" Holt reached for her the moment her feet touched

the wooden floorboards of their room. Kopi flew to his dresser, and Zylah pressed a hand to her chest.

She met Holt's gaze, his eyes flaring and his face paling for a moment before he sat back down on the lounger. He dragged a hand through his hair and let out a quiet breath. "All is well, I trust?"

Zylah sat on the bed, half in a daze, resisting the urge to brush her fingers to her lips. That was *not* what she had expected with Raif. And she knew if she'd gone inside with him, training was the last thing they'd be doing right now.

Holt pushed to his feet and began to pace.

"I'm fine. I'm sorry. I didn't mean to startle you." She couldn't look at him. Not yet. It felt… she didn't know exactly what it felt. Her skin was flushed, her lips swollen, and for some reason, she felt guilty that he had to see that. *In Pallia's name, Zy.* It didn't matter, did it? Holt didn't look at her that way. *I won't touch you.* He'd made it abundantly clear. He was her friend. It worked; *they* worked better this way.

He stopped pacing, sat down, rubbed his palms on his knees. He was far too big for the lounger, even sitting, and he'd never once complained. She should be the one sleeping on it, not him.

"We didn't work on the other part of your training this morning," he finally said. His expression was schooled, but he didn't meet her gaze.

Zylah twisted her hands in her lap, thinking about all the things Raif had told her. "My friend Kara was always giving me books," she said, a frown creasing her brow. "Her

176

favourites were full of stories of faeries overcoming some terrible struggle and finding their mate." Zylah laughed as she said it, at the memory of it. "I loved to watch her talk about them as if they were real." Of all the things she could have mentioned, she'd felt compelled to mention this one particular subject. *Excellent, Zy, waste your questions on ridiculous topics.*

"Why do you think they aren't?" Holt arched a brow, but there was no hint of amusement in his expression.

"A kindred soul? A life mate? Only one person for each of us? What kind of cruel fate would that be, if they didn't choose you, or you never met, or they died?" Rose's mate had been driven mad from the rejection, Raif said. Had he found someone else, like she had? Or would he never get to feel that for someone again, because of something she decided? "I refuse to believe that. We are capable of loving more than one person. We are capable of deep and meaningful love with more than one person, of course we are."

"Not all mating bonds are a good thing," Holt said softly. "Sometimes it goes wrong. Sometimes there are rejections." He let out a breath. "Finding a mate is rare—complications are rarer still. But when it works—when it all falls into place— that's a powerful thing." He looked out of the window, and Zylah wondered if it was the city he was seeing or something else. Someone else. Heat flushed her chest, and for the first time, she questioned if perhaps he already had a partner, a mate even. The heat in her chest became a burning, and she willed the sensation to diminish.

"You've seen it? A bonded couple?"

177

Holt turned his attention back to her. "My parents were mates. They were inseparable. In life, and in death. But their bond got them killed, in the end."

Zylah's heart crumpled at that. He'd barely offered up any information about himself in the weeks she'd known him. To know his parents were gone, *killed*—words failed her. "I'm sorry," she said quietly.

"It's nothing to be sorry about. They tried to save each other, and they couldn't. But their story is unique. I've seen bad matches—seen them end just as badly."

"You said it yourself, not all mating bonds are a good thing." Zylah was still restless from her kiss with Raif, but every muscle screamed as she walked to the window.

"Indeed."

They held each other's gaze for a moment, until Zylah looked away, for fear that if he looked too long he'd know precisely what she'd been doing with Raif. "I've joined the uprising. I want to help other Fae."

When she looked back for his response, Holt was already by the door, a hand resting on the knob. "It's a worthy cause," he said with a tight smile that didn't reach his eyes. "I have to go. No training tomorrow; I have commitments in the morning. Consider it a rest day." His eyes darted to her shoulder for a moment, the one she so desperately wanted to sink in hot water. He didn't wait for a response, the door clicking shut behind him.

Zylah slumped into the chair by the window, pressing a hand to her lips, and for the first time since the incident, thought about the attack by the river. She'd assumed they were there for her, but the way Raif reacted, it was as if it were an everyday occurrence for him. He'd turned one of them to ash with his bare hands. And she'd kissed him. She exhaled slowly, looking out over the city until the lamplights blinked on and her heartbeat returned to normal.

When she finally settled down for the night, she dragged her blanket from the bed and curled up on Holt's lounger, studying the map further and plotting out all the places she'd like to visit. The following day, she'd collect the ingredients for the poultices, but in return, she expected the truth from Raif. She saw no reason why work and pleasure should have to mix, and if Raif intended to bring down Arnir, Zylah wanted in.

17

Raif was waiting for her the next morning. "I've already spoken to Jilah." His smile was wide, and Zylah didn't miss the way his eyes roved over her body. "He's happy to let you go, provided you bring some besa cuttings back for him."

Zylah looked around him, towards the entrance to the botanical gardens as Kopi flew down to her shoulder and quietly hooed. Jilah and the children were nowhere in sight, but that didn't mean they weren't inside the gardens. *Focus on the poultices.* She'd looked over her shoulder at every strange noise on her walk to work, every shout making her want to reach for her dagger. They'd been attacked in broad daylight the day before, and Zylah knew all too well there was nothing to stop it from happening again.

Raif moved away from the wall, his gaze raking over her in a way that sent heat flooding through her body. "Shall we, *Liss?*"

His lips were pressed into a firm line, and she forced herself not to stare at the dimple that had begun to show on one side of his mouth, not to let her eyes drift to his lips. She cleared her throat. "I need to be back by lunch; Jilah needs me to cover for him this afternoon."

"Then we'd better hurry, we've got a lot of ground to cover." He winked, and Zylah rolled her eyes. He held a basket he'd looped his arm through, raising an eyebrow as if waiting for her response.

She almost pushed off her hood to look up at him better. "If you know where we need to look, what do you need me for?"

"I know where to look," he began, tugging at her braid, his eyes lowering to her mouth for a moment before darting back up again, "because I asked Jilah. But what plants to look for, or what they look like, is where you come in."

Zylah held his gaze but knew she'd been turning over replies in her head for a heartbeat too long when he smirked and let go of her hair. She followed him past the morning food stalls, waving politely at the vendors she knew, but not stopping to say hello.

A guard patrol marched by and she jerked at her hood, grateful for Kopi's reassuring weight, however tiny, on her shoulder. The owl hadn't flown on ahead, as if he somehow knew she was going outside the city.

"That basket suits you," she said as Raif waited for her to catch up.

He leant forward in a mocking bow, waving the basket before him in a wide swoop. "Doesn't it just?" A quiet laugh rumbled from him as if he didn't have a care in the world. As if they hadn't just been attacked the day before in the middle of the street. She wondered if the humour was a front, a wall he put in place not just for the benefit of others, but for himself, too.

Whether it was or not, Zylah was grateful for Raif's easygoing presence. She had forgotten what that felt like, to not be always looking over her shoulder or looking out for Arnir's men. To not always be darting away from the posters of herself splattered across the city, just in case anyone noticed her standing beside one and recognised the likeness.

They passed by one of the city's apothecaries, and she shoved aside the thoughts of her father as the scents of saffa spice and alea blossom drifted towards them, carried by the customers that came and went through the glass doors. Was he ashamed of her? Had he sent anyone to look for her?

Kopi hooted softly and flew off towards the trees near the city gates. She watched him land safely before she noticed Raif had fallen into step beside her. She knew she should be using the time to press him with questions about the uprising, about the Black Veil, about all of it, but the scents of the apothecary seemed to cling to her hood, leaving the image of her father's face freshly etched in her mind.

"So how do you know Holt?" Raif nudged her gently with an elbow as they approached the gates, subtly pointing out two guards Zylah hadn't noticed.

She adjusted her hood and lowered her gaze, grateful that Kopi had flown on ahead. Sometimes, walking around with an owl on her shoulder wasn't exactly subtle, but there were enough unusual characters in Virian that usually, no one paid her any attention. The guards at the gate, though, would be a different matter. "I train with him," she finally murmured, head down, her pace in line with the traders up ahead, slow and casual.

Arnir's men were everywhere, now she had begun to recognise them. Not only did all the guards work for the king, but there were others stationed around the city she'd begun to identify, plain-clothed officers always overloaded with weapons, too cleanly presented to be mercenaries or bounty hunters.

Raif sighed through his nose. "So you mentioned."

Zylah didn't dare look up at him as they passed the guards, didn't get to see if the expression on his face matched the irritation that lined his voice.

They crossed the bridge, hugging the wall, and Zylah looked up enough this time to see over it. It was nothing but empty grey sky as far as she could see, but she resisted the urge to lean up to the edge, to peer over. Nothing would mark her as an outsider, as a tourist, more than peering over that wall.

"You're learning from the best, Liss," Raif said when she didn't reply. "Holt's a force to be reckoned with."

"You learnt from Holt?" She remembered his words from a few days before. *I learnt from the best.*

They shuffled past the traders who had stopped in the middle of the bridge, one complaining loudly to the rest about having lost his coin purse. Raif grabbed her elbow and steered her out of the way just as the trader stepped back without looking. "Holt is like a brother to me," he admitted, releasing her arm.

"Funny, he's never mentioned you." She didn't add that Holt had barely mentioned anything about himself at all. *Until last night.*

Raif chuckled. "That doesn't surprise me. He's never been one for many words."

It felt wrong to be talking about Holt with Raif, but Zylah couldn't pinpoint why. The hairs on her arms stood on end as they stepped off the bridge onto the dirt road that bordered the forest. "You must have struggled with that," she finally said to Raif.

"Are you saying I talk too much? I can think of other things we can do instead."

She thought of their kiss, of his body pressed against hers and turned to look back at the city to hide her blush. Virian was so much bigger than she'd imagined when she and Holt had first approached it, weeks ago. The world was much bigger than she'd thought, and she couldn't wait to get away from Virian to see it.

She'd told Raif and Holt she wanted to join the uprising to help, which was true, but it didn't mean she didn't have her own selfish reasons. Like making contacts, connections that might be useful to her in the days ahead. For when she had enough money and supplies to leave Virian for good.

She'd need to know people, have acquaintances, even though she hated the truth of it—hated that she wouldn't be able to do it alone.

One of the guards from the gate strode towards the traders, and Zylah spun back around, checking her hood was still covering her hair. If any of Arnir's men from his prison were stationed here, they'd recognise her. She couldn't risk any of them looking too closely.

Her thoughts drifted to Raif and Holt, to how long they must have known each other for Raif to consider them brothers. Fae ageing was still a mystery to her, but Jilah seemed like an old man. "Is Jilah truly Kihlan and Niara's father? He seems... *old*... even by Fae standards."

"I suggest we do something other than talk and you ask me about that old strip of leather?" Raif nudged her lightly again with his elbow, twirling the basket in his other hand. "He's their grandfather. Their mother died a few years ago."

"And how old are the children?"

"As old as they look."

The Falstin forest spread on both sides of the road leading to the city, and Zylah knew from experience that it spread far. "And Jilah?" Kopi flitted from tree to tree as they walked along the road, keeping out of the way of the horses and carts.

"Who knows? Too old to ask," Raif said with another twirl of the basket.

"I don't understand how the ageing works... Holt is... well I know how old Holt is, and he doesn't look a day over twenty-five. When do you start to age?"

"*Liss*, I never took you for the shallow type." Raif raised an eyebrow as he looked down at her, another smirk tugging at the corner of his mouth. "I see looks are important to you."

Zylah opened her mouth to reply, but Raif cut her off. "Jilah made a bargain, and it cost him."

"A bargain?"

When she looked up, Raif nodded discreetly at a man on horseback. "Humans make deals, do they not? Jilah made a bargain and the cost was his eternal youth. He is still immortal, but as he gets older, he will age and his body will decay."

"But he won't die?" Zylah asked, glancing back at the rider.

"Not exactly, no. A bargain with a faerie is never pleasant. Whatever twisted soul made that arrangement with him, they wanted the satisfaction of knowing that it would one day take his life, but on their terms. He'll reach a point where he'll be so old and frail, he won't want to go on living anymore, and most likely, when he tries to take his own life, he'll discover the bargain won't let him die by his own hand, but some other perverse scheme only a faerie could concoct."

What would have been worth that? And to lose his daughter, too. "That's awful," Zylah said quietly.

"Today's lesson: never make a bargain with a faerie."

Zylah was about to reply when Kopi hooted a warning. She casually looked away from the guard striding past, who had been concealed moments before behind a cart.

"Are you ever going to tell me why you're hiding from them?" Raif murmured, swooping down to pick a weed and place it in his basket for the benefit of the guard watching. It *was* edible, but she'd bet a copper piece that Raif didn't know that.

"Another time, maybe." Zylah's gaze fixed on the guard's back as he walked away. "High Fae and Lesser Fae, what's the difference?"

A narrow path cut away from the road, and Raif looked in both directions before heading down it, waving a hand for Zylah to follow. "Those are old terms; who told you those?"

"I read them." It was an easy lie, and the words just slipped out. Lying had always come easily to Zylah; she'd gotten so used to covering up her strangeness, the odd situations she always seemed to find herself in. Besides, she saw no point in telling him that Holt had told her.

The path became nothing but trampled undergrowth through the trees, the darkness of the forest enveloping them. The sounds from the road disappeared, replaced with the quiet creaking of boughs as they swayed in a gentle breeze.

Raif didn't question her. "Lesser Faeries, as they were once called, are more unusual than their High Fae counterparts. Whereas we look like nothing more than pointy-eared humans, Lesser Faeries come in all shapes and sizes. Some are winged, some have fangs, claws, scales. As a child, I never understood why they coveted pointed ears like mine, they wear metal ear cuffs to mimic the look, but their ears are usually the last thing you're looking at."

Zylah let his words sink in. In all the books Kara had given her, faeries were always beautiful, flawless, fierce. *All High Fae.* "And they still exist?"

"Of course they still exist. Is Dalstead a glass box?" Raif rolled his eyes at her.

Arnir had used fear to stop people from discussing the Fae, and it had worked. Dalstead truly was cut off from the rest of the world. "Evidently. What else should I know? About the Fae?" Zylah pushed back her hood to look up at him better, and he winked back in approval. *Gods above.* He truly was insufferable. A patch of tiny, waxy leaves covered the ground up ahead, and Zylah began gathering the besa leaves into the basket.

"Growing up, I thought all Fae could be split into two groups." Raif gathered leaves with her as she worked, after a moment of observing her actions.

"I can't imagine you growing up." She couldn't imagine Holt growing up either. Amantias usually grew close to besa plants, a good ingredient to include in healing balms and—*ah.* Zylah knelt in the dirt before a tree, unsheathing her dagger to cut the springy mushrooms from the bark.

Raif knelt beside her, closer than he might have done had they not kissed the day before. "Adolescence is a very… volatile time, particularly for males."

"Seven gods, Raif, I don't need details. The two groups?" She knew if they kept looking, she'd find some jupe, but she wasn't ready to make poison just yet. Not when she knew so little about the people she was making it for. Some feverroot and celandia could be good though, so she could make a balm for wounds. Oil and wax would be readily available in Virian. With some besa leaves, she could make poultices for infection and fevers. Hopefully, that would be enough for now.

Raif took the mushrooms as she cut them and placed them

in the basket beside him. "There are the helpers, and then there are the tricksters—the deceivers." His eyes seemed to sparkle as he spoke. "We all use deceits—it's how we hide our ears; conceal things we don't want others to see. But there are Fae who want nothing more than to trick others at every turn, and those who only want to help."

She looked up at him. His eyes were bright, and she remembered the darkness she thought she'd seen there after he'd turned his attacker to ash. "No in between?"

He shrugged. "You'll have to decide for yourself. Let me know what you discover." His fingers brushed hers as he took another mushroom from her, and Zylah rose to her feet, holding his gaze.

"We're looking for a plant with three leaflets; the centre one is pointed like an arrow." She cleared her throat, trying not to think about how fast things could have moved yesterday if she'd let them. Words danced on the tip of her tongue as she looked up to see two eyes staring back at her through the bushes. Kopi hadn't called out in warning. *Sprites.* Zylah knew they were in the forest, she'd seen them with Holt, well, sort of. They'd been watching then and he'd said they were attracted to his magic; they'd helped him take down that bounty hunter.

The eyes blinked and disappeared as she thought of the way Holt had summoned vines like it was nothing, and again the question of her training spiralled around in her thoughts. She couldn't have combat training with both of them every day, that was obvious. Maybe it made sense to continue combat training with Holt and to focus on her... *abilities* with Raif.

They moved on through the forest and she soon came across the feverroot and celandia, filling the basket until it was almost overflowing. Raif helped diligently, cutting the plants exactly as she showed him. She stole glances at him as they worked, telling herself it was just to check he was gathering everything correctly.

He caught her gaze and smiled. "How did you learn about all of this?" he asked, flicking his chin at their collection.

My father, she wanted to say. But she didn't want to think about her father again. Not out here. "I read a lot." It was half of the truth. There had been a lot she'd taught herself over the years, enough to surprise her father a few times.

"Only books about plants and the Fae?" He offered her a hand as she pushed herself to her feet.

She stared at his hand for a moment before placing hers in it. "No. I read storybooks too." He'd pulled her close enough that she could feel the heat coming from him, could see the flecks of silver in his eyes, and she willed herself to hold his gaze, to not back down from the challenge that was written across his face. If yesterday was anything to go by, things could get out of hand very quickly... and the thought sent heat racing through her.

Raif took a step closer and tucked a strand of hair behind her ear, his thumb tracing her jaw. "What kind of stories? Anything interesting?"

There was barely an inch of space between them now, and

his gaze lowered to her mouth as he waited for her answer.

Gods, she was in trouble. Her breath hitched, and she chose her words carefully.

"That," Zylah swallowed, watching the way his lips pressed together as he waited for her response, "depends on your definition of interesting."

Raif didn't reply. His lips were on hers, his tongue sweeping them open. The hand that had been tracing her jaw moments before fisted into her hair and a low, feral sound escaped him that Zylah felt everywhere their bodies touched. Every thought and worry left her head as Raif's hands grabbed her rear and lifted her, and she instinctively wrapped her legs around him.

Her back pressed against a tree trunk as he traced kisses down her neck, his hands warm and strong beneath her tunic. *Gods.* Zylah's back arched as his lips traced lower, then slowly, painfully slowly, back up the other side of her jaw. Raif's shoulders were firm and strong beneath her fingers as she pressed into him, into the thick muscle beneath his shirt. His body was solid and warm against hers, and she wished there wasn't a scrap of fabric between them.

She resisted the urge to rock against the hard length of him pressing between her thighs, unable to help the moan that escaped her lips as he nipped and sucked at her earlobe, his hands stroking up her sides, fingers teasing lower and back up again. It untethered any leash she might have had on her self-control, her hips moving against him to ease the pressure building between them.

Raif's mouth was on hers again just as another moan escaped her, and this time when he made that feral sound, she truly did feel it *everywhere*. He pulled back, his eyes glazed and his breathing ragged, his hands pressing her to him. "Take us to the safe house," he murmured, pressing another kiss to her mouth. "So we can continue this somewhere more comfortable."

"What's the matter?" Zylah breathed as his lips traced lower again. "Don't want to get your clothes dirty?"

She felt his laugh in the puff of air against her neck, in the rumble through everywhere his body touched hers, and she squeezed her legs tighter around him. She knew he wouldn't care about his clothes, but she hadn't decided how far she wanted this to go.

Zylah put a hand on his chest and he released her, the cold rushing in the moment he put space between them—just the tiniest bit of space. They stared at each other, chests heaving, close enough that they could still share a breath.

"I just thought a bed might be better for what I had in mind."

"Ah, so now he's a gentleman?"

"You really do know nothing about Fae." His smile was wicked as she ducked out of his grip, reaching down for the basket just as Kopi landed on the rim.

"I guess you'll just have to show me." Zylah offered her hand, and the moment Raif's calloused fingers brushed against hers, she evanesced them back to Virian.

But it wasn't to the safe house. They appeared in the

grotto, just as Niara ran past them. Zylah's concentration was still in tatters, but she smelt the coppery tang of the wound before she saw it. The girl had cut her knee and had huddled by the wall to inspect it, wiping her eyes against her sleeve.

"A perfect opportunity to practise your healing," Raif murmured, a hand pressed lightly against her back. If he minded that she'd brought them here instead of the safe house, he didn't let it show. Any sign of what they'd been doing moments before had vanished, and in a heartbeat, he was beside Niara, gently coaxing the girl's hands away from her knee to take a look. He waved Zylah over, and she knelt beside them.

She looked between Raif and Niara, guilt settling heavily in her stomach, obliterating any of the desire she'd felt moments before. If the guards found out who she was...

Zylah couldn't get attached to these people. *Fae,* she reminded herself. She had to move on, as soon as she could. She was putting the children at risk; she was lying to all of them.

And if Arnir found out they'd been helping her, he wouldn't hesitate to punish them all.

18

Under Raif's instruction, Niara's wound knitted itself back together after a few failed attempts. Zylah watched in awe as she made it happen, expecting to see light or some indication of the magic, but there was none. She couldn't see the power, the magic, but she could *feel* it, and it made the lump in her back ache a little more than usual, a piece of information she tucked away for later.

Niara threw her arms around Zylah's neck. "Thank you," she whispered before glancing between Zylah and Raif and darting out of the grotto.

"Well, you're certainly a fast learner." Raif offered Zylah a hand and helped her to her feet. He'd pulled her close again, close enough that all she had to do was tilt her head even just a little in invitation. She looked up to meet his gaze, and the way he looked at her made her breath catch in her throat. He was definitely trouble.

Zylah reached up onto her toes and brushed a soft kiss

against his lips. "We should get to the safe house," she murmured. She gestured to the basket of supplies before he could get any ideas similar to the ones bouncing around in her thoughts. "The amantia will turn the other plants if they're left together for too long."

She turned to Kopi as she collected the basket. "If I'm not back by the end of the day, I'll meet you at the tavern, okay?"

"You truly think he understands you?" Raif asked.

Kopi hooed and flew out across the pond to one of his favourite trees, leaves fluttering around him as he landed. Zylah smiled as she watched him go, before turning back to Raif and holding her hand out to him. "I have work to do," she managed to say, just as he took her hand and pressed a kiss to her mouth.

He pulled back, and she evanesced them to the safe house, right into the entrance by the front door.

"How did she break through the wards?" It was Rose, and she marched right out from the counter and circled Zylah. "Arnir is attending the festival," she said, turning her attention to her brother. "It was confirmed today."

"What festival?" Zylah asked, a little out of breath. She'd felt the wards the moment she passed through them, as if she were wading neck-deep through a marsh. The ache in her back had become acute, as though a dull knife was pressing against it. She set the basket down on the counter and tried to conceal the shake in her hands. She didn't want to think about what might have happened if she hadn't been able to pass through the wards and had no idea if she could change direction halfway through evanescing, particularly with some-one else with her. She took a seat on the lounger, pressing her hands to her thighs to hold them steady.

Raif was beside her in one swift movement, a hand pressed lightly to her back. "I think you've had enough of practising your abilities for one day." He wrapped a hand around hers, squeezing gently. His reassuring warmth flooded through her and she looked up to find him watching her, concern etched across his face.

"I'm fine, really. Tell me about the festival." She managed a weak smile as a wave of nausea rolled through her, and Raif rubbed soothing circles on her lower back.

Rose glanced between them, and Zylah didn't miss the dis-approval that flickered across her face, the way her mouth pressed into a firm line and she frowned ever so slightly.

"The Royal Festival is Arnir's way of spitting on our herit-age. It always falls at the exact time we'd have celebrated the Festival of Imala, and it's his way of mocking any who might still favour the Fae ways, to force us to celebrate on his terms." Rose crossed her arms. She hadn't been overly welcoming when Zylah met her, but she'd been polite, at least. Raif had said things between him and his sister were difficult, that Saphi was a buffer between them. Zylah was beginning to un-derstand why.

She thought of the Goddess Imala. Zylah had always known of her as the Goddess of Home, Motherhood, the Harvest. Of all things abundance and growth. It seemed only fitting the Fae would pick her festival to celebrate, although

Zylah supposed she had no idea what other festivals they celebrated. "And the king will be coming here?" she asked, looking to Raif.

He released her hand, but the other still traced circles on her back. "That's what we were hoping for, yes."

"Raif, should she be hearing this?" Rose took a step towards them, thrusting a hand in Zylah's direction.

Zylah opened her mouth to object, but Raif cut in. "You're the one who couldn't wait to tell me. Besides, she's one of us now, Rose, what's to hide?"

"It's a little soon to be giving her this much information, don't you think?" His sister's tone was cold, any sign of the welcoming presence from their introduction entirely gone. Zylah didn't know what to make of it.

Saphi appeared from behind the curtain, strings of glass clinking together as she pushed the beads aside. "Liss, why don't you come with me and we'll get started on those poultices?"

Zylah didn't need to be asked twice. She scooped up the basket and followed Saphi out of the room. "I need a few more ingredients—"

"I'm sorry about Rose," Saphi cut her off. "I know she can be… abrasive." Her bracelets tinkled lightly against each other as she led Zylah through the doorway into a mess room. Tables and benches lined the walls, orblights casting their soft glow onto exposed brick walls.

The room was long and narrow; a hall, Zylah realised as they passed tattered tapestries of creatures with wings and horns and claws and fangs. *Lesser faeries.* She tried not to gawk as she asked, "Did I do something between yesterday and today to elicit that behaviour?"

Saphi sighed. "No, you didn't. Rose is a seer... and sometimes the visions weigh on her. Yesterday was a good day."

"And today?" What if Rose had seen something... what if she *knew*? Zylah swallowed. They reached the end of the empty hall, and with a glance back, she realised just how many might be living there at the safe house. Were they all Fae?

"Today is one of many. What other ingredients do you need?"

Zylah turned her attention back to Saphi as the Fae held another wooden door open for her. "Any vegetable or fruit oil, and beeswax, or just candles will do if you have any. And I'll need a—"

They entered a large kitchen, worktops stacked with baskets and bowls of colourful vegetables. Zylah walked right up to the workbench in the centre of the kitchen and reached across for the pestle and mortar. "These. If the cook won't mind."

Saphi raised an eyebrow at that. "The cook? We're all the cook here. And the cleaner, and the laundry service. Everyone pitches in."

"Are they... is everyone Fae?" Zylah asked, sniffing at an earthenware jug on the counter. *Nut oil. Of course, from the trees in the forest.* She rested her basket on the workbench, pulling open drawers to look for a knife.

"Every member of the uprising is Fae or half Fae; humans

198

are stationed with the Black Veil. Not that everyone agrees with that, but we're just following orders." Saphi's eyes darted to the door.

"From whom?"

The door swung open, and Raif strode in, marching right over to the workbench beside Zylah. "From the boss," he said with a wink.

"I'll be right back with the wax," Saphi offered, glancing between them.

Zylah nodded, her thoughts already back in the forest with Raif, remembering the way his hand fisted through her hair and he'd traced kisses down her neck.

He sat on the workbench, twirling a leaf from the basket between his fingertips. "You don't trust me."

"I don't?" Zylah asked, snatching the leaf from him. She felt Raif's gaze on her as she moved about the kitchen gathering things for Saphi's return. He'd bitten into a brin fruit—gods knew where he'd pulled that from—and she did her best not to catch his gaze.

"You took us to the grotto first, not to the safe house."

Zylah tugged her glasses off, folded them shut and placed them on the table. She was sick of looking at the world through the frames, but out there she still needed to hide. "We've just met, and things have been moving quickly." Part of her didn't want to hesitate; part of her just wanted the distraction.

"I apologise," Raif said with a slight bow. "I keep forgetting you've only recently discovered your Fae side." He snatched up the glasses and tried them on, lowering them down his nose with a finger to look over the top of the lenses at her, and took another bite of his brin fruit.

Gods above. Zylah reached for the glasses just as Raif gently caught her wrist. "And?"

He cast the glasses aside on the table, pulling her into the space between his legs. "Fae are known for their… ravenous appetites when it comes to pleasure." He took another bite of the brin fruit, and Zylah couldn't help but watch as he licked his lips slowly.

"My trust in you could easily be rectified," she said, her treacherous gaze still fixed on his mouth.

He traced his fingers along her wrist, up her arm and across her shoulder, pausing at the opening of her tunic. "Tell me what you need."

Zylah stilled his hand. "Tell me about the uprising. Tell me about the Black Veil. Tell me what it means that Arnir is coming here, why that's so important that Rose couldn't wait to tell you even though she doesn't trust me."

"And here I was thinking my good looks were enough to carry this relationship." Raif set the brin core on the workbench beside him and winked at her.

Insufferable. "Don't deflect. I don't like lies."

"Isn't that what you're doing?" He gestured to the glasses beside them.

"I'm… choosing to withhold the truth; that's different," Zylah said, taking a step back from him.

"Is it?"

It wasn't, at all. She was lying to all of them, except for Holt, and maybe she'd have still been lying to him too if he hadn't found her feeling so vulnerable.

Raif leaned his weight on one hand, never breaking his gaze from hers. "The members of the uprising are scattered across the city in different safe houses. Hang around for a little longer and this place will start to fill up. Or don't, but I think you can see for yourself that there are more than just us staying here. The Black Veil is led by human allies, most of the humans that sign up don't know that, but we mostly use them as a decoy for Arnir's men. Rose doesn't trust you because she just met you, and because she's Rose. And Arnir's visit is important, because of what we intend to do when he gets here."

His information about the uprising and the Black Veil had been vague, but she didn't press him on that. The snippet about Arnir was what snagged her attention. "You're going to kill him?" She'd suspected it but hadn't known how much she wanted it to be true until that moment.

"You said you wanted to help. But you didn't know what you were signing up for. Now you do. Does your offer still stand?" He leaned forwards and twirled the end of her braid around his fingers, tugging her closer again.

"I'm still here, aren't I?"

Raif answered her with a kiss, his lips sweet from the brin fruit and his tongue darting in to claim hers. *Seven gods*, against her best intentions, she took a step into him, her hands reaching up to his chest. She felt safe, in control, certain that if she wanted to stop, he would stop, and the thought eased

201

her, made her sink into him a little more.

If Arnir was dead, everything would change. She wouldn't have to move on. She wouldn't have to run. She could just be this new version of herself, could just be Liss for the rest of her very long half Fae existence.

Someone cleared their throat from behind Raif, and Zylah pulled away.

"Sorry to interrupt," Saphi said with a raised eyebrow. "I brought wax. And I'll be taking notes." She waved a notebook and pencil as Raif pushed himself off the workbench.

Raif shrugged, one hand casually in his pocket. "How long will you need?" he asked, blue eyes still a little glazed as he looked at Zylah.

Ravenous indeed. "A few hours. I'll need to send word to Jilah," she said, taking the wax from Saphi and placing it beside the rest of the ingredients.

"See you in a few then." Raif winked, and he was out of the door before she could think of anything to snap back at him. She smoothed down her apron, taking a deep breath to steady herself. She could still taste the brin fruit on her lips where he'd kissed her, could still feel the heat of him pressed against her.

Saphi cleared her throat again. "Shall we?"

Zylah set to work. She'd already separated the amantias from the rest of the basket, but they'd need to be prepared soon. She made sure not to rush, to allow time for Saphi to observe and take notes, to pause for any questions. After Raif left, Saphi had explained that she knew a little of healing wounds without magic, but that there was always more to learn. Zylah suspected the Fae knew more than just a little.

"When is the festival?" she finally asked as she crushed leaves with the pestle and mortar. Water was boiling on the stove behind them, and she'd readied bowls with cloth for straining.

Saphi paused her slicing of the remaining amantias and set down her knife. "Three months from now." Her eyes darted to Zylah's glasses, still resting on the workbench, but she said nothing.

What was another few months? *You can handle it.* With Arnir gone, she could see her father again, her brother. She could see Kara. Her breath caught in her throat at the thought. What if they didn't want to see her? What if they hated her for what she was? It didn't matter, she decided, if she could see them one more time. Say a proper goodbye.

Arnir wasn't a good man. She didn't doubt he'd taken advantage of countless women over the years. And he was a terrible ruler. Not that she needed any more reasons to want him dead. It was her, or him.

She pounded the leaves a little harder than necessary with the pestle. Raif had asked her if her offer to help remained. But it had felt like a test, a test to see if she was a good fit for the uprising.

If killing the king was what it took, she was in.

19

Virian was winding down for the day, the crowds thinning out for the shift between work and the nightlife that would shortly begin. Zylah walked beside Saphi in companionable silence as she watched the shops close, the restaurants open. After spending the last few evenings after work at the gardens making poultices, they'd spent the afternoon delivering them all to the various safe houses dotted around the city. One had been under the guise of a school, another a religious house, one simply a place for refugees. The rest were so run down and dingy, no citizen in their right mind would care to enter the buildings to investigate.

Zylah had tried not to gawk at the faeries as Saphi explained the poultices. One had walked by with skin as blue as the sky on a summer's day and wings as delicate as a dragonfly's. The blue faerie spoke quietly to a male with scales covering his arms and featherless, leathery wings, before circling the room and talking to each of the Fae that were present. The room was near to full, but she made time for each of them, and Zylah wondered if this was *her* safe house by the way the others seemed to regard her.

The uprising was much larger than Zylah had anticipated. And there were so many faeries—Kara would never believe her if there were ever the chance to explain it. Arnir had turned the Fae out of Dalstead, but Zylah realised now she was a fool for believing they had been wiped out.

Even with Arnir gone, she wasn't sure what place she'd have in Virian. If there were other half Fae like her, she hadn't met any, and Saphi's suggestion that she'd explain the poultices to the other Fae told Zylah all she needed to know. A half Fae would likely not be well received.

The usual array of evening vendors were setting up for the night as they made their way back, the clatter of equipment and the squeak of cartwheels interrupting Zylah's thoughts. *Three more months.* Just three more months and she could go anywhere she wanted. And if her training with Holt continued to go as well as it had been in the past few days, Zylah knew she'd be leaving Virian confident enough to protect herself.

The steady thrum of a guard unit approaching had Zylah adjusting her hood, just as Saphi's hand rested on her arm. "I know what it is to run," she said softly.

Zylah fought the urge to press a hand to her stomach, to quell the twisting inside her. She braced herself for whatever Saphi was going to say.

The Fae's bracelets jingled against each other. "You have

nothing to fear from me."

"And the others?" Zylah wasn't stupid enough to believe whatever she'd gotten into with Raif would be enough to keep her anonymity. Not if they felt she compromised everything they were doing.

"You're not the first one of us to run from a king, Liss." Saphi moved her empty basket to her free hand and looped her arm through Zylah's.

Zylah didn't need to look up to know the Fae was watching the guards walk away. "How did you know?"

Saphi laughed quietly as they stepped onto the bridge that crossed the river. "Aside from the eyeglasses that you don't need, the hair that's always poorly dyed, and the fact you never go anywhere without this cloak?" She tugged at Zylah's sleeve.

"Point taken." Kopi landed on her shoulder the moment the bridge ended, and Zylah stroked a finger lightly over his head.

"Sometimes I think he truly is Pallia's owl, sent to watch over you."

"I don't know about that. But I do know he doesn't like crowds," Zylah said as they turned into the alley that hid the entrance to the safe house.

The door swung open, Rose leaning against the frame. "You're late."

"We missed you, too," Saphi said, pressing a kiss to Rose's lips and gently pushing her aside.

Zylah remained in the alley to give them a moment of privacy and whispered to Kopi, "Sit this one out buddy, it'll be

206

far too busy in there for you." She could already feel the hum of extra bodies from this side of the door and cast aside the twist of nervousness in her stomach. Kopi hooed quietly before flying away, and she watched his little frame bank up and over a rooftop. Whether he was Pallia's owl or not, Zylah was grateful he'd found her.

She let the door fall shut behind her and followed Rose and Saphi into the hall. It was packed, just as she'd suspected, the buzz of chatter filling the room. Again Zylah tried not to stare at the faeries, just like the ones in the tapestries lining the walls; instead, her gaze fell on the blue faerie with dragonfly wings.

Most of the Fae left their deceits in place, but there were a few, like the blue faerie, who concealed nothing. Zylah stole a glance at Saphi and Rose, at their delicately pointed ears on display.

The door to the kitchen swung open, and Raif strode in laughing beside—Holt. *Seven gods. Of course* he was part of the uprising. And for the first time, she saw what he truly looked like. His pointed ears, the brightness of his eyes, his preternatural movements even more fluid than before. He was more than a god. It was as if he was from another world, raw power rolling from him like it had the first time they'd met.

They made their way through the crowd towards her, and although Zylah was vaguely aware of Raif's gaze on her, it was Holt she watched. The way he shook hands, the way he greeted everyone by name, the way the crowd parted for *him*. As if they stepped back in sheer reverence of that power. He was their *boss*, as Raif had put it. Their leader. And she'd been sharing a room with him this entire time, teasing him about his *job*.

She shouldn't have been surprised. Why would he tell her, anyway? *Why wouldn't he?* It shouldn't have mattered if he didn't trust her; they'd barely known each other more than a month… were barely friends. But it still stung. It was Holt who had called her his friend, after all.

It doesn't matter, she told herself. *He doesn't owe you anything.*

Raif walked beside Holt as they made their rounds, an easiness between them that Raif, despite his swagger, didn't have with others. Holt nodded in approval at something, and they both broke into laughter. *Holt is like a brother to me*, Raif had said. Seeing the two of them together, how relaxed Holt was with Raif, Zylah believed it.

"There's our expert apothecary," Raif said as he reached Zylah, looping an arm around her waist to pivot behind her and press a kiss into her hair, his arms wrapping around her.

"Territorial bastard," Rose muttered beside them.

Zylah's attention remained fixed on Holt as he casually made his way through his rounds, his gaze sliding from Raif's arms to meet Zylah's eyes. That feeling twisted over and over in her stomach again. She was nothing like them, nothing like him. If she'd thought him a god with his deceits in place, without it… words failed her.

"*Liss*," he said pointedly, the ghost of a smile tugging at the corner of his mouth. "Nice work with the poultices." He didn't wait for a response, just offered a swift greeting to Rose and Saphi, as if he'd already seen them earlier on, before moving through the rest of the crowd.

The hum of the room was nothing compared to the roaring in Zylah's head, but the chatter soon quietened as Holt took his position in the centre of the hall. "Arnir is visiting in less than a day."

The crowd murmured.

"And no one is to make a move," Holt added.

"So *you* can?" the blue faerie with dragonfly wings asked. "Why not just let the Black Veil do your dirty work again, kill off a few more humans in the process?"

"Mala, hold your tongue," the faerie with leathery wings hissed. Mala shook him off and stormed out of the hall, towards the entrance.

Holt didn't seem fazed by her outburst, or her departure. "The Black Veil work with us willingly to bring down a corrupt king."

The room sounded their agreement as Holt continued.

"Mala is new to our cause," Raif murmured into Zylah's ear. His hands were still around her waist, his reassuring warmth pressed against her, and she leaned into his touch. She hadn't realised how much she'd been anticipating this meeting. She wasn't one of them, no matter how many poultices she made. She wasn't even sure how many other half Fae there were; it was impossible to tell from looks alone. Raif's hand squeezed lightly at her side and she fought back a smile, just as Holt's attention slid to her, to Raif's hand at her waist, and back out to the crowd not even a heartbeat later.

"If we're to succeed, we'll need all the human allies we can get. Without them, we wouldn't be able to gain access to many locations across Virian, and outside the city walls. Rest assured, the Black Veil are compensated for the work they do for us," Holt continued.

Zylah thought of Mala's words about the Black Veil. What *dirty work* did she mean, exactly? Was that what they were being compensated for?

"Arnir is coming to discuss plans for the festival, to make sure everything is going to his liking. I want scouts from every house following him. We need to know who he meets with, where he gets his breakfast, what whorehouses he frequents, all of it. And we need to know who his suppliers are so that we can station members from each house throughout all aspects of the festival." No one spoke as Holt laid out his plan.

Zylah had stepped out of Raif's embrace, offering him a reassuring smile. She was intent on listening to Holt's every word, to work out where she might be able to help. She wasn't the only one; every faerie listened just as intently as she did, no one interrupted him again.

Holt looked around the room from face to face as he spoke, his gaze meeting hers for a moment. He didn't owe her an explanation, and she'd been naïve to think he would trust her so quickly. Holt didn't seem like the type to let humans die, but what did she know? He'd said the Black Veil was working with the uprising willingly, but even Saphi seemed to have her reservations about the working relationship. Still, she couldn't hide the disappointment she felt that he hadn't told her who he was.

"Caterers, festival security, tailors. Scouts over the next few days have their work cut out for them if we're going to cover every part of the festival," Holt added.

Taking down the king wasn't something she'd ever imagined she'd be involved with. It was the kind of thing she'd only ever read about in Kara's books. And maybe before Jesper had died, Zylah might have felt differently about taking a life. *Another life.* But Arnir was a tyrant, and the world would be a better place without him in it. She pushed aside the memory of him in the prison, sneering at her through the bars and talking to her as if she were nothing more than a vessel for his son's enjoyment.

The world *was* a better place without Jesper in it, and it would be a better place as soon as Arnir could follow suit. Movement amongst the crowd pulled Zylah from her thoughts.

"Rose!" Saphi called out, just as Rose staggered forwards and fell to her knees. "What is it? What did you see?"

Raif was beside his sister, pulling her up to her feet.

"What did you see?" Saphi repeated.

Rose's eyes were glazed, her skin clammy and pallid. "An attack," she breathed. "They have Mala."

Someone cried out from the crowd, but the faerie with the leathery wings stepped forwards. "I'll find her." More stepped up beside him, hands resting on weapons.

"All of you will stay where you are." Holt's words cut across the panicked voices, the nervous chatter of the faeries. "They'll be trying to draw us out. All of you are to remain here."

Raif took a step towards him. "You can't keep going out there alone for us."

"I'll go," Zylah cut in. "Kopi will lead me right to her. He'll already be waiting for me outside." She looked from Raif to Holt as she spoke. The faeries might not accept her for who she was, but that didn't mean she'd stand by and let one of them die.

"Liss," Raif began, reaching out to her, but Zylah shrugged him off.

Holt's mouth was a tight line, but then he said, "The three of us go together. The rest of you, you have your orders. Remain here, and *do not* go looking for Mala. There will be no bringing Arnir down if there are none of us left to do it."

That twisting feeling had returned, threatening to slice Zylah's inside to ribbons.

"Three of them took her back across the river… there are more." Rose's words were strained, and she clung to Saphi as she spoke.

"How many?" Raif asked.

Rose shook her head, her eyes still glazed and distant. "Too many to count."

"Let me go with you." It was the faerie from before, with the leathery wings and scales across patches of skin.

"There isn't time to argue," Rose said through gritted teeth.

"Very well, Asha," Holt said. "You're with us."

212

Asha's wings seemed to shudder in anticipation as they made their way out of the hall.

"Don't you want to pick up some weapons?" Asha asked, glancing between Holt and Raif as the faeries stepped aside for them to pass.

Raif shot him one of his insufferable grins. "Oh, you're in for a show, my friend."

Zylah pushed open the door to the alley, heart in her mouth, and waited for Kopi's call. They'd barely made it a few steps into the darkness when the owl called out to them, and the four of them broke into a run.

20

All traces of Fae disappeared the moment they stepped out into the alley. Raif and Holt's ears, Asha's wings—even his skin became a smooth brown, no hint of the patches of scales that had been there moments before.

Zylah followed Kopi down a narrow passage, empty save for a few crates and barrels and a handful of scurrying rats. A hooded figure, just like the one that had broken into her room, and the two that had attacked her and Raif, jumped down into the passage before her—just as Kopi let out a cry in warning. Zylah skidded to a stop. She didn't have a chance to draw in a breath before Holt appeared and swung a right hook so hard the assailant staggered back into a flaking wall.

She looked up for Kopi; there was no use wasting time watching Holt, just as a roar cut through the night. She spun around, only to find Raif and Asha fighting off two more of the hooded figures at the other end of the passage.

All Zylah could think of was those delicate faerie wings

and the look on Rose's face when she'd seen Mala in her vision. Dread danced down Zylah's spine and settled in her stomach. Barely moments had passed since they'd entered the passage, but those were moments Mala didn't have. She looked up at Kopi, patiently waiting on the roof above and made her decision.

Zylah hauled herself up the pile of crates, leapt for a wooden window shutter before she had the chance to question its rigidity, and pulled herself up to the roof.

"Raif, go with her," Holt called out from below.

A heartbeat later, Raif swung up onto the roof beside her, a wide smile lighting up his face in the moonlight. "Shall we?"

"Won't they need help?" Zylah asked, inclining her head to the passage below. She'd continued her training with Holt, but the way he moved against his opponents told her he'd been holding back.

Raif peered over his shoulder in Holt's direction. "You haven't seen everything he's capable of if you're asking that question. Let's go."

Another roar cut through the night, but Zylah didn't hesitate as she darted after Kopi across the rooftops. "What was that?"

"I don't know," Raif managed, just as Zylah grabbed his hand and evanesced them across the space between two buildings.

Kopi dove down to street level, and Raif waved Zylah over to a section of the roof.

"I'll evanesce us down." Zylah rested her hands on her

knees to catch her breath, ignoring the pressing ache in her back.

"No. No one must see you; it's too risky." Raif peered over the edge and Zylah followed his gaze.

"Just like climbing a tree, right?" Zylah muttered as Raif helped her down onto a drain pipe. More roars tore through the streets, from multiple creatures, and Zylah willed the gnawing feeling in her insides to settle as she descended to solid ground.

Raif dropped silently onto the dirt beside her as she was getting her bearings. "We're near the outskirts of the city. This isn't a place I like to frequent in the day, let alone—" Another roar cut him off, only this time it was much, much closer.

Kopi called out up ahead and Zylah broke into a run after him before the kernel of fear she felt in her gut could take root. The buildings became small hovels, shacks and lean-tos that could barely be called homes, but Zylah didn't stop to think about the living conditions within them, even as the rotten, musty stench hit her. She followed Kopi down a gap between two houses, the city wall looming over them. In the dim light, it was difficult to make out Kopi's silhouette, but one minute he was beside the wall, the next, he was gone.

"You're sure he's not Pallia's owl?" Raif asked as he pushed aside the thick hanging ivy covering the wall. The stone had fallen away, leaving a gap just wide enough for one person to squeeze through. "I'll go first," he added.

Zylah slid under his arm and stepped in front of him. "Kopi would never lead me into trouble."

"Damn it, Liss," Raif muttered behind her, close enough she could feel the heat radiating from him.

There hadn't been time for anything between them in the last few days. Zylah had been completely occupied by training with Holt, working at the gardens, and making the poultices. All she'd practised with Raif was healing, and even that she'd practised *without* him, on recruits Saphi brought to her at the safe house but nothing more than superficial wounds so far.

The way Raif had pulled her to him back at the meeting barely an hour before was the closest they'd been since... Zylah thought of the way he'd pinned her against a tree, of how quickly she'd given in and wrapped her legs around him. Her cheeks heated at the wildly inappropriate thought given their current circumstances. *Gods above.* They'd just met. What was she thinking?

"We never did finish what we started in the forest the other day," he said as if he'd read her thoughts.

Zylah spun around to face him, tilting her head up to meet his eyes. The part of her that was Fae had always allowed her to see better in the dark than others, although she'd never known it was that before. "I've been busy."

Raif shrugged as if they weren't in the middle of their crazy pursuit. "That's fair enough. I like to take my time with these things."

"Oh, so now you're patient?"

His grin was feral. "No. Not patient. But time spent waiting for you is a very different matter to how I intend to spend my time *with* you." He tucked a strand of hair behind Zylah's ear, and she could have sworn her traitorous heartbeat was the only sound left in the world.

She swallowed, choosing her next words very carefully, but Kopi's call echoed off the stone. Zylah turned back in the direction they'd been heading, silently cursing herself for stopping in the first place.

Something moved across the opening up ahead, but beyond the stone, Zylah could only make out tree trunks and ferns in the dark. She reached back for Raif's hand.

"Don't worry, I…" he began, as his hand engulfed hers.

Zylah wasn't worried. She evanesced them as far as she could see into the forest, away from whatever was waiting for them on the outskirts of the wall.

"…won't let anything…" He spun her around to face him as realisation registered across his face. "Clever."

But Zylah wasn't looking at him. She was looking at the thing beyond him, an enormous creature standing on two legs that ended in hooves. It swung its great head, not unlike a wolf's, as it searched along the wall for them, spinning around to find them amongst the trees. Two horns spiralled from its head, thick fangs protruding from ghastly lips, and a pair of blood-red eyes fixed right on Zylah.

"Stay here," Raif ordered, before running for the creature head-on.

Kopi called out again, and Zylah didn't stay to watch how quickly Raif would turn the beast to ash. She darted amongst the trees, careful not to trip over gnarly tree roots and loose rocks, the smell of wet earth flooding her senses.

She heard a whimper and slowed to a stop. Her foot pressed into something; the texture so strange her eyes slid to her feet to scan for whatever it was in the darkness. It looked like… little flakes of silver.

The creature roared and Zylah resisted the urge to turn back for Raif, to trust that he would deal with it alone. Instead, she knelt down for a closer look and sucked in a breath. *Dragonfly wings.* She looked around and found the ground littered with silver shards and dark patches of what could only be blood. And there, discarded beside a bush as if they were nothing but a forgotten shawl, were what remained of Mala's wings.

Zylah swallowed down the acid that coated her throat. Willed herself to stay calm as she listened for that whimper in the darkness. Every hair on her arms stood on end as she felt eyes watching her through the trees. She could hear nothing of Raif and the creature. No whimpers in the forest. Only the quiet groan of the trees and the rustle of leaves. And the sound of her own quickened breathing.

She'd left Raif to deal with one of those things alone. He could defend himself but… she looked at what was left of Mala's wings and suppressed a shiver. What if something happened to him?

There. A quiet moan. Zylah darted towards the sound, her arms thrown above her head to shield herself from tree branches.

She smelt the coppery tang of blood before she saw the faerie. Even in the shadows of the forest, Zylah could see the

219

sheen of sweat coating Mala as she hung from a tree in the middle of a small clearing, a rope around her feet and blood dripping down her shoulders and onto the ground.

It could be a trap. But Zylah knew Kopi would have already warned her if there was anyone else nearby. She reached for her dagger, eyeing the places the rope was tied, flicking her gaze left and right, listening for anyone in the darkness. There was no easy way to get the faerie down.

"This is going to hurt," she said softly. Kopi flew into a tree at the edge of her vision, keeping watch, no doubt.

Mala made a sound somewhere between a whimper and a sob. "My wings."

"I know. I'm sorry." Zylah grasped for words of comfort but found none. She evanesced herself to the tree branch above Mala, sawing her dagger at the rope. If she was fast enough, she might be able to catch the faerie when she fell.

She wasn't. The rope snapped, and Mala fell with a heavy thud. A shuddering, broken breath left her as Zylah appeared beside her in the dirt, already working at the rope around her hands.

There was so much blood, it coated her hands and clothes. Had Rose seen this too? Relief washed over Zylah as the rope came free, but she couldn't hide the tremor that ran through her.

"Asha warned me," Mala wheezed.

Seven gods. "Asha's coming for you. He'll be here soon. Just hold on." Zylah rested Mala in the dirt as gently as she could and tried to still the shaking in her hands. She could heal.

220

She'd practised. She could do this.

She swallowed as she looked at the bleeding stumps on Mala's back, hacked off, blow by blow, if Zylah had to guess. She drew in a breath and rested her hands above the wounds, careful not to touch them.

"Asha," Mala murmured. "Give him this." She struggled with something at her wrist, but Zylah wouldn't break her focus.

"Give it to him yourself," she said, as gently as she could. *Don't you die on me.* Zylah's hands were still shaking. If only she had some moss to stem the flow of blood, to give her time to work. *But you don't.* She closed her eyes. Focused on her breathing. Pictured Mala's wound knitting back together and felt something stir at her fingertips. The lump in her back ached and her eyes flicked open. Nothing happened.

Mala let out a wet, broken breath. "Promise you'll give this to him," she whispered. Zylah couldn't see the faerie's face. Couldn't bring herself to look into her eyes. Kopi called out, and she instinctively pressed her body to Mala's, careful not to touch her wounds. A roar broke the quiet of the night, and Zylah's heart sank for the faerie bleeding out beneath her.

She reached for her dagger just as something crashed into the clearing. The creature, with no sign of Raif. Had he been injured, or was this another? If more came... Zylah didn't want to think about the outcome.

She darted away from Mala, to draw the thing away from the faerie, evanescing to a tree behind the horned beast. Red eyes met hers as it lunged for her. Zylah used her height,

221

ducking under its legs, narrowly missing a hooved foot and spinning around to slash against a leg. Wiry strands of black hair became wet with blood as her dagger met its mark and the creature roared, kicking back with a hoof and flinging her across the clearing.

The air was knocked out of her, but she shoved herself to her feet. The beast ran for Mala at the same time Zylah did. Zylah evanesced herself to close the distance, throwing herself over Mala to protect the faerie's broken body. Mala wheezed deeply, and Zylah tried to ignore her own aches with the faerie bleeding out beneath her. Something told Zylah Mala wouldn't survive being evanesced in this state, even if she could manage it.

The creature charged, head lowered, horns first, and Zylah found herself sending a silent prayer to Pallia just like she used to back before all this started. All the air seemed to leave her lungs as the horns came closer.

It couldn't have been less than two strides away when it screamed. Tiny lights whirled around it. At first, Zylah thought they were orblights, but they were far too small for that, far too animated. *Sprites*, some distant part of her mind whispered.

The creature faltered, clawed hands slashing at the lights, at its face to try and swat the lights away. It roared and the lights scattered, blood sprayed and its crimson eyes fixed on her. Zylah drew in another shaky breath just as the creature turned to ash. *Raif*. He was alright.

He was at her side in a heartbeat, his eyes wholly black.

"Help me heal her. I can't do it," Zylah blurted, placing her hands above Mala's wounds. Zylah closed her eyes, begged and begged whatever part of her it was that power came from to pour out of her, but nothing happened. She flicked her eyes open, and Raif rested a hand over her own. His eyes had returned to bright blue, his expression soft, gentle. He showed no sign of injury, that was something, at least.

"She's gone, Liss."

Zylah pulled her hand away from his. "No, she, she's lost a lot of blood, but she's got a bracelet she wants to give to Asha and..." She pressed her fingers lightly against Mala's neck to feel for a pulse, lowered herself to meet the faerie's eyes.

Open. Glassy. Empty.

A curl of leather wound through her fingers; the bracelet, for Asha.

A heaviness settled over Zylah, but she sat tall beside the faerie. She slowly uncurled Mala's fingers, carefully peeled the bracelet away and closed the faerie's eyes. "I couldn't heal her," she murmured.

"It wasn't your fault, Liss," Raif said quietly. She hated that he didn't know her real name. Hated that she was lying to him. That Mala was dead because she couldn't heal her. But she said nothing, just held Mala's hand. She didn't know Mala. But the faerie had stood up for the humans. That told Zylah enough about the faerie's character. About her heart.

Zylah tucked the bracelet into her cloak and brushed a strand of hair from Mala's eyes. She was as beautiful as the faeries in the tapestries back at the safe house.

Raif cleared his throat. "Step back."

"Why? What are you doing?"

He reached a hand to the faerie, but Zylah caught his wrist.

"We can't leave her body, Liss. There could be more of those things."

The heaviness pressed tighter, wrapped around her at Raif's words. "You're right. We can't leave her. But how she is sent into the next life is not our decision to make." Zylah didn't wait for him to argue. She reached her free hand around Mala's and evanesced the three of them to the safe house.

She felt the wards again the moment they passed through them but didn't need to look up to know which room she'd brought them to. The reception area. Away from the business of the hall.

The ache in her back was sharp as she looked at the dead faerie beside her, so acute it pressed right through to her heart. She'd left Kopi behind, but she knew he'd likely go back to the tavern. She didn't have space left for any more guilt.

"Mala!"

It was Asha. He pushed Raif aside and pulled the dead faerie into his arms. "Mala," he whispered.

Zylah didn't speak as she took the bracelet from her cloak and pressed it into his fingers. He didn't look away from Mala, just lifted the faerie's hand to his lips and kissed her knuckles, murmuring something in a language Zylah couldn't understand.

She forced herself to stand, to back away and give Asha his privacy. It wasn't fair. Mala had died for nothing. Had been hunted, like she was nothing more than an animal.

Rose and Saphi pushed through the door from the hall, but Zylah's gaze was fixed on the dead faerie. She was vaguely aware of Saphi's intake of breath, of her resting a hand on Asha's shoulder.

"It was Arnir's men. An elite unit. Holt's still out there," Rose said quietly to her brother.

Zylah didn't look up as Raif spoke. "They had Asters with them."

"That's impossible," Rose said.

Asha was still murmuring, rocking Mala's body against his. The faerie could have been sleeping. Her expression was peaceful, her perfect face tilted up to Asha's.

Except her flawless blue skin was covered in blood. And where there should have been wings, there was nothing but the two hideous stumps Zylah had tried to heal back in the forest.

And failed.

She pressed her hands to her knees, willing herself not to be sick all over the floor.

Mala *could* have been sleeping. But she wasn't.

She was dead.

21

"Here, drink this." Saphi handed over a steaming mug. She'd taken Zylah through the curtains behind the counter, away from Mala and the others. The room was small, dark. Only a candle lit the space, softly illuminating the floor to ceiling shelves opposite the lounger Zylah sat on.

She sniffed at the dark liquid. *Besa leaves.* To calm her. She took a sip and focused on the ache in her back. The pain had become so frequent it was familiar. Comforting, in its own way. Something to concentrate on.

Saphi sat on the floor beside her, a bowl of warm water and a flannel in her lap. "I know you said you weren't injured. But I still need to check. Clean some of this blood up. Okay?"

"Why?" Zylah whispered. "Why does Arnir hate the Fae? Why is he doing this?"

Candlelight flickered off the Fae's earrings and her vanilla perfume filled the space between them. "He's doing what his father did, and his father before him." She dipped the flannel in the water and wrung it out between her hands, took the mug from Zylah and placed it on the floor beside her.

"But there has to be a reason why." Zylah let Saphi take her hand and wash away the blood. She was certain she hadn't been injured. A little bruised from the creature—the *Aster*—knocking her off her feet. But nothing she hadn't endured before.

Saphi's brow scrunched together for a moment before she looked up at Zylah through thick lashes. In this light, her amber eyes were a dark gold—kind, gentle. Like Kara's. The pain seemed to pierce Zylah's chest again.

The Fae turned her hand over and washed the blood away in methodical, gentle movements. "I could tell you it's about balance. About humans wanting to be treated equally. And it might have been about that once. But after a few hundred years of bloodshed, it became clear that it was about greed. On both sides." Saphi wrung out the bloodied flannel and took Zylah's other hand.

Zylah was barely paying attention. She should have stemmed the blood flow right away, should have compressed Mala's wounds. It was one thing for Zylah to come to terms with her part in the plans to take Arnir's life, to accept the fate that awaited him, whether he deserved it or not; a life was a life. But it was another thing entirely to have had Mala's life snuffed out as she lay in the dirt.

"The Fae are not native to these lands. It's said we came here and lived peacefully with the humans at first. But we got greedy. Took too much and treated the humans as glorified slaves. A rebellion was inevitable." Saphi wiped the last of the blood away and set her flannel to one side before handing Zylah the tea. "Drink," she said with a small smile. "Raif will walk you home in a minute."

Zylah took a sip and watched Saphi clear everything away. "I'll evanesce back. I'll be fine." Truthfully, she didn't know if she could.

The glass beads on the curtains tinkled as Raif slipped into the small room and sat beside her. "Asha asked me to thank you. For bringing her back to him." Candlelight danced in his eyes, as bright as endless pools of clear water. Nothing like the darkness that had swallowed them whole when he'd turned the Aster to ash.

Zylah finished her tea and tried to stamp out the image of Asha clutching Mala's lifeless body to him. She knew it was useless. Knew it would be all she would see when she closed her eyes later on.

"Do you want to stay here tonight?" Raif asked, taking the mug from her hands and wrapping a hand around hers. His skin was warm, the weight of his hands a comfort. There was no hint of his earlier playfulness in his expression, only concern.

"No. I want to go home." The word struck her like a stone. Somehow, in the last few weeks, that little room above the tavern had become her refuge. Her one constant.

Raif gave her hand a gentle squeeze. "Come on. I'll walk you."

Zylah half expected to see Mala's body still on the floor in the reception area, but the room was empty as Raif held the door to the alley open for her. She raised her hood as she stepped out into the night, Raif right behind her. Kopi flew across from one rooftop to another, his little shadow snagging Zylah's attention. He was safe. Of course he was. She looked at the stars for a moment and thought of the little lights that had swarmed the Aster. Could they have been sprites? And where had they been when Mala's wings were being hacked off?

"Copper for your thoughts," Raif said quietly as they made their way to the bridge.

There were so many things she wanted to ask. So much she wanted to know. Why Mala? Was it just because she was alone, an easy target? And why had she gone out without any of her deceits in place?

Zylah sighed. "Your eyes. Does it hurt? When you turn things to ash?"

"The cost of my magic. I know it looks unpleasant; I didn't mean to alarm you."

She looked up to meet his gaze. His eyes were still clear, bright and crystalline, with no hint of black. "And it doesn't hurt?" The night air was crisp and cool, but this part of the city always seemed to have a lingering odour of decay clinging to it, even when the streets were empty.

A smile tugged at the corner of Raif's mouth. "Now, now, Liss, anyone might think you care."

Zylah rolled her eyes. "Insufferable." She looked out across the river, inky in the darkness with ripples of silver moonlight

229

skittering across the surface. Would Mala meet with the dead who left the river? Or would she go somewhere else, some faerie afterlife where her wings hadn't been torn from her?

"You did well tonight," Raif said quietly as they stepped off the bridge, Kopi swooping past them.

"Not well enough."

Raif took her hand and gently urged her to face him. "Mala's death wasn't your fault."

Zylah wanted so desperately to believe it. But she couldn't. The faerie's death *was* her fault. "What I don't understand is, why Mala? Why just leave her there? At first, I thought it was a trap, and that I'd walked right into the middle of it, but, no, nothing. *No one.* Why go to all that trouble?"

Raif pressed on towards the tavern but didn't release her hand. "To send a message."

"Because of the festival?" There were no street vendors left at this hour. But there were still signs of life in the city, the smell of warm bread drifting from the bakeries making fresh batches for the morning, delivery carts rolling by.

"Because of Arnir's visit," Raif said as they neared the tavern.

"Don't they realise it had the opposite effect? That now we want to wipe out that piece of shit even more than we did before." She looked up at the bell tower and realised Holt hadn't been at the safe house when they'd returned. Rose had said Holt was still out there. Even now? He could take care of himself, but against how many? She'd told them all she could find Mala, and Holt had believed her. She'd failed him.

Failed Asha. The uprising, all of them.

Raif gave her hand a light squeeze. "Possibly. This war has lasted far longer than Arnir's lifetime, and with Jesper gone, our hope is that a time of peace might follow."

"Do you truly believe it?" She paused at the flaking door to the tavern and looked up at him.

"I cling to that hope, yes." Raif brushed a strand of hair away from Zylah's face, his fingers lingering for a moment before he pulled away. "Maybe that makes me a fool." His hands slid into his pockets as he looked at her. "Will you be alright tonight?"

There were still so many questions on the tip of her tongue, but they could wait. "I'll be fine, thank you."

"Goodnight, Liss. I meant what I said, you did well tonight."

"Goodnight," Zylah said softly. He began to walk away, but she called out to him. "Raif?" He spun back to face her. "You're not a fool."

He gave her a small smile in reply and turned back in the direction of the safe house.

The heaviness from earlier seemed to pin Zylah down as she made her way up the stairs to her room. What had she been thinking? She'd wanted to prove herself to them, that she was one of them. That she could help. And Mala had died because of it. Her stomach twisted over itself as she shut her door behind her.

Everything ached. The Aster hadn't broken any bones, but she would be sore in the morning. She knew better than to soak it off in the bath whilst she was alone though. She let Kopi in at the window and shrugged off her bloodied cloak. The twist in her stomach became a tug, and she pressed her palms to her eyes as she sat on the edge of the bed, breathing deeply.

Her eyes shot open to a heavy thud.

Holt.

"You're bleeding," she said, rushing to the floor beside him.

Holt said nothing as his eyes flickered shut and he groaned. His pointed ears were gone, his face a little plainer than the last time she'd seen it. All his deceits were back in place, yet he still looked like a god.

She pressed her hands over the wound at his ribs. "Why haven't you healed yourself?"

"It's nothing. It will heal." He was covered in dirt and blood, his shirt soaked in crimson and sweat.

She knew it was stupid to feel guilty for leaving him back in that alley. But what if they'd caught him like Mala? What if they'd… Zylah swallowed. "Do you have *any* regard for your own life?" she asked, hoping the uneasiness in her voice wouldn't show.

He eased himself to his elbows and held her gaze. "No."

"Hold still." Zylah closed her eyes and focused. Put herself back in the safe house, healing superficial wounds on recruits that Saphi brought to her. Pictured Holt's wound healing beneath her fingertips.

The lump in her back felt as if someone were clamping it between a vice, and she bit down on her lip against the pain;

the ache was always worse when she used her magic.

"I didn't know you could do that," he said softly when she opened her eyes. He pulled his shirt aside and ran his fingers across the bloodied skin; the wound was closed. Why couldn't she save Mala?

She cleared her throat. Looked up at Kopi, comfortably nestled on his dresser, anything to avoid the intensity of Holt's gaze. "Do you want me to get you something? Help you onto the bed?"

She made to move away, but Holt grabbed her hand. "Just stay. Just sit with me for a while." He released her hand, pushing himself to a seated position and leaned his head back against the table leg.

"What happened?" Zylah asked, looking up at him. Even sitting, he towered over her.

Holt blew out a breath and dragged a hand through his tousled hair. "Asters. Too many of them."

One was enough. Maybe one of the Asters Raif turned to ash had been the one to hack off Mala's wings and shred them. But it wouldn't have been an Aster that tied her up. No, their clawed hands didn't seem dexterous enough to fasten a rope. That would have been Arnir's elite unit.

"You saw them too?" Holt asked softly.

Zylah nodded. Her throat burned, and she shoved aside the memory of Mala's lifeless body in Asha's arms.

His gaze slid to her bloodied cloak on the floor and back to her. "And Mala?" he asked, his brow furrowing.

Zylah willed her voice not to waver. "Dead." She wrung

her hands over each other in her lap. "She…" *She died beneath me, and I didn't even notice.* "I took her body back to the safe house for Asha."

She didn't need to look up to know Holt was still looking at her. But she couldn't meet his eyes. Couldn't tell him the truth. That she'd failed Mala.

"You asked me what the furthest I've ever evanesced was," Holt said, resting an arm on his knee. He closed his eyes again, sadness settling over him so heavily it was palpable. "Most of the continent. For my sister."

Just sit with me for a while, he'd said. He didn't like to be alone, and despite what she'd told Raif, she didn't want to be either. And Holt looked as if he'd barely escaped death at the hands of the Asters. "She's lucky to have a brother like you," Zylah said, watching the way he stared into nothing. "I know you miss her."

A muscle feathered in his jaw. "Memories are fickle things. But sometimes they're all there is."

Zylah thought of her father and her brother. Of laughing in the garden with Kara. That's all they were now. Just memories. Holt didn't like to be alone, but she'd learnt something else about him tonight. He had no regard for his own life. Mala had accused him of as much back at the safe house before she'd stormed out.

"Leader of a Fae uprising. I never would have guessed that. Were you ever going to tell me?" She kept the question as light as possible.

He angled his head to look down at her. "Would you have

234

believed me, if you hadn't been there tonight?"

"Stranger things have happened. For a while, I thought you were a bounty hunter and hadn't made up your mind about what you were going to do with me." A smile tugged at Zylah's lips as she said it, but Holt frowned and looked away.

His gaze fell on Kopi, huddled up on the dresser. "Leading the uprising is one of many… roles."

"A multi-tasker. I see. Why you? Why not someone else?" Raif and Rose seemed capable enough, but she'd seen the way they all looked to Holt earlier that evening, the way each faerie there hung on his every word.

"Because I'd had enough of needless suffering."

And Zylah saw it then, in the tightness of his jaw and his empty stare. How he felt just as responsible as she did for Mala's death.

"It isn't your fault she's dead," Zylah whispered.

His eyes slid to hers. "It isn't yours either."

Zylah drew in a shaky breath. "What happens now?"

Holt rubbed his hands against his knees. "We'll have one chance at the festival. We make it count."

22

Arnir extended his stay. The festival was a little under three months away, and it took all of Zylah's resolve not to seek him out every moment he was in the city. Not that it would come to any good.

Training with Holt had been going well, but she was no assassin. She doubted she could even get past Arnir's guards, his elite unit, who Zylah had now learnt to identify. Three times she'd encountered them: in her room at the tavern, by the river with Raif, and the night Mala died. Holt had known what they were doing, trying to draw the Fae out. He had no doubt known how it would end, too.

It was the fifth afternoon of Arnir's visit as Zylah made her way to the safe house after her shift at the botanical gardens. Six days since Mala's death. Purple banners embroidered with gold thread marked the date of the festival; some even had a silhouette of Arnir's face on them. It turned Zylah's stomach. Mala was innocent. She'd been murdered for nothing more than existing. Zylah paused beneath the drooping branches of a tree and pressed a hand to her chest just as Kopi flew down to her shoulder.

"I'm alright, buddy," she whispered.

It was *her* Arnir was looking for. And yet Mala had been the one to lose her life. She hadn't killed anyone, hadn't been the one to murder the prince. Zylah drew in a deep breath, the sweet smell of venti lilies hitting her as three giggling women walked past and disappeared beyond a gilded door. A restaurant, Zylah had learnt from Raif, that served very little food and a lot of women, as he'd put it.

She left the shade of the tree and made her way to the bridge, focusing on Kopi's wings as he flew across the water. Further upstream, small boats were being loaded with heavy sacks, and Zylah found herself wondering what it would be like to live a life on the water.

"We've got to stop bumping into each other like this," a familiar voice said to her left. Zylah didn't need to peek out from under her hood to know it was Raif.

"Are you following me?" Her mouth twitched as she said it, but she tried her best to conceal her smile.

"I'm just walking in the same direction as you. It's not a crime, is it?" His voice was bright, playful, and it was exactly what she needed to lighten her mood.

She glanced up at him. One hand was in his pocket, the other cradling a white box to his side. His hair was loose, black wisps blowing across his face. Zylah couldn't help herself, she reached up and tugged at a strand. "Doesn't this irritate you?"

This time she didn't hold back her smile.

He caught her hand and twined his fingers through hers. "There's something I need to tell you."

"Oh?" she asked, pulling away from him at his tone. He knew who she was. Knew she'd lied, surely.

He shoved his hand back into his pocket as they stepped onto the bridge. "Mala wasn't the only casualty the night of the attack."

"What?" Zylah knew the colour had drained from her cheeks and willed herself to take steady, even breaths, to not press a hand to her chest or her stomach again.

"We found two more bodies the next day."

"And you're only telling me this now?" Zylah hissed as they passed a pedlar selling tied bunches of purple wildflowers atop a filthy rag.

"Holt ordered me not to tell you. But I wanted you to know the truth."

Zylah couldn't breathe. If she handed herself over, this would all end. No more deaths. No more attacks. But this had been going on since way before she'd escaped Dalstead. Before she'd killed Jesper. She walked over to the stone wall bordering the bridge and looked into the murky water below. Three months. Just three months until she was free. If she gave herself up… Arnir wouldn't stop, would he? He wasn't going to stop until every last Fae had been wiped out.

Dragonflies danced along the surface of the water and she willed herself not to be sick at the sight of them. "And we're just letting him get away with it? Arnir? He's just walking around the city, right now?"

"He left earlier today. He won't be back until the festival."
Raif stood beside her, his arm brushing hers as he looked out
at the water with her.

The first chance she got, she was going to go back to the
forest for some jupe. If there was any way she could get close
to Arnir, she was going to be ready. She might not be able to
wield a sword with skilled efficiency in three months—no, a
sword would never be permitted at the festival anyway—but a
dagger. A dagger was discreet. And she could poison the blade
with jupe. Even a small cut from that would be enough to take
down a king.

Zylah shoved the thought aside for later. "How is Asha?"

"As well as can be expected." Raif turned to look at her,
one arm resting on the stone, the other still looped around the
box, and Zylah thought she saw a flicker of regret cross his
face for a moment.

"Are you going to tell me what's in there?" she asked, eager
to change the subject.

Raif's eyes brightened as he opened the box, a delighted
smile lighting up his face. "It's a gift."

Folds of silk a shade paler than Mala's skin stared up at her,
and Zylah willed herself to hold them up. "A dress?"

"A *hooded* dress. I wanted to take you out for dinner, and I
didn't think you'd be so easily separated from your cloak."

Zylah felt his gaze on her as she took in the fine blue fabric.

The sleeves and most of the bodice below the chest were
made entirely of delicate lace; it was by far the finest thing

Zylah had ever held.

"This is…" The old Zylah would have never accepted it. Would have said she couldn't possibly take such a gift. But then old Zylah would never have done half the things she'd done since leaving Dalstead. And gods above, did she need something to drag her thoughts away from Mala. "It's very thoughtful of you. Thank you."

Raif closed the lid and held out an arm for her to loop hers through. "Come on. Saphi made me promise to bring you to her to get ready."

"We're going tonight?"

"Unless you'd rather not?"

Zylah bit down on her lip. This was far more kindness than she deserved. "No, I… I'd be grateful for the distraction, actually."

Raif squeezed her arm. "*Liss.* You walked right into that one, didn't you? I promise to be as distracting as possible."

The hood was detachable. In fact, the hood *and* the sleeves. They were separate so that the dress could be worn without them but fit flawlessly when worn together. Saphi had tried to convince her to go without the hood, that a few deceits here and there were all it would take to change Zylah's appearance. But Zylah wasn't convinced, not so soon after the attack. The only deceit she'd allowed was one to conceal the knot in her spine, although it had done nothing for the constant dull ache.

She wasn't sure how suited she was to the dress, but Raif's smouldering gaze when she followed Saphi into the reception area had told her all she needed to know about what he thought of it.

"You look beautiful," he said, removing his hands from his pockets and moving away from the door frame.

So did he. His black hair was tied back, and he wore a black jacket with silver—no, pale blue stitching, in the same shade as her dress, and black trousers to match. She'd never seen him so dressed up.

"Where did you say we're going tonight?" Zylah asked, resisting the urge to fidget with her dress. The floor-length skirt was slit up to the thigh on both legs, so it was impossible to walk without exposing her pale skin. The back was entirely open from the bottom of the hood piece to the low scoop of the silk, edged in more of the delicate lace at her waist. The front wasn't much better; it cut low between her breasts, the torso almost entirely lace before flowing seamlessly into the silk of the skirt. She hadn't wanted to explain to Saphi that it was the most daring thing she'd ever worn. Instead, she'd told herself to seize the opportunity of wearing something so bold.

"I didn't," Raif finally said, dragging his gaze lazily down her body as Saphi and Rose said their goodbyes. Zylah mumbled something in response, her attention fixed on Raif as he took her hand in his and pressed a kiss to her knuckles. His lips were soft and warm, and he looked up through his dark lashes and winked. "Insufferable, right?" He took her arm and looped it through his as they stepped out into the night.

Zylah swallowed, heat racing through her despite the cool air. "Right." Saphi had given her a pair of grey silk slippers to wear. Had she been given more time, she'd insisted, she could have 'prepared' Zylah for shoes with a raised heel, something which Zylah thought looked more like a weapon than something to walk in.

She absentmindedly smoothed a hand over her thigh, aware of how little the dress left to the imagination. She'd been surprised to see herself in a full-length mirror, to see just how much muscle had built up in the short time she'd been training with Holt. Her stomach was firmer, her upper arms had built up from the training and lifting boxes at the gardens, and her thighs were more toned. *Strong*, she'd thought, as she'd looked at her reflection; she looked stronger.

Raif wrapped an arm around her waist as they walked, his fingers resting against silk and his thumb against the exposed skin of her back. His touch was warm and gentle, and Zylah fought back a dozen questions for him. She was intent on just enjoying the moment, which was proving rather difficult in her current footwear.

The slippers weren't all Saphi had given her. The Fae had insisted Zylah's bralette wouldn't work with the dress, and she'd been right. Instead, she'd offered Zylah a scrap of lace, several sizes smaller than Zylah would have preferred, but it did what it needed, and it worked beneath the fine dress far better than her bralette did. Saphi had pinned up her hair, too, creating a few soft curls to frame her face.

It was all entirely out of Zylah's comfort zone, but she'd

242

never been the type to back down just because of a little discomfort, and she certainly wasn't going to start now. She was glad of it, as she walked beside Raif, catching glimpses at his profile from beneath her hood. He looked like one of the princes from Kara's books, and Zylah silently scolded herself for such a trivial thought.

They'd already neared the bridge before either of them spoke. "I wanted to thank you—" Zylah began.

"How's the training going?" Raif asked at the same time.

It was a cloudy night; no moonlight broke through the clouds, and beneath a lamp on the bridge stood a young woman playing a stringed instrument Zylah hadn't seen before. The woman plucked at a few strings as if she were testing the tuning.

Zylah laughed quietly as she looked up at Raif, taking in the way his face softened whenever he looked at her. Against her will, her heart skipped a beat.

"You first," he said with a smirk.

How *was* training with Holt going? Zylah was sure Raif already knew the answer to that. Her confidence had grown quickly. Holt was a good teacher, and already she felt as if she could defend herself. "Better than training with you is going." Zylah elbowed Raif playfully; she wanted to keep this evening light.

A dimple made an appearance as he said, "We do need to set aside more time for our one-to-one's, don't we?"

Zylah turned away for a moment as her cheeks heated.

As they strolled past the musician, she'd already begun a

song about forgetting and moonlight, the words sending shivers along Zylah's arms.

"Would you like my jacket?" Raif asked, already reaching for the buttons.

"No, I'm fine, thank you." She glanced over a shoulder as they walked away from the performer, her words about missed chances and a love that got away chasing them to the other side of the bridge.

Raif slid his arm around her waist again, as if it was something he did every day. "I think you've come a long way in, what—not even two weeks of using your abilities. Are you not pleased with your progress?"

Zylah pushed out a breath, forced the thought of Mala's lifeless body from her thoughts. "No."

"Healing is a rare gift. One that takes time to hone. And for you, it will be a foundation for whatever comes next." His fingers splayed across the thin fabric of her dress as he pressed gently, reassuringly.

A foundation. Zylah didn't know what to say to that. She didn't understand what she'd seen so far of faerie magic; Holt's abilities and Raif's seemed to be at odds with each other, and Raif had given her so little when she'd asked about his eyes.

He paused at a doorway arched with pink alea flowers and reached for her hand. "Ready?"

Zylah nodded as a man dressed in white opened the door for them. "Good evening, sir, your booth is ready for you."

"Thank you, Tarin," Raif said, stepping aside for Zylah to follow the waiter.

It was much darker inside than she'd expected, but candles lit up spaces here and there, perfectly illuminating lavish paintings with gilded frames and glittering accents with the most whimsical subjects Zylah had ever seen. Dark swathes of fabric that revealed nothing more than the silhouette of whoever was behind them hung around the tables and booths, the quiet murmur of diners and the occasional burst of laughter erupting from within. Strands of crystal beads looped across sections of the ceiling, interspersed with tiny orblights that made the crystals look like constellations dancing above them.

She caught Raif watching her as she turned back to face him. "What?" she asked quietly.

"I was just thinking something insufferable," he said with a smile, eyes roving over her as he took her in.

The waiter pulled aside one of the fine curtains and Zylah slid inside as gracefully as she could in her dress.

"This place looks fit for royalty," Zylah murmured as she looked at the twinkling crystals draped above and around them. She reached out a hand to touch one and watched the orblight dance off it in tiny rainbows.

Raif entered the booth on the opposite side to her, sliding around the curve of the table to sit across from the curtain and unbuttoning his jacket as he sat. "Royalty is everywhere in Virian, Liss," he said with a wink, patting the velvet cushions beside him. "The best view is from here."

"View?" Zylah could barely see her own hands, the orblights were so small and dim. But she slid along the sofa to sit beside him.

She felt Raif's heated gaze on her even in the dim light. "That dress is…" He swallowed, glancing down at the exposed skin of her leg beside him.

"Scandalous?" Zylah asked with a quiet laugh, watching the way he shrugged out of his jacket and placed it on the banquette beside him. His black shirt was rolled to his elbows, a few buttons unfastened at the neck. Solid muscle pushed against thin fabric, and Zylah resisted the urge to run a hand over one of his biceps.

"You look like a goddess. Sometimes I think you might be Pallia in disguise."

"Jilah said that when I first met him."

Raif traced his fingers along her forearm, stopping at the lace sleeve. "You have her owl, her bravery, her beauty."

The orblights flickered before Zylah could reply, and she looked up to see the shadow of the waiter beyond the curtains.

"Enter," Raif said dryly.

Platters of food were laid out before them, steaming meats and vegetables, bowls of grains and fruit in combinations Zylah had never seen before. The waiter poured wine and left the bottle on the table. "The entertainment begins shortly, sir." He bowed low before adjusting the curtains and leaving them alone with the food.

Zylah had never seen a meal like it. "This is… more food than I have ever seen on one table before."

"Try this," Raif said, smiling brightly as he piled steaming meat onto a plate for her. Everything smelled delicious, and gods did it taste good. The meat melted in her mouth, and the sweet wine complemented everything perfectly. Raif only started eating once he was satisfied with her approval, and Zylah smiled at him over her wine glass. Though he often used humour to coat everything, there were moments when he let that façade slip, moments when she felt he was trying to let her in.

He took a sip of his wine, his gaze fixed on her again. "I wanted to wait a little while longer to tell you, but tonight isn't just about pleasure."

"Oh?" Zylah ate a spoonful of the spiced grains before her expression could give away her disappointment.

"We're here to watch and listen. Boss's orders."

Zylah could tell without peeking out from her hood that he was watching her, waiting for her reaction. "Was dinner part of those orders?" she asked, hoping the question sounded light.

"Not entirely. I did think the distraction would be good for you." He placed a hand over hers. "I wanted to thank you, actually. For bringing Mala back. I didn't think about what it would mean to Asha. Thank you." He gave her hand a gentle squeeze before picking up his fork again.

Zylah decided to push aside the disappointment. He'd asked her to dinner, instead of coming alone. Instead, she sifted through the questions she had for him, the thoughts she'd been waiting for a chance to discuss. She drew in a breath, resting her cutlery on either side of her plate. "Right before you killed the Aster, something swarmed it. I think they might have been sprites."

"They were. They were drawn to you."

"Seven gods. *Why?* Why didn't they help Mala?" She gripped a hand against the edge of the sofa between her and Raif, willing Mala's lifeless body from her mind.

Raif's hand found hers, flexing their fingers together and easing her hand from its vice grip. "You know your gods were Fae, don't you?"

She knew what he was doing. Distracting her from Mala. "Jilah mentioned it when we met, but I never really had time to dwell on it." It was true, so much had happened.

"There were nine of them, to begin with, or so the story goes." He piled more food onto her plate as he spoke. "They arrived here from another world after theirs was ravaged by war."

"Another world?" She took another sip of the sweet wine as she watched him.

"Yes, Liss. There are more worlds than just ours out there. Pallia, Imala, Altais—all seven of the *gods* you know of."

"And the other two?"

A quiet moan drifted from a nearby booth, the dimple in Raif's cheek on display as he caught her raised eyebrows. "They had a different idea for how this world should be formed and began experimenting, using dark magic to make servants and sentinels and all kinds of atrocities."

Zylah held a hand to her mouth. "Like the Asters?" she whispered.

"Like the Asters, yes. But those were not the worst of their creations, by far."

Zylah didn't want to know what could be worse than the Asters. Stringed instruments began to play quietly somewhere in the restaurant, and she willed herself to stay in the moment. The food was incredible. She listened to the quiet chatter as she ate, savouring every bite and trying each new item Raif put on her plate until the word *Dalstead* snagged her attention. Zylah stilled, looking up at him.

He raised a finger to his lips, shaking his head. They could be heard by others just as easily, Zylah understood from the gesture. "Is the food to your liking? The location?" he asked.

"It is." It felt wrong to be enjoying herself when Mala was gone, but she couldn't deny that she was enjoying the experience, enjoying being here with him.

Raif smiled brightly again. "Tell me about your work at the gardens."

She did. Every time she finished an explanation, he asked her a new question; most were serious, but some to elicit a laugh as they ate their meal. They'd long since finished eating by the time Zylah had explained all the new plants she'd been cultivating at the base of the waterfall, ones she hoped would filter the water more successfully, and the young sun lilies she'd planted all along the terraces in the warmer dome.

Raif leaned back amongst the cushions—this side of the booth stretched back further than Zylah had realised—the soft expanse of sofa almost enough to lie down on. Zylah didn't doubt, from the sounds surrounding them, that some were doing just that.

The stringed instruments were still being played

somewhere, soft and sweet, and the orblights flickered just as Zylah intended to steer the conversation back to Raif.

"Enter," he said, pouring another glass of sweet wine for her. He thanked the waiter, his gaze locked beyond the curtains on someone else in the restaurant. "Do you trust me?" he asked as Tarin pulled the curtains shut.

"Do I... yes, why?"

Her breath left her as he scooped her sideways into his lap and looked down at her, but his face was serious, solemn as he murmured, "Just kiss my neck and look like you're enjoying it."

Zylah picked up the sound of soft footsteps approaching their booth as Raif lifted her hand to his chest and mouthed, "Please."

His right arm wrapped around her, pressing her to him, and she felt his body tense beneath her. Not because of her, but because of whoever was about to enter the booth. And maybe it was because of the wine or the quiet easiness that they'd fallen into over dinner, but she leaned in and pressed her lips lightly against his neck, fingers curling into the fabric of his shirt as she kissed the spot just beneath his ear.

"Raif. Busy as always," a male voice said from over Zylah's shoulder as the curtains were shoved aside. She was grateful for the hood covering her face, and for the hand Raif had wrapped around her thigh where the dress had fallen away and exposed most of her leg. The other was pressed to the bare skin across her back, as if they'd just been in the middle of a passionate embrace.

"Marcus," Raif ground out, as if he had indeed just been interrupted.

"No pleasantries still, I see."

Raif angled his head away from Zylah, and she pictured the disinterested look on his face as he stared Marcus down. "Say your piece and leave. You're spoiling a good evening."

"The girl from Dalstead. What do you know of her?"

Zylah stilled, her heartbeat a roaring drum in her ears. Raif slipped his hand under her dress, fingers splayed across the lace over her rear and squeezed lightly.

If he hadn't asked if she trusted him, if they weren't there to spy, she'd have snapped a remark about it. But he'd done it to elicit a response, to urge her to continue to keep up the façade in front of Marcus. It was enough to remind her to trace a kiss beneath his jaw, hoping that Marcus hadn't caught her moment of unease.

"Nothing," Raif finally said, keeping up a good show of enjoying himself, his other hand playing with the lace that edged the very low scoop of the back of her dress. "My scouts tell me she never entered Virian."

"Your scouts? Come now, son. You and I both know they're not your scouts."

Son. Zylah slid her hand under his shirt, her fingers running across his chest, and felt Raif's shrug in response. She leaned back, her face angled to his, lacing her fingers through his hair and studying his expression. Raif turned away from Marcus to capture her mouth with a swift kiss, his lips tasting of sweet wine and his tongue darting quickly over hers.

251

Her breath caught as he teased her lower lip, before pulling back just a fraction to look down at her. His eyes smouldered, and Zylah was certain he could feel her pulse racing everywhere their bodies touched.

Marcus cleared his throat. "Arnir wishes to use the girl. Her escape has sent whispers through the towns and cities. He intends to use her as an example that we will not be allowed to live free."

Let him come, Zylah thought. If not her, there was an army of Fae waiting to take him out.

Raif lifted her hands from his chest and twined his fingers through hers, never breaking her gaze. "And yet that won't stop you from working with him, will it? Are you here on his behalf or your own?"

"I came to visit my children."

"I suspect Rose will give you as warm a welcome as I have." Raif's gaze never left Zylah's as she watched him in the dim light, one hand still playing with the front of his shirt, for Marcus's sake.

"Very well. Perhaps now is too inconvenient a time."

"It is." Raif's mouth was on hers again, his kiss slower this time, devouring.

But the way she tugged at his shirt in response was no act.

"Goodnight, son." Zylah heard the curtain drop, Marcus's footsteps getting further away. But Raif was still kissing her, his fingers working at the fastening at the nape of her neck.

"Aren't we going to discuss the fact that you just hid me from your father?" Zylah asked breathlessly as Raif tugged

252

lightly at the hood, the weight of it pulling the sleeves off her shoulders.

"What if I was hiding *him* from you?" She felt his smile as he kissed her bare shoulder beside the thin strap of her dress. "I've waited all night to see you without this," he said, pressing another kiss to her shoulder before pulling her arm free, and then the other.

"You're distracting me." And gods above, it felt good. His touch. His lips against her skin.

"Isn't that what I promised?" His breath was warm and sweet as he kissed her neck where she had kissed his, pulling her closer to him. He adjusted himself, the hard length of him pressing against her thigh as his other hand slipped under her dress again, resuming its position along the edge of her lace underwear, fingers brushing her navel as his mouth met hers.

He slid a finger down and over the most sensitive spot between her legs, and Zylah gasped into his mouth. Theo had never touched her there before. She knew what she liked from her own exploration and gods… the way Raif's fingers worked idle circles over her underwear, he knew it too.

She twisted round, one leg on either side of him as those circles quickened, needing more friction against the feeling growing within her.

"Greedy," he murmured as his kisses ran along her jaw. He sat back, pulling her dress down from the shoulder, his lips brushing between her breasts.

She arched her back, bracing herself against the table as his fingers moved faster and faster, her thighs pressing together as the tension coiled deeper, lower.

His thumb teased the edge of her underwear as he brought his mouth closed around her nipple, and Zylah fought back a moan. "Raif," she whispered in the dark.

Faster and faster his fingers moved against her, his mouth claiming hers to capture another moan just as release shattered through her, her hands losing their grip on the table. Raif wrapped an arm around her, pulling her with him as he leaned back into the cushions, his fingers slowing and his other hand tangled in her hair as her trembling eased. His kisses were still quick, hungry, and like this Zylah could feel every inch of him pressed against her.

"Like a goddess," he murmured, a hand sliding to her rear as he rocked her against him.

Zylah pushed up, the echo of her release still like a hazy mist all over her as she pressed her hands to his chest. "Was this part of your plan? Make up an excuse to get me in your lap so we'd end up here?"

Orblights reflected in his eyes as he sat up again, rocking her against him deliciously slowly. "I like to deliver on my promises," he said softly against her lips.

Quicker than Zylah could blink, Raif pulled her dress up over her shoulders and rested her hood over her hair. "We have company." He helped her back into the sleeves and gently eased her off of him just as the curtains were shoved aside, and a woman spoke.

"You need to leave. Now." It was Rose, and Zylah didn't need to meet her gaze to know she was furious.

23

"It's Holt and Marcus," Rose explained in a whisper, drawing the curtain closed behind her.

Zylah discreetly smoothed down her dress as she looked from Rose to Raif. *We try not to speak about our father… for fear that it summons him*, Raif had said when she'd asked about his parents a few weeks back. And whatever Rose had seen had worried her, enough to make her come all the way here to find Raif.

"Did he call it in?" her brother asked, pulling on his jacket and throwing a bundle of notes on the table.

Rose shook her head, her brow scrunching together. "No, I… I just saw them together. That was enough." She held a hand to her forehead, and Zylah wondered if there was something else the Fae wasn't telling them. It was no surprise Rose still didn't trust her. Rose had shown little interest in anyone other than Saphi and her brother in the short time Zylah had known her.

"Call what in? What does your father want with Holt?" Dread coiled in Zylah's stomach, and she wished she hadn't had so much of the wine.

"A number of things spring to mind," Raif murmured. "Liss, can you manage two of us?" he asked, flicking his chin in Rose's direction.

She knew he meant the evanescing, but there were people all around them beyond the privacy of their booth. Zylah nodded, reaching a hand out to each of them. "Where to?"

"The safe house." Rose hesitated for a moment longer than Zylah would have liked, the dim orblights bouncing off the crystals and turning the Fae's eyes into glittering pools. Those eyes met Zylah's for a second before Rose placed a hand in hers.

She knew she was taking a chance, risking the wards with both of them. But Rose's concern for Holt urged her to cast aside any worries she might have had. Zylah took them to the reception area, hoping Kopi wouldn't wait outside the restaurant for her as the world came back into focus.

"I see your whore serves more than one purpose." Marcus rested an arm against the counter, wiping his hand idly at an invisible speck of dust. "You always were resourceful when it came to women." His hair was the same shade of black as his children's, cropped short to his head, his eyes the same shade of glittering blue. A sheathed sword hung from his hip; the hilt black to match the rest of his attire.

Rose dropped Zylah's hand, but Raif held onto her, unfazed by his father's presence or his words. "Where is Holt?"

Marcus stared down at his son, his gaze sliding to Raif's hand wrapped around Zylah's and back up again. "Running an errand for me. I needed the two of you together and this was the only way to snag Rose's attention." His gaze roved over Zylah's dress—or lack of it—and she resisted the urge to step behind Raif. Instead, she stood tall and met Marcus's gaze when it finally reached hers, his eyes narrowing almost imperceptibly.

Rose waved a hand as she shifted her weight from her blade to her leg, and it was the first time Zylah had ever seen the Fae show any sign of discomfort. "Spit it out then, Marcus."

The unease in the air was palpable, and Zylah wondered when the three of them had last been in a room together.

Marcus took a step closer to Zylah. "Arnir tells me the girl from Dalstead can evanesce. Such a rare gift." He turned to Rose. "Your mother had the ability, and we never understood why it didn't pass to you, when—"

"Is this going somewhere?" Raif cut in. Had he felt her tense beside him? Had he heard her heart beat faster with each of Marcus's words?

Marcus looked between his children, his expression earnest. "I can protect you, if you come with me."

Rose tilted her chin up to him. "To Arnir's palace? To live as slaves?"

"Do I look like a slave?"

"You look like a fool."

Marcus bristled. "I am still your father. Still King of Feoldran and you will address me with the respect those titles

257

command." *King.* He raised a hand to strike her, but quicker than Zylah could blink, Saphi appeared from behind the curtain, her hand raised, Marcus's stilling in response to whatever she'd done to him.

Saphi walked over to Rose and slipped an arm around her waist, easing her back a step before waving her other hand to release Marcus.

Marcus staggered for a moment, the force of his now unfrozen strike tipping his balance. He straightened his jacket and stood tall. "What did I tell you, little Rose, about keeping what you love from prying eyes. Or will you turn her away, too?" He made for the door without waiting for a response. Perhaps he had seen enough: a weakness in each of his children to exploit.

"Do you think we're just going to let you walk out of here?" Raif asked, releasing Zylah's hand and grabbing his father's elbow.

Marcus stared coldly at Raif's hand on his arm and shrugged out of his grip. "If you want to see your *eminent* leader return in one piece before sunrise, yes, I think you'll allow me to do exactly that." The door shut behind him, and silence fell across the room for a moment before Raif pulled off his jacket and threw it onto the lounger.

"I saw him in the tunnels," Rose said as Raif rolled up his sleeves. Zylah knew that look. They were getting ready to search for Holt.

"How bad was it?" Raif asked.

Rose shook her head, and Zylah felt the breath leave her,

thoughts of Mala dancing behind her eyes. Holt was strong, yet Rose's fear of Marcus told her all she needed to know. "Let me go with you."

Rose raised an eyebrow. "In that dress?"

"Careful, I've already been called a whore once this evening." It must have been the wine, or maybe because now was not the time for one of Rose's bullshit moods. "Holt's my friend, too." Perhaps her only true friend, if Zylah was honest with herself.

"Liss," Raif cut in, taking Zylah's hand. "We can't risk losing any time. Rose's visions, they change quickly." He pressed a kiss to her knuckles and turned to the door. "Make sure word of this doesn't reach the others," he said over his shoulder to Saphi and followed Rose out of the door into the night.

The feelings Zylah had held at bay rose to the surface, and she shoved off her hood, the dress suddenly too tight, too restricting. "I need to get out of this." She pushed past Saphi and headed for the stairs. "Can you get me bracers, some extra knives?" All she could see was Mala every time she closed her eyes, and she wouldn't be able to just sit waiting for the others to return.

"Liss, slow down, you'll trip on your dress," Saphi said behind her, clutching at the hem as Zylah bounded up the staircase.

She felt sick, and it wasn't the wine. "Tell me," she said, as she rushed into Saphi and Rose's room where she'd changed earlier. She caught Saphi's gaze in the tall mirror that stood in the corner. "Tell me what he is to them. Holt."

Saphi sighed, her eyes narrowed as she bit at her lip. "Holt saved them. It's how he got his scars." She brushed Zylah's fingers away from her neck fastening and took over. "He owes Marcus a life debt."

Unease washed over her again. The scars on his arm and neck… "Tell me the part you're leaving out," Zylah said as Saphi helped her peel the sleeves off, her bracelets jingling and her fingers warm against Zylah's skin.

Saphi laid the hood and sleeves on the bed, smoothing out the fabric. "The life debt wasn't for saving them, it was for… something else. When Fae ruled this world, there were four kingdoms, divided into courts, but each kingdom was ruled by two monarchs." She walked over to the wardrobe, crystal beads tinkling on strings as she reached in for Zylah's bundle of clothes. "Courts had High Lords and Ladies, and the royalty became greedy. They wanted one High King and Queen. Or rather, *Marcus* wanted to be High King. Aurelia had already passed, so he sought to take out the other kingdoms, alone. Holt's parents were among them."

Zylah stilled as she gathered the hem of the dress to pull over her head. *Royalty is everywhere in Virian, Liss,* Raif had said. Saphi perched on the edge of the bed, waiting, but Zylah was too busy working through her thoughts. She slipped into her trousers and tunic; the fabric rough against her skin after the delicate silk. Her head was spinning with questions, the effects of the wine overtaken by the unease that had settled in her stomach. "I need weapons."

Saphi nodded and opened a drawer beside the bed, tossing

knives and a set of bracers onto the white sheets as Zylah pulled her boots on. How had Holt saved them from their father?

And the life debt... *A life for a life. Nothing less will repay the debt.* "How does Arnir fit into all of this?" Zylah asked as Saphi helped her strap the bracers on. Only minutes had passed since Raif and Rose had left, and not once had Saphi suggested she stay. She likely knew the words would do nothing.

Amber eyes met Zylah's. "Marcus plays a long game. His alliances only mean something to him until they don't. Until he gets whatever it is he's coveted, no matter how many years it's taken him." The Fae buckled the last of the straps at Zylah's wrist.

"And are you going to tell me how you stopped him earlier?" Zylah asked as she slid a blade into each bracer and one into each boot.

Saphi grinned, turning her palm up to the light. "My magic is mostly limited to tricks. I made him think he couldn't move his hand. If he'd really wanted to hurt Rose, my magic would have merely softened the blow."

"It still looked good," Zylah said with a smirk. "Is this the part where you tell me not to go?" She fastened her cloak over her shoulders and raised the hood. Something told her Kopi would be waiting outside.

Saphi shrugged, folding the dress out on the bed. "You said it yourself. He's your friend too. Just don't get yourself killed. Raif will never forgive me."

Zylah didn't wait for more than that. She took the stairs two at a time and was out the door without looking back. Kopi's quiet hoot told her he was nearby, but it was something else that had her heading for the river. A feeling she couldn't quite place.

She made her way past boarded-up buildings, rotting wooden beams supporting crumbling balconies or leaning into the next building along. This part of the city was a disaster waiting to happen, and for a moment, she longed for the small homes and establishments of her quiet village.

A selfish voice in the back of her mind told her she was looking for Holt because she needed him. She needed his training, the home that he'd offered up to her. She needed him to kill Arnir, so she could be free. But she knew that wasn't what urged her down the narrow path along the river's edge, away from the bridge that crossed over into the main part of the city. He'd saved her life twice, not because he had to, but because he wanted to. Because he was good and kind. And he was her only godsdamned friend in this new life of hers, and she wasn't going to let anything happen to him.

Kopi swooped down over the edge of the riverbank to her left, and Zylah peered down expecting to see water beneath her. Instead, she saw a second path, lined with insect ferns. She crouched low, listening for anything out of the ordinary but heard nothing. She jumped down onto the lower path, and in the dim light, could make out a wooden door in the stone bank up ahead.

Zylah had no plan. A handful of knives to defend herself,

and only her evanescing to fall back on if things went wrong. Holt was ten times more capable than she was at both fighting and evanescing. She ran her hand along the edge of the door, feeling for the lock as she cast her gaze up and down the path. Her fingers grazed iron, and she pulled a pin from her hair and eased it into the lock, holding her breath. She rotated the pin slowly, getting a feel for the inside of the lock and the cylinders within it.

The hairpin snapped, and Zylah swore under her breath. She pulled another from her hair, this time getting down on one knee to press her ear to the lock, to listen to her hairpin tapping the tumblers, and turned, slowly.

The door clicked, and Zylah eased it open, praying it wouldn't creak. She paused to listen to the darkness that stared back at her and held her breath. Only the steady drip of water echoed through the tunnels.

She took a deep breath, pulled herself to her feet, and stepped into the dark.

24

Kopi didn't follow her into the tunnels. Not that she'd expected him to; they were no place for a wild animal. Stones lined the walls, and the air was filled with the stench of dirty river water. It was most likely sewage water, but Zylah cast that thought aside.

She could barely see anything in the dark and reluctantly brushed her fingers along the wall to guide her. The stone was damp and rough beneath her touch, but it gave her something to focus on. Something to distract her from considering what a stupid idea this was.

Going after Raif and Rose would have been the smarter option. *Fight in numbers*, her brother would have said. But they couldn't evanesce like she could. She could get herself out of a tight situation if it came to it. Zylah took a deep breath. She really hoped it didn't come to that.

The sound of a metal gate falling shut echoed through the tunnels. How far away, she couldn't tell, but it had her pressing herself against the wall out of instinct. Not that it would do any good if there were other Fae down there with her. She listened in the darkness for a few moments before continuing until she turned a corner and the tunnel opened out into a chamber. It was divided in the centre by a channel that undoubtedly contained sewage and a questionable-looking plank of wood reaching across to the other side, where more tunnel entrances lined the opposite wall. A rat scurried across the stones on the far side, and Zylah was suddenly grateful for the dark, that despite her keen eyesight she couldn't make out the details or see the water well enough other than to know it was there.

A groan echoed through one of the opposite tunnels, and Zylah reached for a dagger.

"Please. We've done everything you asked, please…" a man begged. A dull thud and the sound of a soft, heavy weight falling onto stone followed.

Zylah crouched down to inspect the plank crossing the filthy water, testing it with the toe of her boot and hoping it didn't creak. It wasn't rotten. Part of her wished it was; that would have been a reason for her to turn back. But she was past logical decisions now, down in the dark with nothing but the rats and whatever floated by in the sewer for company.

She crossed the plank and headed to the tunnel at the end of the chamber, praying to the gods that they would still welcome a stupid half Fae with open arms. *Only they weren't gods*, she reminded herself. Her dinner with Raif felt like a lifetime ago.

265

A distant speck of light lit up the space ahead, and again Zylah crouched low to keep out of sight, dagger in hand as she rounded the corner. Stacks of wooden crates lined this tunnel, and for once, Zylah thanked Pallia for how short she was. Muffled noises sounded from up ahead, but it was still too dark and she was too far away. The tunnel opened up into another chamber, and she'd have to chance getting closer if she wanted a better look at what was ahead.

Zylah darted from stack to stack to get a closer look, the glow of an orblight illuminating the chamber as she approached. The damp air seemed to cling to her skin, the stench of the water settling into her clothes.

"I don't appreciate doing grunt work, Holt. Next time get one of your scouts to do this."

Zylah froze. It was Marcus.

"On your last visit you didn't seem convinced by the numbers, so I thought you might like to take a more hands-on approach this time around," Holt replied, his voice bored, disinterested.

Marcus laughed dryly. "You certainly have come through this evening. If this doesn't send a message to the Black Veil, they're bigger fools than I thought."

The humans. Zylah chanced a look over the top of her crate, to see Holt hauling *bodies* onto a table. Seven gods, what was going on here? Marcus stood watching, arms folded across his chest. As Holt turned back, he caught her gaze, shaking his head almost imperceptibly. *Say* nothing, *do* nothing, his expression seemed to say.

A decoy for Arnir's men; that's how Raif had described the Black Veil. But both Saphi and Mala had voiced their reservations. *The Black Veil work with us willingly, to bring down a corrupt king,* Holt had said.

And Marcus was working with Arnir, that much Zylah had already worked out. *The life debt. It's how he got the scars.* Zylah silently counted how many blades she had on her person to calm her quickening heart. Not enough. There was no doubting it, Marcus was powerful. Dangerous. She glanced up over the crate again, watching Holt pull another lifeless body onto a rickety wooden table. His look had been a warning. To leave. But she couldn't.

She'd barely managed to glimpse the entire room before she had to duck out of sight again.

"Put these on," Marcus said. His voice was commanding, it was the same tone Arnir used when he spoke to any of his servants.

Something heavy fell on wood.

"Vanquicite cuffs?" Holt asked.

Zylah had never heard of such a material.

"Just in case that self-preservation of yours kicks in and you try to evanesce yourself away before we're done here."

Unease settled like a stone in Zylah's stomach. Marcus had made those scars down Holt's neck and arm. Whatever power he possessed, something told her she was about to find out.

The cuffs clicked as if Holt were fastening them, and Zylah considered looking over the crate again, but a shadow against the wall told her Marcus had turned to face in her direction.

She held her breath.

"The girl," Marcus began, and Zylah was certain he'd seen her. She closed her eyes, waiting for a hand to land on her shoulder. "You've seen her eyes, Holt," Marcus continued. "Who is she? I don't care if Arnir wants her." She opened her eyes just as the shadow moved away.

Zylah couldn't breathe. Every instinct she had told her to run, to get as far away as possible.

"She's nobody," Holt said, his tone still bored. "The eyes are a deceit; she favours the colour. Her true eye colour is brown."

"Lies!" Marcus thundered, and something flashed so bright Zylah covered her eyes. Holt groaned in pain, and the stench of searing flesh filled the chamber. *Gods above.*

"You never learn," Marcus muttered. The light flashed again, this time accompanied by a crackle, and Holt ground out another agonised moan. Zylah was going to be sick. She rubbed her sweaty palms against her knees, desperately grasping at ideas. She'd barely seen enough of the chamber to get the layout, hadn't seen enough of it to evanesce further into the room anyway.

Another flash of light, and this time Holt's roar filled the chamber.

"Why are you protecting her? Is it because she's my son's latest trinket?"

Marcus's boots tapped against the stone, but it was Holt's ragged breathing Zylah focused on. She peered over the crate again. Marcus had his back to her, and Holt was doubled over on the floor, but she couldn't see him clearly. Beyond him, another passage led out of the chamber, deeper into the tunnels, Zylah presumed. She could go back the way she came. Go for help. But that would take too long. She could evanesce to the other side of the chamber but—

This time she saw it. "Speak when you are spoken to! Your father never did teach you any decent manners, did he?" Marcus bellowed, lightning flowing from his fingertips.

She ducked down just as he turned, praying he hadn't seen her. Holt was past making a sound, but she could still hear his shallow, wet breaths. It was Mala all over again, and Zylah could do nothing to stop it. A tear slid down her cheek and she brushed it away.

"Pathetic," Marcus muttered. A muted thud followed, and Zylah was certain he had kicked Holt's prone body. She held her breath as his footsteps grew further away, counting to twenty to be sure he'd left the chamber.

She peeked over her crate. Marcus was gone. Holt was lying still. Zylah evanesced to the far side of the room, to make sure Marcus had truly left. There was no sign of him. She evanesced to Holt's side, sucking in a breath as she took in the extent of his wounds.

There was no blood; the cauterisation was so severe his shirt had burned away across his ribs, melted into the flesh in places. "Holt," she whispered, touching a shaky hand to his. His eyes fluttered, and she evanesced them out of there—or— she tried to, but nothing happened. Neither of them moved.

A sob threatened to escape her. He was going to die down

there in the putrid tunnels, and there was nothing she could do to help. She took a steadying breath. "Holt," she whispered again, wiping the hair from his eyes. His heartbeat was weak, but she let the sound anchor her as she looked around the room for anything that might help.

"Cuffs," Holt rasped.

The vanquicite. Zylah pulled the last pin from her hair and set to work on the cuffs, reciting every prayer to Pallia she could remember. The cuffs were a smooth black stone, unlike anything she'd ever seen, and they must have had some kind of dampening effect on their abilities.

Holt's eyes were closed, his skin clammy. She didn't lift her gaze to his wound again; she needed to concentrate. These were different from the last set of cuffs she'd picked, joined by a bar with a single lock in the centre. As she gently turned the pin, listening for the most minute of sounds, she could tell there were two parts to the lock.

A rattling wheeze escaped Holt, and he clasped a hand around her wrist. "Leave," he whispered. If she angled her head up just a little, she'd see the bodies he'd laid out on the table, so she kept her eyes down.

"Stay still, you'll snap my last pin," Zylah pleaded. It took all of her resolve to stop her hands from trembling.

"Zylah, *go*." Holt's eyes fluttered open, and Zylah forced herself to meet his gaze.

She willed her expression to neutral, her tone bored like she'd heard him demonstrate with Marcus as she said, "Shut up." All the colour had drained from his face, and his breathing was ragged and broken. Determination pulled her concentration back to the cuffs. She turned the pin left and right, as gently as she could, until she heard one bar inside the lock catch on the other. She held her breath and rotated the pin one more time—slowly, painfully slowly.

The cuffs sprang open, and Zylah bit down on her tongue to hide her relief. Holt's eyes had closed again, his breathing had become shallower. She pulled the cuffs away with one hand and evanesced Holt out of there with the other.

Zylah brought them to their room at the tavern, pressing a hand over his heart. "Rule number seven," she said as tears pressed at the corners of her eyes. "No dying on each other."

Holt's smile was weak, but it was there. She healed him a little, just enough to take the edge off the pain. But she didn't know how to heal him completely without sealing half of his shirt into the wound. "Stay still." She hoped the tremble in her voice didn't show.

"Yes, boss," Holt said weakly, the corner of his mouth twitching.

She hurried to the bathroom, pulling open the cupboard where she'd been storing supplies. She raced through her options, settling on a vial of celandia drops, a jar of the poultice she'd been making with Saphi, and a handful of besa leaves.

"Chew these," she ordered, grabbing her pillows from the bed to shove under Holt's head as she knelt on the floor beside him.

He took them from her, propping himself up on an elbow to look at his wounds, and it was enough for her to know he would be able to chew the leaves without choking to death. Besa leaves were a relaxant, great for nerves, but they would also reduce the adrenaline that was coursing through him. Calm his heart. She slipped one into her own mouth as she examined the mess below his ribs. She swallowed. "This will hurt."

Peeling the shirt out was the only option. She poured a few drops of the celandia onto her hands, rubbing them together thoroughly to ensure they were disinfected and dripped a little into the wounds. Holt hissed under his breath.

"I'm sorry," Zylah murmured, picking at the shirt as carefully as she could. Every time she peeled a piece away, she delicately smoothed some poultice across the wound, hoping it would be soothing enough until she could work on healing him.

She felt Holt's gaze on her. "You picked the lock," he said quietly.

"Lucky for you I got invited out to dinner this evening," she replied, knowing he knew exactly where she'd been. He'd ordered it, Raif had told her.

"You must have questions." His voice was still strained, and Zylah wished she had a pair of tweezers to pick the fabric out more gently.

She did have questions. Lots of them. But now wasn't the time; she needed to concentrate. "You don't owe me anything," she finally said, setting another scrap of fabric on the floor beside them.

"I see. So we're even now, are we?"

Zylah huffed a quiet laugh. "You saved my life twice; I've saved yours once. No, we're not even yet."

"I think you had the second time under control. Besides, you've healed me twice now."

Zylah closed her eyes and took in a deep breath to focus, to call on that power she'd only just begun to explore. The wounds were still too messy and healing him still didn't feel straightforward. "About that. Can you take over? I think I'm going to do more harm than good from here on in."

His gaze was fixed on her when she opened her eyes, watching her intently. "Not yet, the vanquicite has a lingering effect."

A weapon against the Fae. If Marcus had some in his possession, Zylah had no doubt Arnir knew of the stone and had likely used it to bring down the Fae all those years before. She frowned as she patted the last of her poultice onto the wound. It would have to do. Everything looked clean, at least, though Holt's shirt was ruined. The lump in her back ached and her head was spinning with questions. There was so much information she needed to unpack.

She gathered up the scraps of charred fabric from the floor. "Who were we meant to be spying on this evening?"

"A higher-up in Arnir's elite unite; the unit that I'm sure you're well acquainted with by now." Holt watched her as she tidied everything away.

"One of Arnir's men. Marcus?"

"No. Marcus was a surprise. I... owe him." His eyes shuttered, and Zylah could have sworn whatever pain he was trying to shut down was tangible for a moment.

The life debt. That tracked. But the bodies? "You're killing humans for him?" she asked, handing him the celandia drops to disinfect his hands.

Something in Holt seemed to shut down, like a light had turned off behind his eyes. He squared his jaw. "Yes."

Zylah returned what was left of her supplies to the bathroom, throwing away the scraps from Holt's shirt and scrubbing her hands. "And he's working with Arnir. So you're working with Arnir, by extension." She didn't know how she felt about any of this. She was too exhausted to feel anything but the weariness in her bones, but she needed to piece this together.

"Arnir knows me as a bounty hunter, through Marcus. The Black Veil are how I keep them both away from our kind, keep our plans concealed."

Zylah leant against the doorframe to the bathroom, watching Holt peel off what was left of his shirt and inspect his wound. "By using humans and killing them?" He was ignoring her gaze—and Zylah couldn't decide if that was a good thing. At least he showed remorse. But something about it didn't add up. She'd only known him a short while, but she knew he was good. Kind.

"I can see how it would look that way," he muttered, closing his eyes and dragging a hand over his face.

Killing humans, even if he was protecting others, it didn't make sense. "I'll never find out what you truly do, will I?" She took the remains of the shirt from him. "Get on the bed. I can't lift you, so don't make me try."

He did as she asked without protest, and Zylah knew he must have been weaker than he'd let on. She had no idea how long the effects of the vanquicite would remain, but the poultice would hold. Holt's heartbeat and breathing were steady, which told her Marcus's damage was relatively superficial. This time.

Something tapped at the window. Kopi. Zylah unhooked the latch and watched him swoop in.

"I did tell you to leave," Holt said, watching her from the bed.

She handed him the pillows. "Why? Because you think you deserve to die?" He said nothing, just lay back on the pillows. "I can see you're stuck in something you think you have no way out of. I know whatever you're doing, you're doing it because you've no choice."

He rested an arm under his head and closed his eyes. "We always have a choice, Zylah."

"Even if there's a life debt involved?" She wanted to know—wanted to know what had happened for him to lay his life down for Raif and Rose, or whatever reason compelled him to do it.

"I need to keep Marcus on side if the plan with Arnir is going to go ahead."

"And for what? To replace one tyrant with another? Is Marcus just going to swoop into Arnir's palace once we're done? Was that the plan all along? One asshole king for another?" Zylah was pacing now, dragging a hand through her hair. Would it truly be freedom if Marcus was the one to replace Arnir? Marcus had asked about her, and the selfish voice inside her told her to run, to leave Virian and never look back.

"I'm bound to him, Zylah. There is nothing I can do."

"What happened to we always have a choice? He asked Raif and Rose to go with him. I can't tell if it was out of concern or because he just likes to get his way." It was because he wanted things on his terms; she already knew enough of Marcus to understand that.

"Marcus always gets what he wants, eventually." Holt confirmed her suspicions.

She had no right to be angry. But Marcus had used Holt. To send a message to the Black Veil, he'd said. By having Holt kill them? People who were working for him. It was sick. Marcus was worse than Arnir. She stood beside the dresser, stroking Kopi's head as he settled down to sleep. Holt had almost died. He couldn't heal himself with the cuffs, couldn't evanesce. Would Marcus have gone back to finish the job?

Holt cleared his throat. "I'll be gone for most of the time between now and the festival. Raif will take over your training."

"Why? Is it because of the life debt?"

"Yes." He didn't meet her gaze as he said it, and Zylah wondered whether there was more that he was hiding from her.

Maybe it was to keep up his façade with Arnir or to smooth things over with the Black Veil, or maybe it truly was whatever sick errands Marcus had him running. She waited for him to look at her, but he closed his eyes and squared his jaw. She'd struck a nerve, again.

It felt as if the air had been sucked out of the room, like they'd had a drawn-out argument over who went where.

"Very well," she finally said. She flopped down on the lounger, pulling the blanket Holt usually used over herself, turned her back to the room, and willed herself not to cry. Not to think about what a mess this all was. She was angry, and he was the one who'd almost died. All because he'd been trying to protect his friends. Again.

"Zylah?"

"Yeah?"

"I like rule number seven."

No dying on each other.

Zylah sighed. "Me too, Holt. Me too."

25

Holt was already gone when Zylah woke up. She walked to work, nibbling at the canna cake he'd left for her and working her way through the previous night's events. She took a different route than usual, passing through the market to gaze absentmindedly at the stalls.

She'd decided the night before, lying on the lounger and listening to Holt's quiet breathing in the dark, that after she'd worked with the uprising to take down Arnir, she wanted to hear their plans for Marcus. And not just for her future, but because she saw no point in replacing one tyrant with another. She may only have been half Fae, but her freedom was tied to theirs now, too.

And there was that other matter Zylah had been thinking about since she woke up—Marcus had asked about her eyes. Curiosity prickled Zylah's skin as a woman selling scarves of every colour and pattern waved an emerald scarf at her, and she shook her head and smiled as she walked on. Tomorrow she'd go back to the forest for the jupe, she'd formulate a plan.

Jilah waved her over as she approached the goods entrance of the botanical gardens. He somehow looked older every time she saw him, and she frowned as she wondered if it was because of his bargain.

"Heard you saved Holt's life last night," the old man said, fastening his apron as she slipped off her cloak.

Zylah laughed flatly. "Word travels fast." She wasn't surprised. Holt more than likely would have sent a message in the night; Jilah was well connected. They hauled their boxes side by side, ducking under the wood strings and making their way to the second dome together.

"I suspect he didn't like that much," Jilah mused, handing her his top box of sun lilies that she'd almost finished planting in the terraced levels of the warmer dome.

She thought of how Holt had looked, lying too still on the floor of the chamber with his wounds still steaming, struggling to breathe. How the fabric of his shirt had fused with his wounds. It snatched at her breath to even think of it, and she hastily blinked the image away. "Not really." She glanced around for something to focus on, noting the marantas needed their tops trimming back and added them to her list for after she'd finished planting the lilies.

Jilah sighed deeply. "Just like his father. His mother too."

Zylah paused. "You knew his parents?"

"I served them for many years." The old man stopped beside her, resting his pile of boxes on the pathway for a moment, rubbing at his back and lost in thought.

She thought back to when she'd told Holt she'd got the job at the botanical gardens. She'd asked him if he knew Jilah, and he'd said only in passing. But if he was trying to hide who he truly was, just as she had been, it made sense. "They were royalty. I only learnt that last night," Zylah said softly.

"Not from Holt, I'm guessing?"

Zylah waited patiently for Jilah as he scooped up his boxes again. If she knew he'd agree, she'd tell him to leave them and she'd come back for them. Instead, she said, "No."

Jilah waved a hand as if he'd read her thoughts, swatting her away. "Holt never thought much of the Fae monarchy." He sighed again. "He was right in the end. Got them all killed."

The warmer air of the second dome hit them as they walked in, and Zylah made her way to the first terrace. "I'm glad he still has his sister." She hoped he'd have time to see her whilst he was away.

"His sister? My dear girl, Adina is gone." He was saying something else, but Zylah didn't hear him. She thought of all the times Holt had mentioned his sister. *Seven gods.*

"Such a sweet girl." Jilah was still talking. "Holt would do anything for her. Her death hit him the hardest."

Zylah replayed all the things Holt had told her about his sister as unease twisted in her stomach. The furthest he'd ever evanesced was for his sister. *Memories are fickle things*, he'd said. *But sometimes they're all there is.* He'd as much as told her, and she hadn't been paying close enough attention to realise it. She put her boxes down and took Jilah's from his arms.

"Was it Marcus?" She already knew the answer.

The old man frowned. "Yes."

Anger bubbled up inside her, hot and molten. "Then why are we wasting our time with Arnir? Why isn't Marcus the one we're going after?"

Jilah sat on the edge of the wall, looking out over the centre of the dome as if he were seeing something else. "You're young, Liss. This has been in motion since before you were born. Holt knows what he's doing. He's a strategist. I trust him to set our people free."

Zylah followed his gaze to where the children had chased each other into the dome. *Our people.* It was a world that just over a month ago she hadn't even known had existed. But it was one in which the two children, and countless other Fae children just like them, could grow up to be free if Arnir was gone.

It was late when Zylah finally made her way to the safe house. Training was meant to be daily, but it was the last thing she wanted to do after the previous night's events. She braced herself for the scolding she was going to get from Rose, not at all sure what to expect from Raif. The way he'd touched her at the restaurant... gods above, it had been the best kind of distraction. *He* was the best kind of distraction.

Kopi flew down to her shoulder as she reached for the door, and she gave him a light scratch on his head in acknowledgement. She took a deep breath, steeling herself for whatever Rose was going to throw at her.

"Liss!" Saphi was waiting as she opened the door, and the Fae threw her arms around Zylah. "You did good," she murmured into Zylah's neck as she hugged her. Kopi readjusted his wings as Zylah hugged Saphi back.

Rose appeared from behind the counter, took Zylah's hand and squeezed. "Thank you," she said quietly.

"Have I... did I miss something?" Zylah asked as they led her up the staircase.

They passed their bedroom and carried on up a second set of stairs, pushing open a wooden door to the roof. Stars glittered above them, and a canopy lit with orblights softly illuminated a table. Place settings and platters of food were laid out neatly across it.

"We wanted to thank you properly," Saphi said, pulling out a chair for Zylah. "It was Raif's idea," she added with a smile.

Rose was watching her, but her expression was warm with no hint of her usual demeanour. "Holt means a lot to us, Liss."

Zylah frowned and swallowed down the lump in her throat. Before she could answer, the door burst open and Raif joined them, a tray of drinks in one hand and a basket of bread in the other. His face lit up as his gaze landed on Zylah.

"This was your idea, huh?" Zylah asked as he set down the tray and basket and pulled her in for an embrace, pressing a kiss into her hair.

His hands found hers and he pulled her to one side, away from Rose and Saphi. He sat on the edge of the roof, holding

her hands as he looked up at her. "What you did last night…"
He swallowed. His hands were warm, and he traced circles in
her palms, his eyes as bright as they were in the daylight.
"Punishments from Marcus usually continue for days." His expression darkened, and he closed his eyes for a moment as if
he were steadying himself. "Thank you for finding Holt."

"He's your family. I understand," Zylah said softly. "He
was the only friend I had when I came to Virian. I couldn't sit
by and do nothing."

Raif caught her by surprise, claiming her mouth with a
slow kiss, his hands tangling in her hair. "Thank you," he said
as he pulled back. "Come on." He reached for her hand and
led her back to the table where Saphi and Rose were laughing
quietly.

"I need to return your things," Zylah said as Saphi handed
her the breadbasket.

"Keep them. And wear the bracers, even at work. Jilah
won't question you. I'd prefer knowing you were armed out in
the city every day." She was walking around the table, spooning out servings of grains mixed with herbs, the fragrant scent
mingling with the bread.

"So would I," Raif said quietly from Zylah's side.

Her relief was almost palpable. "Thank you," Zylah said as
Saphi piled more food onto her plate; pieces of steaming
pumpkin in an aromatic sauce. "So that's it, Holt won't be
back now until the festival, and he'll be fine?"

"It was always his plan to go; Marcus just bumped up the
timeline," Raif explained. He lifted his glass of wine, and Rose

and Saphi followed suit. "To Liss. For keeping our family together."

Raif handed her a glass, and she took a sip of the sweet wine with the others. A gentle breeze shook the wind chime hanging off the canopy above them, and beyond it, starlight illuminated the sky. Zylah thought of the gods, the ones that weren't really gods, and how they were said to have come from starlight. Of course, it had all been nothing but fables made up by the humans.

Saphi began talking about the festival, listing off the parts she was excited about and her guesses for some of the entertainment ahead of the scouts' information. Raif and Rose were eating, but Zylah was still as she took it all in; the way the orblights made Saphi's bracelets shimmer, the way Rose smiled at her, the way Raif laughed and raised his glass.

She wanted to see the world. To live free, knowing Arnir would no longer be hunting her down. But she'd missed being part of something, and in that moment, she was. They weren't her family, but they could be her friends.

She managed a few questions between mouthfuls of food, worried she might seem ungrateful for the meal they'd prepared for her. She didn't deserve it, not with the lies she was upholding, the things she'd been keeping from them. Already the wine had begun to muddy her thoughts and thinking of Arnir brought up unpleasant memories of Jesper, so she switched to water, unwilling to let it drag her thoughts somewhere darker.

Holt would be with Marcus by now. What if there were

more punishments? The others didn't seem worried, but they hadn't seen what Marcus had done the night before. She took another sip of water, hoping to drown those thoughts out, too.

Zylah tried to stay present as she ate, to take part in the conversation. But her thoughts kept drifting, no matter how much she willed herself to focus. Rose and Saphi were already clearing their empty plates away, their food long since eaten when Raif flexed his fingers through hers.

"Where are you?" he asked softly.

Zylah blinked at his fingers through hers and met his gaze with a frown. "Here."

The corner of Raif's mouth twitched. "Fine. I'll rephrase. Where did you go? Because it wasn't here with us."

Zylah shook her head. "I'm sorry, I… I was thinking of my family." It was an easy lie, well, half-lie, really. Being there, hearing about how Holt was their family. It had made her miss her own. Her father, her brother. Kara. She had to believe they were safe, that nothing had happened to them after she'd left Dalstead, but some days that was easier than others. Missing them had become a permanent ache that she'd learnt to live with, a memory that she was trying to work out how to carry with her, even if she could never return.

Raif urged her to follow him as he pushed away from the table. "Come with me, I'd like to show you something."

She was quiet as she followed him down the staircase, wondering how Kara had been doing in the time she'd been gone, what books she'd been reading. Raif pushed open the door to a room. A bedroom, with a large bed with dark red sheets, and

285

beyond it, an entire wall of books.

Zylah sucked in a breath as she took in the sight. The door clicked shut, but Zylah's focus was on the small library before her.

"You said you read a lot. That day we went to the forest. I thought you might like to borrow a book or two," Raif said beside her.

Zylah ran her fingers across spines, noticing some titles she recognised, others she didn't. Several were in different languages, and some were old, older than anything she'd ever seen. Her fingers paused as she read: *Song and Shadow*. She leafed through the pages, but they held an unfamiliar language, symbols and markings she couldn't read, had never seen before. She turned to Raif and took his hand. "I would love that. Thank you."

"I'm sorry our evening got cut short last night." He wrapped his arms around her, his warm breath caressing the soft shell of her ear as he spoke.

Zylah tilted her head up, her lips close to his. "You were an excellent distraction, as promised."

"I can distract you again, if you'd like." Raif brushed his lips over hers. "I can be whatever you need."

Gods above. She wanted to. But those memories of Jesper were lingering behind her eyes. "And if I just want to sleep?" she asked quietly, her gaze fixed on his mouth.

"I make an excellent pillow." He stepped out of their embrace and sat back on the bed, patting the spot beside him.

Zylah laughed, reaching for the fastening to her braid and

easing her hair down as she watched him puff up the pillows for her. She settled onto the bed to lay beside him, and for a moment unease washed over her, the sound of her heart loud in her ears.

"How do you like your pillow?" Raif asked, scooping an arm under her and pulling her close, wrapping his other arm over hers and resting a hand on her stomach. Zylah bit down on her smile.

"Insufferable," she murmured as she closed her eyes.

"Liss?" Raif whispered a short while later when the haziness of sleep was already pulling her under.

"Mhmm?"

"Holt isn't your only friend in Virian."

He couldn't have known what it meant, to let her know she wasn't alone in the world. But Zylah couldn't bring herself to admit that to him. Not yet. That ache, that longing for home, eased a little as she settled into Raif's arms and let sleep take her.

A week later, Zylah had settled into her new routine. Work at the gardens kept her busy, and each day after work she'd train for a few hours with Raif before dinner. No matter how exhausted she was, training was the only thing keeping her nerves in check. She walked everywhere, always glancing over her shoulder like she had in those first few weeks in Virian, and was grateful for the weight of Saphi's knives pressed against her wrists and tucked into her boots. The festival couldn't come soon enough.

Zylah was lost in her thoughts as Raif's practice sword came down hard against her own. "Your eyes are getting brighter," he said as she dodged his strike.

"You're just used to looking at me through the eyeglasses." But it made her think of Marcus, questioning Holt in the tunnels about her eye colour. She'd seen nothing of it in the books she'd been reading from Raif's library.

She'd been hoping to find some writings on Fae history,

but all he had were novels—stories of adventure, of heroes exploring the world. Between pages, Zylah had begun to wonder if her real family were out there, if they still lived. Did she have the same eyes as her mother? Her father? Did she have siblings? Were they living somewhere, in safety? She could look for them. No matter how long it took, she would look for them.

With every blow, she saw her freedom, her new life stretching out before her. In just over two months, she'd have it. Raif's sword clashed with hers, and she gritted her teeth against the force of it. He didn't go easy on her, and that only encouraged her. But their training had been limited to the physical kind, much to Zylah's disappointment. "When will we practise magic?"

"Magic should be practised somewhere it can't be tracked," Raif said, swinging around to dodge another of her attacks.

Zylah thought of her room at the tavern, of Holt's training room beneath it. "The safe house is warded. I've been healing minor wounds here; you've had no problems with that." She paused to catch her breath, a streak of anger thrumming through her.

"The house is warded, yes, but not well enough, if you can pass through."

Zylah put her sword back on the rack, her adrenaline dulled by frustration. She couldn't practise with anger clouding her judgement. "What's that supposed to mean? Marcus got through them."

Raif tucked a strand of hair behind her ear, his eyes darting lower for a moment. "Royal lines have the strongest magic. It's no surprise he got through. But that you could, that presents a problem. We need to tighten things up."

Zylah couldn't be certain, but it was almost as if he didn't want to train her. Or maybe he knew she had no real magic besides the evanescing and the healing and was trying to save her the disappointment of discovering that. He took a step back, and she fought the urge to follow him, to continue what he'd started.

Raif's magic, what she'd seen of it, was powerful. Dark. She thought of the way it changed his eyes, how she'd asked him if it hurt. "Can you tell me more about *your* magic?"

She felt Raif tracking her movements as she stretched, his gaze heated, and she was glad for once to be hot and sweaty enough to hide her blush. For all his insufferable ways, he knew when to give her space. Since she'd fallen asleep beside him, in his bed, she'd returned home to her room at the tavern every night, and he'd never once questioned it.

"Magic is about balance," he said, placing his sword back on the rack. He let out a breath as if the subject made him uncomfortable, then picked up her cloak and ran a hand over the buttons. But whatever expression had settled on his face was gone as he held the door open for her with a grin. "We have an assignment this evening, if you're up for it."

Zylah finished her stretches and scooped up her glasses, still thinking about magic. *His* magic. It had a physical effect on him; she'd seen the change in his eyes. Was that the balance he spoke of? Did it take something from him to turn another to ash—his vision, maybe? She thought of the scales the goddess Gentris always held in the drawings that had filled her school books and whether temporary vision loss balanced out turning a person to ash.

"Liss?" Raif asked, his arms folded across his chest as he leaned back against the door.

Zylah cleared her throat as she grabbed her apron. "An assignment. Right. What do you need?"

"We need as much access to Arnir at the festival as we can get. You might not like accepting help, but I'm counting on your willingness to offer it."

Gods, he missed nothing. "*I* can help?" She followed him to the front of the building, fastening her apron behind her back as she walked.

He handed over her cloak with a raised eyebrow. "Florist contracts are released tonight."

"I'm no florist."

"No. But Arnir expects only the best from the citizens of Virian. You have fresh sun lilies growing at the gardens. The terraces are full of them, you told me so yourself. They'll be in full bloom in what… two months from now?"

She threw on her cloak, fastening it as she followed Raif out of the door. She'd told him about the sun lilies at their dinner date. He'd remembered, and a pang of guilt twisted over inside her that he'd done that when she was still lying to him.

She could tell him now. Tell him who she was and that Arnir was looking for her. She glanced up at him from beneath her hood, and he winked at her. "I didn't realise you were paying attention."

Kopi flew down to Zylah's shoulder for a moment before flying off again. He was never far away, and his loyalty always surprised Zylah. Every morning she woke up wondering if he'd return, and every morning he did.

"When it comes to you, Liss, I'm always paying attention." Raif wove his fingers through hers, content with the small amount of contact. Before she could reply, he said, "I think this could get us what we need. Scouts have told me it's the flowers Arnir cares about most. He takes great pleasure in inspecting them every year. This contract gets us one step closer to him."

One step closer to killing him. And one step closer to her freedom. Zylah thought of Kihlan and Niara, of what their future could be like if the Fae were free. A future where they could walk the streets without disguising themselves, where they could play freely with human children, their ears on display. She knew she'd do whatever it took to make that happen.

The weight of what they were about to do hit her, and the cost if they failed. The city passed by in a blur as dread coiled tight within her. She wouldn't let the children down.

"Don't break our cover tonight, no matter what happens," Raif said as they turned down a narrow side street, and he paused, pulling her to him. He rested a hand against her cheek, his gaze on something just down the road.

"Your favourite trick," Zylah murmured. He was watching someone, and she resisted the urge to follow his gaze for fear of drawing attention to them.

His hands dropped to hers and he squeezed. "It's no trick," he said quietly before kissing her. Despite what they were there for, Zylah leaned into his touch. He pulled back, flashing her a smile before leading the way. With his hand still wrapped around hers, her dread eased a little.

They walked past a florist, hanging baskets of lilac cloud violas on either side of the door. *Bloom.* Zylah had walked past many times. On her first day in Virian she'd walked by this florist with Holt, only she'd been too afraid to look up and see the sign and the beautiful hanging baskets. At the end of the street, the owner of the florist turned the corner.

"I'm your assistant, if anyone asks," Raif said quietly as they followed their mark.

Zylah doubted anyone would believe that for a second. "Why don't we go with *bodyguard*? That might seem more convincing."

"Do florists walk around with a bodyguard in Dalstead?"

"No, they don't. Fine. You're my assistant." The stone façade of the Pig's Tail hid the florist in its shadows for a moment before the door opened and the noise and light from within burst out into the street. Zylah had walked past this particular tavern enough times to know it was not the kind of place you went for a quiet drink. As they opened the door after the florist, a bartender shoved a disorderly patron out into the street.

Raif shot Zylah a smile, waving a hand to gesture her in before him. She ran her fingers down the buttons of her cloak, shoved her reservations aside and stepped into the tavern. The heat was overbearing; the air thick with woodsmoke and ale. Raif touched a hand to her elbow, and she followed his gaze to where the florist slipped through a door beside the bar.

They wove through the busy tavern, dodging flailing arms and raised tankards, the floor sticky with ale and bits of food. The Pig's Filth would have been more appropriate, Zylah thought, as they pursued the florist.

A burly man, almost as tall as Raif, with greasy, choppy brown hair and a face that was more frown than anything else, stepped in front of the door as they approached.

"We're here for the contract," Raif said, not even remotely fazed by the man in front of them. "We represent the botanical gardens."

The bruiser's gaze slid to Zylah's apron where her cloak parted, or that's what she told herself he was looking at, as he nodded and stepped aside to let them enter.

Raif shut the door behind them, the racket of the tavern disappearing. Zylah looked around the room, her head high and her gaze meeting each of the occupants as she did. She might not be well practised in these kinds of meetings, but she knew enough to pretend to be. And if Raif was meant to be *her* assistant, well, she had better step up. The room was dimly lit with only a handful of orblights, much smaller than Zylah had expected, and for some reason, that eased her nerves a little.

"And who the fuck is this?" the Bloom florist asked, turning to look them over. His dark hair was peppered with grey, his deep brown skin creased around his eyes.

Zylah met his stare with an easiness she'd so often seen Raif use. "Good evening. We're here from the botanical gardens to negotiate for the contract." There were three other men in the room, all, she presumed, representatives of the king. There was something about the fine edge to their attire, the way they held themselves, and, of course, the swords they each wore at their hip. She prayed they wouldn't recognise her from the posters.

The florist practically vibrated with dissatisfaction. "Negotiate? Bloom has been supplying the flowers for the festival for years!"

"We have the best sun lilies in Virian, an entire dome full of them," Zylah offered, smoothing down her apron and clasping her hands in front of her. Raif stood beside her, arms folded across his chest, emphasising the heavy muscles of his arms. Assistant, indeed. They weren't fooling anyone.

"And what has that got to do with the festival?" The florist took a step towards them, but Raif stepped in front of Zylah.

She eased Raif aside, tilting her chin up to meet the florist's eyes. "Why ship plants in from outside when they are already being grown right here in the city? Our king deserves the freshest, most locally grown flowers, does he not?"

"This is horse shit."

Had Zylah not been training every day, she wouldn't have spotted the change in the florist's stance right before he reached for a weapon. But she had, and as he did, she reached for her own, pressing it to his ribs before he'd so much as wrapped his hand around the hilt.

"You brought a weapon?" one of the king's men asked.

Zylah didn't peel her attention away from the florist, despite the fact that Raif was already at the man's side and could turn him to ash with the touch of a finger. Instead, she sighed, feigning boredom. "Once you've had a delivery stolen from you, you learn to defend yourself. I'm always prepared for someone to pull a blade on me." She flicked her chin to where the florist's hand had slipped into his coat.

The florist made the wise decision to leave his weapon in its sheath and took a step back. Raif took a step back with him.

The tallest of the king's men laughed and clapped his hands together once. "I like you. You can have the contract." He turned his attention to the florist. "You can leave. Attempt to draw a weapon in front of the king's men again and we'll have you imprisoned for treason."

The florist paled but didn't argue as he rushed out the door, the noise of the tavern swallowing him as he disappeared. Zylah sheathed her dagger and waited. There was power in not being the first to speak, she'd often observed. And she would not apologise for drawing her weapon in defence. The other two men remained silent, hands, Zylah now noticed, resting on the hilts of their swords. Perhaps they wouldn't let her misdeed slip either.

"Eirik, Sebastian, at ease," the first representative commanded, and his two companions dropped their hands from their weapons. "I'll send someone in the morning to check everything is satisfactory," he said to Zylah, a smirk still plastered across his face.

Zylah allowed herself to feel the slightest bit of relief.

"I didn't catch your name," he began, reaching out a hand, just as an explosion slammed Zylah into the wall beside him.

27

Zylah's ears rang. Someone was saying something, but the sounds were muffled, like she was underwater.

"Liss!" Raif's hands were on her face, his eyes searching hers. He was checking her over for injuries, but Zylah knew she hadn't been harmed.

"I'm fine," she rasped. "Just winded." And a little dazed, but she wouldn't admit that. His face was all she could see from where he'd rolled her over, his eyebrows knitted together in concern.

He seemed satisfied with either his inspection or her answer and took her hands in his. "Can you stand?"

Vaguely, Zylah registered the smell of burning wood. She nodded, still studying his face, the tightness of his jaw. There were strange sounds, but her hearing was still distorted and *wrong*.

"Remember what I said?" Raif asked.

Don't break our cover tonight, no matter what happens. She didn't need him to explain to understand that he meant *no magic.*

Zylah staggered to her feet, Raif's steadying hand at her elbow and finally cast her gaze around the room. Or rather, what was left of it. Sebastian was slumped over in the far corner, unseeing eyes gazing into nothing. Splintered wood and dust were scattered everywhere. The wall to the room had been blown open, and Zylah realised it must have been Raif that shoved her out of the way just as the explosion went off. Metal on metal clashed, bringing Zylah to her senses.

She reached for a dagger from her boot, just as two men charged at her and Raif, swords drawn. She tossed Raif her dagger, pivoting out of the way as one of the men aimed for her. Her hand was already around the hilt of a second dagger before she stood, her eyes tracking the poorly trained man swinging at her with his weapon.

Zylah's head throbbed, but she schooled her focus on her attacker. He raised his sword again, and she thrust her dagger up and under his ribs, pushing him away and trying not to think about how many lives she'd taken since Jesper's. This was not Arnir's elite unit, Zylah was certain of that as her gaze settled on Raif. He swung at the first man, the hilt of the dagger meeting with his assailant's jaw over and over until he went down. A shiver ran down Zylah's spine at the sight.

Raif looked up and caught her gaze; his eyes had turned wholly black like they did when she'd seen him use his magic, and again Zylah thought of what it cost him. If he could channel his power into fighting. He swiftly looked away, assessing the tavern, or hiding his eyes from her, Zylah wasn't sure which. As she caught her breath she took in the damage, scanning the debris for any sign of her eyeglasses; they'd come off in the explosion.

The tavern was in chaos; parts of the bar had been blown away entirely, tables were upturned, and bodies slumped awkwardly across the floor and the furniture as patrons struggled with swordsmen. Somewhere a woman was screaming, but Zylah couldn't figure out where. Parts of the tavern smouldered, and a group of people were furiously trying to put out a fire on the far side of the bar.

She pulled up her hood, taking a step back as two men barrelled past her in a tangle of limbs, the king's representative who'd just been about to introduce himself, grappling with a young man. A sinking feeling told her he was a member of the Black Veil, that *all* the assailants were, and Zylah couldn't intervene. She took a step towards them, and Raif grabbed her wrist.

"Don't," he murmured, tugging her back. She wanted to leave, to take Raif and the young man away from there. But she couldn't. And, *gods above*, the man she'd just killed had been innocent. Raif's attacker, too.

"They're Black Veil," she said softly, turning to look at him, to brush him away.

His eyes had returned to their normal colour. "Liss, we can't," he urged, just as the king's man's sword pierced through flesh and the member of the Black Veil fell still. Zylah's thoughts swirled into a muddy mess.

This was all wrong. Very wrong.

"Take this. My name is Ambrose; the guards will recognise my seal should the worst happen," the king's representative explained, shoving a piece of bloodied parchment into Zylah's hands. The contract. "The tavern is surrounded, they're trying to choke us out, but if we live, I'll make sure the king hears of your actions here tonight."

Zylah willed herself not to be sick as she shoved the contract into the front of her apron. He expected them to fight with him. He thought that's what they'd been doing. Fighting *with* him, on behalf of the king. There was no time to argue; another stream of the Black Veil poured in from the street just as Eirik leapt over an upturned table and stood beside Ambrose, swords drawn.

It took every inch of Zylah's resolve not to evanesce. She had to stay, but that didn't mean she had to kill any of them. She tightened her grip on her dagger, dread coiling tight in her stomach. She held her position as more men than she could count burst through the door, and Eirik charged into the centre of them, sword slashing and swiping.

A young woman charged at Zylah, both hands gripped around a short sword as if she'd never held one before. The ceiling over the bar collapsed and the woman hesitated, giving Zylah enough time to knock her off her feet and grab the sword.

It was lighter than she expected. Just as Holt had said it would be. "Leave if you want to live." She touched the tip of the sword to the young woman's chest, flicking her chin towards the door. "Go."

Zylah watched the woman scramble away, just as two men charged for her. She threw the sword aside to show she meant no harm, but it did nothing to deter them. She couldn't defend herself without harming them, and even with her training, one dagger against two swords would not end well unless she made each strike count. She raised her dagger just as firelight glinted off the swords coming towards her and sucked in a breath.

It was Mala's face she saw as those swords came closer, and Zylah froze, all the fight leaving her as the two young men charged. One swipe from either of them and she would be in ribbons on the floor, but she couldn't attack them. Mala had tried to defend the humans, too, before she died.

Zylah closed her eyes, and when she opened them, Raif slammed into both men, knocking them sideways. He pulled his dagger from the neck of the first as he pushed himself to his feet, pivoting around to slice at the second. Neither man stood a chance. Three more attacked him, and he slashed and swung at them with preternatural grace. His eyes were black again, his shirt covered in blood, but he seemed oblivious to it, to anything other than cutting down their assailants one by one.

The young woman from before charged at Raif as he fought off the three men, and Zylah moved instinctively, bringing her dagger to the woman's throat.

"Yield," Zylah breathed, praying that she wouldn't have to take another life.

The hostage made to move away, but Zylah pinned an arm

to her back, the dagger still pressing against flesh. "Walk away."

A man crashed into a table beside them as the woman reached for something, a weapon—Zylah couldn't be sure, but she made her decision and plunged her blade into the young woman's neck. The woman staggered back, clutching at her wound, surprise written all over her face. It wasn't a weapon she'd been reaching for, but a piece of parchment that stained crimson as the blood seeped between her fingertips and she fell.

Zylah took a step forwards, but Raif tugged at her hand. "Liss, we need to leave now." He pulled her away, but Zylah kept looking back at the young woman dying on the floor behind them, at the Black Veil missive clutched between her fingertips. She could have tried to heal her. The wound was far more severe than anything she'd healed before, but she could have tried. The thought settled, weighing her down.

"Liss, hurry," Raif pleaded, all but dragging her through the tavern. The night air hit Zylah as he led them outside, through what must have been the goods entrance at the side of the building. "Now," he whispered, and she knew he was waiting for her to evanesce them.

Zylah stopped, pulled her hand out of his and looked down at her bloodied dagger, swallowing down the acid that burned the back of her throat.

"Please. We need to leave." Raif rested a hand on her arm, but she couldn't meet his gaze. Didn't want to see herself reflected in his eyes. A quiet groan pulled her attention down the alley to a man, slumped against the tavern wall, clutching something to his stomach. It was his intestines, Zylah realised with horror. And not just any man, it was Eirik. She couldn't heal him, but maybe she could take away some of his pain.

"*Liss*," Raif pleaded. "Nothing can save him. We have to get out of here."

Eirik met her gaze just as she evanesced her and Raif to his room at the safe house.

Her dagger clattered to the floor as she stumbled, her back hitting the door. She registered the sound of running water as she stared at the dagger and pulled off her cloak and her apron. This wasn't like Jesper. Or the men in the forest. Or the times Arnir's unit had attacked. Those deaths were unavoidable. But tonight…

Her feet carried her to the bathroom, where Raif had peeled off his bloodied shirt and handed her a bar of soap. "Here," he said quietly.

Zylah followed Raif's lead and scrubbed at her hands, watching the blood swirl down the drain. A moment of silence passed, nothing but the sound of them scrubbing away the blood until Zylah finally said, "They were innocent."

"I know."

"And we killed them."

Raif had already walked away from the basin, back out into the bedroom. "I know."

She spun around at the emptiness in his tone, grabbing a towel as she followed him. He sat on the edge of the bed, chest rising and falling as his gaze fell to his upturned hands resting on his knees. She studied his face, the slump of his shoulders, his empty gaze. He'd killed them. For her. To save her.

"Raif?"

He didn't look up, and Zylah realised then; it wasn't just his magic that cost him something. When she'd seen him fight, it was with a ferocity she'd never seen before, and it should have unsettled her, but it didn't. It was *for* her. But it had taken something from him.

"Look at me," Zylah said, taking his hands in hers and kneeling before him. Raif's gaze slowly slid up to meet hers. The brightness had gone from his eyes—they weren't the black of when he used his magic, but a shadow had fallen over them. "Thank you." She rubbed her thumbs in circles on his hands. He had killed for her. So that she wouldn't have to take any more innocent lives, so that she wouldn't have to see their faces when she closed her eyes.

Raif blinked. Once. Twice. As if he were blinking away the darkness that had consumed his eyes more than once that evening. He swallowed. "I just need to… think of something else." Gone was the playful tone, the humour she'd become accustomed to. The insufferable confidence. He looked exactly how she felt, and she couldn't bear to see him that way.

She placed her hands on his thighs and cocked her head to one side, summoning a smile. A distraction. That was what he needed. What they both needed. And she could give him that—he'd given her space when she needed it. Held onto her when she needed holding, too.

"I can help with that," she said quietly, moving to sit in his

305

lap, knees resting either side of him on the bed. She pressed a hand to his chest, his skin warm beneath her palm as his arms wrapped around her. "I can be a distraction." She tilted her head up to look at him, only to find his eyes were closed, his brow tightly furrowed as he held onto her.

Zylah cleared her throat. "I'm sorry," she began, pushing back to ease out of his lap, but Raif moved faster, his hands grabbing her behind and moving to lower her onto the bed.

Any shame she had begun to feel in that moment his eyes were closed disappeared as he looked down at her, his gaze drifting to her mouth. "Like a goddess," he murmured, an arm on either side of her head. Warmth radiated from him, his mint and lemongrass scent flooding her senses.

Zylah reached her hands into his hair, her lips meeting his softly, slowly at first. She pulled back to check it was okay, that this was what he wanted, what he *needed*, and he responded by sliding an arm under her waist and pulling her to him, his lips crashing with hers. There was nothing soft and gentle about the kiss. It was hungry, desperate, and she could feel the evidence of his need pressing between her legs, long and hard.

Her heart was like a beating drum inside her chest. She'd wanted this since their first kiss outside the safe house, yet she'd pushed him away. Kept her walls firmly in place. But seeing his come down tonight had brought hers down, too. And she was tired of keeping him out. Tired of hiding from her feelings. She ran her hands down the thick muscles on his chest, his stomach, and slid her fingers into the band of his trousers, but Raif caught her hand.

"Ladies first," he said, pressing a kiss to her fingers and pulling her arms over her head to pull off her tunic. He knelt over her, tugging her trousers away from her waist and sliding them down her legs.

Zylah watched the way he looked at her, his gaze roving slowly over her legs, her undergarments, over her breasts, her chest rising and falling with each breath. She wanted to take away every dark thought and memory she could from him, to lock them away so he'd never look how he had moments before.

He finally met her gaze; the shadows had gone from his eyes. Instead, they smouldered, and nothing but hunger and desire sparkled in them. He hooked a finger into her underwear, his other hand lifting her off the bed slightly and held her gaze as he slid the fabric down her legs. One arm was still around her as he ran his hand up her leg, his touch feather-light as his hand roamed higher, exploring, teasing.

Zylah's breath hitched as Raif's gaze followed the trail of his hand, fingers coming to rest on the sensitive spot between her legs. Every thought fell away from her as she focused on the feeling of his fingertips coaxing circles against her exposed skin. She eased her hips up against his touch, needing to feel more of him, to have more friction against the sensation building within her.

She threw her arms around his neck, pulling his mouth to hers to kiss him again. It might have only been a distraction for him, but she couldn't deny that it meant more to her. Raif's hand slid lower, a low growl slipping from him as his fingers met with slick wetness and he slid a finger inside her. A quiet whimper escaped Zylah as she moved against him, his tongue sweeping over hers, his kiss devouring. Her hips moved against him; she needed more.

As if he'd heard her thoughts, he slid in another finger, and Zylah cried out against his lips. "Raif," she whispered, as a delicious tension coiled tight within her. She reached for him, her hand skimming beneath the band of his trousers and wrapped her hand around the solid length of him.

"Fuck," he breathed, pulling back to look down at their hands. Zylah moved her hand up and down, once, twice, tugging at the band of his trousers with her other hand to free him. But that didn't stop him; he moved his fingers faster, his thumb resting on the most sensitive part of her, circling in time with his fingers.

Zylah's back arched into his touch, the tension building as Raif kissed around her jaw. His lips against her throat were her undoing. Pleasure swept through her, Raif's fingers slowing as she shook against him. Her bones were liquid, her body heavy and light all at once. The kisses slowed, and Raif eased his fingers out of her as her shaking eased, his hand wrapping around hers as she moved it up and down him.

Another growl escaped him as he eased her hand away, pulling at his trousers and positioning himself over her. Raif paused on his elbows, his breathing as ragged and broken as Zylah's as he looked down at her, waiting. Zylah answered by wrapping her legs around him, and with one swift thrust, he was inside her, easing further and further. Zylah cried out at the size of him, her nails digging into his shoulders as he moved slowly for her to adjust. But she wanted more.

Raif pulled back, but she tightened her legs around him, her hips moving against his and he thrust deeper, his lips claiming hers as she moaned at the building pleasure. He pulled back again to look at her, his blue eyes bright and blazing as he moved inside her.

She didn't just want to be a distraction. And she knew he didn't either. "Raif," she murmured against his lips. He answered by moving faster, his mouth devouring hers again, each thrust faster than the one before.

Every muscle in Zylah's body tightened. She dragged her hands up Raif's corded arms, ran them through his hair, against his neck, his heartbeat pounding against her fingertips. Gone were the shadows of the evening, the darkness that had followed them home. There was nothing left but this moment between them, the burning deep within her.

Release barrelled through her again, and Raif followed, his arms tight around her as she shook, his tongue sweeping across hers as he captured her mouth, hips slowing.

Zylah didn't realise she'd closed her eyes, but when she opened them, Raif was looking down at her, a hand resting gently against her cheek, his chest rising and falling in time with hers. He held her gaze as their breathing slowed, his thumb tracing the line of her jaw.

He pressed a kiss to her lips and moved to lay beside her, head resting on his arm. A tender expression settled across his face, and another piece of the wall Zylah had built chipped away. She wanted to let him in, for so many reasons. He'd been kind to her. Patient. She owed him the truth.

"There's something I need to tell you," she said quietly as he traced his fingers down her side.

Raif flexed his fingers through hers. "I know you're the girl from the posters." He didn't frown as he said it; no anger flared across his face, no frustration.

"Why didn't you say anything?"

"It was for you to tell me when you were ready." He kissed her knuckles, pulled her hand close to his chest and smiled. His hair had come loose from its fastening, like a curtain of black silk spilling over his shoulders. Gods, he was beautiful. And far more patient than she had given him credit for.

She ran her fingers through his hair, words bubbling up inside her, but she pushed them down. Instead, she said, "Did Holt send you to the gardens that day?" It had been on her mind lately—how Raif had turned up so soon after her arrival. Holt had said he had friends in Virian when they were back in his cabin.

Raif smiled again, his dimple on full display. "Holt has a way of making people come together."

"He really is like a brother to you, isn't he?"

"I owe him everything. I can't think of anyone better to lead our people."

Zylah didn't know what to say to that. She traced a hand along his arm, her fingers resting on the tattoo around his bicep. "Does this mean something, or was it part of your *volatile* youth?"

His brows pinched together for a moment. "It's a mourning band. For my mother."

Zylah made to snatch her hand away, but he caught it. "It's alright," he said softly. "You didn't know." He pressed her hand to his chest again, and Zylah closed her eyes, feeling his heartbeat through her fingertips and listening to his steady breaths.

Sleep began to tug at her. She rolled to her side, and Raif pulled her close to him, his body flush against hers, his hand resting across her stomach.

"I never told you my name," she mumbled.

He pressed a kiss to her shoulder. "You chose Liss for a reason. If that's who you want to be, that's all I need to know."

For the first time since arriving in Virian, Zylah thought about the kind of life she could have if she stayed. She let the thought be a comfort as Raif held her close and sleep took her.

28

She hadn't stayed in Raif's bed for long. She'd dreamt of the tunnels, and when she woke in the middle of the night, Raif stirring, she'd told him she was going back to the tavern. But she hadn't. Instead, she'd gone to the tunnels to look for the bodies she'd seen Holt piling up for Marcus.

They weren't there. She should have known Marcus would move them. She'd walked the tunnels, learning every turn, every passageway memorising as much as she could until exhaustion pressed at her skull and forced her to evanesce back to her room at the tavern.

That was weeks ago now. Every day since had been the same: work at the gardens, training after work with Raif, sometimes with Rose and Saphi. Dinner. Nights between the sheets with Raif. But she never stayed the whole night. She would sleep for a few hours and then make her way to the tunnels to practise her evanescing. As she explored, she realised the tunnels must have spread beneath most of Virian, and in time, she'd discovered more of what lay beneath the city than she had above ground. Each night she pushed her evanescing further and further, experimenting with how different substances felt over short distances—a wooden door, a stone wall, tuning in to her senses to learn all she could about her ability.

Without any guidance, all she could do was teach herself. It had never stopped her in the past. And it helped keep her thoughts at bay about what was coming. The festival. The attack on Arnir.

The sun lilies were coming along nicely, tiny buds just beginning to develop. They'd open just in time for the festival, and every day she tended to them, she laughed quietly to herself that it would be flowers that would help secure her freedom.

She'd collected the jupe as a backup on one of her visits to the forest to gather ingredients for the poultices and kept it tucked in the front of her apron; she didn't dare to leave it anywhere else. Her work making poultices had increased, but she didn't mind. Jilah had even set up a table at the gardens for her to work.

Once, on a delivery, she'd seen Asha, but everything she wanted to say had poured out of her at the sight of Mala's bracelet wrapped around his wrist. He'd thanked her for the poultices as if his mate hadn't died under her watch, and when he'd walked away, it had taken all of Zylah's resolve not to evanesce back to the quiet solitude of her room.

Arnir hadn't been back to Virian, but that had done little to ease Zylah's worries. His elite unit hadn't stopped hunting down Fae, and two more lives had been lost since Mala's death.

There were just two weeks to go until the festival, and Zylah thought through the plans Raif had laid out for her as she practised in the tunnels. That night she'd chosen to bring a training sword; she'd wanted to go over a new routine Raif had taught her to sharpen some of the moves she hadn't quite got right earlier that day. Or the day before, she supposed, now it was so late.

She'd been surviving on only a few hours of sleep a night, and she knew it was nothing but adrenaline keeping her going. She swung the sword down against the wooden door she'd been hacking away at, bones shaking with the force of her blow. She slumped back against the wood, wiping at her brow. The lump in her back no longer ached, instead it was an acute pain. It seemed to get worse every day and she felt certain it was connected to her magic. She'd pushed herself too much, but work at the gardens would ease her. She evanesced herself to the tavern, dropping her sword to the floor with a thud.

But something was different about the room. The hairs on her arms raised, her senses on alert. A familiar scent lingered in the air: acani berries mixed with a musky, earthy smell. *Holt.* But he wasn't there. Zylah looked at the table by the window, where a brown paper bag sat. She didn't have to open it to know it was a canna cake inside. A smile tugged at the corner of her mouth as she made her way into the bathroom to freshen up. Some of the heaviness she'd felt in the last few weeks dissipated knowing he was safe; a weight she hadn't even realised she'd been carrying.

If he was back, that meant things were going to plan, and her troubles eased a little further as she walked to work, nibbling at the canna cake. Kopi flew on ahead, touching down onto her shoulder now and then as if he were checking on her. Zylah's thoughts were on the festival—the part of it that would take place before the attack on Arnir.

Saphi had told her it was a Fae custom to exchange gifts at the festival, and Zylah had been looking for the perfect gifts for them all ever since. Even for Rose, who, despite the one night of peace after Zylah had saved Holt from the tunnels, still mostly just tolerated her. She'd found something for Rose and Saphi, something for Jilah and the children, and Raif's was a work in progress, but she'd yet to find a gift for Holt.

She walked past one of the apothecaries, the customer bell jingling as the door opened, and as Zylah took another mouthful of canna cake, she realised she already knew what she was going to get for him. If she could find someone to make it.

Raif was waiting for her when she arrived at the gardens. It didn't surprise her if Holt was back in the city.

"Let me guess, boss's orders?" she asked as she approached him, brushing the canna crumbs from her fingers against her apron. It was getting far too warm to wear the cloak, but her posters were still plastered all over the city; fresh ones seemed to appear in waves whenever the old ones were covered up or worn away. Raif had bought her a new pair of tinted eyeglasses after the night at the Pig's Tail, and out of habit she pushed them up her nose with a finger.

Raif hadn't shown up at the gardens in weeks, which could only mean Holt had asked him to stop by. "How did you know?" He pressed a kiss to her knuckles, looping his other arm around her waist and steered her into the goods entrance.

"He left me a canna cake this morning." Zylah leaned into Raif's warmth. She could fall asleep if she let herself, and she knew she'd need an hour or two working the colder dome before she could tend to the sun lilies in the arid dome later on.

"Jilah won't mind if you take a nap in the grotto," Raif said as if she'd slumped against him just a little too heavily.

Zylah straightened. "I'm fine." She knelt to inspect one of the delivery boxes: *worms*. They aerated the soil and kept it healthy, and she needed them for the sun lilies. She might have known a lot about the uses of plants before she'd arrived in Virian, but she hadn't known all that much about keeping them alive. Jilah had been patient with her, teaching her how to look for signs of mould and rot, how to take cuttings and propagate new plants. She'd even started growing the ingredients for the poultices in the cooler dome, not that there would be enough for months to come, but that she now knew she could grow from cuttings or seeds, take that plant and turn it into a poultice, that filled her with a sense of pride she often longed to tell her father about.

The box was heavier than she'd expected, and Raif took it from her arms as she rose to her feet. "Maybe we should take a break from training tonight. Rest. I could read you a book," he suggested as his fingers brushed hers.

Zylah smiled up at him, her head tilted to one side. "That wasn't what I had in mind."

"I mean it, Liss. You're exhausted. Don't think I haven't noticed. I know you're worried about things going right at the festival, but we've got it under control. Everything's going to plan."

She knew it was the sleep deprivation, but a wave of irrational anger bubbled up inside her. "To plan? You might have spent time training me every day and bedding me every night, but you still haven't taught me any more about magic. Why is that, Raif? Because you like everything to be nice and neat? To keep everything under control, even me?"

His face crumpled for a moment before he had a chance to hide it. But she'd seen the words hit their mark. She knew she should have felt guilty, but she was too exhausted.

"Fae powers are taxing, Liss. You're already working yourself to exhaustion, I didn't want to add to that."

"That wasn't for you to decide. I know my limits." Limits she'd taught herself from hours of training in the tunnels. Alone.

Raif put the box down and rested a hand on her arm, but she shook him away. "Do you? Have you seen the shadows under your eyes? Have you noticed how our training sessions are getting shorter and shorter?"

She had noticed. Both of those things. Although the latter had usually ended because they'd been distracted in other ways—although maybe he'd been doing that on purpose.

Anger shoved the guilt further and further down. Zylah

twisted her fingers into her apron. "I see; lure me to bed in the hopes that I'll fall asleep. So that's what we've really been doing every night. Damage control."

"I don't want to fight with you, I—" His voice caught and he pulled her close, wrapped his arms around her waist. "I care about you a lot, Liss. I didn't want to push you. To do anything."

Cocooned in his embrace, she instantly regretted her words. Seven gods, what was she thinking? She needed to sleep. But Arnir's representatives were coming to check on the sun lilies today. That was probably why Raif had shown up.

She took his hand and led him behind the waterfall, out of earshot of any patrons wandering in. She ran a hand over her hair and realised her braid was a mess. She paced, focusing on the feeling of fixing her hair as she thought about what she wanted to say. Water cascaded down beyond them, the air heavy with the smell of wet rock.

Raif leant back against the railing watching her, his walls already back in place. *I care about you a lot.* She cared for him too. More than she'd wanted to admit to herself. But today was the most vulnerable he'd been with her since the night with the Black Veil.

"Every time I close my eyes, I see them. Mala. The members of the Black Veil." It wasn't all she saw. Memories of Jesper still lingered.

Raif took a step closer. "They all knew what they were getting into, Liss. Mala included." He rested his hands over hers where she was finishing her braid, took the hair fastening from

318

her fingers and fixed it around the end for her.

His gaze slid to hers. *I care about you a lot.* She knew it was a front. The humour, the insufferable ways. But right now, none of that was what she needed. She needed to know things were going to be okay.

"I'm sorry for what I said before." She looked up at him, his eyes still fixed on hers as he wrapped her braid around his hand and tugged gently, pulling her close to him.

Raif's arm slid around her waist, pressing her to him again. It was as if he didn't want to let her go today, and she wondered if that was his way of letting her in. "It doesn't matter," he said quietly, his gaze dropping to her lips. He held her close, so she had to tilt her head back to look up at him. He was waiting, she thought, waiting for her to decide what she wanted.

She reached a hand up to his chest and swallowed. Her throat felt like sandpaper. "Back in Dalstead, with the prince," she began.

"You don't owe me an explanation," he murmured.

"No, I want you to know." Zylah felt his heartbeat beneath her hand, firm and steady. Her brow pinched together as she searched for the right words, for where to begin.

Someone cleared their throat behind them and Zylah instinctively took a step back.

"Liss." It was Jilah. "Arnir's men are here," the old man said, scratching at his neck and looking anywhere but at the two of them.

She nodded, not trusting her voice just yet. Raif took her

hand and they followed Jilah into the second dome, the heat washing over them the moment they entered. Zylah just about managed to explain the flowering cycle of the sun lilies to Arnir's men without slurring any of her words, but the heat was unbearable. They seemed satisfied with the progress, happy to take a good report back to Arnir.

Before Jilah left to see the men out, she heard Raif tell the old man he'd be taking her home for the day. She didn't have it in her to argue; she'd already sat down on the stone ledge to stop herself from swaying on her feet.

Raif knelt in front of her. "Do I need to carry you back?" A smile pushed at his dimple, his hands resting on her knees.

Zylah huffed a laugh. "No." She pushed to her feet, reaching for his arm as she swayed a little. "Get me to the grotto and I'll evanesce us."

Raif did as she asked, and the moment they were safely inside, out of sight from prying eyes, Zylah evanesced them back to the tavern.

Raif looked around them, his arms still around her. "I thought you'd take us back to my place."

Shit. She'd been too tired to think about where they were going. She'd never brought him back here. Something about it had never felt right. It was Holt's place, not hers. And it had always been her safe place. But Raif was her safe place, too. Since the night they got the contract. She shrugged off her clothes, discarding pieces on the floor as she made her way to her bed. Raif may have been holding back these last few weeks, but so had she.

As if he sensed her unease, Raif picked up the worn map she kept beside her bed. "Marking out where all the best plants grow?" he asked, his mouth quirking as he held back a smile.

He knew she wanted to see the world. She'd talked about it often enough. But there was more to it.

"I want to find out where I came from. If I have any family out there." Zylah climbed into bed in nothing but her underwear, sinking into the pillow and not even bothering to pull the sheet up over her. Raif knelt beside her, lifting the sheet over her shoulders and brushing her hair out of her eyes.

"Whatever you want," he said softly. "Whatever you need. I'll make it happen." He pressed a kiss to her forehead and began to move away from the bed, but she caught his hand.

"Stay with me?" She didn't know how bad her dreams would be or even if she was too tired to dream, but she knew she didn't want to be alone when she woke up.

Raif smiled. He kicked off his boots and slipped under the sheet beside her, sitting back against the headboard for her to rest against him. His thumb stroked her shoulder, his other hand finding hers and threading their fingers together.

I care about you a lot. She thought of the way his voice had caught when he'd said it, as if he'd started to say something else.

Whatever you want. Whatever you need. Being with him made her forget everything else. Forget that Arnir was hunting her, that they were plotting to kill him. He made her feel safe, loved, even if it wasn't that kind of love, not yet.

Zylah rested her head against his chest, but she couldn't

close her eyes. As if he'd sensed her unease, Raif launched into a quiet explanation of how training at the other safe houses had been going, the tasks he'd been taking on each day whilst she was at work.

Dimly, in the back of her mind, she realised he was meant to be doing exactly that right now, instead of sitting here with her. A smile tugged at her lips. She let every worry fall away from her as she listened to Raif, murmuring quiet questions every now and then.

He might not have let his guard down entirely, but he was trying. And lying beside him, just listening to him talk about his work, she could almost pretend that he wasn't talking about preparing for the uprising. She could almost pretend they weren't plotting to kill the king.

Almost.

29

Two weeks passed, with less time spent in the tunnels. Zylah still went every day because it was the only thing that could burn off the unease that had settled into her bones, even for a short while. But she slept beside Raif every night. Or rather, he slept beside her. Some nights they would stay at the safe house, sometimes he would come and find her at the tavern after his meetings, the same weariness Zylah felt in her bones reflected in his eyes whenever he arrived.

She had played over the plan a thousand times in her thoughts, but she couldn't shake the feeling that something was going to go terribly wrong. That Arnir would recognise her.

As if he could sense her discomfort, Raif had squeezed her hand as they'd walked to the safe house on the first day of the festival, the city bristling with excitement. Vendors had arrived from across Astaria to set up along every street in Virian for the week, many selling flower crowns and corsages, and citizens had already begun wearing theirs to celebrate. None were as beautiful as the Bloom florist's, and Zylah could already pick out which crowns in a crowd were his from their intricacy.

She found herself staring into Saphi and Rose's bedroom mirror, questioning the outfit Saphi had picked out for her. The first night of the festival was *their* night, Saphi had told her. The night the Fae celebrated for themselves, and the dress code was far less formal than the event at the end of the week when Arnir would be in attendance.

Less formal was putting it lightly. Zylah turned to inspect the scrap of fabric Saphi had called a dress, a gold so pale it reminded Zylah of the evening sun through the wheat fields of Eldham, but with something spun into the fabric to make it shimmer ever so slightly. The neckline was almost as low as the blue dress, folds of fabric draping from fine shoulder straps to fit snugly over every inch of her. It ended mid-thigh, and no matter how Zylah tried to adjust it in the mirror, there was no disguising how short it was.

"You're sure this is appropriate?" Zylah called out to Saphi in the bathroom.

She knelt down to fasten the sandals Saphi had given her. Zylah had accepted a pair with a small heel as a compromise at Saphi's insistence. As she fastened the golden ribbons around her calves, she made a silent prayer to the gods that she wouldn't fall over in them.

She'd almost backed out of going to the party that evening. They were only five days away from the attack on Arnir. Five days until all of this was over, and Zylah could live her life with the certainty that she wasn't going to be followed. *Hunted*. She hadn't broached the subject of her leaving with Raif yet, and a selfish part of her wondered if he might go with her.

"Aren't they wonderful?" Saphi asked, stepping out of the bathroom. "They're Fae made. All the best things are," she said with a wink. She wore a dress a few shades darker than Zylah's, amber coloured, just like her eyes, her jewellery gold to match. The dress crossed tightly at the breasts to wrap around her neck and was as short and tight fitting as Zylah's. Gold cuffs adorned her arms, and she'd added some length to her hair, longer curls reaching down to her ears. She'd been beautiful before and was now even more so. "You sure you won't let me change your hair colour, turn you back to natural for the night?"

If Zylah hadn't been so nervous, she might have laughed.

"No hood and no eyeglasses. My eye colour is as natural as I'm willing to go." She turned back to the mirror, running a hand across the gold ribbons Saphi had added amongst the curls of brown. Her own violet eyes looked back at her, and she'd opted for no jewellery.

The dress and the ribbons were enough, and she had no doubt she'd be wearing a flower crown by the time the night was through.

Saphi picked up a book from the bed and waved it at Zylah. "*Lanaros*. Doing some homework?" She leafed through the pages. "This is about Holt's line."

Zylah frowned. "It is? I had no idea. It says nothing of him or his sister."

Saphi flicked to the back. "Lanaros is his kingdom. This was made after his parents' coronation."

"They were mates, Holt said."

"They were." Saphi handed back the book.

"Does Holt… did he…"

"Does he have someone?"

Zylah nodded. It was none of her business, but the words had slipped out.

"Holt was in love once before I met him. All I know is that she wanted children and he didn't, and she left him and met someone else." Saphi swiped at an invisible crumb on the bed linen.

"That must have been difficult for him."

The Fae looked over her shoulder, a sad smile on her lips. "Yes."

Rose stepped into the bedroom, fiddling with a gold bracelet at her wrist. "We're going to be late." Even though her face was scrunched in concentration, she looked stunning. Her blade leg was a shade darker than the red dress that fell just below her knees, and Zylah wondered if Saphi had insisted on the change.

Saphi was beside her in two strides, easing Rose's fingers away to fasten the bracelet for her. "We'll be there at precisely the right time." She tucked a wayward curl behind Rose's ear, adjusting the strap at her shoulder. She'd styled Rose's hair in a braided crown, ruby ribbons streaked through it, and fine

326

curls cascading around her face. Their matching gold jewellery shimmered in the orblights, and Zylah could have sworn she saw a flicker of unease cross Rose's face for a moment before she looked up to meet Saphi's gaze with a smile.

Zylah cleared her throat. "Your gifts." She picked up two small bundles of fabric from the bed, blue ribbon binding both of them, and handed one to each of the Fae.

Rose opened hers first and, with a pinched brow, inspected the four balls she held. "Well, thank you, Liss."

"They're for the bath. You put them in warm water and petals come out." Zylah blushed as she explained it. She'd seen the bottles lining the wall of the bath next door, and when she'd asked Saphi about them, the Fae had told her it was Rose's favourite way to unwind.

Rose's face brightened. "Oh. Thank you." She sniffed at the spheres—each one was a different combination of fragrances and dried flowers, and Zylah had spent weeks collecting the ingredients.

Saphi had already opened her gift and was dabbing some of it on her wrists, a broad grin across her face as she made an excited squeal. "You made these, didn't you?" The vanilla and cinnamon perfume filled the space between them.

Zylah felt her blush grow. "I did. You always wear the vanilla, I thought you might like a small variation now and then."

"It's perfect. They're wonderful gifts, aren't they, Rose?"

Rose wrapped her gift back up in the fabric with a frown, fastening the ribbon around it carefully. "Yes. Thank you."

"You're already wearing ours." Saphi spun Zylah around to face the mirror again.

The Fae pointed at their reflection with a grin. "The dress is from me, and the shoes are from Rose. Yours. To keep." She put up a hand to stop Zylah from saying anything. "Now, let's go, before Rose shoves us out the door."

Zylah just had a moment to scoop up the golden stringed pouch to match her dress before Saphi ushered her out of the bedroom.

Raif was waiting for them in the reception area, his stare intense as Zylah stepped off the staircase ahead of Rose and Saphi. He wore a black suit, and Zylah smiled as she noticed the pale gold peeking out from beneath his jacket. He'd worn a shirt to match her dress, and she'd no doubt it was Saphi's gift to him.

Zylah watched the way Raif took her in, his hand finding hers and spinning her around.

"This dress," he said, bringing her hand up to his chest. "Is a new favourite." He pressed a kiss to her knuckles, wrapping an arm around her as they stepped out into the night. Despite the warm air, Zylah's nerves from earlier sent a chill dancing along her bare arms and she leaned into Raif's warmth.

Kopi darted down to her shoulder, rustling his feathers for a moment before flying off ahead of them. Saphi launched into an explanation of how good the gardens looked; Jilah hadn't allowed Zylah to leave the dome to see it ahead of the party, but Saphi had been part of the team to set everything up, and now she could barely contain her elation as she told them where the best spots were going to be. But Zylah wasn't really listening. Instead, she tried to commit the moment to memory, walking across the river in the warm night air, surrounded by friends. She knew it was the last time she'd feel part of something for a long while, and that after she left Virian, the days ahead would be lonely. But they would all still be in Virian when she returned. She knew that.

She looked up at Raif and he smiled down at her, and for a moment, she wanted to ask him not to go ahead with everything, to leave with her tonight. But she couldn't find the words.

They reached the gardens, taking the goods entrance into the first dome. Zylah felt the new wards pressing at her skin the moment she stepped through them. Saphi had told her to expect them; only Fae could pass through, and to anyone else, the botanical gardens would appear closed tonight, as they always were at this hour.

Orblights were scattered amongst the trees and along the pathways, illuminating the dome in a soft golden glow and Zylah marvelled at the sight, just as Saphi let out an excited squeal. "You're all going to love it!"

"You both go on ahead," Zylah said, tugging gently at Raif's hand. "I'd like to give Raif his gift first before we go in."

Saphi raised an eyebrow. "I'll bet you would."

Rose elbowed her gently in the ribs. "What have I said about innuendos about my brother when I'm in earshot?"

"We'll be right behind you," Raif said with his most convincing smile.

Zylah led him up the ramp towards the back of the waterfall, and he followed silently, his hand warm around hers. She turned to face him and took a deep breath.

He was holding a narrow black box, tied with a black velvet ribbon. "Ladies first," he said, dimples on full display as he waited.

Zylah bit her lip as she looked up at him, wondering if her gift for him was entirely off the mark. She said nothing of it; instead, she reached up to place a soft kiss on Raif's lips. "Thank you." He'd tied his hair back for the evening, and Zylah traced a hand along his jaw as she wrestled with her emotions.

She turned her attention to the box. The ribbon slipped away easily, and Zylah hoped the tremble in her fingers didn't show as she opened the lid. Nestled on a bed of black velvet sat a delicate silver necklace with a small circular stone in the centre, the same shade of blue as Raif's eyes. *Gods above.* It looked like a sapphire, a gemstone she had only ever seen once before in the prince's quarters. She frowned at the memory.

"You don't like it?" Raif asked, his voice quiet with disappointment.

Zylah shook her head. "I love it, it's just… This is an expensive gift."

"Fit for a goddess," Raif said, one corner of his mouth twitching. "May I?"

Zylah nodded, and he gently eased the necklace from the box and stood behind her to fasten it. She lifted her hair for him to pass the necklace around her neck, his fingers tracing along her shoulders and sending a shiver down her spine. He pressed a kiss to her skin before he let her hair fall back into place. Zylah reached a hand to the stone as she turned to look up at him; it sat right at the base of her throat, the chain a perfect fit.

A week from today, she'd be several days on her way away from Virian. Away from Raif. "It's beautiful. Thank you." Her eyes stung, and she looked away and cleared her throat, gesturing to the waterfall. "My gift is going to seem a bit ridiculous now, I think."

"Ridiculous is never a word I would use to describe you." His playful tone was back, the one Zylah had become so accustomed to, the one she now recognised he used to put her at ease.

Zylah led him down the path that opened up in front of the waterfall, to the small pond at its base. The lily pads had begun to flower, and she admired the way the white flowers turned golden in the orblights, the water glittering in ripples across the pond. She rubbed a sweaty palm against her thigh before pointing. "There."

A small tree sat beside the pond; it stood barely to her waist, thick green leaves hanging from trained branches, the edges already tipped in small violet buds. It had taken weeks to get it looking presentable, although Zylah was disappointed it hadn't flowered yet. She'd wanted it to be perfect. "It's a cousin of the alyssina flower," she began, her nerves getting the better of her. "The flowers are small but plentiful, and it usually flowers for most of summer, but this one is a little late to bloom.

You can see it from above the waterfall, but I thought it would be easier to show you from here. I wasn't sure it was going to survive the transport; half the leaves were gone when it arrived, but—".

"It's perfect." Raif wrapped his arms around her, pressing a kiss to the nape of her neck as he held her back tightly against his chest.

She tilted her head to look at him. "You're sure? It's not, I mean… it's a tree, I know it's not a normal gift, but I—"

"I love it."

"Really?"

"I do. But…"

"What is it?" She turned to look up into his eyes.

He played with the necklace. "I hoped tonight might… convince you to stay. I wasn't going to ask you. I don't want to ask you to give up anything for me. But this. The thought of coming here, and seeing this tree grow, without you…" He let out a shaky breath and smoothed a hand across his hair. There had only been one other time she'd seen him this rattled, and she thought back to the night at the Pig's Tail when he'd killed all the Black Veil members for her.

"Come with me." The words hung in the air between them, and she knew it was a mistake to ask the moment she'd spoken them.

Raif took her hand, his thumb stroking her knuckles. "Liss, I can't. You know that." His gaze remained fixed on her knuckles as he spoke, as if he couldn't look her in the eye.

It already felt like goodbye. And she wasn't ready for it. Not yet. Tears pressed at the corners of her eyes, and she willed them not to fall. For so many months her life had been about just surviving. Leaving Virian after Arnir was gone was her gift to herself: life on her own terms.

"For you, it ends with Arnir. For us, Arnir is just the beginning. I can't abandon my friends. My people."

Abandon. Is that what he thought she was doing? Running away? "That's not what—"

"No, that's not what you're doing. I would never think that, Liss. You have no responsibilities, and I do. It's as simple as that." He held a hand against her face, his thumb stroking her cheek and pressed a soft kiss to her lips. "I wish I could go with you." He rested his forehead against hers. "I would love to go with you."

Music drifted from the gardens and Zylah wished, not for the first time, that things were different. That she wasn't Raif's route to Arnir. That it wasn't him that was to be the one to kill the king. That they could just leave and live their lives. Leave all of this behind. But he wouldn't walk away from his responsibilities for her, and she knew he shouldn't have to, no matter how much the selfish part of her wanted him to.

She gently pulled away from him and took his hand as she looked into his eyes. "Let's go and enjoy the party." It was a question, more than anything. There was no compromise and enjoying the time they had left together was all they could do.

She wondered if he knew how much she needed these last few days with him to feel normal. With their friends. She wondered if he knew how the decision to leave became harder and harder with each day that passed, and how she questioned why she was leaving at all.

She had to do it. She was of no real use to the uprising, and she was a distraction to Raif. And this was what she'd always wanted, wasn't it? To see the world. To live. To find out where she came from and if she had any family left. But the longer she spent with Raif, the more she questioned whether it was what she truly wanted.

30

They followed the orblights out into the gardens, and Zylah gasped at the sight. Saphi was right; the gardens had been completely transformed.

Every tree was strung with lights, every pathway lined with orblights. There were faeries everywhere. Some had antlers, some had scaled faces. Others had delicate wings like Mala's. They stood around upturned barrels, sat at benches, some danced. Zylah tried her hardest not to stare, but she'd never seen this many faeries in one place.

Tables overflowed with food, and dancers weaved in and out of the crowd, some with ribbons and flowers, some with bells. Zylah still couldn't see where the music was coming from, but there were lively strings and drums, and a male voice singing about summer love. Joy radiated from every faerie, and it might have been the knowledge that in a matter of days Arnir would be gone, but Zylah couldn't help but wonder if it was simply that they were happy to be there, together. Safe in this little bubble in the heart of the city, if only for one night.

Raif squeezed her hand as they eased through the crowd and Zylah caught sight of Jilah, hand in hand with Niara and Kihlan.

"It looks wonderful, Jilah," Zylah said as they approached. "I wish you'd let me help." She waved a hand at the lights in the trees. It must have taken all day, but she hadn't been allowed to leave the domes, Jilah's orders.

The old Fae shrugged. "And ruin the surprise? I'm not so old that I've forgotten what it feels like to be awed by something." He patted Niara on the head as she looked up at him, the lights dancing in her eyes. "Alwen was looking for you, Raif." He inclined his head towards a table where a few faeries were gathered.

Raif looked down at Zylah as if he was reluctant to go. She'd hoped that the evening would be free of business matters, but she wouldn't keep Raif from his duties. "Go," she said, with a gentle squeeze to his hand.

He pressed a kiss to her forehead and said his goodbyes to Jilah and the children. A faerie with antlers had walked up to talk with Jilah, and the children had run off into the party, so Zylah left the old Fae to his friend and set off to explore the food tables.

She toyed with her necklace as she inspected the spread before her. Cheeses, meats, nuts, berries; every space was filled with food. And as appetising as it looked, Zylah's stomach had other plans. She willed the unease to settle as she hovered a hand over some grapes, debating whether she'd be able to keep them down for the night.

"Don't believe what you've read about the food," a male voice said beside her.

Zylah smiled and looked up to meet Holt's gaze. "Oh?"

"It's harmless," he said, biting into a brin fruit. He wore a notched black jacket, with fine buttons at the front over fitted black trousers, and under one arm he held a long bundle of cloth. "The wine, on the other hand, that truly will have you dancing the night away. It can make you forget who you are, for a while." He discarded the brin core in a bucket beside the table and smoothed down the front of his jacket. Gold threads caught the orblights, and Zylah could make out some of the fine stitching down the front, a little at the cuffs. Understated, but elegant. If she hadn't already known he was a prince, she'd have wondered at that moment if he was one.

Perhaps it was something he wanted to forget. Zylah understood what that was like. "That doesn't sound like a bad thing."

Holt frowned. "No. It doesn't." His eyes lowered to her necklace for a moment, and then he surveyed the table of food intently.

"I'm sorry," Zylah said quietly. She wrapped a hand around an arm, chewing her bottom lip.

"For what?"

"For bringing Raif to the tavern. It's your home and I—" She glanced up to see him frowning, but he didn't meet her gaze.

"Who you take to your bed is no concern of mine." The words were cold, emotionless. He dragged a hand through his hair and sighed, finally glancing down at her. "I'm glad you feel at home here, Zylah."

She willed her cheeks not to flush. It shouldn't have mattered. She knew he didn't see her that way, and guilt washed over her for a brief moment. She rested a hand against the necklace Raif had given her, staring at the food before them. "Why did you send Raif to the gardens that day to look for me?"

"Raif has always had a good relationship with Jilah, it seemed like a logical choice."

Because she was too much trouble. He'd said as much before they'd even entered Virian. She toyed with the necklace again, looking for Raif amongst the crowd. *I wish I could go with you.* She knew it was going to be harder to leave than she'd let herself acknowledge.

She followed Holt's gaze to a trio of dancers, flower crowns in their hair and ribbons in their hands, spiralling through the party-goers. One rang a bell in time to the beat of the music, and Zylah cleared her throat. "I hear it's customary to give gifts tonight." She reached inside her little pouch for a small box and handed it to him.

He looked at her, surprise lighting up his eyes for a moment before the expression faded, and not for the first time that night, Zylah felt embarrassed by her choice of gift.

Words poured out of her to fill the silence, eager to smooth over whatever crack she had just made between them. "I made a bracelet for Kara once. It's stupid, really. I just wanted to say thank you. For being my friend. For everything." Holt lifted the lid as she spoke. Inside sat coils of black braided leather with a bell, just a small silver sphere nestled amongst the braids. She didn't expect he'd wear it, but he took it right out of the box and wrapped it around his wrist. Zylah's fingers twitched with the urge to fasten it for him, but she watched as he did it himself, positioning it exactly how he wanted, the bell at the centre of his wrist when his palm faced up. "I made the leather braid," she added, "but I had help with the bell. I had a pin added to stop the pellet, since, you know, rule number six. *No bells.*"

Holt's mouth twitched. "Technically, that was rule number five." His fingers curled as he looked at the gift for a moment, then his eyes met hers, his expression soft.

"Oh?"

"Rule number three wasn't really a rule, just a question."

Tell me what you want from me, was what she'd said to him as she'd held up three fingers back in his cabin. "I didn't realise you were paying such close attention."

Holt smiled, inclining his head to the bracelet. "Thank you, Zylah." For a moment she thought he was going to say something else, but he said only, "Your turn," and handed her the bundle of cloth he'd been carrying.

Zylah carefully unrolled the fabric, revealing the polished metal beneath. She looked up at Holt, barely able to contain the smile that stretched across her face, and he smiled back. It was a short sword; vines and leaves carved into the blade and continuing around the gilded hilt, set with a single violet stone in the centre.

339

Her very own sword. Zylah could barely contain her excitement. She took a few steps back, holding the weapon in one hand to test the weight. It was much lighter than a training sword, just as he had said it would be. She sliced once through the air; it felt perfect in her hand. "Holt, this is…" She swiped again, spinning the blade to the hilt to test how easily she could use it for blunt strikes.

"I thought you might like knowing you had an adequate weapon to defend yourself on your travels." He watched her as she examined the blade, arms folded across his chest.

She threw one arm around him and gave him a hug, his comforting scent washing over her as she willed herself not to cry. "Thank you," she whispered.

Holt hesitated for a moment before unfolding his arms to hug her back, and it felt like another goodbye as he leaned his head against hers. Everything she had now was because of him. Everything.

"My brother would never believe I could use a real sword," Zylah said against his jacket.

Holt eased her out of his embrace and looked down at her. "Why don't you visit him before you go? I'll take you to him, if you'd like."

Zylah shook her head, looking at the sword again. "I can't do anything that might jeopardise his position with Arnir. Zack's worked so hard for it."

"Your brother is the King's Blade?"

"You know my brother?" Zylah's heart raced, and a thousand questions filled her thoughts.

Holt nodded, then picked up the fabric where Zylah had dropped it on the floor. "He's usually the one to deliver requests from Arnir when Marcus is... unavailable." He motioned for Zylah to hand him the sword.

"Requests?"

Holt slowly wrapped the blade, taking care to cover every part of it in the cloth. "Arnir knows of me as a bounty hunter, remember."

Of course. That was likely how he'd found her the first time they'd met. It was strange to think her brother had met Holt before she had, that they had been connected somehow without ever knowing each other. And how if she'd never taken Kara's shift, she'd never have met him at all. "Is he... is he well?"

"Yes. He's in good health, Zylah."

She tilted her head back to look at the sky. Despite the lights in the gardens, the stars were bright, and Zylah could easily pick out familiar constellations. "It was Zack who first taught me about the gods. How they were born of storms and starlight. He would tell me stories on the nights he knew it bothered me most that I had no idea where I'd come from." She wrapped her arms around herself. "As if hearing where the gods had come from would be a comfort."

"And was it?"

She looked up at him, his gaze fixed on the stars. "Sometimes."

Holt's hands were empty, but he looked down as if he'd felt her watching him. "It's at the tavern, I didn't think you'd want

341

to hold it for the rest of the night. There's a scabbard and belt to go with it."

"I don't know how to thank you."

"You already did." He waved his hand to the bracelet she'd given him. Before she had a chance to reply, an arm came around her shoulders, and Raif's mint and lemongrass scent filled her senses.

"My two favourite people." Raif clapped Holt on the back, and Zylah wondered if he'd had some of the wine.

Holt laughed. "Don't let Rose hear you say that."

"Hear you say what?" Rose asked as she made her way over to them.

"That we need to excuse ourselves for a moment to discuss business," Raif said with a wink in Zylah's direction.

"Good to see you, Rose," Holt just had time to say, before Raif ushered him away, leaving Zylah standing alone beside her. Zylah watched the two males leave, Raif roaring at something Holt had said.

"It isn't right, you know," Rose said quietly beside her. "To be with one of them when you want the other."

Zylah wrapped her arms around herself. "It's none of your business." Guilt prickled beneath her skin as she fought for an explanation. Holt was her friend. He'd made that perfectly clear. Raif was good and kind. And she knew how she felt about him. Had known it for a while now, and it made it all the more difficult to leave. But she'd been afraid—afraid after what happened with Jesper. The running. Not knowing if she could stop. That if she let herself love something—someone—

it would be taken away from her, as punishment for what she'd done.

"I know what it's like to have someone love you so much and to not return it." Rose placed a hand on Zylah's arm. "To hate yourself for not returning it."

"That's not—I don't—"

"There you are!" It was Saphi. Zylah spotted Asha amongst the crowd and didn't want to miss another opportunity to speak with him; there was no use trying to convince Rose of her feelings for Raif. Besides, that was a conversation she needed to have with him before she left. She just hadn't decided yet if it was kinder not to.

Saphi pressed a finger to Zylah's necklace. "Beautiful, isn't it Rose?"

Rose said nothing.

"Raif gave it to me," Zylah said.

Saphi smiled, tucking a piece of hair behind Zylah's ear. "We know. He asked us if we thought you'd like it. Come on, let's go and dance."

"I'll be right over. There's someone I'd like to speak to first." Zylah flicked her chin in Asha's direction and Saphi nodded in understanding. It needed no explanation, and without another word, Zylah made her way over to Asha's table. Kopi flew down to her shoulder as she weaved through the crowd. "Hey, buddy," she whispered as he ruffled his feathers. Despite his sharp little claws, he never once scraped her skin. Zylah supposed since he was so tiny, it didn't take much effort for him to stay upright.

"What does Kopi think of the party?" Asha asked as Zylah approached his table.

Zylah gave Kopi a scratch on his head, grateful that the little owl had given her something to talk about. "I think he's wondering when everyone will leave him to his gardens in peace."

"Interesting." Asha turned his attention back to a pair of dancers.

There was so much Zylah wanted to say about Mala. That she was sorry she hadn't made it in time. That she hadn't brought her back to him sooner. That he didn't get to say goodbye. But the words seemed to tie themselves around the tip of her tongue. Nothing she could say would bring Mala back, she knew that.

They watched the dancers; two had strings with tiny orblights on the end that reminded Zylah of sprites when they moved. The dancers were telling a story, she realised, as others joined them, the sprites circling around the newcomers. Saphi had told her the dancers traditionally told tales of Fae history, and that at Arnir's festival it was another way he'd spat on their culture by having dancers tell the human version of events. This year, they'd planned something different, Saphi had promised her.

"I heard the sprites helped you protect Mala," Asha said, breaking their silence. "Did you know they're older than the first Fae?"

Zylah didn't know that. "Is that the story they're telling here?"

"This is the story of how they saved Imala." His voice caught on the word save, and Zylah wanted desperately for him to know she'd done all she could, but even she questioned whether that was the truth of it. She should have tried to evanesce Mala away sooner. Should have risked it.

"They gave Imala her freedom, and this is why we celebrate. This festival is about *our* freedom."

Zylah looked at the Fae around her. Laughing, dancing. Fighting for something. Even being there at the party was an act of rebellion. She didn't belong with them, no matter how much she wanted to; she barely knew her own history.

Asha looked up at Zylah, before inspecting the contents of his glass. "They tell me you're leaving next week."

"I am."

"Why?"

"To see the world. To find out where I came from. To discover where I belong."

The faerie finished the last of his wine. "Mala and I moved around a lot over the years. For most of it, we were alone, and I was content. But Mala said it was time to stop running. To stop searching for something that was right in front of us the whole time, even if it was broken, that it was up to us to help fix it." He toyed with Mala's bracelet as he spoke, and then looked up to meet Zylah's gaze. "Here is where you came from. Here is where you belong."

Zylah opened her mouth to speak, but Asha added, "Your work has not gone unnoticed. Don't underestimate how much your actions have contributed to mending what's broken."

She knew he didn't just mean the poultices and the healing,

but all Zylah could see when she closed her eyes were the fragments of Mala's broken wings. "I'm sorry I didn't bring her back in time for you to say goodbye."

"You brought her back to me. That's all that matters."

"There you are." Raif's arm slipped around her waist. "Mind if I borrow Liss, Asha?"

Asha held up a bottle of wine, ready to refill his glass and nodded. "By all means."

"I have a surprise for you," Raif murmured, steering Zylah away.

She looked over her shoulder at Asha, and he raised a full glass in goodbye. "You do?" she asked, looking up at Raif.

He winked. "I know, I know, two presents in one night. I know what you're thinking, you could get used to this level of worship, right?" He placed a flower crown on her head. "This is for you. It's not the surprise, I just thought you'd like to have one."

Zylah smiled as she reached a hand up to the soft petals, her eyes meeting with Holt's for a moment as he stood talking with Rose and Saphi. Emotion flickered across his face before he shut it down, raised his glass and turned his attention back to his friends.

Raif led her to the grotto, to the cut-out in the rock overlooking the water. Food and wine were laid out on a small square of cloth. "Fae parties can get a little... out of hand." He led her to one side of the window, gesturing for her to sit. "I thought you might like a little quiet."

"Raif, this is... Thank you."

She worried if she spoke, tears might follow.

He handed her a plate of food, launching into an explanation of what Rose and Saphi had gifted him, the orblights reflecting off the pond and lighting up one half of his face.

In just a few days, Arnir would be dead. And her life could start over; for Mala, and for all the others who had had their life cut short. But maybe starting over was always meant to happen in Virian. She'd have her freedom. A family of sorts. Friends who could help her find out about where she came from. And she could help. Make a difference in the days ahead. Maybe Asha was right.

"Liss?" Raif rested a hand on her knee. His skin was warm, and he traced circles with his thumb out of habit.

Zylah set aside her food and took the wine glass Raif handed her. "Sorry, I… was just enjoying listening to you talk."

"Now, now, you know how easy it is to fluff my ego." He touched his glass to hers, one dimple on display in the glow of the orblights.

Zylah reached for the flower crown, inspecting the flowers. Cream roses with small gold flowers threaded between them, to match her dress. She met Raif's gaze. "When we first met, I wasn't sure about you."

He pressed a hand to his heart in mock offence. "What's not to be sure about?"

"But Saphi told me you had a good heart. And she was right. You do." She took a deep breath, her confession on the tip of her tongue.

Raif looked out across the water. "You asked me once if my

magic hurt me. The truth is, the cost is more than I like to admit." He sighed deeply. "I feel it take something from me every time I use it. Like a little piece of me is chipped away. Before I met you, I'd begun to wonder if there was anything left." He turned away from the water so that his whole face was in shadow, and it snatched Zylah's breath away to hear that he'd ever thought that about himself.

She reached up for his face, and he turned to look at her, his eyes dipping to her mouth and back up again. She'd never given much thought to what his life must have been like; he was always so reluctant to talk about the past. And now she understood why. Her hands tangled in his hair as she pressed a kiss to his lips, leaning into him until his lips parted for her and their kiss deepened.

"You are good, Raif. In here. No magic will ever change that." Zylah rested a hand against his chest, as Raif lifted her closer to him. She kissed him again, her tongue sweeping along his, and he pulled her even closer, bringing her knees up around his waist and kissing her until they were breathless.

He released his grip and took her hand, leading her deeper into the grotto.

"This dress has been taunting me all night," he said, kissing her shoulder.

He lifted her again, one hand bracing against the wall behind them, one hand pinning her to the hard length of him. Zylah arched back, just a little. Just enough to make him suck in a breath through his teeth.

"I apologise on behalf of the dress," she murmured against

his lips, fighting back a smile, and then gasping into his mouth as his fingers ran along the top of her underwear. Heat bloomed between her legs and she arched further into his touch.

"Have I told you how much this drives me crazy?" Raif asked, tracing kisses down her chest.

"What?" Zylah asked, as all her thoughts and words seemed to eddy away from her.

"The scent of you when you're turned on."

Zylah stilled in his arms. "What?"

Raif laughed against her skin, his fingers still teasing, stroking, dipping and pulling back up again across her underwear. "Sometimes I think you forget you're Fae. Fae have exceptional senses. We can scent arousal, and your scent…" His fingers dipped beneath the fabric and found their mark, his mouth capturing Zylah's moan.

"That explains a lot," Zylah whispered, her breaths ragged and broken as Raif moved his fingers in circles. She didn't want to wait, she needed to feel him, and her hands reached between them for the belt of his trousers.

He caught her hand gently, pausing to look into her eyes. "I'll never forgive myself if I don't ask," he said quietly.

"Ask what?" Zylah stilled at the question.

He rested his forehead against hers, his chest rising and falling with his heavy breathing. "Stay. Just for a little while longer."

Here is where you belong. A tear rolled down Zylah's cheek, and Raif kissed it away. She couldn't speak, or she knew more tears would come, so she nodded. Raif eased into her then, his lips crashing against hers as he moved slowly at first, pressing her back against the rock.

Then his movements matched his kisses, and Zylah moved with him, focusing on nothing but the feeling of him, his hands around her, his lips against hers.

Just a little while longer.

31

Zylah left the party alone. Raif had offered to walk her back, but she knew he had more people to meet with, and all she wanted was her bed, so she'd told him to stay. She'd evanesced to the tavern out of habit, peeled out of her party clothes and slid into bed, exhausted. Raif's scent clung to the sheets, and with a blush, she realised Holt would have been able to detect it too.

She awoke once in the night to Holt's scent in the air, her bed dipping as he sat beside her. It was his scent, mixed with venti lilies, and she'd thought of the dancers he'd been watching earlier. She'd listened to his quiet breathing in the dark— was that avenberry liquor she could smell?

It isn't right, you know. Rose's accusation had played on repeat in her thoughts.

Holt didn't move. She thought he might have had his head in his hands, but she'd kept her head to the pillow.

She'd been too tired to do anything but focus on Holt's

steady breaths until sleep claimed her.

Zylah woke before Holt did. She took a moment to study his face, head resting on his arm as he lay on his back on the lounger. How did he sleep like that without waking up with a numb arm? She stifled a laugh. His messy hair was even messier with sleep, his jaw peppered with stubble. His lips were slightly parted, and his eyes fluttered as if he were dreaming. He hadn't even removed his jacket.

She opened the window for Kopi, warm air hitting her at once and padded to the bathroom to get ready for work. She'd need to look for a new place to stay. She could stay with Raif, but she preferred the idea of having her own place—even if just to give them space away from Rose. She dressed and towel-dried her hair, working her way through her thoughts.

When she came out of the bathroom, Holt was up, his jacket on the back of a chair, his hair a little smoother than it had been moments before. He held a mug of tea in his hand as he looked up at her, and not for the first time, she wished she could read his expression.

Zylah cleared her throat. "How was your evening?"

"Fine."

"Good." She sat at the dresser and brushed out her hair, glancing back at him in the mirror. Something was off, but she didn't know what.

"May I?" Holt was behind her, waving a hand at her hair.

"You know how to do it?"

Holt nodded once. Perhaps he was worried about Arnir's arrival; she knew she was. Zylah's brow pinched. "Go ahead."

He separated her hair and braided it slowly with sure, steady movements, his fingers incredibly nimble for someone so big. Kara used to braid her hair. But this… this felt different. She could feel the heat from him, the avenberry liquor and venti lilies from the night before long faded, leaving only his familiar scent. He was careful not to brush his fingers against her neck as he gathered more hair, but each movement was considered… gentle.

"Who taught you to do this?" Zylah asked, watching him in the mirror.

Holt didn't look up from his work, his expression neutral as he said, "I used to braid my sister's hair."

Zylah tried not to flinch. She knew loss, but not that kind. Leaving her family and Kara behind was something entirely different, and she couldn't imagine how it would feel if one of them were… gone. She wanted to put a hand over his, to offer some kind of comfort, but instead, she twisted her fingers over themselves in her lap.

"What are you thinking?" he asked as he reached over her shoulder for a strip of leather, and again Zylah noticed how careful he was not to touch her. She thought back to that day in the cabin. *I won't touch you.*

It was safe here, in their little room. But Arnir would be gone soon, and she could defend herself now. She didn't need Holt's protection anymore, and she shoved down the flicker of guilt that surfaced as she admitted that to herself.

"I saw a beautiful little building near the botanical gardens yesterday with a room for rent. I was thinking it would be nice

353

to have my own place. Make it a home." It wasn't exactly a lie, but she needed a way to broach the topic with him. She was staying, but that would still mean some changes were needed. Like where she lived.

Holt was quiet as he fastened her braid and rested it gently against her back. In the mirror, she could see his brow furrow and his intake of breath.

Pedlars called out their wares to passers-by in the street below, and a man laughed enthusiastically at something.

"I can pin it up for you, if you'd like?" Holt asked.

Zylah snapped her fingers. "Hairdresser!"

"Is that your third guess, Zylah?" Amusement flickered across his face, and Zylah's toes curled over the edge of her stool at the way he said her name.

"No, I was just saying thank you, hairdresser. No pins today, good sir." Zylah stepped away from the dresser and gave him a mock bow before sitting at the table by the window.

Some of the tension seemed to ease out of him. "You'd need two jobs to afford a room near the gardens," he said, taking his seat opposite her.

Zylah picked at the canna cake he'd left for her. "You only have one job and you can afford this place."

She waved a hand at the room. It was far from palatial, but she had a feeling that was more to do with his taste than his money.

Holt leaned back in his chair, arms folded across his chest. The honey-coloured flecks in his eyes were luminescent in the morning sun. "That's because I own the tavern."

Zylah almost choked on a crumb. "The Pedlar's Charm. *You're* the pedlar?"

The corner of Holt's mouth twitched. "Is *that* your third guess?"

"No. So Arran, is he…"

"He's an old friend. Besides, you know what I do. You've seen it first-hand." He held her stare as he said it, as if he were waiting for her judgement. He was talking about the bodies in the tunnels. The members of the Black Veil.

Zylah looked out of the window. It was a clear day, and from here, she could see the purple and gold banners across buildings, ribbons hanging across the streets. If it hadn't been for Arnir's arrival, she'd have thought it a wonder to behold. Instead, the decorations were a constant reminder of what was coming, of what needed to be done. She turned back to meet his eyes. "I know what you do, but I don't know why."

Holt shrugged. "Does a baker know why he bakes?"

"You tell me. You seem pretty good at making canna cakes." She shoved another piece into her mouth, wiping the crumbs off her hands.

Holt looked across the rooftops, taking in the sights of the city, Zylah presumed. "My sister taught me."

"What was she like?" It was the first time she'd acknowledged that she knew his sister was gone, that he hadn't been the one to tell her. But she thought he might like to speak of Adina, for her to be more than just a memory for a moment.

A muscle feathered in his jaw, and Zylah wondered if he would reply. "She was kind. She would do anything for

355

anyone. She hated violence." He recited the words as if he'd repeated them to himself many times, and Zylah knew why. She could see it in the pinch of his brow, the slope of his mouth. He had to be violent, likely had had to be violent more times than she could imagine for Marcus, for the uprising. All with the knowledge that his sister would disapprove.

"Why did you kill those members of the Black Veil?" Maybe it wasn't her place to ask. But they were friends. And if he was in trouble, she wanted to help.

His eyes met hers. "They weren't Black Veil."

Interesting. They'd been wearing the uniform of the Black Veil. "But you killed them?"

He wiped some crumbs off the table, depositing them on his empty plate. "I twilight as a bounty hunter, it isn't difficult to come across an array of assholes who deserve a worse fate than I gave them for what they'd done to others."

"Why didn't you tell me that before? And why didn't you tell me you're a prince?" For some reason, she felt a flash of anger, adrenaline spiking through her veins. She had no right to be angry, not with him.

Something flickered across his face, but he quickly shut it down. "Would it have changed anything?"

It was Zylah's turn to look away. It wouldn't have, but she pushed aside the weight of that question. The lump in her back ached again, and she made a mental note to ask Saphi about it the following week. Maybe she might know someone who could help remove it.

"You're staying?" Holt asked when she didn't reply.

356

Zylah turned her attention from the window, watching the way he ran a thumb over the bracelet she'd given him. "I am."

He met her gaze and drew in a breath. "I didn't want it to be Raif. To be the one to kill Arnir."

"Because you wanted it to be you?" Her anger flared again, and this time Zylah felt the flush in her chest.

Holt said nothing.

"Why does everyone else's safety matter above your own?"

He looked away, still toying with the bracelet. "Because I have nothing to lose."

"Do you truly believe that?"

Kopi flew in through the open window, landing on the table between them. Zylah stroked his head in greeting and he ruffled his feathers.

Holt rested his hands on the edge of the table, his attention on Kopi. "Raif is confident Marcus will be less inclined to interfere this way."

"So it's Marcus you're worried about?" Guards marched their morning route on the street below, and Zylah wondered whether Arnir had anything on Marcus at all, whether the Fae was just, as Saphi had said, playing a long game. Going along with the king's demands. Biding his time.

Holt followed the guards until they were out of sight. "Marcus is always a concern."

Zylah hated that she'd been right. That they were getting Arnir out of the way only to have another tyrant take his place. "What's the plan, once Arnir is dead?"

"This has taken years to prepare, Zylah. Every puzzle piece

affects another." He reached out for Kopi, just as the little owl shuffled towards him.

The dread that she'd managed to shove down had begun to resurface. "That wasn't an answer. Do the others know what you do for Marcus? The extent of your debt?"

"No."

"Is it… is it because of your parents?"

Holt leaned back in his chair. "My parents? No. I wasn't there when Marcus took their lives. But my sister. He promised me he'd keep her safe." He looked out of the window, across the city, as if he were looking at a memory. "He saved her so that I would owe him. And then he left her to die."

Zylah pressed a hand to her stomach, wrestling with her nausea. A quiet sense of foreboding wrapped around her heart. She didn't like any of this. Not one bit. Marcus was trouble, and not even his own children were enough to change him. "That's why saving Raif and Rose was so important to you." Her voice was quiet as she spoke, almost a whisper as she pieced together everything Holt had done for his friends.

"Yes."

A life for a life. The bastard. And they were as good as handing Marcus the throne. Zylah would spend the rest of her life hiding from Arnir if it meant ridding this world of Marcus. If she ever got the chance, she was going to kill Marcus herself. For Holt and Adina. For Raif and Rose.

She thought through everything Marcus had said the night she'd met him, everything he'd done. "Back in the tunnels— with Marcus. He mentioned something about my eyes. Do you know what he meant?"

Holt carried Kopi over to his dresser, opening his hands for the owl to hop out. "Your eye colour is not just rare for humans."

Zylah stilled. "Marcus... recognised me? Do you think he might know my family?"

"I think if he does, he'll never tell you. He'll use it against you."

Like he'd used Holt. The unspoken words hung in the air, but Zylah said nothing. She'd seen Marcus's power. Arnir must have had something, some reason he had Marcus parading around as his pet. "Why aren't you going after Marcus at the festival? Raif, I mean. Why isn't Marcus the target?"

Holt pulled a fresh shirt from the chest of drawers. "A life debt is... I can't harm him. I can't even hear of any harm coming to him..." He pulled off his shirt, and Zylah looked away.

"And you're telling me Raif and Rose have never once thought of this for themselves?"

"He's still their father."

"You choose your own family," she said, turning back to him. He raked a hand through his hair before rolling up his sleeves, ready to leave for the day. Zack and her father had found her, brought her up as family, and every day they chose her. Every day she chose them. That was what family was, and she knew Holt understood that. The way he'd chosen Raif and Rose and Saphi.

He rested a hand on the doorknob. "Marcus will be at the festival, Zylah. Just stay out of his way." The door clicked shut behind him before Zylah could reply.

She grabbed her apron, tying the fastenings behind her back as an idea took shape. She'd need to find Asha. She wasn't sure she could trust him, but he was the only one she could ask, and something told her he would want to help fix this. She reached for her eyeglasses and didn't dare let herself hope that her plan might work.

Zylah would not replace one tyrant with another. She would not let Marcus win.

32

Asha had been more than willing to help. Zylah looked at herself in the mirror, her unease causing the hairs on her neck to stand on end. Saphi had given her a floor-length silver dress for the festival, so fine it looked like liquid metal when she moved. She wore the necklace Raif had given her, and on her head sat a fine silver circlet that dipped onto her forehead.

She ran a hand through the unfamiliar shade of her hair— bright red, chosen by Saphi—and pale blue eyes. Zylah had been taking lessons from Saphi in how to achieve these small deceits, but tonight she'd let the Fae carry out the task. They couldn't risk Arnir recognising her, and looking at her reflection in the mirror, Zylah barely recognised herself with her red hair falling over her shoulders in loose waves. Tonight they'd be taking down the king *and* his puppet; only her friends didn't know that yet. They didn't know it was them she was doing it for. Because she knew that if Marcus was allowed to live after Arnir died, Raif and Rose, Holt, and Saphi, would all be answering to Marcus. Even Jilah and the children. They all would. And she'd seen his power. What she was counting on was that he wouldn't risk using it at the festival, wouldn't risk showing up the king in such a public setting.

Zylah adjusted her blade, sheathed against her thigh, just in case. Whilst Raif took down Arnir, she and Asha would take on Marcus. She didn't have the luxury of hiding copious weapons beneath her dress, but Asha had confirmed weapons would be easy to conceal on his person. Weapons that Zylah had made sure were heavily poisoned.

Like all the Fae outfits Zylah had so far encountered, this dress left little to the imagination. The lace bralette was cut low, the fabric of the dress even lower so that the lace was exposed. It skimmed over every inch of her body like a second skin, pooling slightly at the hem into a small train. It was sleeveless, only the straps of the bralette on display, but naturally, Saphi had chosen a set that looked as if it were part of the dress. One side had a slit almost up to the lower thigh, and just above that was where she had strapped her weapon. A hastily whispered deceit had been enough to conceal the outline of the strap beneath the dress. The blade was small, no longer than her hand and as thin as a pencil. But it was all she would need. Threaded through her arms and across her back Zylah wore a shawl in the same liquid silver fabric.

Hushed voices whispered to each other outside the door to Raif's bedroom, pulling Zylah from her thoughts.

"I saw our mother." It was Rose.

"That's not possible," Raif replied.

362

"I know what I saw, Raif. She's alive."

Zylah didn't know enough of Rose's visions to know how accurate they were, or whether the Fae could see the past. But it sounded as if she were speaking of the present. She kept her focus on her reflection in the mirror, adjusting her shawl over her shoulders and then pulling it back down to where it was before.

The door swung open, and Raif stood alone in the doorway, hands in his pockets as his gaze roved slowly over Zylah in the mirror. "I think we need to make these festivals a weekly thing."

He wore a silver-grey suit, a few shades darker than her dress, his hair tied up and neat, rounded ears on display.

"Making a demonstration of your humanness, are you?" Zylah asked, reaching a hand up to touch an ear. With the deceit, they felt round, like human ears. Magic was incredible.

Raif captured her hand with his, pressing his face into her palm. "I'll demonstrate anything you like if you'll say it again."

Zylah rolled her eyes with a smile. In the few days since she'd agreed to stay, he'd wanted to hear her say it, over and over. "Insufferable," she murmured, looking up into his eyes as he wrapped his free arm around her and held her close. Heat bloomed low in her belly, and one of Raif's dimples made an appearance as the corner of his mouth twitched into a smile. He moved her hand to sit over his heart and held it there, waiting.

"I'm staying," Zylah whispered, her eyes drifting to his lips.

His mouth was on hers at once, his tongue sweeping across

hers. She'd told him she was staying. But she hadn't told him the words she'd decided would be kinder *not* to tell him if she was leaving. She'd never said those words to anyone.

A knock sounded on the door. "Come on, you two, we can't be late." Zylah stepped back from Raif's embrace to see Saphi beaming at them.

Kopi flitted between Zylah's shoulder and the surrounding rooftops as the four of them made their way through the streets. The citizens of Virian were out in full, countless flower crowns already trodden into the cobblestones at their feet. Drums were beating somewhere in the distance, each strike echoing in Zylah's heart. Raif, Rose and Saphi seemed unfazed. They all knew what they had to do tonight to get Raif close to Arnir, where they were meant to be, and what part they had to play.

Zylah had overheard snippets of other plans involving different members of the uprising and Arnir's elite unit. Her role tonight was in her job at the botanical gardens, and she said a few silent words to Pallia that she wouldn't have to talk to anyone about the sun lilies she'd prepared for the king.

They made their way past the gardens, where they would no doubt be celebrating later that evening, until they reached the wall of the palace district. This area of the city was usually kept closed to citizens, but not tonight. Tonight the doors were wide open, entertainers and revellers alike pouring through them to the lush green area beyond. The sun was setting, and floating lanterns drifted across the expanse before them, the palace illuminated with orblights and mirrors, the white marble glowing orange like the sun.

A wide path lined with trees led to the palace, in the centre of which, a troupe of dancers weaved their way through the crowd. It was another play, Zylah realised, like the one at the botanical gardens a few nights before. There were nine dancers, one with a toy owl pinned to her shoulder, and at once, Zylah knew they were meant to be the gods. The original nine. This was what Saphi had spoken of.

Kopi had flown on ahead into the trees, and for once Zylah was grateful that he was out of sight. Raif's hand was warm around hers as they made their way amongst the dancers, but Zylah couldn't take her eyes off their performance.

The gods danced hand in hand, around and around until two of them broke away, the drums from earlier beating, metal sheets clashing together to mimic the sound of thunder. More dancers ran amongst the crowds waving black ribbons, swirling and snaking around the revellers.

The two gods that had broken away pulled horned masks from somewhere among the crowd, the black ribbons weaving around them and binding them together. When they parted, more dancers emerged between them, dressed in tattered black rags and wearing more of the ghoulish masks. Some had fur attached to their faces, some had fangs like wolves.

The gods had used dark magic to make servants and sentinels and all kinds of atrocities, Raif had told her a few months before. She came to a stop amongst the crowd, watching transfixed as the *atrocities* attacked the dancers with the ribbons, and the seven other gods rushed in to help.

"The ones with the fangs were called vampires. They were meant to feed on humans, but when they started feeding on Fae, Ranon and Sira realised the severity of their mistake." Raif pulled her closer as they watched.

The seven gods worked together until the atrocities were defeated, but Ranon and Sira fled amongst the crowd, nowhere to be seen. Zylah felt a chill watching the gods disperse, the crowd cheering and whistling as the drums and the music faded. Only they weren't gods, she reminded herself. They were Fae.

Raif shifted his hand to her back, ushering her forwards.

"What happened to them?" she asked, looking up at him.

"Hmm?"

"Ranon and Sira, the two gods, the Fae who broke away. What happened to them?"

"That depends on who you ask," Saphi said at her other side. "Some say the seven destroyed them. Others say they fled. None of them have been seen or heard of in centuries."

Zylah looked back over her shoulder at the dispersing dancers. Some took off their masks and smiled; others still weaved through the crowd. She'd seen the Asters. She didn't dare dwell on what other *atrocities* remained.

Rose had been quiet for most of the walk, and at first, Zylah had wondered if it was to do with what she'd overheard the Fae say about her mother. But when Zylah had stopped to watch the dancers, Rose had seemed eager to move away. It couldn't have been easy, standing by knowing her brother was about to take on Arnir. If something went wrong, if she'd had a vision—Zylah shut the thought down before she let it take over. She squeezed Raif's hand as he led her towards the palace doors, where musicians with stringed instruments walked through the crowds.

All citizens were allowed into the palace district, but only those with an invitation were allowed into the palace. Zylah instinctively averted her gaze from the two guards as she walked up the steps beside Raif, even though she looked nothing like the wanted posters anymore.

Two more guards stood at the other side of the steps, and Zylah knew if she turned in a slow circle, there would be pairs of guards as far along the palace façade as she could see. She was eyeing out spots she could evanesce to if needed, the most direct routes back to the district gates away from the crowds. She'd opted for sandals with a small wedge—Saphi had tried to get her into heels—but Zylah wanted to be able to move. No, *to fight*, if it came to it.

Raif reached into his jacket and pulled out four invitations. How he'd managed to get Rose and Saphi an invite, Zylah wasn't sure. No doubt he'd put them down as employees of the botanical gardens.

Zylah's mouth was as dry as sand as the guard closest to Raif took the invitations and gave them all a once-over. She stood as tall as she could beside Raif, her head barely reaching his shoulder, and looked up to meet the guard's piercing gaze. She gave a sweet, close-lipped smile and leaned into Raif's arm as playfully as she could.

She hoped if she faked the giddy excitement for long

enough, it might wash away some of the dread.

The guard nodded to his companion at the top of the step, where another guard waited to usher them inside. They were too low down to see what lay beyond the palace doors, but music and laughter carried to them down the steps.

Zylah began listing all of the ways this night could go horribly wrong as they made their way to the open doors. She hesitated at the last step, and Raif turned back and held out a hand for her.

His smile was warm, his eyes calm and reassuring, so at odds with what he was about to do. She doubted he had any weapons under his jacket; his raw power was all he would need to take down Arnir, to obliterate the king from existence. And though that thought was reassuring, something about all of this felt off.

It had been only a few nights since she had told Raif she was staying in Virian. The start of something new. But as she took his hand and walked up the last of the steps to the open doors of the palace, it was that moment that felt like her new beginning.

Zylah took a deep breath, cast aside her worries and followed Raif into the palace.

33

Zylah's stomach turned over itself as they entered the palace. Sweeping staircases of white stone wound up on either side of the doors, and in the centre sat a fountain with five white-winged carved stone horses flying over the water of the fountain. Zylah had never seen anything like it.

She paused for a moment to steady her breathing, her gaze falling on the horses' wings. "Beautiful," she murmured.

She took a moment to note the doors coming off of the entrance hall; three on either side, the only ones open were those ahead of them, laughter echoing against the stone from the room beyond.

"This way, please," another guard called out over the chatter and music escaping from behind him.

Raif touched a hand lightly to her elbow and she followed, Saphi and Rose close behind them.

A waitress passed with a tray of drinks, and Zylah recognised her from the safe house. She was Fae. Raif took two glasses from her and muttered something under his breath, handing a glass to Zylah as the waitress turned back into the crowd. Behind her, Rose and Saphi had glasses of their own, and Saphi raised hers in a toast before taking a sip.

They weren't inside, as Zylah had first thought. It was a courtyard space, and it stretched further than she could see. The palace swept around them, bordered with white pillars and trellises that were heavy with vines. Above them, orblights were strung across the open space like chandeliers.

Many of the guests wore flower crowns, men and women alike. Only they weren't just men and women. There were Fae, everywhere. Zylah recognised them all from the different safe houses. Some were waiters, some were entertainers, some were even guards, all hidden in their deceits to fit in amongst the humans.

Humans who would have been Arnir's most avid support-ers, Zylah suspected. She didn't like it. Any of it.

She slid a hand around Raif's neck, easing him towards her as if beckoning him for a kiss. "Why do I feel like we're walk-ing into an ambush?" she murmured against his lips.

Raif threaded his fingers through her hair, tilting her head up so he had better access to her mouth, and kissed her slowly.

"Just stick to the plan," he said quietly, biting at her lower lip before he drew back.

Zylah nodded, stepping back as a familiar scent caught her attention. It was Holt. He greeted Rose and Saphi with a kiss on the cheek each, laughing at some comment Rose made about his suit. It was midnight blue, the jacket notched at the neck with silver stitching. His hair was a little shorter, and Zylah thought he might have attempted to tame its unruliness with a comb.

"Your sun lilies are the talk of the festival," he said to Zylah as he clasped a hand to Raif's shoulder in greeting.

"They are?" Zylah looked around but couldn't see them through all the people. In the centre of the courtyard was a flowerbed, but from here, all Zylah could see and smell were the Bloom florist's roses.

Holt's mouth twitched as she turned back to him. "They're up with Arnir."

Zylah stretched up onto her toes to try and see across the crowd, and for the first time, she caught sight of the uniform of Arnir's elite unit. Instinctively she fell back to the balls of her feet, positioning herself out of sight of the one she'd spotted. She brushed a strand of hair from her eyes and cleared her throat. *They won't recognise you like this.* She hoped to Pallia that was the truth.

Raif pressed a hand to her back, rubbing soothing circles as if he'd heard her thundering heart. They probably all had. Saphi launched into a description of the dancers they'd seen on their way in, questioning Holt on what the best entertainment of the evening had been so far, but Zylah was focusing on her breathing. On making her breaths even and steady.

She looked around the courtyard as discreetly as she could, counting guards. Five, and that was only as far as she could see—Zylah pressed a hand to her stomach and froze.

"Liss?" Raif asked beside her, his reassuring warmth

pressing against her side.

"Zack," she whispered. "My brother is here." Her brother, the King's Blade, stood talking with an elderly man, laughing at something the human had said.

Holt followed her gaze and glanced back at her. "Look at me," he said calmly.

Zylah forced herself to look away from her brother and met Holt's eyes.

His eyebrows pinched together for a moment. "You know his position. He had to be here. For tonight, it might be best to stay out of his sight. You can visit him after. Agreed?"

After Arnir is dead. Holt didn't need to say it. But there were too many Fae in the palace grounds, too many members of the uprising. Zylah looked into Holt's eyes, silently praying to the gods he would tell the truth. "Do I have your word he'll walk out of here tonight?"

"I swear it. Now let's keep moving."

Zylah looked back one more time at her brother and swallowed. She wanted to push through the crowd and run to him. Throw her arms around his neck and ask how he was. How their father was. But she couldn't. Not yet. *After*, she told herself.

Holt was already moving through the crowd, Rose and Saphi beside him as if they were simply there to enjoy the evening. Zylah drew in a shaky breath and released it through pursed lips. She didn't even want to think of how Asha would find his way in, of where he was in the palace at that precise moment. But she knew he'd be there.

Zylah focused on the flowerbed as they made their way through the courtyard, admiring the Bloom florist's display. The roses were white, to begin with, but as they made their way further into the courtyard, creams and pale yellows were dotted through them, getting brighter and brighter the further across the courtyard they walked until they were gold, the white roses replaced with purple ones.

String instruments played a lively melody from somewhere under one of the ivy trellises, and dancers weaved in and out of the crowd with gold and purple ribbons. For once, Zylah didn't feel like her outfit was out of place as they eased past countless purple and gold gowns, most likely worn in an attempt to impress the king. Zylah had no doubt Saphi had picked out the silver dress as an act of rebellion, and she smiled at the thought.

But her relief was short-lived. They were reaching the end of the courtyard, and the guards had doubled. She placed her untouched glass on a passing waiter's tray and twisted her cold fingers over themselves. Every instinct told her to leave, to evanesce away from there. But she had to face him.

They reached her sun lilies, and she might have taken a moment to admire her work if not for the fact that at the end of the flowerbed a small staircase stretched up to the doors of the palace, and before the doors sat King Arnir.

He sat on a throne draped in purple and gold fabric, and Zylah had to force herself not to stare, to keep her gaze fixed on the sun lilies. It was difficult to swallow as she gazed at the golden flowers. The Bloom florist had arranged them, and

Zylah tried to appreciate his work as she willed herself not to fidget.

Still no sign of Asha. But there had been no sign of Marcus either. She was vaguely aware of Rose and Saphi departing through the crowd, and a third voice joined Holt and Raif behind her.

Zylah turned to the voice she recognised. "Ambrose." The king's representative from their meeting at the Pig's Tail... and the attack that followed.

"Good evening," Ambrose said with a smile.

How much of the plan did he know? Were there more of Arnir's guards working with them? Her brother, perhaps, but Zylah didn't let herself hold onto that hope, not yet. She looked from Ambrose to Holt. "He works for you."

Holt dipped his chin almost imperceptibly. Of course, he'd never admit it here. Zylah wondered if Raif had known when they went to meet Ambrose.

"Ready for your introductions?" Ambrose's eyes sparkled under the orblights.

Raif hooked Zylah's arm through his. It was too soon. Asha wouldn't have found Marcus yet. But she couldn't stall them, for fear it might draw attention.

Her throat was so dry, all she could manage was a nod.

"Everything's going to be fine," Raif murmured beside her.

Ambrose made his way up a few steps, bowing low to the king before speaking into his counsel's ear.

The counsel nodded, casting his gaze over Raif and Zylah. Holt had moved away from them, but Zylah didn't dare look behind her into the crowd.

Seven gods.

She kept her head low, looking through her lashes. King Arnir nodded, beckoning for them to approach. They walked a few steps, pausing halfway to bow before the man who'd tried to have her hanged. Raif had released her arm, one of his hands held behind his back, the other at his side, waiting.

This was it. No more running. No more hiding. Zylah willed her racing heart to be still.

"You grow sun lilies and you come dressed as the moon," Arnir said, his jowls vibrating even more than Zylah had remembered.

She held her head high, praying to all seven gods he wouldn't recognise her with Saphi's deceits. The slight with the dress might have been a step too far. "What better tribute to the sun than the moon herself?"

Arnir's shoulders shook as he laughed silently. He held a heavily jewelled hand to his chin and held her gaze. "Is that so?"

Shit. Zylah bowed her head. "One cannot exist without the other, Your Majesty."

Arnir laughed, a short bark this time. "Let me look upon you. Bring your friend, I mean no harm."

Zylah looked up, and her eyes met with Zack's, standing beside the king. His eyes widened, but Raif had already threaded her arm through his, easing her up the steps beside him, gently tugging her to the stone steps to kneel before the king.

Zylah didn't dare look up again as her knees touched the cold stone.

Arnir leaned forwards, and the purple fabric slid to one side to reveal the polished black stone of the throne he sat on. Vanquicite. *In Pallia's name.* Raif's power wouldn't work. They'd be exposed, they'd—

"Your Majesty!"

Zylah closed her eyes, silently praying over and over.

"I do apologise, Your Majesty." It was Marcus, which could only have meant one thing. A pair of feet came into view in front of them. "He was discovered in my quarters, Your Majesty, he attempted to take my life with this."

Zylah couldn't look up, couldn't risk exposing them all. She'd poisoned all of Asha's blades herself. Something heavy fell onto the stone steps nearby and Zylah swallowed. Asha.

If Marcus recognised his son kneeling on the steps before him, he didn't let it show. Raif needed to be close enough to touch Arnir for his power to work, but if he hadn't noticed the vanquicite, it was too late to warn him. And her brother was right beside the king. Holt had promised he'd be safe, but things had already gone wrong so very quickly.

She was certain Marcus could hear her heartbeat. Certain every Fae nearby could hear it. Her hands were clasped together at her front—she could reach for her dagger, just one cut of the king's flesh... but then that left Marcus to deal with. And Asha. Only the sound of his ragged breathing told her the Fae was still alive.

"Well, well, well. If it isn't the whore. What gifts has she bestowed upon you this evening, Your Majesty, or is she a gift for later?" Marcus's voice was almost sing-song in his mockery.

Zylah held her breath. Marcus had recognised her. Zack still hadn't said anything. She focused on the sound of Asha's breathing, vanilla perfume carrying to her from somewhere over her shoulder. Saphi. Followed by acani berries. Holt.

Arnir's feet shifted in front of them, covering the vanquicite in another fold of fabric. "She grew the sun lilies. You know her?"

If he had been any other Fae, Zylah knew he wouldn't have risked exposing his son. But this was Marcus. "Look at your king," he instructed.

Zylah raised her chin slowly, first looking through her lashes until she was holding her head high before Arnir. His eyes widened and then narrowed.

Several things happened at once. Raif lunged for Arnir. Zylah reached for her blade with one hand and Raif with the other. Arnir was shouting, and as Zylah pulled her blade from its sheath, a hand clamped around her wrist.

She looked up to meet her brother's eyes just as she evanesced her and Raif away.

34

Zylah vaguely registered the wards as she took them to the reception area of the safe house and fell to her knees. Zack had stopped her. She blinked at her wrist where her brother had held it, her blade still in her hand. She let it clatter to the floor.

"What just happened?" Raif asked, kneeling in front of her.

Zylah didn't look up to see if he was angry or concerned. *Asha.* Marcus wouldn't spare him; he would torture him, just like she'd seen him torture Holt. She pressed a hand to her stomach, the other bracing herself against the floor.

"*Liss.* What happened? I had him."

"Vanquicite," Zylah whispered. The weight of that throne… Zylah could well imagine how a man like Arnir wouldn't go anywhere without it, coward that he was. How he would make his servants suffer carrying it, no matter the distance. And he'd concealed it on purpose, to lure out any Fae at the festival. Could it lift deceits? Asha had looked human when they left, but if the vanquicite dampened magic…

"Shit," she said under her breath.

"Liss, look at me. What was Asha doing there?" Raif placed a hand on Zylah's arm, and she finally looked up to meet his gaze. His eyes blazed.

"You're angry," Zylah rasped. She'd ruined their plans, messed up everything. He had every right to be angry.

"What happened?"

"I think we'd all like to know what the fuck just happened." Zylah looked up to see Rose beside Holt and Saphi. Holt must have evanesced them in. Rose had her arms folded across her chest, waiting for an answer.

"The throne," Zylah whispered again. Asha. She had to get to Asha. She reached for her blade, sliding it back into its sheath as she pushed to her feet. "I need to go back for Asha."

"What was he doing there, Liss, and again, what the fuck just happened? Do you have any idea how long this took to plan? How many Fae died for this, for tonight?" Rose took a step closer with each question until she was close enough to stab a finger into Zylah's chest. Her eyes narrowed, and it was the same expression Zylah had seen on Raif's face moments before.

"Rose, that's enough." Holt swiped Rose's hand away, waiting until she took a step back. "The throne was made of vanquicite. If Raif had laid a hand on Arnir, every guard in there would have jumped him."

Zylah pressed a hand to her stomach again. "My—" She cleared her throat. "My brother saw my blade. It's poisoned, I couldn't..." If she could just see Zack for a moment. If she could just explain, smooth things over. *And say what?* "I need to go back for Asha."

"Why was Asha there?" Raif asked. He hadn't touched her since she'd risen to her feet. His eyes had darkened, and he mirrored his sister's pose, arms folded across his chest.

Guilt settled in Zylah's stomach. She looked at Raif, but he wouldn't meet her gaze. "He was there for Marcus." She tore off the silver circlet, feeling a fool in her dress. "I poisoned Asha's blades. While you took out Arnir, Asha was going to take out Marcus."

Saphi whistled. "Poisoned blade. A fitting death for that bastard."

Zylah thought so, but she wasn't about to agree with Saphi. Not when the air was so thick she could almost slice through it with her blade. She needed to get out of her dress. Get to the tunnels. That's where Marcus would have taken Asha.

"The vanquicite must be how he keeps Marcus under his thumb. I should have known." Holt dragged a hand through his hair. "Marcus had the cuffs. If Liss hadn't noticed the throne was made of vanquicite, we might not all be standing here right now."

Rose took another step closer. "How could you evanesce so close to that much vanquicite?"

"You're the seer. You tell me." Zylah took a step towards Rose, her whole body tensing. She had no idea how or why she could evanesce near the throne. It had been the same with Holt and the cuffs. If she was touching them, nothing. But with no contact, she'd been able to evanesce him out of the tunnels. She held Rose's stare, refusing to back down. She might have messed up with Asha, but she'd got Raif out of there.

"That's enough." Holt stepped between them. "She just saved your brother's life. You might want to thank her instead of getting ready to swing at her." He gestured to Rose's hand, curled into a fist at her side. Then he turned to Zylah. "We can't go back for Asha tonight. After you left, everything was chaos. They'll be packing up Arnir and already on their way back to Dalstead, and the guards will be on high alert. Looking for Asha now would not be wise."

He didn't need to say why. Zylah didn't want to think of what Marcus could have done to Asha in the few minutes since they'd left.

"He won't kill him," Holt said, searching her face. "He'll question him for as long as he can. I'll go as soon as the guard reduces."

Zylah began to speak but thought better of it. She looked at Raif, but he still wouldn't meet her gaze. There wasn't time to wait for the guard to reduce. Marcus wouldn't wait.

Holt looked at each of them, his cool façade back in place. "Everybody get some rest. We'll talk in the morning."

"I'll be at the tavern," Zylah murmured, before evanescing herself back to her room. But she had no intention of staying there. She changed her clothes, slid her dagger into her boot and evanesced to the tunnels, searching for any sign of Asha and Marcus.

But they weren't there.

Three days passed. She'd spent the entire night searching the tunnels but had come across nothing more than a few sewer rats. Holt had given her an update each morning; there had been no sign of Asha. Or Marcus.

Zylah hadn't been back to the safe house, and Raif hadn't come to meet her after work. She doubted that would change after she finished off for the day. A butterfly landed on a celandia, azure wings fluttering delicately, and Zylah loosed a sigh. She'd seen Raif's reaction, the way he wouldn't meet her eyes. He was angry. Disappointed. Just like Rose was.

Asha had gone to seek out Marcus willingly… but only because Zylah had asked him. And Pallia only knew what Marcus would be doing to him for information. Asha would never speak. He'd go to his grave protecting his people, and the thought made bile rise in Zylah's throat, not for the first time that day.

She raked over the last of the soil where the sun lilies had been, preparing it for something new. Jilah waved at her from the far end of the dome, his signal that it was time to go home. He hadn't been at the festival, but he'd heard what had happened. And he'd been kind to her. "You and Raif are still with us," was all he'd said. But she'd felt his disappointment. Arnir was still alive, and the children were still hiding who they were. Still hiding in plain sight.

Kopi flew down to Zylah's shoulder just as she pulled on her cloak to leave. It was far too hot for it, but she couldn't be without it now. The little owl gave a quiet *hoo* in greeting and Zylah sighed. "I know, buddy. I have to face them at some point." She had to deal with Raif and the others and knew all she'd been doing was putting off the inevitable argument. Better to get it over with.

She walked to the safe house rather than evanescing there, working through her thoughts. If she couldn't fix things here, maybe she could fix things with her brother. Either way, she needed to try.

She stepped over discarded flower crowns as she made her way across the river—this part of the city hadn't been cleaned up yet, partly, Zylah assumed, because the citizens were disappointed that the festival had been cut short. She reached the door to the safe house and drew in a deep breath.

Zylah cleared her throat and knocked once.

Raif opened the door, and before Zylah had a chance to speak, he pulled her into an embrace. "I'm sorry," he breathed into her hair.

Zylah frowned against his shirt. "I thought you were angry with me?" she murmured against his chest.

Hot breath huffed against her hair. "I was angry with myself. For putting you in that situation. For not noticing the throne was vanquicite."

Zylah closed her eyes and breathed him in. "Why haven't you come to see me?"

Raif laughed again, taking her face in his hands. His eyes were bright and clear, full of emotion. "Because I'm an insufferable asshole." He loosened his hold, taking Zylah by the hand and closing the door behind her and Kopi. She shrugged out of her cloak as he led her to the lounger then knelt before her. Zylah swallowed. His walls were down. She recognised it now. One of the few times he let her in.

He took her hands in his. "Liss, I—"

Holt evanesced to the centre of the room, his gaze meeting Zylah's. His clothes were unmarked, with no signs of any struggle but he looked utterly defeated.

"Tell me," Zylah demanded.

Holt shook his head almost imperceptibly. "He's gone."

The world tilted. Zylah pulled her hands back from Raif's, smoothing them over the front of her apron. *Don't underestimate how much your actions have contributed to mending what's broken*, Asha had told her.

This was her fault. All of it. Her eyes stung, and she willed herself not to cry.

The glass beads of the curtain clicked together and Saphi and Rose walked through.

"We heard," Rose said quietly.

Kopi flew to Zylah's hands, and she stroked his head, but all she saw was Asha's face, agreeing to her plan. He'd been so confident. He'd said nothing would go wrong, that by the end of the night, both tyrants would be dead, and they'd truly be free. Zylah swallowed down the lump in her throat, vaguely aware that Holt and Raif had left the room.

"This is your fault. Asha. Marcus." Rose stood in front of her, so close Zylah had to tilt her head back to meet Rose's eyes.

Saphi reached for Rose, resting a hand on her arm. "Rose, that's enough."

"Asha made his own choices. I didn't make him do anything." Zylah said it more for herself than for Rose's benefit. "You've never liked me." It was the truth. Rose had tolerated her, at best.

Rose barked a bitter laugh. "You want to know why?"

Kopi didn't move. Even with Rose as close as she was, he stayed still in Zylah's hands, as if he knew she needed the comfort as she braced herself for whatever Rose was about to say.

"Rose, please." Saphi tugged on Rose's arm again, but Rose brushed her away.

"Because I've seen Raif's death," Rose spat. "And you're there. You need to leave, *Liss*. You don't belong here. You know it. I know it. Raif knows it. We all do."

Zylah's head was spinning, her breaths coming faster and faster. She cupped Kopi to her chest as Raif and Holt came back into the room. A hot tear rolled down her cheek and she sucked in a ragged breath. They'd heard. They must have. Worse than that, they would have known. Rose would have told them all, the moment she'd had the vision.

For a second, the life she could have had in Virian played out before her. It was all a lie. If her staying meant Raif would... that he could *die*, because of her. Just like Mala and Asha. No. She wouldn't let that happen.

Another tear fell as her eyes met with Raif's.

"Liss, no," he pleaded, reaching for her.

But it was too late, Zylah had already evanesced away.

35

It was Kara she thought of as she evanesced. That she was somewhere safe, far away from all of this. Zylah's feet hit the floor of her father's cottage, and Kopi flew out of her hands, resting on a beam. It was the furthest she'd ever evanesced, but her practise in the tunnels had told her she could do it. Holt had told her she could do it when he'd confessed he'd evanesced most of the continent for his sister.

She looked around the cottage as she caught her breath, gritting her teeth against the ache in her back. Everything was exactly as it had been when she'd left. The fragrant besa leaves and alea blossom that always permeated everything hung thick in the air… and the coppery tang of blood.

A shiver ran down Zylah's spine. "Father?" she called out. Kopi hooed quietly above her, ruffling his feathers. Zylah listened carefully, the sound of strained breathing carrying to her from her father's bedroom.

She eased the wooden door open, sucking in a breath as

she saw her father lying in his rickety old bed. "Father?" She rushed to him, kneeling beside him on the rough floorboards to take his hand. He was sleeping, but it looked wrong. His skin was ashen, his lips almost blue. She could barely hear his heartbeat. He was far beyond her healing capabilities.

A rusty patch stained his threadbare blanket, and Zylah reached out to take a look, just as Kopi hooed a warning. Zylah knew her brother's scent before he walked through the door, but she didn't release their father's hand as Zack stood in the doorway, watching her.

"The king had him beaten within an inch of his life after he returned from the festival. To teach him a lesson," Zack said, his eyes firmly on their father. Dark shadows bloomed beneath his eyes. He looked as if he hadn't slept in the last three days. If this was what he'd come home to, he probably hadn't.

"Have you given him any celandia?" Zylah asked, lifting the blanket to reveal the stained bandage tied around their father's chest.

Zack grabbed her arm, pulling her away. "He is *dying*." His grip was tight enough to bruise, but Zylah didn't shake him off. She had to explain.

Their father wheezed behind her. "I knew you'd come. I waited for you."

Zylah shrugged out of Zack's grip and took her father's hand, smoothing back his sweat-slicked hair. "I'm here," she whispered. "I'm here." His eyes slid to hers—not bright like they once were, but hazy, distant. As if he was looking through

387

her. She held her hand to his face and kissed it as her tears fell. The calloused skin was just as she'd remembered it, just as it had always been. How many times had he held her face in his hands, looking upon her with eyes filled with nothing but love?

Her father drew in a rattled breath to speak. "Oh, my darling girl. I thought we'd have more time." The ghost of a smile tugged at the corner of his mouth, and he slid his thumb over a tear, the haze lifting from his eyes. Guilt gnawed at Zylah's insides, and she loosed a shaky breath.

"You were never like us," her father said softly, his mouth still a faint smile. "That day you fell from the weeping eye tree, you should have broken every bone in your body, but you didn't." His voice was scratched and strained, barely a whisper. "You can run faster than anyone we know; you can hear things we can't." He wheezed. "You can probably hear this old ticker of mine giving up on me." He lifted a hand, but it fell to his chest. "I knew. I always knew and tried to hide it, to keep you safe." Speaking had made his breathing worse, and the haze had returned to his eyes.

Zylah's tears fell freely as she held his gaze. She wouldn't look away. Couldn't. A faint smile tugged at her father's lips, and he clasped her cheek as he let out a breath like a soft sigh.

"I'm sorry," she said. "I'm so sorry." She searched his eyes, waiting for words that would never come. Zack took a step closer, and Zylah pressed another kiss to their father's hand as a sob shook through her. He was already gone.

Her brother moved to the far side of the bed, taking their

388

father's other hand, resting it on his chest and straightening the sheets. He'd always been the same, cleaning and tidying the cottage, the garden, the space out front whenever anything had unsettled him.

"I knew he was holding on for you. With his injuries, he shouldn't have lasted more than a day," Zack said quietly.

Zylah wasn't ready to let go. Not yet. She held her father's hand, his eyes still fixed on hers, and still, she couldn't bring herself to look away. "I'm sorry," she whispered again.

She laid his hand gently over the other, smoothed aside his hair the way he liked it. Zack closed their father's eyes and eased his head until it was resting straight on the pillow. Zylah wiped her tears away as another sob escaped her. She pressed a kiss to his forehead; his skin was warm, but he was still, and she couldn't make those two facts make sense. He was gone.

"The moment you evanesced from the gallows they knew what you were." Zack turned to look at her then, and it was fear she saw in his expression. "They will hunt you down until they find you. They're afraid of you."

Zylah twisted her fingers against her apron. Her brother had always looked after her. Fought for her. Taught her how to defend herself when he couldn't. "And you. Are you afraid of me? Your own sister?"

"You're not really my sister."

The words seemed to slice through her skin. She couldn't find her voice to respond.

Zack waved a hand at their father. "You brought this on him."

A shaft of evening sunlight poured in through the window behind their father's bed, but Zack's face remained in shadow. "I'm still the same person I always was, Zack," Zylah whispered. "I'm still me." Kopi made a noise in the next room, but all Zylah could hear was, *you're not really my sister.*

Zack sighed, resting a hand on their father's. "Go. The guards check here regularly. Go before they find you."

"But I... we need to bury him. His funeral." Zylah looked at her father, at the way the sunlight turned his hair golden, how it gave some warmth to his ashen skin. Kopi cried out again, but Zylah couldn't leave, not like this. Not yet.

"They'll kill me if they find you here," Zack whispered. "Go."

A floorboard creaked in the next room, but Kopi was silent. Zylah was on her feet, dagger in hand as she heard the creak of a bowstring being pulled back. But she wasn't fast enough.

"Pull your little party trick, and I'll kill the King's Blade." The man had an arrow pointed at Zack's chest, and Zylah didn't doubt for one second that he wouldn't follow through on his threat. He was a bounty hunter, just like the ones that had attacked her and Holt that day in the forest. Kopi screeched in the next room, and a man cried out.

"Cal?" the archer called out, his arrow still pointed at Zack, his gaze unwavering. Zylah was fast, but not fast enough to catch an arrow. Maybe she was, but she couldn't risk it. Couldn't risk harming Zack.

Another man spat on the floor behind the archer. "That fucking owl almost took my eye out." He clasped a bloodied hand over an eye, glaring at Zylah. "Let's hope your pet is

390

trained, I could quite go for some bird for my dinner."

"He isn't mine," Zylah said, calculating if she'd be fast enough to throw a dagger from her bracers before the archer could release an arrow.

"Cal," the archer demanded. "The cuffs."

"Oh, yeah." Cal shoved a hand into his shoulder bag and pulled out a pair of vanquicite cuffs. He took a step closer to Zylah, removing his hand from his face and squinting against the wound. Kopi *had* almost taken his eye out. Three gashes ran from the centre of his eyebrow, across his eye and around to his ear. It was an effort not to smile at quite how spectacularly Kopi had wounded him.

She shot a look at her brother, praying he'd have a way out of this. His head moved just a fraction, as if to say, *don't*. But she could do this for Zack. To keep him safe. She held out her hands for the cuffs, the cold stone clicking shut far tighter than necessary over her wrists. She didn't dare try to pull on her power to test how effective the cuffs were. Not with the archer's arrow still pointed at Zack.

Cal pulled a sack over her head, and something hard hit her across the face. A fist, maybe. Zylah staggered back. She'd taken enough fists to the face in her training, but her brother still called out.

"Don't hurt her, she's going willingly," Zack said, his voice marking him as closer than he had been a few moments before.

"Not in much of a position to make requests there, son," the archer said. "Cuff him."

"He's human," Zylah said, her breath hot inside the sack. It reeked of horse and rotten potatoes, and Zylah could only see enough through it to make out where each body was positioned in the room.

"Doesn't matter," Cal grumbled. "Cuffs are cuffs." Another pair of cuffs clicked shut, followed by the sound of a sack being pulled over Zack's head. The archer's bow creaked, and she knew he'd finally put the arrow away.

"Our father," Zylah pleaded. "He needs a proper burial."

"Cremations are faster," the archer said flatly.

Zack sucked in a breath. "Please, let the villagers bury him beside our mother."

"Now, now, Little Blade. What did I say about making requests?" the archer taunted as he grabbed Zylah's arm and shoved her through the doorway. "Sunrise, Cal. Don't be late." They were splitting up. But Zylah didn't let her rising panic take over. She was focusing on Zack, on any sound that would let her know what they were doing with him.

A match struck, and then another and another.

"No!" Zylah pleaded. "Zack?"

"I'm alright, Zylah."

They were torching the cottage. Zylah could already smell burning cloth as the archer shoved her outside. The smell of warm rain hung in the air, but it wasn't enough to cover what was drifting from her home.

A hinge creaked. "Get in." The archer shoved her against a rough platform. The back of a cart.

She hauled herself up as best she could with her bound

hands, and the tailgate slammed shut behind her. Only once she was inside the cart could she hear the huffing of the horses, the scraping of their hooves impatiently against the dirt. "It's spelled," she murmured. She was alone. "Zack!" she cried out. "Zack!" But he wouldn't be able to hear her over the spell.

She could still smell the burning cottage. Could hear the crack and pop of wood, and she scrambled to her knees to try and see out the patches of the canopy where the light filtered through. But she saw nothing but the weave of the sack over her head.

She lost her balance as the cart pulled away, smoke clinging to the sack even when she knew the cottage must be long out of sight. Zylah slumped against the side of the cart, her head throbbing and her ears ringing. She wasn't sure if it was the effects of the cuffs or the spell, and she reached up to yank at the sack, but it was no use, Cal must have fastened it.

Her father was gone. But no tears came. She could still find a way out. Could still find Zack. *And then what?* He couldn't work for the king anymore, not after this. He'd be hanged. No, she'd have to evanesce him somewhere far away from here. Maybe he wouldn't want to go with her. *You're not really my sister.* But he'd tried to protect her. Tried to tell her to leave.

She couldn't go back to Virian for help either, even though she knew Raif would help her, no matter what Rose had told her. She'd seen it in his face right before she evanesced.

Zylah hadn't just lost her father. She could never see Raif and her friends again.

36

Zylah wasn't sure when she'd fallen asleep. But when she woke up, she was no longer in the cart, and there was no longer a sack over her head. Her bracers and boots had been removed, both of which had held her only weapons. But she was still clothed. She patted her apron, the cuffs still tight at her wrists. Aside from the bruise throbbing on her cheek where Cal had struck her, she was fine. Another spell, perhaps, one that ensured she wouldn't be disturbed whilst she slept. She shivered at the thought of being touched without invitation, thoughts of Jesper fighting their way to the surface.

She shuffled up to a seated position, her eyes adjusting to the darkness. For a human, it would have been pitch black. But Zylah could make out the walls of a cave, could see where the rock curved around into a passageway. She took in as much detail as she could, determined to stay calm, to find a way out of this.

"If you try anything, I'll send the signal to end your

brother's life. Understood?" It was the archer, and Zylah hauled herself to her feet at the sound of his voice.

He'd spelled himself in the same way he'd spelled the cart, so she couldn't hear his breathing or his movements. A bounty hunter who hunted the Fae and used their tricks against them. Zylah resisted the urge to lunge for him.

She looked around, feigning disinterest in his threat. "Signal from within a cave?" she asked, hoping she sounded far more confident than she felt.

The archer shoved aside a piece of heavy cloth Zylah hadn't noticed before, and moonlight streamed in through a hole in the rock. "One strike of a match and your brother goes over the side of Mount Rinian."

They were in the mountain range. Even though it was warmer now, she could smell the crisp snow outside. "Why aren't we in Dalstead?"

"Negotiating a better price." The archer's face gave nothing away. If he hunted Fae, he knew how good her sight was.

She kept her face in shadow as she said, "Seems fair. I'm Liss." Her voice was steady, her expression as schooled as Raif and Holt's. "You know my brother. I know Cal. Who are you?" He might have known her real name, but she wasn't about to give that up just yet.

The archer was silent for a moment. "You knew my brother. Eirik. I'm Oz."

Eirik. The king's representative who'd died during the Black Veil's attack in Virian. A blade glinted in the moonlight. One of the thin blades from Zylah's bracers. Oz inspected it carefully. "I always told him he was a fool for serving in the King's Guard. Told him he could still work for the king as a bounty hunter. But he said it wasn't honest work. Wasn't honourable." He laughed dryly. "There was nothing honourable in the way I found him, half his guts hanging out on the streets of Virian. Will you deny that was your handiwork? Or one of your friends?"

He pointed the blade in Zylah's direction, his eyes on hers, and even in the dark Zylah could see that they were a dull brown, just like the rest of him. Dull brown hair that looked as if it hadn't been washed in weeks, filthy beard, and drab clothes in varying shades of brown and tan, all patched up in places by a skilled hand.

That didn't bode well for a bounty hunter, and it was that small detail that set the hairs on the back of her neck to standing. Not that he'd removed her weapons and her boots whilst she'd been sleeping. Not that he'd threatened Zack. Bounty hunters were usually brutes: brash and clumsy. All muscle and nothing much else. And in Zylah's experience, the only people who could stitch with such a steady hand were tailors or undertakers.

She cleared her throat, saying a silent prayer to Pallia that in a previous life, Oz had been the former. "Nice to meet you, Oz. And no. It was the Black Veil that killed your brother. I'm sorry for your loss."

Oz's shoulders moved as he chuckled and pressed her blade into the dirt at his feet. "The thing about Fae is, Liss…"—he reached into his coat pocket, rummaging—"…you're all a bunch of fucking liars." He ceased his search as if a better idea had struck him, and instead reached for something at his feet, resting it in his lap. It looked like a coiled piece of rope, but then Oz picked up the thick end and coiled the rest of the material between his hand and his elbow in a practised movement.

Seven gods. It wasn't a rope. It was a whip, moonlight glinting on the spurs of metal studded through the end. Zylah sized him up. She might not be stronger than him, but she'd be faster than him. And even with her hands bound she knew she could get him off his feet, she was confident enough in her training that she could do that. But then what? If she made it to the blade he'd shoved into the dirt, she couldn't wield it properly, not with her cuffed hands. She had no pins in her hair and nothing tucked in her apron, with the exception of a few dried leaves as always.

The faintest cry of an owl carried to her through the hole in the rock, so quiet Oz couldn't have heard it. Kopi. He must have followed the cart. Oz cracked the whip on the ground beside her, and her attention snapped back to him.

"I hate liars," Oz said calmly, winding up the whip again. "Cal will be here at sunrise. You'd better hope he's got good news because Delilah here has been itching to taste flesh again."

Shit. Zylah swallowed. "You named your whip?"

"She's got a real thirst for Fae blood." Oz lovingly ran a hand along the leather, like the whip was a pet, a terrifying grin stretching across his face.

Zylah didn't dare move. Didn't want to show any second of weakness to this asshole.

"Sit," Oz commanded.

Zylah blinked and then did as he asked. She couldn't do anything that might put Zack in more danger.

"Sunrise," he said. Zylah didn't want to know what would happen if Cal didn't bring good news, or what *good news* meant for her. She couldn't lean against the rock; it was too cold. And she certainly wasn't going to lie down and go to sleep. So she sat there, eyes fixed on Oz, hoping she could stay awake until morning.

⊱⋅⊰

Cal didn't bring good news at sunrise. Arnir hadn't been interested in the new price Oz had offered him, and Cal suspected they'd only have a few days before Arnir's elite unit were sent after them. All of this Zylah heard from within the cave, as Oz and Cal spoke in hushed voices. Her brother was still alive. She'd almost cried when Oz had asked about the *Little Blade*. Cal left, and all Zylah could do was sit and wait.

⊱⋅⊰

A day passed, and another. There had been no news. No word from Cal. Oz's spell was beginning to wear off because Zylah could hear the shuffle of his feet, could smell the stench of his clothes. The smoke from a fire. And something else. Tea.

398

More than a week old, but it made her dry, cracked lips sting even more than they already did. Oz had given her a crust of bread on the second day, and half a cup of ice-cold water, but nothing else.

On the third day, Oz's spell had worn off entirely, and she could hear his sigh of dissatisfaction when he took the last sip of his tea. She stared out of the gap in the rock from her place in the dirt as she listened to his footsteps coming closer.

"You know," she said, every movement of her throat hurting. "I make excellent tea. I've been working in a tea shop since I arrived in Virian." Oz was quiet, but he took up his position opposite her, his hands running along the length of Delilah.

Zylah didn't let the movement distract her. "The best black tea in Astaria comes from the Rinian mountains." She flicked her chin to the hole in the rock and waited.

Oz sighed. "I've looked nearby. Can't find any."

Zylah tilted her head back and sniffed. "I can smell some. Under snow, but it's there." She couldn't. Not from this far away. But she knew she would be able to as soon as she was outside, and she just needed to figure out where she was.

Oz unfurled Delilah and then wound her up again between his hand and his elbow. "Walk. Any horseshit and I won't bother to whip you, I'll just wrap Dee right around your pretty little neck."

"Understood." Zylah made it to her feet without wavering; only the gods knew how. She hadn't left the cave since they'd arrived, and she was frozen stiff from sitting in the dirt, even though this was the warmer season. She wished she'd had her cloak. Still, she was about to step barefoot into snow, so she supposed it had been good preparation.

Oz led her through the tunnel. It was further than she'd realised, but the light ahead of them was bright as soon as they turned the third corner. A sack leaned against the opening to the cave, beside which was a pan and a few rudimentary supplies. The bastard had been cooking. And right beside the pans were her boots. *Asshole.*

Zylah staggered forwards a few steps and fell into the snow, shoving handfuls against her mouth and letting it melt against her tongue.

"Up," Oz grunted, yanking at her arm when she didn't listen.

Somehow, Zylah made it to her feet. Gods, what she wouldn't give for her cloak. Cold snow bit into her bare feet, and she was certain if she didn't keep moving, she might lose a toe. She looked up, pretending to sniff for the tea leaves, but instead used the opportunity to take in as much of her surroundings as she could. Not that she could see far. They were up high, and everything was grey. An expanse of forest lay below them, but it was too far to make a run for it without her boots.

Not that it mattered. If her plan worked, Oz would be lying face down in the snow before long. She caught the smell of some tea shrubs. Faint, buried beneath snow, but nearby. "This way," she said, pointing to a patch of snow beside a rock.

Oz flicked his chin, threading Delilah through his hands, but Zylah ignored the threat. Either he was going to whip her or he wasn't. She didn't have time to dwell on it. She fell to her knees where she hoped to find the shrub, scooping away the snow with shaking hands. She loosed a breath when she caught the first sight of green. "See," she said triumphantly, beaming up at him. She tore up what she could with her cuffed hands, pushing herself to her feet. She was soaking. Her feet were numb, her fingers were numb. But this was the only idea she had.

Oz seemed moderately pleased as she shuffled back up to the cave, forcing herself to keep moving. Her brother. She was doing this for her brother. As she approached the opening of the cave, she saw the spot where Oz had been having his fires. The ground was free of snow, but there was no sign of any firewood.

"Sit," Oz instructed.

Zylah lowered herself to her haunches as gracefully as she could. She needed her boots, but she was too cold to do anything but watch as he retrieved a bundle of firewood from inside the cave and lit the fire.

He wasn't about to let her rest; instead he dropped a pan at her knees. "Fill it with snow."

She held out her cuffed hands. "You'll get your tea a lot quicker if I don't have these on."

He'd disappeared behind her again, back into the opening of the cave, and the moment Zylah registered the cracking sound, the whip bit into her back. She cried out as the metal studs sliced through her tunic and into her skin, biting down on her lip not to cry out a second time. She pressed her hands into the dirt to steady herself, staring at the way the flames reflected in the pan. *Just breathe*, she told herself as pain rolled through her.

Oz knelt in front of her, inserting a key into the cuffs as stars danced before her eyes. "Exposure to vanquicite for as long as you've had these on for means you won't be able to evanesce for days. Try anything stupid, and I'll whip you again. Cry too loud and I'll whip you again. Fuck up my tea and I'll whip you again. Understood?"

Zylah nodded as he pulled the cuffs away and she rubbed her aching wrists. She winced as the movement pulled at the fresh wounds across her back, but she didn't falter. She pushed against her magic, and just as he'd said, she felt nothing. She picked up the pan and made herself walk over to the snow, scooping in a few handfuls to boil. She didn't dare slip a hand into her apron. Not yet.

She knelt in front of the fire, hooking the pan on the stick hanging above it. Her back was to Oz. A risky choice, but she needed access to her apron without him seeing. She warmed her hands in front of the fire, balled them up and pulled them close. This time she knew to brace herself, and as the whip came down, she bit on her lip so hard she drew blood.

But it had been all she needed. She pressed her fists to the ground as the pain racked through her, clinging tightly to the jupe leaves and praying she'd tucked them well enough out of sight.

"Take too long, and I'll whip you again," Oz spat behind her.

Zylah nodded, reaching for the bundle of tea leaves, the jupe tucked under her thumb. She hoped it was enough as she let it all fall into the pan. She closed her eyes, listening to the sound of the water boil and focusing on her breathing. He'd hit the lump on her back with that last lash, and Zylah was certain, from the warm press of blood, that a section of skin had come away entirely. She let out a shaky breath through pursed lips and turned to Oz. "Cup?"

He threw it at her, and she barely caught it. She dipped it into the pan, the water burning her fingers, but she didn't care. She willed her hands not to shake as she rose to her feet and took it over to Oz.

"Set the tea down slowly, then turn around."

Zylah's insides twisted. She knew what was coming, and she didn't know how much more she could endure. She did as he asked, setting the tea down and turning around. She wasn't close enough to lunge for him, and even if she had been, she didn't have it in her. She didn't know how much longer she could stay standing.

"Take three steps," Oz instructed. She heard his quiet groan as he bent over for his tea, heard his deep inhale. She winced as she licked her bleeding lip. The bastard was making her wait on purpose.

Her heartbeat pounded in her chest as she waited for the whip. Oz took a sip of his tea, and Zylah held her breath. The whip cracked, and Delilah sliced through her skin again and again, and she fell to her knees as a third lash came down, a quiet whimper escaping through her gritted teeth.

But Oz didn't stop there.

Three more lashes and Zylah couldn't see her hands anymore, could see nothing but stars and blotches of light dancing in front of her eyes. She sucked in a shaky breath as the lashing stopped, willing herself not to be sick. Oz's breathing was heavy, but he said nothing. Zylah blinked until her vision cleared, waiting.

Another sip. Tears rolled down her cheeks and she blinked them away. It hadn't been enough. The jupe. It hadn't been enough, and she was going to die up here alone in the mountains, and gods knew what was going to happen to her brother. She was shaking, her fingers curling with pain.

"Good te—" Oz began, but the word ended in a strangled cough.

Zylah couldn't turn to watch, not yet; she didn't even know if she could get up. But it didn't take long. Oz struggled for a few more moments before he fell to the ground with a thud. Zylah held her breath, straining to listen for his as she lay still. Nothing. No heartbeat. A sob escaped her, and she staggered to her feet and turned around.

Oz lay on his front, his purple face in the snow, froth staining the white a sickly yellow. Zylah wanted to kick him, but she didn't think her toes could take it. "Bastard," she spat, wiping at her tears.

She grabbed his whip and threw it into the fire, and then she searched him for weapons, the pain in her back so acute it felt like a dozen white-hot blades were still slicing through it. She pulled on her boots with shaking hands, her wounds splitting further with each movement, but she pushed through the pain. She had to. She was so close. She couldn't stop moving, not even for a moment.

Zylah tipped open the sack and found her bracers and weapons, a roll of bread and a tattered blanket. She fastened the bracers, tears rolling down her cheeks as she gathered her weapons. Oz had enough equipment to remain in the mountains for weeks. *Bastard.* She tucked the bread into the front of her apron, wiggling her toes to try and bring some life back into them as she threw the blanket around her shoulders. She wanted to lie down. Wanted to curl into a ball and close her eyes against the pain. But she had to find Zack.

The mountain was silent. Only the sound of her heavy breathing and the wind, no matter how much she strained to hear anything else. But Zack was out there somewhere, and she was going to find him.

Zylah took one last look back at Oz and ran out into the snow.

37

The patch of forest never seemed to get any closer, but Zylah kept running. She kept running until every few steps were a stumble, her lungs burning. She couldn't feel the pain in her back anymore, at least, that's what she told herself.

Everything ached. She was cold, the only warmth from the blood seeping through what was left of her tunic under the blanket. A strangled sob escaped her whenever the rough fabric scraped against her broken skin. She fell again, her stomach twisting in knots. She would die if she didn't make it to shelter, and the thought made her push on harder, as if a single word was carried to her on the wind. *Live.*

A wave of nausea washed over Zylah, and she whispered a prayer to Pallia as the feeling turned itself over in her stomach, like throwing a line for anything, *anyone* to find her. To help her. But still, she kept moving until she reached the edge of the forest, tears blurring her vision the moment the canopy blocked out the light.

The wind stopped, and the world fell silent.

She felt eyes on her, watching from the depths of the forest. Sprites. "Help me, please," she whispered as she paused to catch her breath. Nothing. No birds, no snapping twigs underfoot. The sprites weren't going to intervene, not this time. She wiped at her tears, just as an owl call broke the silence. Kopi.

"I'm here," Zylah rasped through her tears, her voice broken and scratched. "I'm here." She stumbled, pushing herself up again as she ran between the trees, every bone in her body begging her to stop, to lie down, until a voice cut through the quiet.

"Zylah!"

It was Holt, and all Zylah could do was let out a pathetic whimper in response. She peered ahead and caught sight of him through the trees as she stumbled again in the snow, another broken whimper escaping her.

When she glanced up again, Holt was right in front of her. "Zylah," he breathed, as she fell into his arms. "What have they done to you?"

Zylah couldn't speak. All she could do was lean into Holt, breathing in his reassuring scent and willing herself not to fall apart. She felt his hands pass over her back; he was trying to heal her.

"Cuffs," she murmured.

Holt held her closer. "How long?" he asked, his breath hot in her hair.

"Three days."

407

"Shit." He lifted her just as she was, wrapping her legs around his waist so her front pressed against his, careful not to touch her back.

In any other circumstance, Zylah would have commented on how undignified it was, and a delusional laugh almost escaped her, thinking back to when they'd first set foot in Virian together and she'd mentioned how she must have looked like a child beside him. But she wouldn't have been able to make it up onto his back without tearing at her wounds. She closed her eyes as she leaned into him, her heartbeat pounding in her head.

"What happened?" Holt asked quietly.

Zylah fought back a sob. "I went to see my father. He…" She swallowed. Took a deep breath. "He died. Arnir had him beaten. Two bounty hunters came and took me and Zack… I don't know where he is, Holt; I need to find him."

"How did this happen?"

She knew he meant her back. "One of the bounty hunters. I killed him."

"Good."

"How did you find me?" she asked quietly.

His grip tensed for a moment. "Kopi."

Zylah was vaguely aware of him moving through the forest, of trees coming in and out of focus. "My brother," she murmured, trying to twist back in the direction of the cave and instantly regretting it. Raw skin rubbed against cloth, and Zylah swore under her breath.

"I'll go back for him."

Zylah nodded against him, too tired to reply. She focused on the sound of his breathing, of his feet crunching through the snow. If he couldn't heal her because of the lingering effects the vanquicite still had on her, he likely couldn't evanesce with her either.

Trees passed by, but his breathing remained steady and even, as if he ran around forests carrying wounded women every day.

The forest grew thicker, darker, the world coming in and out of focus. Zylah felt weak, boneless, and she knew it wasn't a good sign. "You're shaking," she murmured against his neck, her lip splitting open again as she spoke.

Holt's hands carefully tightened around her, pulling her closer. "It's you, Zylah."

Her eyes closed, and all she wanted was to sleep. To sleep and never wake up. To be free from the pain that coursed through her body.

"Hey." Holt's voice pulled her from an almost dream. "Remember rule number seven?"

"Hmm?"

He pressed a thumb against her thigh to get her attention. "Rule number seven. No dying on each other."

Zylah huffed a quiet laugh, the rhythm of Holt's footsteps lulling her closer to sleep. Or maybe it was the state of her back, she couldn't be certain. "Technically, that was rule number six."

"Six, seven, pick any number you want. The rule still stands." He ducked to miss a low branch, his hand cupping the back of her head for a moment.

"Mmm." She was so cold and so tired, but if she stayed still enough, she couldn't feel the pain in her back. She focused on Holt's warmth, on each of his steps, sure and steady despite his speed.

"Zylah." Holt's voice sounded so far away. "Stay awake. Raif will be here soon, he's in the forest looking for you."

Raif. She hadn't told him how she felt. And now she would probably never get the chance to. The world was slipping away from her; she didn't know how much longer she could hold on.

"Zylah."

She thought of the words she would say to Raif if she got the chance and remembered Saphi's story. "Saphi said you were in love once." Zylah's voice was barely a whisper as she spoke.

"Saphi does a lot of talking."

"Tell me about her."

Holt sighed. "What's there to tell? We were together, and then we weren't. She wanted children, and I wasn't ready. We went our separate ways."

"Do you regret losing her?"

"She's happy now. She has a family. So no, I don't regret it."

An immeasurable sadness settled over her at the thought of him alone. That she'd never see him happy. *You deserve to be happy, Holt.*

"Wake up, Zylah." Holt shook her gently. "Hey, *hey*." The

urgency in his voice jolted her awake. "I thought you wanted to live."

She groaned, shifting in his arms so she could look at him. His mouth was set into a firm line, his brows pinched together in concentration. "I do. But no promises, remember." She couldn't tell him how afraid she was, how the thought of dying stole the air from her lungs. At least now, she wouldn't die alone.

His eyes darted down for a moment, and he swallowed. "And what would Kopi do without you?"

Zylah rested her head against his shoulder, too weak to hold herself upright. She shrugged against his neck. "Stay with you. I hereby leave you my owl that isn't mine to give. He's a terrible pet, but an excellent friend."

"Pallia would never approve."

"Gods, not you as well."

The briefest hint of a smile tugged at the corner of Holt's mouth. "What?"

Zylah rolled her eyes, looking over Holt's shoulder to the path he'd cut through the snow. "If I had a copper for every time someone has told me Pallia had an owl just like Kopi."

"You'd have three coppers?"

"Shut up." Zylah patted her hand against his arm in the most pathetic attempt to punch him.

Holt huffed a laugh into her ear, and if it wasn't for the trees blurring by, she could almost forget for a moment that he was running. Could almost forget that she hadn't just been starved and whipped. If she let herself focus on the pain, even just for a second, it was all consuming, and she involuntarily dug her fingers into Holt's shirt.

She focused on his steady steps again, breathing through the pain. "Holt?"

"Yeah?"

"Look after him for me."

Holt's arms tensed, and he shifted her against him. "We're almost there."

Too late, Zylah thought. Darkness was pressing in, so consuming it drowned out every sound in the world.

"Zylah." Holt's thumbs pressed against her thighs again. "I'll make a bargain with you." His voice was stretched, strained, and she wondered if he needed to rest.

Her eyes half opened. "I thought Fae bargains were unpleasant?" She knew what he was doing, trying to keep her awake, conscious.

"Not as unpleasant as you dying on me."

Zylah laughed against his neck. "Good point. And we did make it a rule already."

"Live, and I'll help you find your real family."

That truly was something to live for. She fought to keep her eyes open, willed her mouth to form the word. "Agreed."

Something pulsed between them, Holt's grip on her tightening as a wave of pain rolled through her. Magic. Too late, she thought, her eyes already closing. Thoughts of her brother and father muddied into one. A creaking, cracking sound had her flicking her eyes open, and Holt slowed to a walk. He'd brought her to his cabin.

"Oh good, I can have a bath," she murmured, the thought of the warm spring water melting her frozen bones pulling a soft sigh from her lips.

The door shut behind Holt, and he strode over to the table. He pulled back to look at her, his eyes full of concern, his hair ruffled from running and falling across his forehead. "I need you on the table so I can inspect your wounds. It's going to hurt. A lot. Ready?"

Zylah nodded. She wasn't ready. She didn't want to move. She just wanted to sleep. Holt lowered her to her feet, and a searing pain broke out across her back. Zylah made a sound somewhere between a gasp and a cry, wishing she could bite down on her lip.

"Do you want me to lift you onto the table?"

She let the blanket fall off her shoulders, not wanting to see how much of her blood had soaked through to it. "I can do it."

She didn't think she could, but she still had a shred of dignity left, despite the noises she made as Holt helped her onto the table. Every movement felt like her back was splitting open, every touch of the fabric against the wounds like hot needles. But somehow she made it onto her front, her cheek resting on one arm, the other lying beside her. When she tried to move, it pulled at the broken skin and sent an involuntary whimper from her lips.

Zylah closed her eyes, listening to Holt pulling open cupboards and gathering materials.

He placed something down on the table beside her, glass

413

clinking together. Zylah was afraid to die, but maybe the world would be better off without her in it. For Raif. Her brother. Her father would have still been alive if she'd just stayed on the gallows that day.

"Zylah." Holt squeezed the hand that lay at her side. "I can't heal you until the effects of the vanquicite wear off, so I have to do things... by hand."

Zylah nodded once. He meant he was going to have to peel out every scrap of her clothing, try to separate cloth from flesh. She was certain he'd be able to see right through to the muscle, and gods knew what that looked like.

Holt shuffled beside her. "This is—"

"Going to hurt? I've got this, Holt. Just do it. Please." She wasn't ready to die. Not yet.

Holt uncorked something beside her. Celandia. She focused on her breathing as he poured it onto a cloth and paused. His fingers brushed the first piece of fabric, and Zylah jolted from the pain as he pulled it away. He didn't press the celandia to her back, not yet.

He sucked in a breath as he eased away another shred of fabric, and Zylah winced again, a hot tear rolling down her nose.

"What is it?" she asked, quietly sniffing back her tears.

Holt moved another piece of fabric, tearing at a piece that wasn't in contact with her wound. "It's your..."

"My lump? What about it?" Zylah waited as Holt tore away more of her tunic.

He let out a quiet breath, and Zylah wondered how he

sounded so composed. "It's split open."

"And?" She tried to look over her shoulder, but pain coursed through her.

"There's something inside it. It looks like vanquicite."

"Vanquicite? How? That doesn't make any sense." She'd always had the lump in her back, for as long as she could remember.

He peeled away another piece of fabric and Zylah bit down on her lip, splitting it further. "I've never seen anything like this, it looks like it's—" He paused, and Zylah strained to listen to whatever he might have heard out in the forest.

"Holt," a voice called out from outside. Raif. Against Zylah's will, more tears fell.

Holt disappeared for a moment, returning by the time Zylah had breathed in and out. He'd evanesced, which meant that he could call on his powers if he wasn't touching her, that the vanquicite must have some effect only on the blood of the person that had touched it. But that didn't make any sense, if there was a piece of vanquicite in her back, Holt must have been mistaken—

"Liss." Raif's hands were on her face, in her hair. He knelt in front of her, his features etched with worry as he pressed soft kisses to her face and wiped at her tears with his thumbs. Zylah tried to speak but the words lodged in her throat.

Kopi landed on the table beside her, nuzzling into her hair. Zylah couldn't make a sound for him, either, but she closed her eyes as she blinked back more tears. Kopi must have brought Raif, but how if he'd led Holt to her? It didn't make any sense. Maybe he really was Pallia's owl. *Gods.* A delirious smile tugged at her mouth at the thought.

"Liss?" Raif's eyes were bright and glassy as she willed her own to open, another tear rolling down to the tip of her nose.

"I was just thinking he really must be Pallia's owl," she said, her voice barely a whisper.

Raif huffed a laugh, wiping away the tear and pressing a kiss to the corner of her mouth, careful not to touch her split lip.

"I can't heal her," Holt said from the far side of the cabin, as if he'd been waiting, giving them space. "She's been wearing vanquicite cuffs for days. It's only her Fae side that's stopped her from bleeding to death."

Raif stood, but his hands stayed on Zylah's. "Is that what I think it is?"

He must have seen the vanquicite. If it *was* vanquicite. Holt hummed in acknowledgement.

"That explains why she could evanesce to the grotto," Raif said quietly.

"It explains a lot of things."

"It doesn't explain anything to me," Zylah said dryly.

Holt carefully peeled away another piece of fabric. "You've built up some small amount of tolerance to the vanquicite. The effects won't last as long as they would for Raif and me. It's how you could evanesce me out of the tunnels, and in and out of the grotto. Wearing it for three days seems to have been your limit."

"Three days?" Raif's voice was lined with vitriol, and he

squeezed Zylah's hand gently.

The celandia swab pressed lightly against her back as Holt said, "I'm going to seal the perimeter, and then I'll be back with Saphi."

Seal the what? Zylah wondered if she'd misheard Holt's words. Kopi hooed quietly and flew away, but something told her he was still nearby. And he'd brought Raif right to her.

Raif kneeled in front of her like before, brushing her hair out of her eyes and let out a shaky breath. "I haven't stopped looking for you. None of us have. The moment you left I checked the whole city. Holt took out five guards trying to find you." His words came faster and faster, his thumb stroking her cheek. "I love you, Liss. I should have told you a hundred times. When I asked you to stay, *no*, before that. You had me from the moment you cut me with your dagger at the safe house."

He kissed the corner of her mouth, and Zylah couldn't help the tears that fell. She'd wanted to tell him. So many times. But she was afraid. And now the fear of losing him…

Raif wiped away her tears. "We can leave Virian. We can go wherever you like. All over Astaria. I can take you to Iskia, you'd love the ocean. Kopi might not like it, but we can keep him dry. Just stay with me."

The life he described played out in her thoughts, like it was right out of the pages of one of Kara's books. But that was all it could ever be, a story. If Rose's vision was true, Zylah knew she had to get as far away from Raif as she could. If she made it out of the cabin.

"I had to leave," was all she managed to say. "I can't risk... I can't lose you." She let out an unsteady breath, her fingers tightening around his.

Raif stroked a thumb across her cheek, pressing his forehead against hers. "I'm not going anywhere," he said softly.

Zylah nodded; it was all she could manage.

A thud sounded against wood, and Zylah knew Holt had returned. Two more heartbeats told her he'd brought Saphi... and Rose.

"Oh, Liss," Saphi said quietly as she approached. Zylah couldn't see her face, and for that she was grateful.

Raif gently squeezed her hand as Saphi's delicate fingers touched an unbroken patch of skin on Zylah's back.

"The vanquicite will be too dangerous to remove. It's going to need someone with far greater skills than mine. But I can clean the wounds and dress them for you." Saphi's voice was soft, soothing.

Zylah nodded again, just once.

"Raif, Holt, go and bring me as much moss as you can find," Saphi instructed. "Rose and I will get started."

Zylah didn't know how she felt about Rose helping, but she was in no position to protest.

Raif pressed another kiss to the corner of her mouth. "I'll be right back," he murmured.

The door clicked shut, and Zylah knew they'd gone back out into the snow. Saphi knelt before her, her top dipping low and revealing the scar that ran up the centre of her chest.

"Who did that to you?" Zylah whispered. If there was ever

a time she could ask, she figured it was now.

"I did. Here, put this in your mouth." Saphi's face gave nothing away about the scar, and Zylah couldn't understand why anyone would need to do something like that to themself. She sniffed the besa leaf Saphi held in front of her lips and held her mouth open. Zylah doubted it would do much to calm her but took it anyway.

She felt Rose move closer, heard her intake of breath. "I'm so sorry, Liss. I never meant for this to happen."

Zylah chewed on the leaf, wishing she could see Rose's face, but she didn't dare try to look over her shoulder again. She closed her eyes, willing herself to relax. She was safe. She wasn't going to die. She said it to herself over and over. But it wouldn't be without sacrifices. Raif's mint and lemongrass scent lingered in her hair, and she sniffed back another tear. She would live, but she couldn't stay. She couldn't risk his life with her selfishness.

"Zylah," she said at last, as she felt the besa leaf working, her muscles relaxing. "My name is Zylah."

38

Two days passed in the cabin. Saphi had moved Zylah to the lounger, where she'd spent an entire day sleeping. She pulled on her power every chance she got, testing it to see if she could evanesce from one end of the cabin to the other, but nothing happened. That meant she wasn't healing fast enough.

Raif barely left her side. He didn't speak much with the others around, none of them did, but he moved as if he was frightened she might disappear. Zylah wished he wasn't right to think that but no matter how much she wanted the future he'd painted for them, she couldn't put him at risk. Besides, Arnir was still out there, and that meant she'd always have a target on her back. She never should have stayed in Virian. Should have moved on the moment she had a few coins to her name.

"Copper for your thoughts?" Raif asked quietly beside her. Saphi was washing supplies in the bathroom, Holt and Rose were outside keeping watch—where they'd spent most of their time for the last few days.

Zylah ran her tongue over her lip where it had scabbed. "Just thinking about Zack." Holt had been out to look for him, but each time there was no news, no sign of her brother.

Raif placed a hand on her arm, his elbow resting on the back of the lounger beside her. She'd been able to sit up that morning, and she'd taken to leaning her front against the back of the lounger, elbows on the top for support. His fingers twitched, and he traced the seam of her shirt to her wrist, uncurling her fingers with his and placing a kiss onto her palm.

"He'll be fine, Zylah. He's the King's Blade for a reason."

It was so strange to hear him say her name. But since she'd told Rose, none of them called her Liss anymore. Enough hiding, she'd decided. If she was going to leave Raif, leave all of them, they deserved to know who she was. Even Rose.

She pulled at a thread on the back of the lounger, listening to the crackle of the fire and the steady beat of Raif's heart.

"None of this is your fault." His fingers brushed her chin, and he gently moved her head to look at him. "Knowing you has been a gift. I'm sure your father felt the same. I'm sure Zack does, too."

A tear threatened to fall, and Zylah blinked it away. She'd tried not to think of her father since arriving at the cabin. She didn't want to face what those thoughts might do to her, not in front of the others. "I feel like a curse, not a gift," she whispered.

Raif's lips twitched. "Can I say something insufferable?"

Zylah smiled, resting her hand on his where his thumb

421

stroked her cheek. If they could just stay like this, safe in the cabin, safe from the world, no harm could come to him, could it?

His eyes fell to her mouth, and gently, so very gently, he kissed her, resting his forehead against hers. "If this is what it feels like to be cursed... curse all of it... my mind, my body, my heart. It's all yours."

Zylah sat back on her haunches, ignoring the shudder of pain it sent through her back, and threaded her fingers into Raif's hair, pulling him closer. "Insufferable," she murmured against his lips, kissing him as much as her broken lip would allow.

She winced, a burst of pain snagging her breath and pulled away to lean on the lounger once more. "Rose's visions... are they ever wrong?"

Raif looked away, shadows dancing across his face from the fire. He squared his jaw. "Nothing is going to happen to me."

Zylah had already known the answer. But she'd needed to hear it. Needed to know if there was any chance she could be wrong.

"What she saw could be years from now, Zylah. But I'm not walking away from you over the possibility that it isn't. Nothing will keep me away from you." He turned to look at her, more of his face cast in shadow, and Zylah could have sworn his eyes darkened for a moment like they did when she'd seen him use his magic.

The door to the bathroom clicked shut, and Saphi's vanilla perfume seeped into the room. "Wound check."

The Fae didn't wait for Zylah's response, just sat beside her on the lounger and rolled up her shirt. Raif had already stood and begun pacing. Zylah knew he was watching as Saphi rolled up Holt's shirt—just like the one she'd worn when he'd first brought her there—and inspected the wounds.

"You're starting to heal," Saphi murmured as she replaced a bandage. "Even if you can't evanesce by then, tomorrow you'll be well enough to make the walk back to Virian."

But that was the wrong direction. She had to go back to the mountains, had to search for her brother.

Raif stopped his pacing in front of the lounger. "I'll carry her," he said, as if there was no discussing it.

Arnir's men would have been all over the mountain range, were likely already in the forest. They were all taking a risk, staying there with her, but when she'd protested on the first day, Raif had told her they were all there because they wanted to be.

Zylah rested a hand on Saphi's arm, pulling herself to her feet. She wouldn't be a burden. Raif was at her side immediately, one hand at her elbow.

"I'm fine," Zylah said through gritted teeth, testing the pain. "I need to try."

Saphi watched her and Raif from the lounger but didn't reach out as Raif had. "You need to rest."

Kopi called out, the call far away in the forest, but it was enough to send Zylah's heartbeat racing. She took a step towards the door, and he called out again. Raif reached out to stop her, but she brushed him away, making for the door as

Kopi called out a third time, much closer now.

Zylah wasn't dressed for snow. She only had a pair of Saphi's slippers covering her feet, but she didn't care. She ran out of the cabin, a few steps into the icy powder, then stopped.

For the first time, she saw the *perimeter* they'd all been talking about. Vines and roots twisted over and over each other as if they'd been pulled right from the forest floor, weaving together so thickly they formed a wall right around the cabin. Zylah had to tilt her head back to see the trees; the wall reached higher than Raif. Only magic could have made something like this. Holt's magic.

She felt Raif beside her, but he didn't reach out for her again. He was listening. Something was wrong.

Zylah looked up into the canopy for any sign of Kopi, just as Holt evanesced himself and Rose back inside the perimeter.

"Arnir," Holt said, weapons appearing in each hand from wherever he'd summoned them. He handed a sword to Rose, the other to her brother before summoning two more.

"How many?" Raif asked.

Holt's eyes flicked to Zylah for a moment and then back to Raif. "Fifteen, maybe more."

"Zylah, get inside with Saphi. Lock the door." Raif's hand was around her wrist, gently easing her back towards the cabin.

She shook him off. "My brother. He could be with them."

Kopi cried out again. Saphi had come out of the cabin to join them, her gaze snapping to Rose first.

"The bounty hunter who took me, he used a spell to

conceal his scent, to mute any sounds he made—his breathing, his footsteps," Zylah said quietly, so quietly she knew only Fae ears would hear her.

They all looked ahead as branches snapped in the forest.

"Esteemed friends," a voice called out. King Arnir. Zylah would never forget his voice. Saphi touched a hand to her elbow, just as Raif positioned himself in front of her.

The king cleared his throat. "Let me propose a simple trade. My hostage for yours."

Her brother. He had her brother. "Zack!" Zylah called out, just as Saphi's hand clamped down over her mouth.

"It could be a trap," Saphi murmured.

"Prove it," Holt called out. "Let us hear him speak."

A moment of silence stretched between them all.

"Zylah?" It was Zack's voice, and Zylah held a hand to her mouth to stifle a sob.

Holt raised a hand, and the vines creaked and cracked. It was the sound Zylah had heard when he'd brought her there a few days before. The vines uncoiled from each other slowly, until a space wide enough for a single person to walk through opened up in the wall. Beyond it, Zylah could see a handful of Arnir's elite unit, weapons drawn.

"Now, now, perhaps a little show of faith. You can't expect my men to walk in there one by one, can you?" Arnir called out.

"I don't expect any of them to walk in here at all. Hand over Zack, and we'll allow you to leave with your unit intact," Holt said firmly.

Arnir clicked his tongue. "That will never do. Drop the walls, or he dies."

"Holt, please," Zylah pleaded.

Holt lowered the wall further, and it was only Saphi holding her back that stopped Zylah from running to her brother. He was bound, his face bloodied, kneeling at Arnir's feet like a dog.

"Zack!"

"Ah, there she is. You shall not escape your punishment a third time," the king spat.

I didn't mean for him to die. But there was no use telling Arnir that. His son deserved what he got. Zylah looked at the rope Arnir held, the other end tied to her brother, and her attention fell on Arnir's hands. Instead of the gaudy jewels he'd worn at the festival, he wore only one ring this time. A vanquicite ring.

"Do you see the jewellery?" Zylah said quietly for the others.

"Fucking coward," Rose murmured under her breath.

Kopi cried out again, and the forest floor seemed to erupt with movement.

Saphi held Zylah back with enough force to split open one of her wounds. "I'm sorry, Zylah. You'll only be in their way like this."

Holt, Raif and Rose moved together as one unit, swords raised. Raif and Holt used their abilities to complement their swordplay, while Rose moved about Arnir's men as if she were dancing. As if she could see every move before it was made.

Zylah didn't know where to look, but Saphi kept a firm hold on her arm as they stood on the deck of the cabin. She kept pushing at her magic, testing it to see if she could reach Zack, but she felt nothing.

A soldier knocked Rose's sword from her hands, but she was already one move ahead of him, launching onto her hands to swipe a kick at his chest with her blade leg. Crimson stained the soldier's chest as he fell, and Rose touched down on her foot, then her blade, swiping down to gather her sword.

Holt used the forest to fight. Tree roots and branches did his bidding, wrapping around soldiers and holding them in place as his weapons did the rest. He cut through three soldiers as if they were nothing.

Every soldier Raif touched turned to ash. Zylah wondered if he'd used his weapon even once. She was certain she felt eyes on them all, watching through the trees, and she knew, somehow, that it was the sprites. But still, they didn't intervene. Kopi flew down to her shoulder just as Raif turned another soldier to ash.

They didn't stop until every soldier was dead.

Arnir's laugh cut through the silence. "Marcus told me you were good."

"Shame he couldn't join you," Rose spat.

"I had another task for Marcus today. But my request still stands. Her, for him."

Nobody moved.

Arnir drew a sword from the sheath at his belt, the black stone of the blade glinting in the last of the light through the trees. More vanquicite. "Last chance. The girl, or he dies."

Zylah stepped forwards, just as Arnir made a pained sound, and blood pooled at his chest.

"Zack!" Zylah called out, but Saphi held her back.

Blood dripped from the corner of Arnir's mouth as he dropped the rope holding Zack and pressed a hand to his wound.

The king looked up at Zylah, his lips moving but no sound escaping them, and fell to his knees.

39

Zylah blinked once. Twice. She was looking at a ghost. She had to be. Beside the lifeless body of Arnir stood Prince Jesper, wiping his hands clean on a pristine piece of white cloth he'd pulled from his pocket. He wore his finest purple jacket, his golden hair perfectly smoothed back.

"Impossible," Zylah breathed.

Jesper looked right at her as if he'd heard her. He smiled, revealing two perfect fangs pressing against his lips, eyes as dark and empty as a starless night.

Zylah watched in horror as the prince leaned over his father's corpse, pulling off the vanquicite ring and sliding it onto his finger, admiring it as if it had just been gifted to him. The dancers at the festival wove through Zylah's thoughts, masked figures spiralling through the crowd, and at once she knew Jesper was one of those monsters created by the gods.

"Vampire," Saphi murmured beside her. "You didn't kill him, Zylah. He just faked his death to preserve his identity."

The colour drained from Zylah's face. All of this, everything she'd been through, was because of a lie. Zack shuffled back a few steps in the snow, but Jesper didn't seem to care. His gaze was fixed on Zylah, his dead eyes taking her in. She held her breath, pushing and pushing against her powers, but there was no response.

She hadn't needed to though; Holt disappeared and reappeared beside her brother, just as Jesper moved impossibly fast and pressed a hand to Zack's shoulder. "He stays with me."

Zylah couldn't see what Jesper did, but Holt staggered back a few steps. *Shit.* Holt was the strongest Fae she knew. And with the vanquicite ring... Jesper had just made himself untouchable.

She should have been afraid, but she was more afraid for her friends than herself. For her brother, who could do nothing but cower beside Jesper like his pet.

Rose had backed up to the cabin, to protect Saphi, Zylah suspected. She knew Saphi could fight, but she also knew the Fae wouldn't leave her side. Holt resumed his position beside Raif, unfazed by whatever Jesper had done to him a few moments before.

Again and again, Zylah pushed at her abilities: to evanesce, to heal herself, anything. She thought something within her stirred, but when she remained rooted to the spot, she cast it aside as nothing more than a desperate hope. Injuries or not, if she had a weapon, she would gladly join Raif and Holt. Her eyes darted to Arnir's vanquicite sword, and back to her brother. He was the only one of them who could wield it without any lasting effects, but his hands were still bound. If she could just reach him...

Jesper shoved a hand in his pocket, surveying the piles of ash before him. His eyes didn't linger on his father for even a moment. "Well, you're a quiet crowd."

"I think we're all wondering why you just killed your father, although I have to say I can think of several reasons to take down my own," Raif said calmly.

Jesper's smile widened. "Arnir wasn't really my father."

"He raised you like you were his own fucking son," Rose said quietly, too quietly for human ears to hear.

The prince didn't flinch. "Aurelia warned me about your mouth."

Aurelia... Zylah recognised the name... Raif's mother. Zylah paled as she recalled Rose's words from a few nights before. *I saw our mother.*

But Rose wasn't finished yet. "Our mother has been dead for far longer than you have drawn breath," she said, this time loud enough for Zack to hear her.

Jesper clicked his tongue, one arm sweeping wide. "Come now, is this hostility any way to welcome a family member?"

"We are not family," Rose spat, but something in her voice told Zylah the Fae wasn't so sure.

Jesper held out his hand to examine the vanquicite ring, the other still firmly planted on Zack's shoulder. "Well, in the loosest sense of the word. Aurelia found me over a century ago. Made me into what I am."

Zylah shrugged out of Saphi's hold and took a step

431

forward, but Kopi landed on her shoulder, as if in warning. Zylah didn't like any of this. Not one bit. She kept pushing and pushing, praying to the gods to give her back her abilities.

Raif had taken up position at Holt's side, his sword lowered, but Zylah knew that meant nothing. She'd seen how fast he moved. How fast they both could move. And she worried Jesper might be faster.

Jesper circled his father's corpse, never further than hand's reach from Zack. "Mother saved me when no one else would. Raised me when the bloodlust took over me for decades. I was meant to take Arnir's place, but by the time the bloodlust eased, it was his son whose place I took instead."

"Where is the real prince?" Zylah asked, though she was sure she could guess.

Jesper grinned, and it was the look he'd used on her in his bed chambers, only this time, those two very sharp fangs were on display. "Dead, along with anyone who knew him as a boy." He admired the ring again. "Arnir's memory was wiped many times. Compulsion—such a gift. Such a simple task to perform, perhaps the favourite of my acquired abilities." He looked at Zack before his gaze rested on Zylah once more. She read the unspoken threat and took another step towards her brother, Saphi close behind her. *Compulsion.* Zylah recalled how it had felt to stand before Jesper in his bed chamber, as if she were frozen to the spot. *Bastard.* How many women had he used his *gift* on?

This was years in the planning. She tried to think back on how old the prince was supposed to be, a few years younger than her, and how many people he would have killed to make them all believe he was the true prince. She could think of dozens at the palace alone.

"But it isn't him I've come for. It's you." Jesper pointed a long finger at Zylah, and she could almost feel it drag up her thigh and claw at her shirt. She swallowed back the bile that burned in the back of her throat.

But she wouldn't show him fear. Zylah kept pushing at her abilities, testing, pushing against the lingering sensation of the vanquicite. And felt something stir.

Raif circled back to the cabin, and Zylah wanted nothing more than to stand beside him, but Saphi still held her back.

"Why?" Raif asked. "Come to finish what you started in Dalstead? Our kind have a particular punishment for your choice of misconduct."

Misconduct. That was certainly one way of putting it. Zylah knew what kind of punishment she felt was most fitting for Jesper's crime.

But Jesper's smile didn't falter. "Because I owe a debt to Marcus, for keeping our mother safe."

Raif took a step closer to Jesper. "Marcus can go fuck himself."

"Ah. He warned me you were protective of her." Jesper cocked his head to one side, as if he were sizing Raif up.

They needed to leave. All of them. She glanced at Holt, willing her expression to say, *gather them all up, take them away from here, please.* But he just moved his head almost imperceptibly, as if to say, *don't try anything.*

"What does Marcus want with me?" Zylah asked, her attention sliding back to Jesper.

The prince shrugged. "He didn't say. Just that I'm to bring you to him using any means necessary." He tapped a finger against his chin, as if he were recalling some long-forgotten memory. "I believe his exact words were, *bring me that little whore no matter what.*"

Raif growled. He lunged for Jesper, dangerously close to Zack. Faster than Zylah could blink, Jesper had Arnir's vanquicite sword in his hands, bringing it down to clash against Raif's.

Zylah didn't know where to look. At Raif, moving around Jesper faster than she could keep track, or at Zack, perilously close to the blades swiping at each other.

Jesper's sword came down as Raif pivoted out of the way, grazing the dirt beside Zack. Zylah pushed again at her abilities and felt the wounds on her back begin to knit together slowly. But she still couldn't evanesce, not yet. Kopi hadn't moved from her shoulder, as if he were telling her to stay where she was.

Holt was one step ahead of her again. The second Jesper moved away from Zack, Holt evanesced to her brother and brought him back to the cabin. Holt summoned vines and roots from the forest floor, all in an attempt to make Jesper lose his footing, but nothing got close to him with the vanquicite ring.

Zylah still felt those eyes on them all, watching, waiting. As if the sprites were holding their breath. And she wondered why they still hadn't intervened, what made them decide when to help and when not to. Holt had told her they responded to his magic; did they recoil from Jesper?

Saphi took another step closer as Holt darted around the perimeter, building and lowering walls from the forest to trap Jesper, but Raif barely landed a blow. Jesper moved faster than anything Zylah had ever seen, the vanquicite blade nicking and slicing at Raif so frequently little welts of blood pooled across his shirt.

Jesper was toying with him, trying to tire him out. Holt evanesced closer, his sword raised to strike the prince, but Raif spun, his sword slicing Jesper's arm just as the prince pivoted away. He touched a hand to the blood, his eyes darkening as he glared at Raif.

Zylah held her breath. Even Kopi seemed transfixed, claws digging into her shoulder, but she didn't care. Saphi had grabbed her wrist again, holding so tight it would bruise.

"Raif, please," Rose begged, as Holt tried to get closer to Jesper.

Zack's hand slipped into Zylah's, and she didn't dare let out her breath. Not until Raif was away from Jesper.

"Stay out of it," Raif spat, swinging again at Jesper.

Holt landed a strike to Jesper's arm, but the prince didn't baulk, his attention fixed entirely on Raif.

"Take him, Holt, please," Zylah whispered. Away from here, away from all of this. Anywhere Raif would be safe.

Holt's green eyes met hers for a moment. "We're not leaving you."

That wasn't the answer she wanted to hear. Zylah's lungs burned. Her head was pounding from pushing against her abilities, and she swiped at tears she hadn't realised had fallen. Jesper's sword sliced into Raif's thigh, and Holt surged forwards on a tree root, sword raised. But Jesper slammed him back with nothing but his fist.

Raif lunged for the prince, but Jesper saw him coming, disarming Raif so fast Zylah couldn't work out how he'd done it. Her breath left her in a half sob, half gasp, and she pushed and pushed, willing her body to evanesce, to reach him, to get him away from there.

Rose was screaming as Raif fought with his bare hands, swinging blows at Jesper that were never going to land. Zylah couldn't take her eyes off Raif. Holt moved at the edge of her vision, just as Raif cried out. Just as Jesper's sword slid out of Raif's abdomen.

"Raif!" Zylah screamed.

He fell to his knees in the dirt, one hand pressed against the wound, his eyes fixed on Zylah's. Jesper grabbed him by the collar, lifting him into the air as if he were nothing. Holt evanesced beside him, but Jesper shoved him back with that preternatural strength, his gaze on Zylah.

A sickening grin spread across Jesper's face. "Marcus sends his regards." His fangs sank into Raif's neck, tearing away flesh.

Zylah's world tilted as Raif slumped to the forest floor.

40

Someone was screaming. Zylah thought it was Rose, but then she realised it was her. Both of them. Saphi was holding onto her, pulling her and Rose back, Zack at her other side. Holt was shouting something, but all Zylah could do was push and push against her abilities. She had to get to him; she had to reach Raif. She couldn't hear his breathing from this far away, couldn't hear his heart.

She pushed again and felt the hands that were holding her fall away into nothing as she closed the distance between her and Raif, passing through the aether to reach him. But something slammed into her when she reappeared beside Raif. Or tried to. It was a wall of vines. No, not a wall, a cage, spreading over Raif's body everywhere she reached for him.

"Holt, stop it," she screamed, tears blurring her vision as she clawed at the roots and vines.

A hand landed on her shoulder. "It isn't me," Holt rasped.

Zylah looked on in horror. It was the sprites. And they'd

chosen this moment to intervene, to trap Raif with Jesper, away from her.

She clawed and clawed at the roots until her fingernails split, screaming Raif's name. If she stopped, she'd be admitting it was over. And she couldn't. Couldn't breathe at the thought—

"Zylah," Holt said softly, touching a hand to her arm, but she smacked him away.

"Why won't you help him?" Zylah sobbed, pressing a hand over her heart as she watched the roots twist and thicken.

"Zylah, listen."

Something in Holt's voice made Zylah pause. She held her breath. Closed her eyes. She knew what she was listening for. The sound that had sent her to sleep on so many nights in Virian. The heart that had held hers gently. That had asked her to stay.

Silent.

Raif was gone. And the moment Holt sensed the recognition in her face, he evanesced them back to the cabin, where hands grabbed at her shirt, and they evanesced away.

Away from Jesper. And away from Raif.

41

"Marcus is coming for her," Rose said through a broken sob, the moment they arrived at the safe house.

Zylah stared at her hands, tears mingling with her bloodied fingers. Silent. Raif's heart was silent. He was gone.

"How long?" Holt asked.

Rose pressed a hand to her stomach, wiping at her tears. "Tonight."

Zylah was shaking. It couldn't be real. He couldn't be dead. His scent still lingered in her hair and on her clothes where he'd touched her, held her. She pressed a hand to her heart against the sharp ache that made her want to curl up on the floor and never move.

Holt swore under his breath. "Saphi. Gather as many supplies as you can. I'll be back with the rest of her things."

"Where are you taking her?" Zack asked.

Zylah didn't care that they were talking about her as if she wasn't there. Raif was gone. And she hadn't told him. Hadn't told him how much he'd saved her these last few months in Virian. How he'd made each day easier for her. How she loved him. Her breath caught in her throat, and she clutched at the necklace he'd given her. She hadn't deserved it. His love. Any of it. And now he was gone.

"She isn't safe here," Holt said quietly.

Zack was on his feet, and despite how filthy he was, how his face was crusted with blood and one eye barely open, he stood tall as he looked up at Holt. "I'll go with her. I can protect her."

"No," Zylah demanded. No one else. She'd been right. She *was* a curse.

"I'm not leaving you." Zack was on his knees before her, his hands resting on her arms.

"I tried to leave." Zylah's voice came out as a whisper, tears streaming down her face as she took in how badly his face was bruised. "Before I came to see Father. I should have stayed away." She wiped at her face, willed the tears to stop. "You said it yourself, I'm not your sister. Just look at what my being here has done. What *I've* done. I'm leaving."

"It isn't safe for her here until we can deal with Marcus," Holt murmured. And then he was gone, back to the tavern, Zylah presumed.

Zylah pressed her face into her hands. She felt arms around her shoulders and someone sobbing. It was Rose. Gods. The Fae had just lost her brother. Zylah rested her hands over Rose's, and they sat in silence together.

"None of this is your fault. But especially this," Rose said quietly, her head on Zylah's shoulder.

"I loved him," Zylah whispered. She had to say it out loud. For someone, anyone to hear it. Saying it out loud made it real.

Rose brushed a piece of Zylah's hair back and tucked it behind her ear. "He knew. We all do."

"I'm not leaving you," Zack said again. He hadn't moved from his spot in front of her, and like this Zylah felt safe. Loved. But she didn't deserve it. She was a curse to all of them.

Zylah took a deep, steadying breath. "Stay with them. Help them. Whatever comes next, Zack, there's nothing left for you in Dalstead. But you'll have a family here."

Zack held her hand, and that was all Zylah needed to know he thought she was right. He wouldn't be able to keep up with her; he'd learnt that so many times as a child. Her friends would look after him. And he knew Holt. Gods, Zylah had no idea how long they'd known each other, how much more time she might have had with them all, and the thought sent another sob shaking through her.

Rose's arms tightened around her, soothing her. Zylah let the tears fall. She'd had so little time with Raif. And it had been snatched away from them. All the plans he'd described to her, the places he wanted to show her, all gone. She prayed to Pallia that it was all a bad dream, that she would wake up at any moment. That he would stride through the door, that insufferable grin of his spread across his face...

The three of them huddled on the floor together, silent, only the sound of their breathing filling the space. Zylah didn't know how long they sat until Kopi's soft call broke the quiet and Saphi brushed aside the glass bead curtain.

Zack got to his feet first, reaching out a hand for Rose. Zylah stood alone as Saphi rested a canvas bag beside the counter, the space seeming to close in on her. Zylah closed her eyes to steady herself, Saphi's vanilla perfume hitting her as the Fae's arms wrapped around her shoulders.

"Do you want to see his room before you go?" Saphi asked into Zylah's hair.

Zylah's stomach twisted. "No. Thank you." She couldn't see it. Couldn't look at all the places they'd been together, didn't want to feel his lingering presence when he wasn't there to hold. To hold *her*.

Saphi pulled away, and Zylah wrapped her arms around herself.

"We'll see each other again," the Fae said quietly. "Rose has seen it."

Zylah nodded. It didn't matter what they said. Whether Marcus was gone or not. Or whether Jesper was still out there, running Marcus's errands. She was never coming back.

"Will you have a funeral?" Zylah asked. Her father's body was gone, but it brought her some comfort to know that they could do that for Raif, even if she couldn't be there for it.

A dull thump sounded on the floor behind her, and Zylah turned to see Holt with her things. "His body is gone; I went back there first."

Zylah's hand went to her necklace. "Jesper?"

"The sprites, I think." Holt dragged a hand through his hair.

"Maybe they wanted to protect him from Jesper."

Wild heat flashed through Zylah. "Why didn't they protect him before Jesper killed him? Why didn't they protect him when he needed it?"

Holt shook his head. "I don't know."

The anger left her then, when she saw the anguished look on Holt's face. The loss wasn't hers alone. They had all lost Raif. And Zylah knew Holt would be feeling just as responsible for Raif's death as she was.

"Now what?" she asked quietly.

"Put these on." He handed her a fresh apron and her cloak. "There are horses waiting for us on the south side of the city."

"Horses?"

"Magic has a trace, remember. We can't risk Marcus tracking us, so we'll take the horses for a while." Holt fastened the bag again after handing Zylah her things.

She didn't question the clothes, just did as he asked, tugging her apron on over her head. "I'm not putting anyone else at risk." Holt might have had his reasons for getting her out of Virian and if he thought this was how they could protect her, let him believe it. But Zylah held onto the truth. She was protecting them instead.

Holt frowned. "Zylah, please."

She read the unspoken words in his eyes. *Let me do this.* He hadn't been able to help Raif. But this was something he could do. She turned to Saphi and Rose, made her goodbyes as if she were floating somewhere outside of her body, watching.

Zack hugged her tightly. "I love you, Zylah." She didn't

deserve his love. She didn't deserve any of them.

She smiled weakly as she tugged up her hood, and Kopi took that as his cue to fly down onto her shoulder. This was why she'd left the way she had before. To avoid this moment with them. This look on their faces.

Holt handed Zylah her sword, slung the bag over his shoulder and grabbed the one Saphi had packed. Then he reached out a hand to her. "Ready?"

Zylah looked up at her friend. "Ready." She put her hand in his, took one last look at her brother, and Holt evanesced them away.

They reappeared on the south side of the city, just as Holt had said. But only one horse was waiting for them, a note tucked under the bridle in the dusk. Zylah peered over Holt's arm as he read the scrawling ink. *This was all I could manage at short notice. Please accept my apologies.*

"Shit," Holt breathed. "We'll make slower progress, but this will have to do." He fastened the bags on either side of the saddle and helped Zylah up, passing her the sword. "Keep the belt on. Do not take it off." He pulled himself up behind her carefully.

The horse took off into a canter, its feet fast in the dirt, and Zylah let the sound wrap itself over her thoughts. It was fitting, she supposed, that Holt had been the one to bring her to Virian, now he was the one to take her away from it. She replayed the moment Jesper's fangs sank into Raif's neck over and over, wondering if she'd just tried a little bit harder… whether she could have reached him in time.

"Did he teach you to shield yourself?" Holt asked over her shoulder as the horse cantered further into the forest.

"Hmm?" It took her a heartbeat to realise he was talking about Raif. "To shield? No, I can defend myself, just like you both taught me."

"There are other ways to be attacked, Zylah."

"What kind of ways?"

"Mental attacks. They are... a violation of everything that we are."

He said it like he knew. Like he'd experienced it.

"Raif didn't teach me, no. He didn't teach me much when it came to Fae abilities."

Holt was silent at that. Zylah had wondered about it many times—Raif's reluctance. He'd been so encouraging with the healing that day in the grotto with Niara, but since then... he'd always had an excuse, something else for them to do instead. Whether it was training, making her laugh, distracting her with his insufferable ways.

Her heart hurt even more at the thought of that word, as though at the same moment Raif had fallen she'd taken a blade to the chest, too. Why hadn't she told him she loved him? So many times she'd wanted to. So many times she should have. She pressed a hand over her heart again and sucked in a breath against the pain.

"Breathe, Zylah," Holt murmured behind her. Daylight had long since disappeared, and Zylah knew Holt had chosen the forest bordering Virian where Mala had died. Where the Asters lingered. She didn't care. In that moment, she was just as much a monster as they were.

A monster just like Jesper. "Jesper... he's a vampire," Zylah said quietly, resting her hands on the front of the saddle. It took a lot of effort to keep herself upright; her wounds were healed, but she was still exhausted, and she was certain they weren't healed entirely, at least, the pain in her back told her that was the case. Perhaps it was her lump—the vanquicite—and it had been dislodged by Oz's whip. Maybe she'd healed it wrong.

"The vampires were created by the original Fae—your gods. Two of them, anyway. Ranon and Sira."

Raif had told her as much at the festival.

Holt continued, "The vampires are immortal like we are, but they need blood to sustain them. But there were complications Ranon and Sira hadn't anticipated, the vampires began creating more of their kind and developed a particular taste for Fae blood, and when the gods realised that they tried to destroy them. Vampires haven't been seen since I was a child." Holt spoke quietly as they rode through the forest, branches and tree trunks a blur as they passed them in the darkness.

Zylah followed Kopi's tiny silhouette flying ahead of them, darting out of view every now and then, flying faster than she'd ever seen him fly before. They were moving downhill; on this side of Virian, she knew the forest stretched for miles.

"None of this is your fault, Zylah," Holt said after a while.

"It isn't yours either." She knew he'd likely been replaying it all over and over in his head just as she had. Wondering what more he could have done. How he could have intervened. But he'd moved so fast around Jesper and Raif, Zylah had wondered if there would be a limit to his power, if he would stop to catch his breath, but he didn't, not once. He did everything he could to help Raif.

They were silent for a moment.

"I don't know how to grieve for them both at once. My father. Raif. It's like I don't know how to feel." Only Holt's quiet breathing told Zylah he was listening behind her. "Did it get easier when Adina died? After you lost your parents?"

Holt sighed, shifted in the saddle. He was being careful not to touch her, although, sharing one saddle, it was practically impossible. He adjusted the reins, one hand at a time. "It doesn't really get easier. You just learn to carry the weight of it."

Zylah rested a hand on his. It was all she could offer at that moment. He'd lost so many people. Raif wasn't hers alone, she reminded herself, even though the thought brought selfish tears burning at the corners of her eyes. Was it wrong to want him to be? When she was alone, she supposed it wouldn't matter anyway.

They rode through the night until the grey light of dawn seemed to cling to everything. Holt pulled the horse to a stop at the edge of an even darker expanse of forest, a wet, musty odour lingering in the air. The horse whinnied and took a step back, and Kopi flew down and rested on its head, as if to calm it. Zylah swallowed, staring into the dark depths of the forest ahead. The hairs on her neck stood on end.

"Asters and vampires are not the only dark creatures the gods

447

created," Holt said quietly as he dismounted. "There are more out here in the wilderness. No one will expect you to go that way."

He helped Zylah down, holding her steady when her legs wobbled from so long on the horse.

"And you're confident I'll make it through to the other side?" She looked into the dark, shadows moving through the trees in the distance, but Kopi didn't cry out.

"I am. You're far more resilient than you know."

Zylah huffed a quiet laugh. "You didn't even ask me if I could ride a horse."

Holt's face paled.

"I can ride a horse, Holt, relax." A smile tugged at the corner of her mouth for a moment, but it immediately felt wrong. How could she be smiling when Raif was gone, when she would never see his smile again? She pressed a hand to her chest.

Holt reached into his coat and pulled out a paper bag. "One for the road?"

Zylah sniffed at the air, already knowing what was inside. A canna cake. Holt's mouth quirked, but Zylah couldn't bring herself to say anything other than a quiet, "Thank you."

"Give me your apron. I need to mark your scent, create a diversion." Holt held out a hand as Zylah began to shrug out of her cloak.

She handed him the apron and pulled her cloak back on, fastening the buttons with fingers that somehow didn't tremble.

She let out a breath, willing the tears not to fall. Another goodbye.

It was what she deserved. And yet... "Will I ever see you again?" She looked up at him, studying the lines of his face.

A tear fell down her cheek and Holt brushed it away, so lightly she barely felt his skin touch hers. "I'll find you." His jaw was tightly clenched, as if there was more he wanted to say, but he just held her gaze.

Zylah threw her arms around him, breathing him in for the last time as he hugged her back. "Thank you. For everything." Holt's arms enveloped her, pulling her close.

The thought of asking him to go with her crossed her mind. But she knew she was being a coward. She couldn't put a target on his back like that. She knew she had to keep moving, alone.

Holt pulled back but didn't meet her eyes. He helped her up onto the horse, adjusting the stirrups for her and sliding her feet into each one. "Daylight is the safest time to travel through the Kerthen forest. Keep one hand on your sword the entire time, and if Kopi alerts you, don't ignore him."

Zylah nodded. She didn't think she could speak. Not anymore. Her whole body ached, and for the first time since they'd left Virian, she was afraid.

"I'll find you, Zylah," he said again, his voice hoarse. She studied his face, the way his hair fell across his eyes, the way he'd squared his jaw, and committed it to memory. He patted the horse's flank, and with a huff, it set off into the forest.

Zylah couldn't bring herself to look back, but she could feel

Holt's eyes on her until he would have had to follow to keep her in his line of sight. She heard the rush of air when he finally turned to sprint off in another direction, to mark her scent as he'd said he would.

Kopi ruffled his feathers, still nestled on top of the horse's head like its own personal mascot. It was just the three of them now, and a twisted thought crossed Zylah's mind: this was what she had waited for, for so long. To be free. To explore the world.

"Now what, buddy?" Zylah asked quietly, brushing a finger over Kopi's head.

The little owl flew off into the trees, his cry not one of warning, but one of elation.

As if he were telling her to do the only thing he knew how. To live.

ACKNOWLEDGEMENTS

Thanks, hugs and memes go to the following:

Belle Manuel, Holly Hoffmann, Jozanne Fernandes, Amy Eversley, Kayla Maurais, Brie Tart, Charlotte Murphy, Melanie Underwood, Franziska Stern, Elina Yatsenko, Alexandra Curte, Andrés Aguirre Jurado, Helena Craggs, and all the incredible bloggers and bookstagrammers who've shared my work.

Thank you, wonderful reader. Your support means I get to continue doing what I love.

To Ali: for the endless support and love. I couldn't do any of it without you.

Made in the USA
Coppell, TX
04 March 2022

74465791R00267